Dee Williams was born and brought up in Rotherhithe in East London where her father was a stevedore in Surrey Docks. As a child Dee was evacuated during the war, although she kept returning to London because she was so homesick, and in 1940 she witnessed the night of the Blitz. Dee left school at fourteen, met her husband at sixteen and was married at twenty. In 1974 she and her husband opened the first of several ladies' boutiques in Hampshire but eight years later they moved to Crete and subsequently to Spain, where Dee first started writing. She and her husband now live near Portsmouth, close to the rest of her family. *Hannah of Hope Street* is Dee's fourth novel set in Rotherhithe.

Hannah of Hope Street

Dee Williams

HEADLINE

First published in 1994 by
HEADLINE BOOK PUBLISHING

First published in paperback in 1994 by
HEADLINE BOOK PUBLISHING

20 19 18 17 16 15 14 13

ISBN 0 7472 4605 X

Typeset by Avon Dataset Ltd, Bidford-on-Avon

Printed and bound in Great Britain by
Clays Ltd, St Ives plc

HEADLINE BOOK PUBLISHING
A division of Hodder Headline PLC
338 Euston Road
London NW1 3BH

I would like to dedicate this book to the memory of my daughter Julie, who sadly, at the age of thirty-four, lost her battle with cancer on 3 August 1992. You are always in our thoughts, Julie.

Chapter 1

Hannah Miller rested her head against the brick wall.

'Are we safe now?' whispered Alice as she snuggled against Hannah.

'I think so,' answered her sister, putting a comforting arm around her and drawing her close.

Hannah looked down on the blonde, ruffled, untidy head leaning on her chest. Under the closed lids were the bluest of eyes. Alice was so different from her, in ways as well as looks but she loved her young sister dearly. Hannah brushed aside a troublesome strand of her own long dark hair which she wore pulled back and tied with a thin piece of frayed black ribbon. Her high cheekbones, a full, sensuous mouth and dark, smouldering eyes, were a legacy from her father whilst Alice, who was three years younger than her, had a small pixie face and dimpled cheeks. Her face, Hannah thought fondly, always reflected her feelings: lighting up when she was happy, her mouth quick to turn down when she was sad. Hannah herself had learnt to be more careful about what she showed to the world. Alice, who was still a baby in so many ways, only came up to her sister's shoulder, and because her right leg had been badly set after a fall a few years ago, had a slight limp.

Hannah shivered. Although it was May it was warm, but she knew they would be cold again tonight if they didn't find proper shelter. She looked towards the pile of rubbish they were hiding behind, terrified the old woman would find them. Scared and breathless, they had run as fast as they could and had been

1

lucky to find a few loose boards in a wooden fence at the end of a dark alley. They had squeezed through, and were surprised to find the yard full of old and broken furniture. Swiftly and quietly they had concealed themselves, then slid to the ground exhausted.

If only they had some decent clothes, thought Hannah, brushing the mud from her pinafore; then they wouldn't look so much like dirty ragamuffins. Yesterday had been her birthday: she was now fifteen. Since they had moved to Uncle Harry's, she had had to grow up very quickly. Hannah reflected on the past few days, the living from hand to mouth, sleeping where they could, and eating anything anybody threw away. Slowly tears filled her eyes. Everything had happened so quickly. Why did Uncle Harry drink so much? If only Papa was still alive. Hannah sighed. Dear, dear Papa, how they missed him. He'd been so gentle, always cheerful despite everyone saying he couldn't bring up two girls on his own.

Alice stirred. Hannah knew she had to look after her; they only had each other now. She gently brushed the hair away from Alice's face. I've got to protect her, just as I promised Papa, she told herself, as if saying it would make it happen. First she had to find somewhere to live – but where could she start? If only they could find their way back to Richmond, back to their old home, back to the green fields and the nearby river. But Hannah knew that was impossible. They were hopelessly lost, and besides, a new man was living in their old home. Hannah tried desperately to stop any of her tears from falling on to Alice's head. After all, she was the eldest, and she had to put on a brave face.

'How long are we going to sit here?' asked Alice.

'A little while longer.' Hannah ran her sleeve under her nose and cocked her head. The sound of horses' hooves and the steel rims of the cart wheels rattled over the cobbled street that ran along the bottom of the alley, mixed with general distant noises of dogs barking, women shouting, and men whistling. The sun had moved round and its rays were now warming her. She relaxed and for a moment felt safe, reluctant to move.

'I wish we were still with Miss Jordon,' said Alice.

'So do I, but you know she couldn't look after us.'

Alice nodded. 'I know, but that doesn't stop me from wanting to see her. Why couldn't she take us to America with her?'

'Alice, don't start. We've been over and over this for years. She was marrying her young man, and they didn't want two orphans hanging round them.'

'We're not babies,' Alice said sulkily.

'I know that.'

'I thought she liked us.'

Hannah couldn't see Alice's face, but she knew from her tone she was pouting. 'She did. But she was only our teacher.'

'I still think she should have taken us.'

She also knew Alice had to have the last word, and so held her tongue.

Hannah brought her hand up and quickly brushed away a tear as she sat and thought of all that had happened in the last few years. She'd been ten when dear Papa had been killed by a horse and, that day, their lives had changed.

At first they had lived with Miss Jordon, their teacher at the village school. When they told her they had an aunt living in Fulham, Miss Jordon had written to Aunt May telling her of the girls' plight. She had also told her about her planned new life in America, and that she couldn't take the girls.

Aunt May was their only living relative, and finally, when Miss Jordon went away, they were sent to live with her and Uncle Harry. They had never been to Fulham before and were upset at all the dirt and grime around them, and the squalid room they lived in above the stables. Although Aunt May worked hard to keep it clean, it was run down and dilapidated, with the rain continually dripping through the roof. Poor Aunt May; Hannah almost felt ashamed that they had run away from her. Perhaps Aunt May needed them – Hannah prayed for her to get better. Oh, if only Miss Jordon could have looked after them, then they wouldn't be here now, hiding like common criminals.

Guilt filled her. They shouldn't have left Uncle Harry like that, not like that. What if he was dead?

She looked down at Alice's dark print frock. It was faded, and far too small for her; Hannah cringed in sympathy when she remembered the multicoloured bruise that was hidden under her long sleeve. Hannah knew all too well how much it would hurt: she winced when she recalled the pain she had felt the many times Uncle Harry had thrown her against the wall, or beat her with his wide leather belt if she had accidentally upset his jug of ale, or just got in his way. Again Hannah wondered if Aunt May was all right. She had often talked about their mother who had died many years before. Hannah could barely remember what she looked like, though Aunt May had told them many times how lovely she was, and that Alice resembled her. Poor Aunt May was nothing but a drudge: the tired look on her pale face and the sad blue eyes would always be with Hannah. She could almost feel the rough red hands trying to comfort them when Uncle Harry was in a black mood. Why had he been so hard on them? Was it because he and Aunt May had never had children, and he was jealous of his wife's sister having had them?

Suddenly there was a noise in the yard, and Alice's head jerked up. 'Will she catch us?'

'No,' whispered Hannah, 'not if we're quiet.' She prayed they were safe and out of sight. She wrinkled her nose at the smell of the rotting vegetables and rubbish they were hiding behind, thankful at least that the pile of old doors and broken furniture was offering some form of refuge. Something was scratching around in the rubbish, making a rustling sound. Hannah held her breath and pulled Alice closer.

In the far corner of the yard a great commotion broke out. A dog started barking and an old woman's high-pitched voice screamed out, 'Ger out o' it.'

The dog began yelping and they could hear a stick hitting the ground. 'I said git out o' it yer dozy flea bag. Ger after it, then.'

Suddenly their protection was being dragged away. Two little beady black eyes peered through the ripped cloth of a three-legged chair. Its nose twitched as it sniffed the air, its long whiskers trembled. Hannah froze. She hated rats, and to be this close was more than she could stand. Alice began to cry.

'Shh, shh,' said Hannah, pushing her head down.

'I'll git yer, yer dirty filthy little . . .' The voice was getting louder.

The sound of boxes and furniture being tossed aside was almost on them, and the noise of a stick thrashing about came nearer. Hannah's eyes were riveted on the large brown rat with a long thin, sleek tail. With a chorus of squeaks, he jumped over her head and disappeared.

'Well, well, well, what 'ave we got 'ere then?' An old woman was standing over them.

Hannah couldn't speak as she gazed up at this large blob of a woman, wearing run-down slippers and wrinkled stockings. Despite the warmth of the day she was wearing a man's long black overcoat, frayed at the sleeves and much too large for her. Her face was bloated, and Hannah couldn't see her eyes: as she squinted against the sun they were lost in her podgy face. Most of the mass of ginger-coloured hair was scragged on top of her head, the rest hung limply down. It made her look like a witch Hannah had seen in a picture book. She felt Alice shudder.

'Well, bugger me if it ain't the bloody kid wot pinched me bread.' As the woman shuffled towards them they squashed themselves against the wall, trying to make themselves as small as possible.

'Bonzo,' she yelled over her shoulder. 'Come 'ere, yer daft git. Come and sort these two out.'

A big sandy-coloured, mangy-looking dog pushed past his mistress and bounded towards the girls. Alice screamed and started to cry again.

Although Hannah was shaking with fear, she stood up and confronted the dog. 'Go away,' she shouted, flapping her hands.

''Ere, don't yer shout at me dog,' the woman ordered.

Alice, who was still crying and clinging on to Hannah's leg sobbed, 'I'm sorry. I was ever so hungry.' She struggled to her feet.

'I don't bleeding care.' She wagged her finger in Alice's face. 'Yer ain't pinching me bread from out me mouth.'

'She didn't,' said Hannah, smoothing down her torn, dirty pinafore. 'She took it out of your shopping bag.'

'Don't yer git saucy wiv me, gel.'

'I can't give it back,' said Alice cautiously, patting the dog that was now sniffing round them, wagging its tail.

'What yer doing 'iding round 'ere?'

'Nothing,' said Hannah.

'Don't give us that.'

'We're having a game,' she said, desperately forcing herself to think of some excuse.

'Who yer running from?'

'No one,' said Alice weakly.

The old woman threw her head back and laughed. ''Ere, it ain't the rozzers?'

'No.' Hannah nervously looked down at her well-worn black button boots and began to straighten her black stockings, but they had so many holes in them that she gave up. She suddenly jerked her head up and, trying to control her panic, asked, 'You won't tell the police, will you?'

'I should cocoa,' said the ginger woman drily.

'Thank you. Come on Alice.' Hannah took hold of her sister's hand and they started to move away.

''Ang on 'alf a mo. Looks like me dog's taken a shine ter yer. Why don't yer come back ter my place, I can give yer a bowl of soup.'

Hannah stopped. 'Why?'

'Yer looks 'alf starved. And I fink I can find yer a little job ter do.' She cast her beady eyes over Alice.

'Doing what?' asked Hannah suspiciously.

'I'll tell yer later. Come on.'

'Doing what?' asked Hannah again.

'Come on, if yer wants a nice big bowl of soup.'

Hannah looked down at Alice who was nodding eagerly. She could almost see her drooling. Well, they *were* both very hungry.

As they followed the old woman, Hannah noticed that for the first time in days there was a smile on Alice's pixie face, the dog, who had big feet and a long bushy tail, bounding at her heels as she limped along. Alice, she thought proudly, had a way with animals, one of her few sources of pleasure at the stables.

'I only lives just round the corner, in 'Ope Street,' the woman shouted over her shoulder. 'By the way, you two can call me Maudie. Everybody else does.'

They squeezed through the fence and followed Maudie along the road, passing a pub, a grocer's and a butcher's. They turned the corner and walked down a narrow street that had a row of dingy terraced houses on both sides, the front doors opening straight on to the pavement. Hannah was sure she saw some of the yellowed lace curtains twitch. Two women who were standing at their front doors stopped talking as they approached. When the three of them had gone past, one of the women shouted, 'See yer got yerself some more bloody strays then.'

Maudie quickly turned. 'Mind yer own bloody business, yer nosey old cow.'

'That's very nice, I must say.'

Hannah and Alice stopped to look at the thin woman who, with a pinched, sallow face, nervously folded her arms and leant against her front doorpost, staring back at them. 'Wot yer gonner do wiv 'em then?' She inclined her head towards Hannah and Alice.

Maudie came up to them. 'Come on, gels, don't take no notice of 'er,' she said, gently pushing them forward.

'Who is she?' asked Hannah as they moved on.

'Don't worry about 'er,' Maudie sniffed. 'Dunno 'er name, everybody calls 'er Mrs Nosy, been 'ere fer years, she 'as.'

Hannah was worried, and quickly gave her another look before hurrying on.

A large building dominated the end of the street. It looked empty and, with all the windows boarded up, sinister. As they got nearer, Hannah could see Hope Street was a dead-end.

Maudie stopped in front of a pair of rusty old gates. 'Frough 'ere.' The gate's hinges squeaked in protest.

Trembling, Alice grabbed hold of Hannah's hand.

'In here?' asked Hannah. 'You live in here? It looks empty.'

'Yer, it is. Come on, don't 'ang about.'

The girls tagged behind, reluctant to enter the cobbled yard. They passed an ancient warehouse towering above them and, moving round the back, stopped in front of a long, low building whose chimney was almost as tall as the red-brick building.

8

Puffing and blowing, Maudie pushed aside a sheet of corrugated iron that had been wedged in front of a doorway.

They went down a long passage, and through a door that led into a large room; gradually their eyes, after coming in out of the bright sunlight, became accustomed to the dim surroundings. There was a musty smell of damp and washing. Hannah stood and looked around her. It had light coming in through the very high windows; they were streaked with dirt and paint. In one corner was a pile of old mattresses, most of which were split and had the flock spilling out. There were several chairs, most of them in a dilapidated condition. Some had great tufts of horsehair stuffing sprouting from them, and the large table in the middle of this vast room had a brick wedged under one leg to even it up. Maudie shuffled across the room, took her coat off and threw it on a chair. Much to Hannah's surprise her brown frock was covered with a very clean white wrap-around pinafore. She watched the old woman go over and plonk herself in one of the two wooden armchairs that stood in front of a black stove.

'This was the boiler 'ouse. It's real cosy in the winter.' Maudie tucked some hair behind her ear.

Hannah suddenly felt very grubby, and she too pushed a few strands of tangled hair away from her face.

The dog, wagging his large tail, wandered around then blew noisily through his nose, sniffed, and walked round and round in a tight circle a few times before settling on a moth-eaten rug at Maudie's feet.

'Well, gels, this is me 'ome. Now wot's yer names?'

'I'm Hannah, and this is my sister Alice.'

'Very nice. Now, d'yer wonner tell me where yer comes from?'

They both looked down.

'Well please yerself, but it ain't from round 'ere, yer don't

9

talk like us. Just as long as we don't 'ave the law round 'ere looking for yer yer can stay.'

Hannah felt her face flush. 'Thank you,' she whispered, grateful Maudie wasn't going to ask too many questions, wondering if this was really what they should be doing.

Maudie stood up. 'Right, well, now we know each ovver I'll put the kettle on. Don't stand there wiv yer tongues 'anging out. Come over 'ere and I'll show yer where all me fings are.'

As Hannah moved forward, she put her hand behind her for Alice to grab hold of. 'What sort of work do you want us to do?' she asked.

'If yer gits up first yer 'as ter light the fire. There's plenty o' wood outside,' said Maudie ignoring the question. 'Watch. And the matches stay 'ere in this cupboard. I don't want yer running off wiv 'em ter light yer fags, savvy?'

Hannah noticed the cupboard had an assortment of mugs and cups, some cracked and without handles. There was an array of plates, and a few bowls and the deep chipped sink had a wooden draining-board either side. Against another wall stood an old and large carved oak sideboard, with shelves up one side holding many pretty ornaments. A mirror hung over it.

Maudie lifted the kettle and shook it. 'There's enough in 'ere fer us. This used ter be a wash-'ouse, so there's plenty o' water, and a tap and bog outside. I try ter keep the place nice,' she said proudly. 'But some I've 'ad 'ave been right little cow-sons, right dirty little bleeders. Some ain't never been inside a wash-'ouse before. Ain't even 'ad a wash, some of 'em, that's except Dolly and Jack.'

'You've got other children?' asked Hannah in surprise.

'Yer, five. Now it's seven wiv you two.'

'Have you got a husband?'

'Na, they ain't my kids really, I just took 'em in orf the street.'

'Where are they?'

'At work.'

'What do they do?'

'Yer a nosy little cow, ain't yer?' Maudie said accusingly.

Hannah hung her head. She was worried. What did this woman want from them? 'Sorry, it's just that . . .'

''Ang on, the kettle's boiling. Bet yer fancy a cuppa?'

'Please,' said Alice. 'We've not had one since . . .' Hannah pulled at her hand. 'Since this morning,' she added quickly.

Maudie took a brown enamel teapot from the cupboard and carefully measured out one teaspoonful of tea from a tin caddie, added the boiling water, and stirred it vigorously. 'As yer can see I like ter keep everyfink nice and proper-like. Gawd 'elp anyone wot lets me down.' She picked an enamelled milk jug from out of the galvanized bucket resting on the stone floor, took the wet cloth covering the jug off, and sniffed it. 'It's on the turn, but it'll do. Put this lot on the table. D'yer want sugar?'

'Please,' said Alice sweetly, and the dimples in her cheeks deepened.

Maudie brought a bowlful of sugar from the cupboard and plonked it on the table. 'Yer a pretty little fing and no mistake – 'ow old are yer?' she asked Alice as she poured the tea into two chipped cups.

'I'm nearly twelve,' she replied confidently. 'And Hannah's fifteen now.'

'Fifteen, eh?'

'It was her birthday a few weeks ago.'

Hannah quickly shook her head at Alice. She didn't want to talk about the past.

'I like birfdays,' said Maudie smiling. 'Always try ter give the little 'ens a bit extra.'

'That's nice,' said Alice politely.

Hannah lifted the spoon, caked with tea-stained sugar, from

11

the bowl, put one spoonful in hers, and one in her sister's cup.

'Thank you,' said Alice looking up at Maudie, her big blue eyes shining. 'This is very kind of you.'

Hannah shot her a worried glance. She had heard about people who sold children into service, and other things. 'What do you want us to do?' she asked quickly. She was aware it was the second time she'd asked the question.

Maudie took a fine white bone-china cup and saucer with pretty violet flowers all round the brim from her cupboard. She held it in front of her. 'Now, remember, this is mine. I told yer I likes nice fings, and if I ever catches anybody ser much as looking at it, I'll 'ave their guts fer garters. Savvy?'

They both nodded vigorously.

She sat at the table and began to fill her cup. 'Right, now we've got that all settled, I'll tell yer what I want yer ter do.'

Chapter 2

They watched Maudie slowly stir the tea in her cup. After pouring some in the delicate saucer, she picked it up and, with loud slurping noises, gulped down the light brown liquid. She then sat back and wiped her mouth with the back of her hand. 'That's better, always feel better after a nice cuppa. Now, after seeing yer pinch me bread, wot I've got in mind fer you two little darlings is – I'm gonner teach yer 'ow ter do it prop'ly.'

'I didn't mean to take your . . .'

Maudie put her hand up to silence Alice. 'I knows yer was 'ungry, that's why I didn't set me dog on yer. But if yer gonner pinch fings, yer gotter do it proper-like.'

Hannah's mouth fell open. 'What? You want us to steal for you?'

'Well, if I'm gonner look after yer, yer gotter 'elp yerselves. I ain't a charity, yer know.' She poured more tea in her saucer.

Hannah stood up. 'Come on, Alice, we're not staying here.'

Alice struggled reluctantly to her feet. 'But Hannah . . .'

'We are not going to steal for you or anyone,' said Hannah indignantly, and took Alice's hand.

'But Hannah,' repeated Alice. 'Where are we going?'

'I don't know, but we're not staying here to take things for this old woman.'

Maudie put the saucer on the table. 'Now sit down and stop being ser daft. I'm offering yer a 'ome and food fer a little favour; and she's right, yer know – where are yer going?'

Hannah slowly slid back on to the chair, her confidence

13

slipping away. 'I don't know.' The last few days of worrying about Alice and very little food, and the fear of the police catching them, suddenly proved too much for her, and the tears began to fall, slowly at first, then in great torrents.

Alice threw her arms round her sister, and cried with her.

After a while Maudie came and put her big fat wobbly arms round both of them. 'There, there.' She patted their backs. 'I fink yer better sit down and tell me wot this is all about.'

Alice went to speak but Hannah quickly wiped her eyes on the bottom of her dirty pinafore. 'I'll tell her,' she sobbed. She wasn't going to let Alice blurt out that they thought they had left Uncle Harry to die. Starting from the beginning, Hannah went into great detail of how their mother had died when Alice was very young, and then their father had been killed by a horse a few years ago. Miss Jordon, their teacher, had looked after them for a while, but she was going to America with her young man, and couldn't take them, so they had had to go and live with their Aunt May and Uncle Harry. At first he was all for sending them to a home – they didn't have any children and he didn't want them till he was told they came with a legacy. As they got older he became annoyed at what they cost to keep. Hannah told how she'd worked in the brush factory for a while but had been given the sack.

'I didn't get a lot of money,' said Hannah sadly.

'Her fingers used to bleed,' added Alice, screwing up her nose.

'It was very hard work, sweeping and picking up all the bristles. D'you know they used to get stuck between the floorboards and you had to dig them out? If you left any the forelady used to scream and shout.'

'The forelady didn't like her,' butted in Alice again. 'Said she spoke too posh.'

'That really annoyed Uncle Harry,' said Hannah. 'But I

didn't like it there anyway: all that dust got up my nose, and I only got two shillings a week, and it was very hard work.' Hannah stopped to wipe her eyes again. She glanced at Maudie, who said nothing. 'I know the money Papa left for us to be looked after had all gone,' Hannah continued. 'Uncle Harry did drink a lot.'

'He was a blacksmith,' said Alice. 'And when he got drunk he hit Aunt May, and us. Look.' She pulled at the flap of torn cloth on her sleeve and showed Maudie her bruised arm.

''E did that?' Maudie tutted, speaking for the first time. 'The cow-son.'

'We lived over the stable,' said Hannah quickly, afraid of what Alice was going to say next. 'And when he told us we had to go into a home, we ran away.'

Alice looked at Hannah. 'Yes,' she repeated slowly, backing up her half truth. 'We ran away. That's why I stole your bread, we were ever so hungry.'

Maudie nodded. 'That's all right. I guessed it must 'ave been sumfink like that. Those sorta blokes are worse than animals when they've 'ad a few. Where did yer live before yer went ter live wiv 'im?'

'Near Richmond.'

'Richmond?' repeated Maudie. 'That's up-river, ain't it?'

Hannah nodded and allowed a faint smile to lift her dirty tearstained face. 'It has lovely country all round.'

'Yer, so I've 'eard,' Maudie sniffed. 'Someone told me about it once – 'e'd been up-river, said it was all posh-like.'

'Papa used to run the stables for a gentleman,' said Alice proudly.

'Aunt May was our mother's sister,' continued Hannah, beginning to relax. 'We lived over the stables at the brewery, in Fulham.' She screwed up her nose. 'It didn't half stink.'

Maudie threw her head back and laughed. 'Talk about going

15

from the bloody sublime ter the ridiculous. If yer uncle was that worried, why didn't 'e send yer *both* out ter work?'

Hannah stiffened. That had been one of the arguments between him and Aunt May. 'I don't know,' she said. 'He made me go out but when I lost my job I think that was the last straw.' She wanted to quickly gloss over the last few days.

'So 'ow come yer finished up round 'ere, in Roverhive?'

'We were trying to get back to Richmond. We knew we had to cross the Thames, so we went over the first bridge we came to,' said Hannah.

'It went up and down,' interrupted Alice.

'It wasn't the right one,' said Hannah, 'and we got lost. We had followed the river for quite a while, but we must have been going in the wrong direction.'

'I fink yer was. Wot did yer wonner go back ter Richmond for?'

'I don't know.' Hannah's tears began to fall again. She was beginning to warm to this woman who was willing to listen to their story without reprimand. 'When Papa was alive we lived over the stables in Richmond, the part where all the carriages were kept and it was warm and clean. The lady of the house was so kind, we thought she might give me a job.'

'It was much nicer than Fulham,' said Alice, running her hand under her nose.

Maudie took a clean handkerchief from the pocket of her white overall, and gave it to Alice. 'Well, that's settled then. Yer gonner stay 'ere wiv me and my lot. Now, as I said before, yer gotter earn yer keep. I ain't looking after yer fer nuffink.'

Alice squeezed Hannah's hand and smiled up at Maudie. 'Thank you.'

Hannah knew then she couldn't refuse Maudie's offer.

'Right, first, 'fore the kids come in, we'll 'ave that drop o' soup I promised. I ain't got no bread, mind,' Maudie smiled.

'Some little cow nicked it.' Her little eyes twinkled.

Alice giggled nervously. 'I'm ever so hungry.'

When they'd finished the soup, Maudie said she would show them round. 'The bog's outside. We've got a wash-'ouse and washing line as well. There's one place I don't let any of yer in, and that's me bedroom.' Silently they followed her as she shuffled her way to a door at the far end of the room. When she opened it, Hannah and Alice couldn't believe their eyes. Maudie's bedroom was a lot smaller than the other room, and Hannah guessed that long ago it must have been an office. In this room was a bed with a big wooden headboard, a brown velvet chair, the back of which had been neatly patched, a wardrobe and a dressing table that had dozens of ornaments on top. Maudie stood in the doorway looking round with pride. 'I told yer I liked nice fings, and when the kids brings me sumfink really pretty I can't bear ter sell it, so I keeps the best pieces in 'ere. I got me bedspread orf a widder woman; she'd just buried 'er old man, and wanted a few pence. She said 'e didn't die in the bed it was on, so that's all right.'

Hannah and Alice gazed in wonder at the brown and white folkweave bedspread, the prize exhibit in this Aladdin's cave.

'Pretty, ain't it?'

They nodded.

'I didn't ask where she got it from. I expect 'er old man pinched it. D'yer like me rug?'

Again they only nodded.

'Made it meself out a bits o' rag.'

Maudie, Hannah decided, was like no other person they had ever met. She taught street children to steal, and yet Hannah knew she was kind, and beneath her gruffness soft-hearted. Walking back into the large room, Maudie showed them where they could sleep.

'You'll 'ave ter take pot luck ternight. I expect young Jack might 'ave sumfink ter say about it.'

'Who?' asked Alice.

'Jack. 'E must be almost seventeen be now, and Bert, but we don't see a lot of 'im now – 'e likes ter come and go as 'e pleases; 'ad 'im from a baby. Mind you, I can't make 'im out at times, though, sorta sullen-like, keeps 'imself to 'isself when 'e's 'ere, but I can't turn 'im away. 'E's a funny bugger. Jack's a couple o' monfs younger than Bert, so I reckon. 'E's a nice lad, been wiv me fer years.' A smile crinkled her eyes. 'Next is Tom. 'E's a nice boy, 'e's twelve, found 'im at the side of the Thames. Don't know a lot about 'im, 'e don't 'ave much ter say. Then about a year ago I found Dolly and 'er young brother Freddie. They were being chased by the police, bit like you two, I s'pose, only they were running away from their old man.'

'And they all steal for you?' asked Hannah in amazement.

'Na, not just fer me, but for 'emselves as well – we all gotter eat.'

'Do Bert and Jack go to work?' asked Hannah, intrigued.

'Jack don't, 'e reckons 'e couldn't take orders from a boss, likes ter be on 'is own.'

'What about Bert?' asked Hannah.

A nearby clock struck five.

'That's the church clock,' said Maudie. 'Right, let's get cleared up before they gits back.' She took a gold watch from the pocket of her overall and flicked open the lid. 'They should be 'ome soon.'

Hannah stared at the watch. 'That's very nice.'

'Yer,' Maudie smiled. 'I told yer I like nice fings.'

Hannah wondered if she could tell the time, or if it was just for show – after all, it sounded as if she had the church clock to rely on.

Shortly after that the dog stood up and began wagging his tail.

''Ere comes someone now.'

The door opened and a young skinny girl about the same age and height as Alice came in carrying a basket. Her long dark hair was falling over her face, and she tucked the loose strands behind her ear. She was wearing, over a dark print frock, a white smocked pinafore, which Hannah noted was clean; her neat black stockings made Hannah feel dirty and untidy, though the girl's black boots were scuffed and run-down. At her side was a small boy with the same colouring. His clothes were ill-fitting and not as tidy as the girl's. Hannah guessed this was Dolly and her brother Freddie.

'Didn't 'ave a bad day terday, Maudie. Just seen Tom. 'E'll be . . .' Dolly's voice trailed off when she caught sight of Hannah and Alice. Freddie quickly hid behind his sister.

'Come and meet yer new mates,' said Maudie, pushing the girls forward.

Dolly's dark eyes were full of suspicion, and quickly darted from one to the other as she looked them over as Maudie told her their names. Then, completely ignoring them, she put her basket on the table. 'Got a few apples, some taters, and greens.'

'Is that all?'

'Freddie 'ere managed ter git a bit of meat. Bin in 'is pocket all day, so it smells a bit 'igh, but it looks all right. 'Ere, we gotter share it wiv them?' she nodded towards Alice and Hannah.

Maudie put her big fat arms round the two girls and drew them close. 'Yer, we're all gonner be one big 'appy family.'

Dolly carried on emptying her basket. 'Yer, well, I don't s'pose Jack'll be none too 'appy about it.'

'I don't bloody well care wot Jack finks. This is my place, and I'll bring in who I like.'

The dog, which had been busy sniffing round the table, rushed over to the door wagging his tail when it was pushed open again and a boy wearing a well-worn jacket and trousers that, like his boots, were far too big for him, came in. His blond hair, sprouting out from beneath his large cloth cap, hung over his forehead, and he had to hold his head up in order to see.

''Allo Tom, come and meet 'Annah and Alice.'

''Allo,' he said shyly, snatching the cap off his head.

'Well, wot yer got fer us?' asked Maudie, pushing to one side the things Dolly had put on the table.

'Not a lot. The rozzers kept looking at me.'

'Well, what d'yer expect?' said Dolly suddenly. 'Look at the state of yer. If yer tried ter smarten yerself up a bit, yer'd blend in more.'

'She's right yer know, Tom,' said Maudie. 'Look, it's market day termorrer. Take Alice and 'Annah wiv yer down Jamaica Road, and try ter pinch sumfink off the second-'and barra wot fits yer. And fer gawd's sake try ter git yerself a decent pair a boots, yer keeps walking out o' them ones.'

Tom blushed and began to empty his pockets. There were two reels of black cotton, a couple of marbles, a handful of cherries, and a small coloured china dog wrapped in a grubby piece of rag.

'Is that it? Is that all yer got?' Dolly looked angry. 'Yer bin out all day and that's all yer got – yer'd bloody well starve if me and Jack didn't git the food.'

'I'm sorry, Dolly. But I know 'ow much Maudie 'ere likes nice fings, and I fought she'd like this.' He lovingly handed Maudie the small china dog. 'D'yer want me snot-rag?'

'No ta,' Maudie said. 'Dolly, stop going on, 'e tries ter 'elp. Fanks, Tom, this is really nice.' She smiled as she took the dog from him. 'I'll put it on me shelf. P'raps 'e'll do better wiv Alice and 'Annah 'ere ter 'elp 'im,' she said over her shoulder, and stood back from the oak sideboard to admire her new ornament proudly displayed with the other pieces. 'Right. You, Tom, can do the taters. Alice, in the drawer over there you'll find some knives and forks. Bring 'em 'ere. Where you going, Dolly?'

Dolly stood in the doorway. 'I'm gonner 'ave a wash.'

Maudie tutted. 'She'll wash 'er bleeding self away one a these days.'

'I like to be clean,' Dolly retorted, disappearing out of the door with Freddie at her heels.

'Just a good excuse ter git out of a few chores if yer asks me,' said Maudie, and with a lot of clatter fished a blackened frying-pan out from the array of pots and pans in the bottom of the cupboard. 'Put those few cherries and apples on a plate, 'Annah. There's a nice one in the sideboard.'

Hannah was astonished to find such lovely china, and as she arranged the fruit, couldn't help wondering at this strange woman's taste for nice things. The smell of the meat frying was making her stomach churn in anticipation. Even living with Aunt May they didn't have meat very often; it had always been saved for Uncle Harry.

Alice came and sat next to her sister. 'I can't believe we'll be eating tonight, and sleeping in the warm,' she whispered, gently fondling an apple.

Dolly came back in, with Freddie at her heels. She carefully wrapped a bar of soap in a piece of frayed white towelling. 'Wot yer whispering to 'er for? And wot yer sitting at the table for? And leave that apple be.' She snatched the apple from Alice's hand. 'I told yer, yer ain't gitting none o' our food, and this is my bit o' soap.' She sniffed the towelling. 'It's lily of the valley, so keep yer 'ands orf it.' She waved the soap in the air before carefully placing it in the bottom of the cupboard.

'Leave it out, Dolly,' said Maudie, and raising her voice added, 'And I told yer, we're all gonner be tergevver, and that's that. Good job I didn't sling you two out, yer would 'ave been in a fine old state be now.'

21

'Wot's all the shouting about?' A new voice rang out.

Hannah looked up at a tall lad wearing a large cloth cap pulled down to his ears. His striking blue eyes were swiftly glancing over her and Alice. His clothes were far too small, Hannah noticed, wanting to laugh at his trousers, which looked as if they had a row with his boots, and the sleeves of his jacket, which were half-way up his arms. His pockets were bulging, however.

'Who we got 'ere then? Blimey, you two royalty or sumfink? See we got the best china out then, Maudie me old love.' He nodded towards the plate of fruit.

''Allo Jack.' A warm smile filled her face. 'This is 'Annah and Alice, they've come ter live wiv us.'

'O yer. More bloody strays.' He sat next to Alice. 'Where're yer from then?'

Alice quickly looked at Hannah, then said confidently. 'We've run away from our uncle.'

Jack laughed. 'Cor, don't she talk posh?'

Dolly too looked up. This was the first time she had heard Alice speak.

Jack continued. 'And yer finished up 'ere. Well I expect Maudie'll look after yer, but, like she's probably told yer, yer got ter earn yer keep.' He stood up and began to empty his pockets.

Hannah couldn't believe what was in them. There were oranges, bananas and, last of all, and with a great flurry, he took from his large inside pocket a small rabbit, complete with brown fur. Jack held it up by its feet, and its dead eyes bulged. Hannah was laughing, and she felt like applauding. He was almost like a magician they had seen many years ago.

'How did you get all this?' she asked, her big brown eyes wide open.

'Ere, 'ark at this one.' Jack was still holding the rabbit and laughing with her. 'Been round the market, easy pickings round there. Didn't git nuffink worf flogging though, Maudie. When yer seeing Frank?'

'Not fer a week or so.'

'Good. I'm going over the water termorrer, I'm gonner stay a couple a days as they'll be a lot a toffs over there jostling ter git a good view of the funeral.'

Maudie sat down. 'Yer. Shame about the king going – 'e didn't last as long as 'is muvver.'

'Well, 'e didn't start ser young.'

Hannah too felt sad at the death of their king. One of her earliest memories had been of his coronation which her father had taken her to see.

'Still there's always a bit of a scuffle breaks out over there, and there'll be a few well-lined pockets worf dipping inter,' said Jack lightheartedly. 'Right, now gel,' he said to Hannah. 'Put this stuff on the posh plate, then we'll 'ave a bit a dinner.'

Hannah blushed as she looked at Jack with admiration. Quickly she picked up the fruit and began arranging it with the rest. She glanced at Dolly who was also looking at Jack. Hannah knew that if she wanted his attention, she was going to have to fight for it.

Chapter 3

Hannah couldn't believe the chatter and good humour as they sat at the table and ravenously stuffed food into their mouths. Maudie certainly knew how to make a real meal out of a few bits and scraps.

'What about Bert?' asked Alice with her mouth full. 'Don't you wait for him?'

'Not likely,' said Jack. 'Never know when 'e's gonner show 'is ugly face.'

'Oh,' said Alice, not looking up as she continued mashing her potatoes in the lovely thick gravy.

''E's a bit of a loner is our Bert,' said Maudie. ''E's not a bad lad.' She threw a piece of meat to Bonzo – it disappeared in a flash.

Jack laughed, a hollow, disbelieving laugh.

''E's not bad,' said Maudie brusquely.

'She's got a soft spot fer 'im,' said Tom quietly.

'Well, 'e's a good lad.'

''E's what?' Jack waved his fork with a piece of meat stuck on the end at Hannah. 'Don't yer listen to 'er. 'E goes orf fer weeks, monfs sometimes, then turns up again like a bad penny, and always causes trouble, or brings it wiv 'im.' He stuffed the fork into his mouth.

'Not always,' said Maudie, determined to have the last word.

Hannah was intrigued to know more about the mysterious Bert, but knew by Jack's furrowed brow and his grim expression as he chewed on the meat that this wasn't the right time to ask.

When they finished their meal they took their chairs and sat outside in the yard. It was a warm evening and everybody was busy making plans for the next day; for the first time in years Hannah felt happy and contented. She pushed to the back of her mind the doubts she had about what they'd have to do to stay here.

'Right you two,' said Maudie to Hannah and Alice, as the last rays of the sun began to disappear. 'This is wot yer do. Grab it and walk away.' Maudie lumbered to her feet and, with a surprisingly deft movement, took Jack's packet of cigarettes from his coat pocket. 'Savvy?'

They both nodded.

'Yer see,' said Jack. 'When yer nicks sumfink, don't stand around looking ter see if someone's spotted yer. Just pick up the stuff an move on a bit sharpish, but don't run and draw attention ter yerself.'

'But then if someone 'as spotted yer,' said Dolly confidently, 'then yer runs like 'ell.'

'D'yer fink yer got it?' asked Jack.

'I think so,' said Hannah nervously.

Jack stood up. 'Oh, I think so,' he mimicked and, placing a hand on his hip, walked up and down. He grinned at Hannah over his shoulder.

They all fell about laughing, and Hannah could have cried, she suddenly felt so happy. She didn't care if stealing was what she had to do to stay here, the important thing was they belonged. Alice seemed happy too, she thought. Having taken in Maudie's lesson she was busy watching Freddie playing with Bonzo. They threw a stick, but the dog was so lazy he wouldn't fetch it, so they had to run after it themselves.

'And try ter git yerself a pair o' stockings,' said Dolly. There was a hint of disgust in her tone.

'Yes, yes, I will, and a bar of soap,' said Hannah.

'Christ, looks like we've got anuvver one,' said Jack sitting back in his chair and puffing away on his cigarette.

'By the way,' said Maudie. 'Yer better git me some more baccy, me tin's nearly empty.'

'What sort?' asked Hannah.

Jack nearly exploded with amusement, laughing so much he began to choke. 'What sort? 'Ere, yer going in a shop and ask fer a special brand ter pinch? She ain't fussy wot yer gits, just ser long as she can fill that bloody old clay pipe of 'ers.'

Tom, till now, had been very quiet. 'I'll show yer when we go out termorrer. Is Alice coming wiv us?' he asked shyly.

'I should cocoa,' said Maudie. 'I've got enough ter do, got that rabbit ter skin and clean fer one fing, got some carrots and onions left from yesterday so I could make us all a nice rabbit stew, so I don't want 'er under me feet all day. Might even go round ter where I found 'em – looks like they've 'ad some new stuff dumped, might find meself a decent chair.'

It was beginning to get dusk, and the church clock struck ten.

'Right now,' said Maudie, gently banging out her pipe and picking up her chair. 'Let's git some shut-eye. Yer've all got a busy day in front o' yer.'

After a lot of sorting out, Hannah and Alice settled down on an old horsehair mattress that nobody else wanted. As she pulled it to the far end of the big room, she hoped it didn't have any fleas or bed-bugs in it.

Maudie, with her dog at her heels, shuffled to her room with the proper bed. Very soon Alice was fast asleep, but Hannah was too excited, and sleep wouldn't come. She could hear Dolly in another corner singing very softly to Freddie. She felt safe. Tom was restless, and Jack was lying on his back, smoking. She watched the glow on the end of his cigarette lighting up his fine features. He had short dark hair, and she

27

knew that his blue eyes had long lashes, and his nose was a lovely shape, not bent like Uncle Harry's. Uncle Harry. Despite the night being warm, Hannah shivered at the thought of . . . Was Uncle Harry dead? Or did . . . ? Her mind went back to what had happened. Was it only a few days ago? She could go over and over it, almost minute by minute.

Hannah had been in the yard helping Aunt May with the Monday wash. As she leant over the tin bath that was balanced precariously on two stools, the water soaked her sacking apron. Her hands hurt through the cuts and blisters she'd got in the brush factory. She winced: her knuckles were red and sore and, as she rubbed the scrubbing brush up and down the wooden washboard in the cold water, she let her thoughts go to the brush factory. She'd hated it there, and the overlady who'd thought she was posh and given her the sack. Sorting out the hard stiff fibres that stuck in her fingers had made them bleed and though Uncle Harry was furious, part of her was glad about what had happened.

'Hannah. Hannah.' Her aunt's voice brought her out of her daydream. 'Ain't you finished that vest yet?'

'Could do with a bit more soap.' She was trying to get stains out of Uncle Harry's vest, but with the small amount of soap she had, she couldn't get any lather, and no matter how hard she scrubbed at it, she still couldn't get it clean.

'I don't think your uncle would give me any more money for soap,' said Aunt May. 'Alice, give these a rinse.'

Alice left the mangy black dog she was playing with and staggered over to the tap with the bucket, heavy with wet clothes.

'Then, when yer done that, get the pegs and 'ang 'em on the line,' called Aunt May.

There was no tap upstairs, and come rain or shine all the water had to be carried up, and the slops brought down. Every morning, even before Hannah went to work, they had to empty the chamber-pot, which was always full to overflowing, then scrub the closet, and the step outside. It seemed that every morning Uncle Harry took a great delight in stepping on their work leaving great muddy footprints.

The early morning sun was beginning to filter through the smoke from the brewery's chimney. The smell of the hops brewing filled the air.

'Looks like it's going ter be a nice day,' said Aunt May looking up. 'Alice, wring those out a bit better than that, otherwise they'll never dry.'

'Don't know why you ain't got a wringer,' moaned Alice as the water from the tap splashed over her feet.

Hannah threw the vest she had been scrubbing back into the tin bath. 'I'll help her.'

They took the towel between them and twisted it round and round so the water ran out. They were pulling at it, and laughing and giggling, when Uncle Harry stormed into the yard.

'Wot you two larking about for?' He shouted and, turning to his wife, added, 'You should send 'em both out ter work instead of letting 'em sod about round 'ere all day. 'Bout time yer got yerself anuvver job,' he growled at Hannah.

Both the girls knew better than to answer him back, even though Hannah had only been out of work since Saturday.

'They're all right,' said Aunt May, pushing her hair back from her wet forehead with the back of her bony hand. 'They're helping me, and Hannah's going out this afternoon to get a job, ain't yer love?'

Hannah nodded.

'Git me a beer,' he bellowed at Hannah.

She raced up the iron staircase to the room above the stable to get the jug of beer that always had to be full. As she ran back down, some of the beer slopped out.

'That's right, go on, spill it, yer dozy bitch.'

Hannah quickly stepped back when he raised his hand to hit her. Over the years she had learnt to swiftly duck out of his way.

'I 'as ter work bloody 'ard to keep you and yer sister, and all you do is upset me beer,' he growled, snatching the jug from her and drinking its contents down almost without taking a breath. He ran his fingers across his moustache; his short, greying beard caked with food and yellowed with beer and tobacco. He grabbed Hannah's long hair and jerked her head back. 'Right, now go and git it filled up again.' He forced the empty jug into her hand. 'And bring it over ter the smiffy.'

Hannah went to run, but he was still holding her hair. He put his face close to hers and she tried hard not to breathe in the fumes from his beery breath. 'And don't yer dare spill a drop, else yer feel the back of this.' He lifted his hand, it was large and dirty. His bare arms were thick and sinewy. Hannah knew he was very strong, for she had felt the weight of his hands many times before.

Tears welled in her eyes as he hung on to her hair, but she dared not cry out in pain for fear of more punishment. He gave her a push and she fell sprawling in the pool of muddy water that always lay near the tap. He roared with laughter as he marched off whilst Hannah lay quite still till the sound of his boots striking the cobbled yard died away. Alice was crouching in the corner, not daring to move.

'Get up, Hannah, and when you get back, take that dirty wet apron off,' said Aunt May apprehensively. She was still shaking, even though her husband had left. 'Now hurry round and get his beer.' She looked behind her, her face red and fearful.

Hannah raced round the corner to the pub. She pushed the door open and put the jug on the counter. 'Would you fill this, please?'

''Allo there, 'Annah. It's a bit warm terday. Christ, you look a bit of a mess. Wot 'appened?' Hannah turned and saw Alf, one of the carter's apprentices, sitting in the corner. She didn't answer. She didn't like him, for he was always chasing Alice, making her run, then laughing at her limp. He came over to Hannah. 'I see old 'Arry's started early terday.'

'Well, it is warm work. And by the way, shouldn't you be at work?'

He laughed in a rough way, showing the gaps in his yellow teeth. 'Yer. The boss sent me out fer a pie, so I fought I'd 'ave a swift 'alf while I was 'ere.' He leant closer, and his bad breath made Hannah turn away.

The barman put the jug on the counter. 'Did yer tell yer uncle 'is slate's gitting a bit 'igh?'

'Yes, yes I did.' Hannah quickly crossed her fingers. She didn't like telling lies, but there was no way she was going to tell Uncle Harry that he owed a lot of money.

'Well tell 'im I'll 'ave ter stop serving yer if 'e don't start paying it orf soon.'

'Yes, I'll tell him.' Hannah picked up the foaming jug of beer with both hands, and carefully made her way out of the door.

'Bye, 'Annah, see yer around,' called Alf after her.

Aunt May was still busy with the washing, helped by Alice, when Hannah returned to the yard. She didn't stop to speak, but kept her head down and made her way to the blacksmith's shop.

The heat from the fire in the smithy was suffocating, and the smell from the horses nauseating. Uncle Harry was bending over holding the foot of one of the big shire-horses between his knees, banging a new shoe on to it. Flies buzzed all around them.

'Shove it down there, gel,' he said without looking up.

Hannah put the jug on an upturned box, and slowly backed away. How she hated this man. It was hot, and she knew he'd be yelling for beer all day. What would happen if the pub wouldn't let her have any more? If only they could go back to Richmond. Out in the yard, Alice was still trying to hang out the washing. She was short and the line was too high up. Aunt May, a nervous, jumpy woman, looked flustered. 'I'll go on up and start getting the bubble-and-squeak ready. You two carry on down 'ere. Don't forget to 'ang the bath up, and sweep down when yer finished.'

When they had hung the last of the clothes on the line, Alice helped Hannah lift the heavy bath of water from off the stools, and tip it away.

'Cheer up, Hannah,' said Alice, grabbing a broom and marching round the yard with it on her shoulder. 'I'm a soldier, look.'

Hannah laughed and, going over to her sister, put her arm round her shoulders. 'Alice, what am I going to do?' She sat on one of the rickety stools, her face growing serious. 'I've got to tell Uncle Harry he can't have any more beer till he's paid up his bill.'

Alice stopped laughing and sat beside her. 'I don't know. He'll be ever so angry. Couldn't we run away? Let's go back to Richmond.'

'How could we? Miss Jordon's gone; who would look after us?'

'I don't know.'

'And what about Aunt May?' continued Hannah. 'I'm sure Uncle Harry would kill her if he thought she had helped us.'

'I don't want to live here,' said Alice, her big blue eyes filling with tears.

'Come on, cheer up. I'm sure everything will work out all right.'

'If only we could go to school instead of mucking out the stables and helping Aunt May.'

Hannah knew Uncle Harry would never spend the money on them. 'I thought you liked the horses,' she said.

'I do,' said Alice quickly. 'But I would like to go to school and meet other girls.'

'Oh, so you're fed up with my company?'

Alice smiled. 'No, silly.' She stood up and hugged her sister. 'I'll always love you.'

Hannah patted her back. 'Come on, let's get this yard cleaned up before Uncle Harry comes in for his dinner.'

'What about his beer? You know he always has to have a jugful at dinner-times.'

A worried frown wrinkled Hannah's brow. 'Yes, I know.'

'Couldn't we ask Aunt May.'

'I don't know. She's as frightened of him as we are.'

'You could try.'

'You wait here. I've got to go up for a clean pinny, I'll ask her then.'

Hannah stepped inside the gloomy room. Aunt May was sitting at the table with her head in her hands. 'Don't you feel well?' asked Hannah, her voice full of concern.

Aunt May looked up and a faint smile lifted her pale face. 'It's this weather, fair takes it out of me it does. Lay the table, there's a good girl.'

'I'll just get me clean pinny first. Aunt May . . .' She hesitated. 'The pub said they won't give me any more beer till Uncle Harry's paid his bill.' The words came out in a rush.

With both hands flat on the table, Aunt May slowly pushed herself up. 'If only 'e didn't drink 'is week's allowance in one go,' she sighed. 'I'll go down and see if I can get some money for you.'

As Hannah watched her leave the room, she suddenly

realized her aunt was ill, her footsteps heavy and laboured. 'Aunt May,' she called after her, 'what's wrong?'

Aunt May turned on the stairs. 'I'm all right, love. I'll be back in half a mo.'

Hannah was busy putting the knives and forks on the bare wooden table when she heard shouting. She hurried to the door and saw Aunt May shaking her head and screaming as she ran through the yard.

Uncle Harry was following her and yelling. 'Wot yer done wiv it? Christ, woman, I gave yer a shilling at the end a last week. If yer spent it on those kids, I'll murder yer.'

Hannah saw him raise his fist. 'Git out the way, yer silly cow,' he bellowed, Hannah couldn't see who at. He brought it down, and Hannah knew he had hit Alice.

She raced down to her sister who was lying face down on the ground, covering her head with her hands and screaming. Uncle Harry kicked her to one side. The thin worn sleeve of her frock split, and a large red patch appeared at the top of Alice's arm.

Aunt May didn't stop running. Outside the yard they heard Aunt May scream, then came the whinnying of a horse, a lot of shouting, and a great commotion. The sound of heavy boots thumping on the cobbles stopped Uncle Harry in his tracks. He walked slowly to the yard's entrance.

Hannah helped Alice to her feet, gave her a hug and wiped her tears on the bottom of her pinny. 'Quick, we'd better see what's happened.'

They followed Uncle Harry. Outside many people were gathered round a coalman's horse and cart.

'I couldn't stop,' said the driver, removing his hat with the leather protector hanging down the back. He mopped his dirt-streaked brow with a red handkerchief. 'Came out o' there like a bullet, she did. Is she dead?'

Hannah and Alice edged their way closer. On the ground lay Aunt May. They both cried out and dropped to their knees. Her face was covered with blood. 'Aunt May, Aunt May, are you all right?' asked Hannah.

She slowly opened her eyes. 'Yes, yes I think so,' she whispered.

A man who was leaning over her, said, 'We'd better git 'er round ter the doctor.'

''E only lives round the corner,' said another.

Uncle Harry, who had been standing back, pushed his way through. 'Out the way, I'll take 'er.' She must have been very light, for he swept her up in his arms and walked away.

'Hannah, should we go with him?' asked Alice.

'No, we'd better not, we might be in the way.'

The chattering crowd dispersed and the girls slowly wandered back into the yard and sat in the sun.

''Allo gels.' Alf poked his well-greased head round the gate.

'What do you want?' said Hannah.

'Someone said yer aunt's been knocked down.'

'Yes, Uncle Harry's taken her to the doctor,' said Alice.

'That's a shame. I'll be back later ter see 'ow she is. Bye.' He didn't tell them what he wanted.

The smell of burning suddenly filled their nostrils. 'The dinner,' yelled Hannah, racing up the staircase. She pushed open the door and a cloud of black smoke billowed out. She ran inside and knocked the frying-pan off the stove then, carefully wrapping the dishcloth round the handle, threw the pan outside.

At that moment Uncle Harry returned to the yard, to be greeted by the black, burnt frying-pan crashing and clattering down the iron stairs, and landing at his feet. Hannah trembled as his face turned scarlet, whilst Alice ran and hid.

'What's this?' he roared, staring at the black baked mess

lying in the mud. 'Was that me dinner?'

Hannah stood at the top of the stairs, and nodded.

'Git down 'ere.'

Hannah was too frightened to move.

'I said git down 'ere.' His bellows filled Hannah's ears and echoed round the yard; her uncle's face had now turned from scarlet to purple.

Alice crept out from her hiding place and stood at the far end of the yard. 'It wasn't her fault. Leave her alone,' she cried, tears streaming down her face.

He turned. 'Somebody's gonner pay fer this.' He moved towards Alice.

'Don't you touch her,' yelled Hannah.

'Why you little . . .'

Alice began to run. 'I'm going to tell on you,' she cried out.

'Yer wot?' He started to run after her.

Hannah raced down after Alice as she dodged towards the smithy. Alice could never run very fast because of her leg, and Uncle Harry was gaining on her. Hannah was screaming. 'Leave her alone. Please, don't touch her.'

When she reached the smithy, Alice was struggling to climb up into the loft, Uncle Harry holding on to her foot as she tried to shake him off. Hannah pulled at his arm but he just shrugged her aside and she fell to the ground. She quickly looked round for something to hit him with, and the first thing that caught her eye was a hammer. With both hands she raised it above her head and, with all the force she could muster, hit him in the middle of his back. He fell face-down in the dirt. The dust and chaff filled his mouth and he started to choke. Alice, who was half-way up the ladder, was sobbing, clutching the top rung, unable to move. Hannah stood over him with the hammer in her hand.

'No, don't Hannah,' screamed Alice.

Uncle Harry lay on the floor, writhing and fighting for breath as he clawed at his mouth, trying to remove the chaff. He turned over and his eyes were bulging as he stared up at Hannah. Pieces of straw were sticking out of his beard, and he was making strange choking noises in the back of his throat.

'Come on, Alice,' she said calmly. 'Let's go.'

'We can't, Hannah. We can't leave him. Not like this.' Alice fell to her knees and quickly began brushing the chaff from his mouth. He grabbed her hand, unable to speak.

Hannah pulled Alice away. 'Leave him,' she yelled. 'He'll kill us if we stay here. Come on, quick, let's go.' She pulled Alice to her feet.

Uncle Harry reached out feebly to grab Alice's leg, but Hannah pulled her away. 'Come on, Alice, we've got to get away from him.'

'We can't . . .'

'Shh,' said Hannah. 'There's someone in the yard.' She edged towards the door and looked out.

Alice was close behind her. 'Is it Aunt May?'

'No. I can't see them, but it's someone wearing hobnail boots.'

'Hannah. Hannah, look,' screamed Alice in panic. 'We can't go and leave him, not now. Look, he's stopped breathing.'

Hannah turned. The colour drained from her face and she began trembling. Tears blurred her eyes. 'We must.'

'But Hannah . . .'

'We've got to get away from here, and away from him,' her voice was stern. 'So don't argue. Quick, let's run.' She grabbed Alice's hand and with their heads bent they ran through the yard and out into the main road . . .

The hobnailed boots were chasing her. They were getting closer. Hannah cried out and woke with a start. She sat up, sweating with fear, tears filling her eyes. What had she done?

She ran her hand over her face. Where was she? In the half-light, the room looked eerie. Alice turned in her sleep and mumbled. Hannah lay beside her and, pulling her close, gently stroked her hair. She smiled in relief. She knew they were both safe here with Maudie. At least for now.

Chapter 4

The following morning when Hannah opened her eyes, sunlight was just beginning to seep through the high window. She blinked, it was early, and she was still a little disorientated. Alice stirred beside her and Hannah smiled when she recalled the previous day. She lay quite still, unable to believe their good fortune, at last they had found some sort of home. A flurry of excitement and conscience washed over her when she wondered what the day would bring. Could she steal? But they did have to eat. A noise in the far corner of the room caused her to lift her head slightly; she could see Jack sitting at the table drinking tea, the tell-tale end of his cigarette glowing.

Hannah quietly stood up and wandered over to him. 'Good morning,' she whispered.

''Allo gel, sleep all right?'

She nodded.

'Yer was doing a bit a shouting earlier on. I was gonner wake yer, but yer quietened down – did yer 'ave a bad dream, then?'

Hannah blushed, confused. What if she'd . . . 'Yes, yes, I did. I'm sorry if I woke you – did any of the others hear . . . ?'

'Na. I'd just got up fer a jimmy when yer started carrying on. Na, yer didn't wake any of 'em.'

Hannah felt uneasy. 'Jack, did I say anything . . . you know? Could you understand?'

'Na, just a lot a mumbling.' He grinned. 'Why's that, got sumfink ter 'ide?'

She laughed, but it sounded false to her ears. 'Course not. You look very smart this morning,' she said, quickly changing the subject.

'D'yer like me whistle?'

'Whistle?' she repeated.

'Yer, me whistle and flute, suit.'

'Yes, you look very smart – but why?'

'Going up wiv all the toffs, so I gotter blend in, ain't I?'

'Yes, I suppose you have.'

'There's a cuppa in the pot, gotter be orf, can't stand 'ere chatting all day.' He pulled at his tie. 'See yer Sunday.' He picked his cap up from the chair, placed it on his head at a jaunty angle, and disappeared.

There were movements coming from all quarters, as one by one the others left their beds.

Tom was rubbing his eyes. 'Better put yer mattress over there on the pile,' he said to Hannah as he dragged his across the room. 'Ovverwise Maudie'll go mad.'

Hannah knelt beside Alice and gently shook her. 'Come on, lazy bones, it's time to get up.'

Alice quickly sat up. 'Hannah.' She threw her arms round her sister and began to cry.

'What's wrong?' asked Hannah as she gently patted her back.

'Oh Hannah, I had a terrible dream,' she sobbed, clinging to her sister. 'I dreamt Aunt May was calling us, and Uncle Harry had just got hold of me when you woke me up.'

'There, there. Don't worry. That's all over now.' She quickly looked over her shoulder to see if the others had heard or were watching them; fortunately they were all busy with their own chores. 'We're safe here. Now come on, dry those tears and help me put the bed back in the corner, then we can have a nice cup of tea. Tom's up, look.'

Maudie was still in bed when they left.

'She don't like gitting up too early,' said Dolly when they were outside. She was stuffing her hair under a blue woollen beret. 'Got ter try and look a bit different,' she announced, taking Freddie's hand. 'And remember, we ain't a charity 'ere, so make sure yer brings back plenty. Cos if yer don't, don't fink yer sitting at our table again ternight.'

'It's not up ter you,' said Tom. 'It's up ter Maudie.'

'Yer, but if yer don't bring nuffink back, I'll make sure fings . . .' Dolly stopped. 'Come on Freddie, let's be orf.'

Tom, Hannah and Alice stood at the bottom of Hope Street and watched her go off in the opposite direction to the one Tom said they were going to take. Hope Street wasn't very long, and it didn't have a pub or shop on either of its corners like most of the streets round here had. Before Freddie disappeared round the corner, he turned and poked his tongue out.

'Did you see that?' said Hannah in disgust.

'Take no notice,' said Tom. ''E's a funny little fing, don't say a lot. I fink 'e's scared stiff of Dolly.'

'I don't blame him,' said Hannah. 'I wouldn't like to upset her.'

Tom shrugged. 'She's not too bad, got a bit of a temper sometimes though. Come on, let's git ter the market down Jamaica Road.'

The excitement of what they had to do was building up inside Hannah. She was thrilled by the noise and bustle as they pushed and wandered around the stalls looking for anything that had fallen into the road. Men were shouting out about their wares, and the different smells all added to the wonder. Tom squeezed round the back of the stalls and found a box with some oranges in; most of them were mouldy, but he managed to find four good ones which he quickly stuffed into his pocket. Alice was

41

giggling, and her face glowed when she took an apple and wasn't seen. Hannah stood gazing at the clothes piled high on one of the many second-hand stalls. A white smocked pinafore and a pair of black stockings were hanging over the edge. The old woman tending the stall looked at Hannah suspiciously.

'Go on, clear orf.' She flapped her hands at Hannah, who was looking dirty and unkempt, then, turning back to her customer said. 'Yer 'as ter 'ave eyes in yer bloody arse wiv sum of 'em round 'ere. Pinch anyfink, sum of 'em would.'

Hannah walked on. There was no point in waiting, the woman had seen her.

Further up the road they were in luck. A barrow had tipped up and a sack of potatoes split open and spilled over the road. As they rolled away Tom, Alice and Hannah lunged to snatch them whilst kids appeared from everywhere picking them up. Despite all the owner's shouting and shaking of his fists the potatoes were cleared away in a flash.

Hannah, Alice and Tom raced round the corner. Hannah, holding up the bottom of her pinafore full of potatoes, fell against the wall laughing.

'That was good fun,' she gasped. 'Here Tom, put these in your pockets.'

'We could do with a shopping bag,' panted Alice. 'I'll ask Maudie if she's got one we can take out with us.'

'Yer know what she'll say ter yer, don't yer?' Tom rammed the potatoes in his pockets.

'No, what?' asked Hannah.

'She'll say if yer wants a shopping bag, yer better nick one.' He laughed. 'I'm glad I've got you two ter talk to.' He kicked the wall with his big boots, scuffing them even more. 'I feels a bit out of it at Maudie's.'

'Why's that?' asked Alice.

'Well, Dolly's got Freddie, and Jack's a lot older, and

well . . .' He continued kicking the wall.

'Well, you've got us two now,' said Hannah. 'And we're all going to stay together. A bit like the Three Musketeers.'

'Who're they when they're out?'

'They're men we've read about. Haven't you ever heard of them?' inquired Alice.

'Na. 'Ere, can you two read?'

'Yes, of course we can. Can you?' asked Hannah.

'Na.' Tom looked uneasy, he blushed and looked down. 'Well, not very well. I ain't been ter school fer years, not since me mum run orf wiv some bloke.'

Hannah looked shocked. 'Your mother ran away and left you?'

He looked sad. 'Yer, she took me little sister, but me uncle didn't like me. 'E wasn't me real uncle, just some bloke she took in.'

Alice was all eyes. 'Where did you go?'

'All over. I managed ter find a bit a food, and I kipped anywhere, then Maudie found me sitting by the river.' He laughed. 'I fink she fought I was gonner chuck meself in.'

'Were you?' asked Hannah, her dark eyes opened wide with interest.

'I 'ad fought about it. Wonner orange?' He dived into his pocket. 'There's a park near 'ere, let's go over there and 'ave our breakfast.'

The girls followed him, and they sat on a bench eating their oranges.

Alice, with juice running down her chin, asked, 'Will Maudie be cross with us for not getting very much?'

'Na. We've got plenty of taters. 'Sides, the market ain't finished yet, should find a bit more when they move orf.' Tom sucked loudly on his orange.

'I saw a nice white pinny like Dolly's, and a pair of stockings on the stall, but the woman was looking at me,' said Hannah, wiping her hands on the bottom of her grubby pinafore.

'When we've finished these we'll go back and 'ave a look, and if she's busy I'll try and take 'er mind orf yer, yer might be able ter git 'em then.'

Hannah hesitated. 'I don't know if I could steal. I mean, that's really stealing, don't you think?'

'S'pose it is, but we gotter eat, and git clothes. We're lucky really, Maudie does look after us.'

'Why does she do it?' asked Hannah.

'Dunno. We fink she was an orphan 'erself, and was ill treated. But we don't really know.'

'That's really nice of her,' said Alice.

Tom shrugged his shoulders. 'We dunno if that's right. I fink Dolly just made it up fer sumfink ter say.' He stood up. ''Ere, d'yer fink yer could teach me ter read prop'ly?'

'We could try,' said Hannah.

'And write,' added Alice.

'We'll 'ave to pinch some pencils and paper,' said Tom enthusiastically. 'Come on, let's see if we can git some clothes fer yer first.'

Every time they wandered past the second-hand stall the old woman kept her eyes on them, so for the rest of the day they picked up anything that seemed to be lying around. They laughed when they found a bag of sweets someone had left on a bench, and quickly stuffed their mouths full.

Hannah couldn't believe they were having so much fun, and really what they were doing wasn't stealing.

At one point Alice was walking close to the wall when she suddenly stopped, looked about her, bent down, picked up something, and quickly moved on.

'What have you got there, Alice?' asked Hannah.

'Nothing,' she said not turning around.

'Oh come on, show us.'

'Later.'

Hannah turned to Tom. 'She can be so – so maddening at times. Come on, let's walk on.'

They passed Alice, and had almost reached the park gates when Hannah turned and noticed her sister was beginning to look apprehensive on her own. 'Wait for me,' she called out.

They stopped and Alice limped towards them. 'Look, look what I've found,' she said in a loud whisper, her blue eyes shining. She unclenched her hand to reveal a sixpence, then quickly closed it again.

'Crickey,' said Tom. 'A tanner, that's an 'ole bloody fortune.'

Hannah stared at Alice's clenched hand. 'What're you going to get with that?'

'Don't know.'

'We could get some sweets,' said Tom enthusiastically.

'Or some cakes,' said Hannah joining in.

'I found it, and I'll decide what to get,' Alice announced.

Hannah was taken back. 'Well, yes, it is yours, but I thought that seeing as how we're all together, you would have shared . . .' Hannah's voice drifted off when she saw the expression on Alice's face. She was reminded of the time a long while ago when her doll got mysteriously broken, and Alice refused to share hers with Hannah. 'Come on, Tom, let's go and see if we can find something else.'

They began to move away from Alice. 'Wait, wait a minute,' she called, hobbling towards them. 'Let's sit down and try to work out the best way to spend it.'

After a lot of deliberating, Alice decided to buy some meat, and tobacco for Maudie. Hannah smiled. Alice would now be the golden girl in Maudie's eyes.

'The stalls'll be clearing away soon,' said Tom. 'Should find some bits left. The veg stall's always the best.'

They kicked over the rotting veg and found a couple of good apples, some cabbage leaves that weren't too yellow, and a large onion. Their pockets were quickly bulging and Alice pulled the ties round her pinny tighter and filled her bodice with the potatoes they had picked up earlier.

'Maudie's gonner be real pleased wiv us,' said Tom. 'Don't ever remember gitting ser much.' He pushed the apples under his cap.

Hannah laughed. 'Now I know why you've got such a large cap.'

They wandered past the second-hand clothes stall again where the old woman was busy reaching up and taking the clothes from off the top of her barrow. She wasn't looking at Hannah. Tom nodded to her and started to chase Alice, making her scream.

The old woman yelled 'Bloody kids, yer frightened the bloody daylights out of me. Go on, clear orf.'

Hannah knew this could be her only opportunity, so she grabbed the stockings and pinny and quickly walked off in the opposite direction to the one Alice and Tom had taken.

Two minutes later she sat in the park breathless and trembling, the noise of her heart beating like a hammer filling her ears, her face flushed. She felt guilty but elated as she cuddled her new clothes to her – this was easy, and if she thought about it she didn't feel as if she had done anything really wrong.

After a while Tom and Alice came into view and she walked over to meet them.

'Yer got 'em then?' asked Tom.

'Yes, yes,' said Hannah. 'Look. Feel it, it's lovely cotton, and all that pretty smocking. This must have been very expensive.'

'You should give it to me,' said Alice sullenly.

'What?'

'You should let me have it. I could have easily bought that with the money I found, but no, you two decided I should buy meat.'

'It was your idea as well,' said Tom.

'Well yes, but I knew that was what you wanted me to do.'

Hannah looked at Alice. Her sister was changing. It was living with Uncle Harry that had done it, made her so much more bitter and concerned for herself than she'd been before. She dearly loved Alice and didn't want things to be difficult between them. She'd had a hard time with their uncle, for which Hannah had felt partly responsible. She deserved a bit of pleasure now. Hannah stood up, she had to give in, it was her duty. 'Here you are, you can have the smock, I'll keep the stockings. Come on let's get back.'

'Thanks, Hannah.' Alice threw her arms round her sister's neck.

'Cor, ain't yer done well? Look at this lot, Dolly,' yelled Maudie as Tom, Hannah and Alice tipped their pickings on to the table.

They were all laughing excitedly, even Bonzo trying to join in, with his large paws resting on the table and his great tail swishing back and forth.

'Did yer git yer soap?' asked Dolly.

'No I didn't.' Hannah giggled. 'To tell the truth, I forgot all about it.'

'Well yer ain't using mine.'

'Now Dolly, don't start,' said Maudie.

'Got some meat though,' said Tom quickly. 'Alice found a tanner and she got some meat and yer baccy Maudie.'

Maudie's face lit up. 'Yer found a tanner, an 'ole tanner and spent some of it on me?' She clasped Alice to her ample bosom. 'I knew yer was a good 'en the minute I set eyes on yer.' She took Alice's head in her hands and plonked a resounding kiss on her forehead.

'I got Alice a new pinny,' said Hannah softly. She was feeling a little put out at all the fuss being made over Alice. 'And meself some stockings, look.'

'That's very nice. Now let's put all this stuff away and start finking about sumfink to eat.'

'That stew smells good, Maudie,' said Tom. 'And I see yer got yerself a new chair.'

'Yer, got it round where the gels was 'iding. It's been a good day all round.' Maudie affectionately patted the high back of her new brown velvet chair. 'It ain't as good as me bedroom one, but wiv a bit of a clean up and a bit o' patching, it'll do.'

'Did you bring it home on your own?' asked Hannah.

'Na, Bob round the news-stand give me 'and. Mind you, that nosy old cow in number six gave Bob a bit o' lip. You should 'ave 'eard 'er. Reckoned I'd pinched it. I tell yer, gel, it took me all me time ter keep me 'ands orf 'er.'

'I don't like that woman,' said Hannah. 'She gave me a funny look this morning.'

'She gives everybody a funny look,' said Tom. 'We all call 'er Mrs Nosy.'

'Yer, well, let's git cleared up, and let's 'ope Jack's bin as lucky as us,' said Maudie, standing back to admire her chair.

'I'm going to have a wash and put my new stockings on,' said Hannah.

'Yer can 'ave a bit of me carbolic, but don't be too long gel,' yelled Maudie after her.

Outside Hannah wondered about Jack. She wished she could have kept the pinny, it would have been nice to look clean for him, but she knew Alice would make a fuss. He wouldn't be back today, and tomorrow everything would be closed because of the king's funeral. The stockings felt good and, as she laced up her boots, Alice came out wearing the new pinny.

'That looks very nice,' said Hannah.

Alice did a pirouette in front of her. 'That was very kind of you.' She kissed her sister's cheek.

Hannah hung her head. 'It's all right. I'm glad it fits. If you give me your old one I'll wash it out, and if Maudie's got some cotton perhaps I could mend mine a bit and give it a wash.'

'Hannah, will you be thinking of going out to work again if we stay here?'

'I don't know, why?'

'It's just that . . . well, it's just that if we settle here, I'd like it to be, well – you know?'

Hannah frowned. 'No, I don't know, what're you talking about?'

'Well, what if we get caught taking things, will we go to prison?'

Hannah was taken aback: she had been having such a good time today she hadn't really thought about all the awful consequences it could bring. If Uncle Harry was dead and they were caught stealing, would the police find out where they were from and put two and two together? The colour drained from Hannah's face. Could they be hung? 'We mustn't take anything else,' she nodded. 'I'll have to get a job.'

'I'm sure Maudie would let you stay here if you brought in some money every week,' said Alice quickly.

Hannah looked thoughtful. 'I'll do anything, though I'm not sure what. But I couldn't get a job looking like this, now could I?' Hannah pulled at her pinafore.

Alice shook her head and, despite her worries, Hannah suppressed a smile. Was her sister beginning to feel guilty at taking the pinny?

'Look, let's give it a few days to see if we really like staying here, then I'll have a word with Jack. He might know of somewhere that's looking for workers.' Hannah stood up. She had to protect her sister and, though the thought of going to prison really upset her, she didn't want Alice to see that. 'Right, let's go and tackle that rabbit stew Maudie promised us.'

The following day, as nothing was open, Hannah and Alice decided to take a walk to explore their new surroundings.

'Can I come with you?' asked Tom.

'Course,' said Hannah. 'You can show us round.'

Outside they wandered along Hope Street.

'I wished we had a home like this,' said Alice as they strolled past the row of houses, the front doors of which opened straight on to the pavement.

It wasn't a very long street, and one end was dominated by the old red-brick wash-house. Today the street was quiet, no gossiping women standing at their doors, or noisy children playing. Hannah guessed it was because of the king's funeral; no doubt that was why most of the curtains were drawn too, as a sign of respect. Quite a few of the houses were very shabby, grimy and dirty, with paint peeling off the doors. Hannah noticed that inside some of them, where the curtains didn't reach, dead bluebottles were lined up along the windowsill. But some did have spotless white steps and pretty lace curtains up at the clean windows.

'Cost yer a few bob a week in rent,' said Tom.

'Hannah might be going to work,' said Alice pertly.

'Oh, when?' asked Tom.

'Alice,' said Hannah sharply. 'Don't take any notice of her, Tom.'

'But you said—' whined Alice.

'I said I might. Besides, I told you, how can I go for a job looking like this?' She tried to tug down the sleeve of her frock, but it was far too small for her. 'Come on, let's get a move on,' she said tetchily.

They wandered into the park and Alice picked up a stone. She scratched it on the ground, it was made of chalk. 'Look, Tom. We'll be able to teach you to write your name,' she said, writing the word 'Tom' on the paving-stones.

'Is that me name?' he asked, standing back to admire it. ''Ere, let me try.' He went down on his knees, his tongue stuck out with concentration as he began copying Alice's letters.

Alice laughed and giggled at his attempt. Hannah sat on the ground with him and guided his hand.

'Cor, fanks,' he said. 'We'll 'ave ter git 'old of some paper, then we can 'ave a go indoors.'

'Let's try and find an old newspaper, then we can have a go at teaching you to read,' said Hannah, catching Tom's enthusiasm.

Alice ran on to the park's shelter. 'Over here,' she called. 'We're in luck – look, there's a paper in here.'

Tom put the chalk in his pocket and they hurried across the grass to Alice.

'It's a few days old, but that doesn't matter,' said Hannah, busy folding it to a manageable size before settling down to read to Tom.

He was a very bright boy and willing to learn. Although the news about the king's death was very sad, they had to laugh at Tom's attempts to read, and it was only when Alice said she was hungry they realized they had been out for a very long while.

Chapter 5

All Sunday, Hannah eagerly awaited Jack's return. Alice and Tom were studying the newspaper, and even Maudie and Dolly listened as the Miller girls took it in turns to read to them.

'Looks like yer got yerselves a full-time job now,' said Maudie. 'Always wanted ter know wot was going on. I'll ask old Bob at the newspaper stand fer some old ens.'

'Could you ask 'im if 'e's got any clean paper we can use ter write on?' asked Tom.

'And a pencil,' said Alice. 'We need a pencil.'

'I'll see wot I can do.' Maudie sat back in her armchair and, with Bonzo at her feet, puffed on her clay pipe. The smile on her face told Hannah she was happy with her family, and Hannah was happy to be part of it.

It was well into the afternoon before Jack returned. Maudie greeted him almost like a long-lost soul.

''Ave I done all right!' he said triumphantly, tossing his cap on the chair. 'Wait till yer claps eyes on this little lot, Maudie me old love.'

They all sat at the table in wide-eyed wonder as Jack started to empty his pockets. First coins appeared, then, greeted by gasps of astonishment, two ten-shilling notes were laid on the table.

'It's a bloody king's ransom,' said Maudie, eagerly sweeping up the money. 'That's wot it is, a bloody king's ransom.' She began counting out the coins.

Jack laughed as he took out a gold watch and chain from his pocket. 'Should get a few bob fer that,' he said, carefully placing it on the table.

'Does it work?' asked Maudie.

'Course it does.' He held it to his ear. ''Ere are, you 'ave a listen.' He passed it over to Tom. 'And what d'yer fink about this?' With a great flurry he took from the inside pocket of his jacket a gold bangle. 'Solid gold, I reckon. Go on gel, try it on.' He rolled it along the table to Hannah.

She quickly put her hands out to stop it rolling on to Dolly. As she slipped her wrist through it she felt rich. She had never seen real gold before and her fingers gently ran over the bracelet's ornate scrolls. It was very heavy.

'Let's 'ave a look then,' said Dolly, pulling at Hannah's arm.

''Ang on there, Dolly,' said Jack. 'Give 'er a chance. Well, gel?'

'I think it's lovely.'

'Come on, 'urry up, it's my turn ter wear it now,' said Dolly impatiently.

Hannah was still twisting it round her arm. 'Where on earth did you get it?'

Jack touched the side of his nose.

'But how could you get it off . . . ?'

Jack smiled. 'We don't ask questions like that round 'ere, do we, Maudie love?'

Maudie smiled. 'No, Jack. Now, wot d'yer want me ter do wiv all this?'

'Well, I've kept a few quid back fer meself.' He patted his chest. 'Got it in a nice leather wallet. But you can flog the watch and bracelet. Let us know what old Frank wants ter give yer fer 'em first. Yer see, I fink 'e's likely to pull a fast one; I reckon they could be worf quite a few bob.'

'Wot about the money?'

'Put it in the kitty. I expect there's a few fings yer wants ter git. But no fancy stuff, mind.'

'All that? Christ, it's a bloody fortune. Fanks Jack, yer a real gent,' said Maudie. 'Always fought yer was one of the best.'

Jack looked embarrassed. 'Go on wiv yer. Yer could start be gitting that one sumfink decent ter wear,' he pointed to Hannah.

Hannah felt dirty and ashamed. She hated the idea of Jack feeling sorry for her. She wanted to have money herself and be free of hand-outs. Stealing and living from hand to mouth wasn't for her, she decided. She had to find a job.

Now it was Alice's turn to wear the bangle. She sat turning it round and round on her wrist. 'I'd love to have something like this. It's really lovely, and I'm going to get someone to buy me one when I'm older.'

Dolly laughed. 'Oh yer, and where d'yer reckon yer gonner meet a toff like that?'

'I don't know – yet,' she said, tossing her head. 'But when I grow up . . .' She quickly stopped.

'Oh yer, and what d'yer wonner be when yer grow up?' asked Dolly.

It was Alice's turn to be embarrassed. She looked down at her hands and whispered, 'I'm not telling.'

'Oh go on,' urged Tom. 'Tell us.'

'Yer, come on,' said Dolly.

Alice pulled herself up. 'I want to go on the stage and be a fairy princess.'

With that they all fell about laughing.

'Gawd bugger me,' said Maudie. 'Well, I've 'eard it all now. A bloody fairy princess – well, when the time comes, gel, yer can grant me a few wishes.'

Jack too was laughing, but he put his arm round her shoulders and said kindly, 'There ain't no point in going frough life if yer ain't got no ambition. Right young lady?'

Alice nodded.

''Sides, I reckon yer'd make a real cracking fairy princess wiv yer blonde 'air and those baby-blue eyes.'

Alice blushed and smiled, her dimples deepening.

'And what about you?' He was speaking to Hannah.

'I want to get a job,' she said confidently.

'Cor, Maudie, yer've gone an' picked up a right pair this time,' said Jack, giving Hannah a wink.

Hannah blushed too, and quickly looked away.

'Come on, put the kettle on, Dolly,' said Maudie, 'and we can 'ave a cuppa tea.'

'Why is it always me?' she grumbled.

'It ain't always you.'

'I'll do it,' said Hannah, glad to get away from the table.

'I reckon the shrimp and winkle man could be in 'Ope Street. Go round and 'ave a butcher's, Tom. I just fancy a nice plate of winkles,' said Maudie smacking her lips. 'Alice, you'll find some pins in that drawer over there.'

'I'll just take me whistle orf 'fore tea.' Jack smoothed down his jacket. 'Gotter look after it; cost a few bob, I can tell yer.'

'It's very nice,' said Hannah shyly.

'Keeps me trousers under Maudie's mattress – 'er weight keeps 'em looking smart.'

'Not ser much of it, yer saucy sod!' Maudie laughed as Jack took off his jacket and, pulling down his braces, wandered into Maudie's bedroom.

'I don't mind 'im using me cupboard. 'E's a good lad,' she nodded and, collecting up the money and jewellery, followed him into her bedroom.

* * *

Night was falling and, out in the front yard, Maudie and Jack were talking and having a quiet smoke by the street's gas-light before retiring. Hannah stood at the door for a few moments looking at Jack. He was so handsome. Now she'd got over feeling hurt at his remarks about her clothes she decided she was pleased he wanted her to look nice. Tomorrow they were going to another market, but this time she would have some money to spend.

Leaving Jack and Maudie outside, the others began to settle down for the night. Suddenly there was a commotion outside the back door. Bonzo was barking and someone was shouting. Tom, who was nearest the door, sat up.

'What is it?' asked Dolly in a loud whisper.

'Dunno,' replied Tom. 'Can't make out what they're talking about.'

Hannah didn't think they were talking; it sounded more as if they were having a row.

Alice sat up. 'What's going on?'

'Don't know,' said Hannah in a hushed tone. 'We think Jack and Maudie are having a row.'

Alice giggled. 'I thought he was her blue-eyed boy.'

'Listen,' Hannah cocked her head. 'Sounds like someone else is with them.'

'It's Bert,' said Tom. He threw himself back down on his mattress. 'What does 'e wonner come back for – 'e always brings trouble.'

Hannah could see Dolly draw Freddie closer. Who was this Bert that everybody was afraid of? Even Jack spoke his name with hate. She was intrigued. 'I'm going to have a look,' she said, getting up.

'I shouldn't if I was you,' said Tom, resting on one elbow. 'You'll 'ear 'im soon enough.'

'Does he come back very often?'

'Na, but 'im and Jack always 'ave a row. Seen 'em fight once.'

'What is it that makes everybody except Maudie dislike him so much? How long has he been here?' asked Hannah.

'Dunno. 'E was 'ere before me,' said Tom. 'Ain't 'ad a lot ter say ter 'im. 'E just comes and goes.'

'Just lie down and shut up,' said Alice peevishly. 'Don't start looking for trouble.'

'We fink 'e must 'ave some sorta 'old over Maudie,' said Tom.

Hannah sat down and hugged her knees. 'Really? What, sort of like blackmail?'

'Don't fink it's as strong as that.'

'Well, what then? Does she give him money?'

'We dunno,' said Dolly irritably. 'Do as yer sister told yer, just lay down and shut up.'

The noise outside had died down. All they could hear was the sound of a normal conversation taking place.

'Fink 'e's gone orf,' said Tom. 'Good-night all.'

'Night,' mumbled Dolly.

Hannah lay on her back, staring up at the dark. She would have dearly liked to go and look at this black sheep. He must have done something really bad.

It was pitch-dark when a gentle swishing noise startled Hannah out of a deep sleep. Slowly she brought her head up. As her eyes got used to the blackness, she could see the outline of someone moving about. It wasn't the shape of anyone she knew. This must be the mysterious Bert. But what was he doing moving a mattress? He must be stopping the night, but did Jack and Maudie know? She looked over at Jack who was asleep. She quickly put her hand over her mouth to suppress her nervous giggles. She couldn't wait till morning to see what he looked like.

As soon as it was light, Hannah sat up and looked across the room to where she thought Bert was. She could just about make out a figure over on the far side of the room, quite apart from everyone else.

Jack began to stir. Hannah slid back down into her own dark corner. She knew she would have to wait. Jack lit a cigarette. He was lying on his back; if only he would get up.

At the end of the room, Bert began to move, and in an instant Jack was on his feet.

Hannah sat upright and watched him go over to Bert. He bent down and said something. Jack waved his fist and pointed towards the door – he was speaking in a loud whisper. Although Hannah couldn't hear what Jack was saying, she knew by his actions he was angry.

Hannah looked down at Alice, willing her to move, call out, do anything to give Hannah the excuse to get up. Hannah even thought of pinching her, but knew she'd yell out too much.

Bert stood up. He wasn't as tall as Jack, Hannah noticed, but he was broader. She wondered if there'd be a fight – she couldn't lie there any longer.

'Good morning,' she whispered politely as she passed them to go out to the lav.

''Allo, gel,' said Jack without turning from Bert.

In the closet she sat with her hands resting on the wooden seat. Swinging her legs, she tried hard to think of what she could say to break the tension outside. Someone banged on the door. 'Go away,' she shouted.

'Sorry 'Annah,' said Tom. 'Yer gonner be long?'

'No.' She pulled up her drawers, pulled down her frock and opened the door. 'Did you see Bert?' she asked eagerly. 'Is Jack still glaring at him in there?'

'Na, don't fink so,' said Tom casually.

'I wonder how long he's staying?' Hannah stood in the doorway smoothing down her clothes.

'I dunno – 'urry up and git out the way.' He began dancing up and down. 'I'm breaking me blooming neck.'

'Sorry.' She put her hand in front of her mouth and giggled. 'Don't want you wetting your pants.'

There was plenty of activity when Hannah returned. Jack was making tea, and the others were putting their beds away. Bert was sitting at the table.

'So Maudie's got a couple of new ones. You two sisters, so this one says.' He pointed his thumb at Alice who looked frightened as she edged towards Hannah.

'Yes, that's right.'

'They talk posh, don't they?' he said to those sitting at the table.

'Git you and yer sister a cup if yer wants a cuppa,' Jack growled at the Miller girls. Hannah got the cups and sat at the table between Alice and Dolly. 'I suppose you're Bert?' she said confidently.

He nodded.

Hannah noted he had a slightly strange accent: still Cockney, but a bit different from the rest of Maudie's household. 'Well, you don't talk like these. Where're you from?' She felt Dolly stiffen as she reached across for the teapot.

Bert jerked his head up. 'Nosy, ain't yer? And what's it to you?'

'Come on, Freddie, we've got to git ready.' Dolly quickly left the table with Freddie scurrying behind.

Tom slid into Dolly's vacant seat. 'You gonner ask Maudie fer some money to buy new fings, like Jack said?' he whispered to Hannah.

'Is that all right, Jack? Did you mean what you said yesterday?' She knew she was trying to put on an act, trying to appear grown-up and self-assured. She wasn't going to be like the rest of them and cower down in the presence of this Bert.

Jack was busy lighting his cigarette. 'What? Oh yer, course I did.'

Hannah looked at Bert. He had dark eyes and short black curly hair. His skin was a lot darker than Jack's, almost weatherbeaten.

'Have yer finished?'

'What?' asked Hannah taken by surprise.

'Have yer finished staring?' Bert's thick black eyebrows came together.

'Sorry, I was thinking about what I'm going to buy today.'

'Buy? Buy? Since when did any of Maudie's waifs and strays buy anyfink?'

'Jack's given Maudie some money, and he kindly said I could get myself a new pinny because I'm going to start looking for a job.'

Bert burst out laughing. 'Get a job. That's rich. Doing what? Street-walking?'

'I beg your pardon?' Hannah was deliberately talking poshly: putting on airs and graces, as Uncle Harry used to say. Alice was pulling at Hannah's frock.

Bert leaned back in his chair. 'And where did Jack get enough money from ter start chucking it around? What poor sod did yer rob then, Jack?'

Jack slowly stood up and pushed his chair back from the table. 'Watch yer mouf. Yer've bin told before, yer not welcome 'ere. Now git out before I frow yer out.'

'And I told yer before, this is Maudie's place, and what she says goes.'

Tom jumped to his feet. 'Come on, 'Annah, we best be orf.'

Alice was standing up, her face white with fear. 'Come on. Let's go and ask Maudie for some money,' she whispered.

'Yer go on, clear off.' Bert began pouring out more tea.

''Ang on a minute, gel,' said Jack, walking to the door with them and hustling them outside, and turning to make sure Bert wasn't following. 'Don't go waking Maudie. I'll give yer a couple of bob. Git yerself sumfink decent.'

Hannah's face flushed. 'Thank you. But why are you doing this for me?'

'Git yer sister sumfink as well. And 'im,' He pointed to Tom. 'The second-'and barras 'ave a lot o' good stuff, and it's only a couple o' pence. Now be orf wiv yer.'

They walked off in silence.

'I wonder why Jack's given us this money?' asked Hannah, looking at the two-shilling piece Jack had put in her hand, half hoping that someone beside herself might think Jack had a special reason for being so generous to her.

''E did the same fer Dolly a while back,' Tom said, 'just after she came ter Maudie's. I fink 'e's got a soft spot for gels – and I fink 'e 'ad a rotten time before 'e met Maudie.'

Alice laughed. 'I don't like Bert, but I think Jack's nice. What you going to get with the money Hannah?'

Hiding her disappointment, Hannah smiled. 'A new pinny, and some soap, a new ribbon, and a comb.' She tugged at her hair. 'This lot's in such a tangle.'

'So's mine.' Alice fluffed up the back of her long blonde hair. 'And I could do with a new pair of . . .' Alice giggled and buried her head in Hannah's arm. 'You know?' She said nudging Hannah.

'So could I.'

They ran down the road laughing, all thoughts of Bert gone from their heads.

Chapter 6

It was late afternoon by the time Hannah, Alice and Tom hurried home with their wares.

'Maudie, Maudie, look what we've got,' yelled Alice. They tipped everything on to the large deal table. There was fruit and veg as well as clothes, but Hannah couldn't shake off the feeling of guilt; not everything had been bought. 'D'you like my new frock?' Hannah held up a grey dress that had cost her sixpence.

'It's very nice.' Maudie sat at the table, and Hannah thought she looked sad.

'Is everything all right?' Hannah asked gently.

'Where's Bert?' asked Tom.

''E's gorn. Right, let's 'ave a look at wot yer got.'

Hannah looked at Maudie suspiciously. 'Has he upset you?'

'Na, course not. See yer got yer soap then. If yer wants yer can keep yer fings in that side of the cupboard. Dolly 'as the ovver side.'

'Thanks, Maudie.' Without thinking, Hannah quickly kissed her cheek.

Maudie smiled and gently touched the side of her face, a smile slowly lifting her round features. 'Wot d'yer do that for?'

Hannah felt awkward and giggled. 'I feel so happy I just felt like it. Did you mind?'

'Mind? Course not.' Maudie looked away. 'I'd better start gitting the tea ready.'

'Come on, Alice, let's go and get tided up,' said Hannah, gathering up their belongings.

Outside, they laughed and chuckled excitedly as they washed themselves all over and changed into their clean clothes. For the first time in weeks Hannah felt good as she sat in the sun brushing her clean hair dry.

'Yer got a mop there, gel.'

Hannah looked up at Jack and smiled. 'We'll never be able to thank you for giving us the money to get all these things.'

'Maudie said yer done all right. She's right pleased wiv yer. Spent it real good, so she said.'

'Why did you give us that money?'

'I 'ad a good day, and fought yer'd like somefink new.' Jack sat on the wall. 'You're a bright kid, so 'ow comes yer finished up 'ere?'

'It's a long story – I'll tell you all about it one day.' She tossed her hair back and began tying it with a clean mauve ribbon. 'There was a funeral and, as we followed it, one of the ribbons came fluttering down off a wreath, and landed right at my feet.'

'Oh yer?' said Jack.

'Really,' said Hannah. 'Alice, go and ask Maudie if we can have some of her carbolic soap to wash out our dirty things.'

Alice, with Bonzo at her side, went without an argument.

'She's a pretty little fing,' said Jack watching her move away.

'Yes, she's supposed to look like our mother.'

'Shame about 'er leg. Maudie told me yer 'ad a rough time wiv yer uncle.'

Hannah quickly looked away. 'Yes, we did.'

'Is it 'im what gives yer yer bad dreams?'

'Yes, yes it is.' Hannah began gathering up the dirty clothes.

'D'yer know, you two remind me a bit of the "Babes in the Wood".' Jack laughed.

'That's a fairy story.'

'Yer, that's right.'

Hannah sat beside him. 'Can you read?'

Jack grinned at her. 'Yer dead nosy, ain't yer?'

She smiled. 'Well?'

'Yer, I can read, and write.'

'I thought so. So how come you don't go to work?'

He fumbled in his jacket pocket and, bringing out a dog-end, lit it. 'Cos I wouldn't git as much working fer someone, that's why.' He blew the smoke into the air.

'But don't you worry about getting caught?'

'Na, I'm good.' He wagged his finger in her face. 'I dunno why I'm telling yer all this. Don't yer go letting on ter them in there what I just told yer.'

'About what?' asked Hannah.

'Being able ter read and write.'

She shook her head. 'Jack, do you know of anywhere round here where I could get a job?'

'What d'yer wonner get a job fer?'

'I would rather go to work than . . .'

He laughed. 'Yer could try the biscuit factory, it's orf Jamaica Road, or there's the tea factory, but that's a fair trot away. What d'yer wonner do?'

'I don't mind. I did work in a brush factory for a while. All I did was sort out the fibres and sweep up. I got the sack for being too posh.'

Jack laughed. 'There's the cottage 'ospital not too far away: they might want cleaners.'

Hannah screwed up her nose. 'Can't say I fancy that.'

'There's some nice little darlings work there.'

'You know some of the girls?'

'Yer. Took one of 'em out once, but she wanted ter go ter one of them there suffragette meetings, and I wasn't 'aving none of that.'

Hannah nodded wisely.

Alice came rushing into the yard. 'I've got the soap, d'you want me to help?'

'You can rinse them and put them on the line.'

Jack began to walk away.

'Where did Bert go?' Hannah called after him, her curiosity getting the better of her. He shrugged his shoulders. 'Dunno. You sure ask a lot o' questions, gel.'

The following morning, Hannah felt very grown up when she put on her new grey frock. Tom was going to show her where the biscuit factory was and Alice wanted to go too.

After a few minutes' walk they were standing in front of a smoke-blackened red-brick building. She had seen the tall impressive chimney from a distance, belching its black smoke high into the air, but up close it looked drab and over-powering.

'You going to work in there?' Alice pulled a face.

'If they'll have me.' Hannah was suddenly feeling very apprehensive. 'You wait here.'

She pushed open the gate and made her way to the entrance. There wasn't much noise coming from the building, but the sweet, sickly smell of cooking filled her nostrils. Inside she stood gazing open-mouthed at the women taking biscuits from off benches and filling large boxes with them. Someone touched her shoulder.

'Wot d'yer want?'

Hannah quickly turned to find herself face-to-face with a well-built woman, white from head to foot with flour.

'I'd like a job,' she blurted, trying not to sound unnerved.

'Yer better see the foreman, that's 'im over there.' The woman pointed at a man with his back towards them. He was bending over and had his arms round a couple of women.

Tentatively, Hannah made her way over to him. 'Excuse

me,' she said, but he didn't hear her above the clatter all around them, so she spoke louder. 'Excuse me.'

He turned. ''Allo, what we got 'ere then?'

Hannah was shaking with fear. 'I'd like a job please.'

'Would yer now?'

Hannah nodded; bit by bit feeling her courage slipping away.

'Yer better come ter me office.' He smoothed down his shiny straight black hair and began walking away. Hannah followed. Although he was a short podgy man, he walked very fast, and she had to break into a trot to keep up with him.

In his small office he sat behind an untidy desk. He pushed some papers to one side and, picking up a pencil, licked the lead. 'Right, what's yer name?'

'Hannah Miller.'

He began writing. 'How old are yer?'

'Fifteen.'

''Ave yer been ter work before?'

'Yes. I worked in a brush factory for a while.'

He leaned back in his chair and, holding the pencil in both hands, studied Hannah. She felt uneasy.

'What made yer leave?'

'We moved.'

'Oh, I see. Yer might find it'll be 'ard work – are yer afraid of 'ard work?'

'No,' said Hannah.

'When can yer start?'

'Right away if you like.' She looked down and shuffled her feet. 'Please,' she asked. 'How much will I get?'

'I'll start yer orf wiv 'alf a crown a week, and we'll see 'ow yer gits on. Yer starts at seven, 'as an 'alf-'our at lunch-time, and finishes at six. OK? And yer gits an 'alf-day Saturday, and a pound of broken biscuits.'

Hannah nodded. 'Thank you. I'll be here at seven tomorrow.'

'Don't be late, cos if yer late I stops it out yer money. OK?'

Hannah went to move away.

'I'll git Elsie ter show yer where yer clocks on.'

Once more, Hannah found herself following him, though at a much slower pace this time; as they went through part of the factory, some of the older women called out to him and gave him a wave.

A skinny woman, who looked to Hannah about fifty, came over when he beckoned. 'Show 'er 'ow ter clock on,' he said, and marched off towards his office.

'This way,' said Elsie. 'When d'yer start?'

'In the morning.' When they were in the relatively quiet area of the entrance, Hannah asked. 'What's it like here?'

'Not ser bad. Old Wally can be a bit of a sod if yer starts ter muck about.' Elsie walked up to a large clock with cards stacked in a rack on one side. 'This is wot yer does.'

'I've done this before,' said Hannah eagerly.

'Yer been at work before?' Elsie looked surprised. 'Where was that?'

Hannah wished she'd kept quiet. 'A long way away. We've just moved here.'

'Didn't fink yer come from round 'ere. I best git back, see yer termorrer.'

Hannah nodded. 'Bye.'

A minute later Hannah was outside with Alice and Tom. 'I've got a job,' she said excitedly. 'I start in the morning.' She suddenly clasped her hand over her mouth.

'What is it? What's the matter?' asked Alice.

'I've got to be here at seven. I haven't got a clock, so how will I know the time?' She sat on the low concrete wall and leaned against the black wrought-iron railings.

'Yer'll 'ave ter listen out fer the church clock,' said Tom.

70

'But what if I miss it chiming the hour? I won't know what time it is.'

'Dunno,' said Tom, sitting next to her. 'P'raps Maudie'll lend yer 'er watch.'

'Or the new one Jack gave her,' said Alice, joining them on the wall.

'I could ask if I could borrow it, then perhaps later on I could get myself a clock from the pawnshop.' Hannah smiled. 'I'll be getting two-and-six a week to start with.'

'Blimey, is that all?' asked Tom.

'It's only to start with,' Hannah said defensively, 'and at least I'll be getting it every week.'

'Yer, I know, but yer 'as ter go out every day. What yer gotter do?' Tom stood up.

'I don't know.'

'Yer won't 'ave any time ter teach me ter read.'

'Of course I will and, anyway, you've got Alice. And you must promise me you'll look after her.'

Tom smiled. 'Course I will.'

Alice jumped up. 'Come on, let's go to the market.'

As they wandered along the road, Hannah's mind was in a turmoil. Would she like being stuck in a factory all day? Now she'd got it all arranged she was having doubts. She hadn't liked the time she was in the brush factory, but perhaps biscuits would be different. At least the work would be cleaner. And what about the other girls? Would they think she was too posh to work with as well?

She watched Tom and Alice talking and laughing together. Their lives were going to be very different from now on.

At the end of the day they made their way back home. Hannah hadn't been too eager to be pulled into the tasks of gathering bits and pieces of thrown-away rubbish, or pinching off the barrows. She was worried she might get her new frock dirty, or even torn, and now she'd got over the novelty of it, stealing seemed both wrong and risky. But Alice and Tom had enjoyed themselves, and much to Hannah's distress, she began to see Alice wouldn't really miss her. If only she could get a good job later on, then perhaps Alice could go to school. She'd have to find out what they charged to go to school round there. It shouldn't be very much as it was a very poor neighbourhood; she was sure Maudie wouldn't throw them out if Hannah was bringing in a decent wage every week. As she ran a stick along the park railings her mind raced with possibilities for the future.

After showing Maudie their goods, they wandered outside into the yard and Hannah told Maudie her news: now seemed like a good moment.

Maudie didn't seem displeased. 'Working in the biscuit factory, well I never. We won't be short of a biscuit or two from now on then. Let's 'ope yer gits some of those new chocolate ones I've seen in 'Erman's shop. Could be very partial to a chocolate one, I could,' said Maudie. 'By the way, yer frock's dry. I brought yer washing in, it's on the chair.'

'Thanks, Maudie.' Hannah went and sat next to her. 'You don't mind me getting a job, do you?'

'Na, why should I?'

'Well, I won't be able to bring in so much stuff, but I'll be getting half a crown a week, and if I could keep sixpence you could have the rest.'

'Wot will yer do wiv yer tanner?'

'I'd like to send Alice to school.'

'Fought as much. So she won't be out gitting any swag neither? And yer reckons two bob a week will keep the both of yer?'

Hannah hung her head. 'I don't know. I hope I'll get more

after I've been there for a while. We could still go to the market on Saturday afternoons,' she added, trying to sound enthusiastic about the prospect.

'Well I dunno wot Dolly'll 'ave ter say about it. She can be a right little . . .'

'Oh yer, and what can I be? And what yer talking about me for?' Dolly stood in front of Hannah, her face full of anger – they hadn't heard her creep into the yard.

''Annah's got a job,' Maudie said calmly.

'Oh yer, doing what?'

'She's gonner work at the biscuit factory.'

'Only 'opes she gits enough ter be able ter feed 'em both. And what was yer talking about me for?'

'Maudie was just wondering what you would say about it,' said Hannah sweetly, trying to keep the peace.

'Ain't none of my business, is it? Not if yer reckons yer can keep yerselves and don't rely on me and the rest of us ter feed yer. Come on, Freddie, let's go and wash yer 'ands.'

When they had moved away, well out of earshot, Hannah turned to ask Maudie. 'Can Freddie talk?' she asked. She realized she hadn't heard him say a word since they'd arrived.

'Not very good. 'E's got a terrible stutter. Dolly said it came on after their old man started bashing 'im.'

'Poor little lad,' said Hannah. 'Oh Maudie, can I ask you a favour?'

'Depends. Wot d'yer want?'

'Do you think I could borrow the watch Jack gave you?'

'Ain't got it.' She stood up. Suddenly her attitude had changed. 'Gotter git the dinner on.'

'Oh, did that man come round to buy it then? What's his name? Frank?' asked Hannah, following her.

'No; I mean, yer.' Maudie seemed confused. 'Don't be ser

73

bloody nosy. 'Sides, wot d'yer want a watch for?'

'I've got to be at work at seven, and I haven't any way of telling the time.'

'Yer got the church clock.'

'I know, but if I don't hear the chimes . . .'

'Yer should 'ave fought of that 'fore yer told 'em yer'd start. Yer'll 'ave ter git yerself a clock from the pawnbrokers then, won't yer.'

Hannah's heart sank. 'I haven't any money.'

''Ard luck.' Maudie stormed inside leaving Hannah standing open-mouthed.

Tom and Alice were sitting in the corner. Alice had kept her head down, reading to Tom all the while Hannah was talking to Maudie. When Maudie walked in, Alice went to her sister. 'What you going to do about a watch?'

'I don't know. I'll ask Jack if he can talk Maudie into letting me borrow hers. I'm surprised she let that man Frank have it. Didn't Jack tell her to find out what he'd give her for it first before she sold it to him?'

'Yes, yes he did.'

'D'yer know what I reckon?' said Tom, joining them. 'I reckon she's gorn and give it ter Bert.'

'She wouldn't do that, would she?' asked Hannah.

'Dunno. Mind you, 'e could 'ave pinched it, and she don't wonner say.'

'I don't believe that. She keeps her valuable things in her room. No, I don't think she would let him do that.' Hannah was shaking her head.

'Yer, well, we'll know soon enough when Jack comes 'ome. Yer gonner ask 'im if yer can lend it?'

'I don't know now.' Hannah stood up. 'Oh, why does life have so many problems?'

Dolly walked past. 'You poor old soul. Yer got problems

then? Yer got yerself a job, and still yer ain't 'appy. What do you want, eh?'

Hannah sighed. She knew what she wanted, but it was no good telling them.

Chapter 7

When they were seated at the table, Hannah told Jack that she'd got a job.

He seemed pleased for her. 'If that's what yer wants,' he said, digging into his stew.

'I have to start at seven in the morning,' she said tentatively, looking at Maudie.

'Well I finks she's mad. I wouldn't fancy being stuck in a noisy factory all day,' said Dolly.

'It's not very noisy.'

'How much they giving yer then?' asked Dolly.

'Well, I only get two-and-six to start with,' answered Hannah.

''Alf a crown, 'alf a bloody crown – that fer a week?'

Hannah nodded. 'Yes. But it's only to start with.'

'Watch yer language, Dolly,' said Maudie sharply.

Jack sat forward and laughed. 'Yer gitting 'alf a crown fer being stuck in a factory all week. Now yer sees why I don't wonner work fer someone.' He leaned back in his chair 'Yer saw what I brought in fer just a couple o' days work.'

'Yes, but that was stealing, and I . . .' Hannah was getting flustered.

'It might be in some people's eyes, but then, on the ovver 'and, how did some of them there toffs git it? I bet a lot of 'em do a lot of dodgy deals, so in some ways it's the same. Except mine's more direct.'

'But it's still not . . .'

''Ark at Miss prim an' proper,' interrupted Dolly. It was her turn to sit forward to emphasize her point. 'But yer don't mind eating what's been pinched though, do yer? Or wearing fings that fell off a barra.'

'She's right, gel,' said Maudie, laughing very loudly along with Dolly.

Hannah knew she was up against it. She looked across at Jack who only shrugged his shoulders. She wanted to ask him about the watch but didn't want the others listening.

When they finished their meal they sat outside, but Hannah felt restless. All evening she'd been trying to think of a way to get Jack on his own, but it was hopeless.

As the light started to fade, Alice began yawning. 'I'm going to bed. You coming, Hannah?'

'In a while.'

Dolly and Freddie also moved away, and when Tom followed them he gave Hannah a wink.

Maudie stood up. 'It's been a busy day, so I fink I'll be turning in.'

Hannah panicked. What about the watch? If Maudie went to her room she'd never get it, and if she didn't know the time tomorrow morning . . . She jumped to her feet. 'Maudie, please let me borrow your pocket-watch?' she blurted out.

'Wot?'

'Please, just till I can afford a clock.'

Maudie looked worried. 'I told yer no.'

Jack quickly glanced at Maudie. 'What d'yer wonner watch for?' he asked Hannah.

'So I'll know the time in the morning.'

'Yer knows what Maudie's like with that posh ticker of 'ers.' He turned to Maudie. 'Say, why don't yer let 'er 'ave the one I gave yer? Old Frank ain't coming yet, is 'e?'

Maudie shook her head stubbornly. 'Na, she might overwind it and bugger it up.' She quickly looked across at Hannah.

Hannah cringed. Jack didn't know she hadn't got it, and Maudie wasn't going to tell him.

'Course she won't. Go an git it,' said Jack. 'I'll wind it up. Can't 'ave 'er late on 'er first day.'

Maudie didn't move.

'What's up, old gel?'

'I ain't got it,' she said softly, and slowly sank back down on the chair.

'I fought yer said . . .' Jack stood up, his brow furrowed. ''E's pinched it, ain't 'e?' His face turned red with anger. 'Bloody Bert. 'E's pinched it.'

'Jack, Jack . . .'

He wasn't listening to her, and continued his shouting. 'D'yer knows every time that bloody bloke steps back in 'ere 'e's trouble.' His knuckles went white as he clenched his fists. 'What else did 'e pinch? What about the money? Where was yer? Yer shouldn't 'ave left 'im alone. Did yer know 'e'd been sneaking round yer room?'

'Jack, 'e didn't pinch it,' Maudie took a deep breath as Jack finished his outburst and sat down.

'What?'

'Bert didn't pinch it . . . I gave it to 'im.'

Jack's face was now ashen. 'What?' he asked, slowly drawing the word out. 'Not again. Not after yer promised.'

It was Maudie's turn to get agitated and she turned on Hannah. 'It's your bloody fault. Keeping on about the damn fing.'

'Never mind 'er,' said Jack. 'What about Bert?'

'Yer see 'e's 'ard up. He wanted some money real quick,' Maudie's voice changed to a whine.

'I bet 'e did.'

'I knows yer don't like 'im staying 'ere, so I fought yer

wouldn't mind if I . . .' Her voice trailed off.

'What about the bracelet? Yer give 'im that as well?'

'No. Na, course not.'

Hannah sat on the edge of her seat, dumbfounded. She couldn't believe her starting work could have caused so much trouble.

Jack lit a cigarette, and for a few moments it was very quiet.

It was Hannah who broke the silence. 'I'm very sorry, Maudie, I didn't think it would start . . .' She didn't know what to say.

'Yer, well . . .' Maudie too was fumbling for words.

'Look, I knows what Bert means ter yer,' said Jack in a low voice. 'But I've told yer before, 'e's trouble. What if 'e takes that watch ter the police?'

Maudie's head shot up. 'Why'd he do that?'

'To get me inter trouble, that's why!'

''E wouldn't do that: they might fink 'e pinched it.'

Jack seemed a little calmer. 'Yer, yer that's true.'

''Sides,' said Maudie, looking down at her feet. ''E said 'e needed the money.'

'What for?'

Maudie didn't answer.

'Well, it's gorn now, no good crying over spilt milk.'

Jack sniffed contemptuously. 'Look, why don't yer let 'er 'ave yer own watch just fer ternight.'

'Oh, all right then.' Maudie turned to Hannah. 'I'll wind it up, and don't play wiv it, cos if yer breaks it I'll kill yer.'

Hannah trembled. With a threat like that hanging over her, she doubted if she would even sleep.

Maudie left her and Jack to get the watch.

'I'm sorry I've caused so much trouble,' Hannah said quietly.

'That's all right, gel. I guessed she'd give 'im the watch or

the bracelet; she always manages ter give 'im sumfink of value
when 'e comes back.'

'He's not from round here, is he? Where's 'e from?'

'Yer orf again asking questions, ain't yer?'

'I'm sorry.'

'Christ, yer've only been 'ere five minutes and yer wants ter
know everybody's life 'istory.' He moved closer. 'But yer ain't
told us nuffink about you and yer sister, now 'ave yer?'

'I told you, it's a long story,' Hannah said quickly.

To her relief Maudie came back out. ''Ere are, and don't
play wiv it.'

'Thank you, thank you very much. As soon as I can, I'll get
myself a clock. Good-night.'

'Night,' they said together.

Alice was asleep when she settled down beside her, but
sensed Dolly was still awake.

Tom grunted sleepily. 'Tell us what 'appened termorrer.'

Hannah smiled. She'd have a lot to tell.

After a fitful night, Hannah woke as the dawn's early morning
light crept through the high window. She looked at the watch.
Five o'clock. She decided to get up, get herself ready and take
a nice slow walk to work, leaving the watch high on the shelf
of the sideboard, just as Maudie had instructed.

Hannah was amongst the first arrivals at the factory, and as
she stood nervously waiting at the gate, Elsie came over to her.

She smiled. 'Yer nice and early then. Wally'll like that.'
Her voice was drowned by the sound of a loud hooter rending
the air. It made Hannah jump, and Elsie laughed. 'Come on
gel. By the way, wot's yer name?'

'Hannah.'

'Oh, that's nice. Come on then, 'Annah, let's git clocked
on.'

Inside, as Elsie had instructed, Hannah stood in line to wait her turn to clock on. She looked round and bit her bottom lip apprehensively as one by one the women went to their places waiting for the whistle to blow, and the biscuits to be packed into boxes. Elsie had told her they were on piecework, and only got paid for how much work they did.

When Wally caught sight of her, he came over with a broom in his hand. "Ere are, sweep up all the bits that falls off the bench and put 'em in the bin over there, and when yer done that yer can run any errands the gels want, and make sure them round the ovens gits plenty of drinks.'

Hannah was left holding the broom. As she began sweeping she started to take in what was happening around her. All the women were doing things automatically, and they all had the same blank expression on their faces – the one thought that kept coming into her head was, is this what I really want to do? Would she eventually be put on the bench, and if so could she stand there all day doing the same thing? She tried to look on the bright side. Perhaps there were some more interesting jobs in the factory but, she told herself firmly, for now this would have to do.

When she went round to the back of the ovens, the heat was unbearable. Most of the men and women had their sleeves rolled up revealing large, thick arms. As she wiped the sweat from her face, she knew she never wanted to work near the ovens, even if they did get extra money.

At lunch-time Elsie took her under her wing and told her about some of the other women, but Hannah wasn't really listening, nor could she understand all the ribald remarks that brought forth gales of laughter from the others.

It was with a sense of relief that she heard the hooter for six o'clock, the signal that she could walk away from the noisy factory. 'Well, that's the first day over,' she said out loud as she hurried home.

As she walked in she was surprised to see Alice combing Maudie's hair.

'That looks nice,' she said, sinking on to a chair.

'Yer, she's a clever kid wiv 'er 'ands. Does it look all right? She chopped a bit orf round the back. She reckons it'll stay in me bun a bit better. Did yer 'ave a good day?'

Hannah opened her mouth to answer, but quickly Alice said, 'Managed to get Maudie a new hairnet.'

Maudie turned and affectionately tapped the back of Alice's hand. Alice smiled her best smile down at her.

'Well,' said Alice, finally coming and sitting down next to Hannah. 'What was it like?'

'It was all right.'

'Did you make any biscuits?'

'No.'

'Did you manage to eat any?'

'Only a couple that Elsie gave me.'

'Who's Elsie?'

'The woman I first saw.'

'Is she nice?'

Hannah nodded.

'Me and Tom had a good day, didn't we, Maudie?' Alice leant on the table. 'We pinched some eggs from the grocer's. He was helping some poor old dear load her shopping bag,' she laughed excitely. 'Tom nearly dropped 'em. Then we got some bones from the butcher. I told him I was an orphan and was hungry – well, I am really – and he felt sorry for me.'

'Alice, you didn't?' Hannah could see by her sister's face she was proud of what she'd been doing.

'Yer should 'ave seen 'er, 'Annah. She limped in, an' even cried,' said Tom.

'It wasn't from the shop round the corner, was it?' asked Hannah in alarm.

'No, course not, silly.' Alice smiled at Maudie. 'We mustn't take anything from those, must we?'

'I should cocoa, too close ter 'ome. I gotter git me bits from them, and I can't walk in there if they've been nicking old 'Erman's stuff.'

'See,' Alice said, 'I know what's what.' She did a little curtsy.

Maudie laughed. 'She'll end up being a bloody actress one day, you mark my words.'

Hannah was beginning to get angry.

Alice giggled. 'Do you know what else . . . ?'

'Alice, don't keep on, I'm tired. I've been on my feet all day.' Hannah yawned; she didn't want to hear any more about their day.

'Pardon me for being interested in you.'

'I'm sorry, Alice,' said Hannah wearily.

'I'm glad I don't go to work, not if it turns you into a misery,' said Alice petulantly.

'It was you that suggested I get a job,' said Hannah, annoyed that nobody really seemed interested in her day.

'Yes, well, I didn't think you'd change. Come on, Tom, let's go outside. Coming Bonzo?'

The dog reluctantly got to his feet and, with its tail wagging very slowly, followed Alice and Tom.

'Hummh,' said Maudie, giving her a long look. 'Don't looks like going ter work agrees wiv yer.'

'I'll be all right. It's just that it's my first day, and . . .' She stopped, what was the point in telling them she hated it – they didn't want to know. She wanted to cry she felt so miserable, but knew she couldn't give in. She couldn't lose face, and after all she knew Alice had to continue her schooling. Perhaps it would get better; and it was ten times better than the broom factory.

Jack came in while they were having tea. The first thing he did was walk over to Hannah. ''Ere are, gel.' He passed her a brown paper parcel.

Hannah looked up at him shyly. 'Thank you. What is it?'

'Well, open it, then yer'll see.'

'More presents for 'er?' said Dolly, licking the jam off her fingers.

Hannah quickly glanced at her as she tore at the paper. Inside the box was a clock. 'This for me? Thank you!' she grinned.

'Who's the lucky one, then?' Dolly was clearly put out.

Jack looked embarrassed. 'It's fer all of us, really. Just in case any of us 'as ter git up early.'

Hannah smiled. Even if she hated the job, at least she wouldn't be late for work now.

It was a great relief when Saturday came, Hannah's half day off. She collected her wages and, as promised, gave Maudie the two shillings and the broken biscuits.

Alice and Tom had told her they would meet her at the market. It was crowded as usual, and Hannah found herself wandering around for quite a while before she caught sight of them hanging round the ribbon and button stall. She went to raise her hand to attract their attention, but then stopped, stood and watched in appalled fascination as Alice went up to the stall and picked up some ribbon, running her fingers over the shiny satin. The owner must have said something, for Alice looked up and smiled and, her big blue eyes wide open, put the goods back. With her limp exaggerated she moved on but immediately the owner turned away, Alice calmly walked back, picked up the reel of ribbon and hurried on. The owner was none the wiser.

Hannah was shocked. It looked so professional. How could her sister have changed in such a short time? Who had taught her? Tom wasn't as good as she was. Hannah was angry. It was Alice who had wanted her to get a job because she was frightened of them getting caught, but now she seemed to be almost flaunting herself; she was certainly enjoying her antics.

'Hello, Hannah,' yelled Alice when she caught sight of her, her face flushed to a pretty pink. 'We've had a good morning. Let's go into the park and we'll show you what we've got.'

Hannah followed Alice and Tom in silence.

'Everyfink all right?' asked Tom.

'Yes, yes,' replied Hannah.

'Did you get paid?' asked Alice.

'Yes, and Alice, when the new term starts in September, I want you to go to school.' Her voice was firm.

'What? Do I have to?'

'I think you should.' They sat on the first empty bench.

'Why? I can read and write, and I'm getting good at tea-leafing.' She threw her head back and laughed.

'She's got it all wrong,' said Tom. 'What she means is, she's gitting ter be a good tea-leaf – feef.'

'Who's been teaching her?'

'Me, o' course. We work good tergevver.'

Hannah sighed. She knew there was a thrill in taking things, but she also knew what the consequences would be if they got caught – she hadn't told Alice of her fears about the police and Uncle Harry. 'Alice, please. Papa would like it if you continued your schooling.'

'I fought you said 'e was dead?' said Tom.

'He is,' said Alice, turning her back on Hannah. 'It's my birthday in September, Tom. Did you know that?' She smiled and her dimples deepened.

'Mine ain't till next year. How old will yer be?' asked Tom.

'I'll be twelve.'

'I'm twelve already.'

'Hannah will be sixteen in May,' she chattered on.

'Alice, about school?' Hannah tried to sound assertive.

'Hannah,' Alice said with a show of patience. 'You can't afford to send me.'

'It only costs a penny a week, so Elsie told me: she sends her two boys.'

'Yes, but I'm a girl, and Maudie says girls don't need an education as they soon get married.'

'Not all of them, and if you have a good education you can get a good job. Be a teacher, or a nurse.'

'Agh. I don't want to be a nurse, not with all that blood,' she laughed. 'And I don't want to end up like you, sweeping floors all day.'

Hannah was at a loss for words. They were drifting apart after all they had been through together. Alice was still giggling at what she had said. 'Please yourself,' said Hannah, fighting back the tears. 'I'm going back.'

All the way home, Hannah was feeling low. How could she make Alice see it was only good sense to go to school. Their papa had always wanted them to have an education. She sighed, remembering the times they used to sit on his lap while he read to them. Those days were so far behind them now.

She turned into Hope Street which was full of noisy kids. They rushed about seemingly without a care in the world. As it was a hot day, most of the front doors were wide open, and Hannah couldn't help looking in at all the paraphernalia lining the passageways. The smell of cooking drifted out, not all of it pleasant. As usual there were a couple of women Hannah often saw standing at their front doors. Today they had their heads bent together, gossiping and as she passed, they gave her a nod. 'Yer lives wiv that Maudie, don't yer?' one of them said.

Hannah nodded and moved on. She wasn't in a mood to talk to them now.

On the other side of the road there was a lot of shouting coming from inside number twelve. Its half-open door was suddenly flung back, and a large woman dressed all in black, with a wide black hat perched precariously on top of her head, rushed out.

'That's it. I'm leaving yer!' She stood in the doorway for a few moments. 'Yer can look after yer bloody self, I'm leaving yer, d'yer 'ear? Yer drunken sod.' Tucking her handbag under her arm, she yelled back. 'And I'm taking me money wiv me.' She stormed off down the street. As she walked all her fat wobbled, and the deep rim of the hat began undulating like the wings of a bird about to take off.

All the kids in the street began cheering. Hannah stood and watched, fascinated. She began to giggle.

'Don't take no notice, love,' called one of the women who was leaning against the wall of number eight. 'That's the battling Barkers, they always carry on like that when 'er George comes 'ome drunk.'

Her neighbour was laughing. 'Look at that bleeding 'at. If she ain't careful, it'll take orf.'

The first woman who had nodded to Hannah laughed and said, 'Seem's 'e's bin out celebrating 'er birfday, but forgot ter take 'er wiv 'im. Don't worry about it, she'll be back.'

Hannah felt guilty at stopping and listening to their conversation, and quickly moved on. Walking in front of her were two young girls, who had completely ignored Mrs Barker's outburst. They weren't particularly well dressed, but one of them was pushing a large, well polished bassinet. They were talking quietly together and, as she passed them, one of the girls, who could hardly see over the pram's hood, stopped and rearranged the covers inside, giving the impression she'd done this many times before.

How can they afford such luxuries? wondered Hannah, admiring the shiny pram. A group of boys ran past her, yelling and shouting as they approached the girls.

The eldest of the two stood her ground. 'If you lot don't shut yer gobs,' she yelled out, 'I'll give yer all a pasting. Yer'll wake the baby up.'

One boy put his tongue out and, with his thumbs against his head, waggled his fingers. 'Old muvver Dobson don't care if the kid cries, just ser long as it's out the way, so there.'

'Wot yer worried about? Yer gits yer money. So don't tell us ter shut up, Katie Linton,' said another.

The young girl's face darkened with anger and she hurried along, rocking the pram with such gusto that it made Hannah smile. She'll have that baby out of that pram if she's not careful, she chuckled to herself. And another thought quickly filled her mind. How much did this girl get for looking after a baby all day?

Chapter 8

It was the beginning of September, and with summer almost over, Hannah had been busy making plans for her sister to start school. Today was Alice's birthday, and Hannah was pleased that she had managed to save up enough to buy her a pair of second-hand shoes. Although Hannah knew most of the things were stolen, she couldn't argue with the joy on Alice's face when, in the evening, the others gave Alice their presents. Dolly gave her some new ribbon, from Maudie she had some sweets tied up in a pretty handkerchief, and Tom had proudly presented her with a small doll. But it was Jack's present that brought forth the most delight.

''Ere are, gel. Pin this on yer frock.' He handed her a lovely brooch in the shape of a small silver wishbone.

Hannah gasped.

Jack quickly turned on her. 'And 'fore yer say sumfink, I didn't pinch it. A bloke I knows was selling it – 'e said it was 'is muvver's, and 'e only wanted a few pence for it. Seems 'e's fallen on 'ard times. Anyway gel, d'yer like it?'

Alice threw her arms round his neck and kissed his cheek. 'It's the best present I've ever had,' she said, carefully pinning the brooch on to her dress.

'It looks very expensive,' said Hannah.

'Yer, well, it ain't real. Remember, all that glitters ain't always gold.'

Hannah loved these funny sayings Jack came out with, especially when he got them wrong.

Dolly looked far from pleased at Alice's present. 'Seems it's you that's taken 'is fancy now,' she said sullenly. 'I ain't ever 'ad nuffink like that fer my birfday.'

'That's cos up ter now I ain't been in a position ter buy fings like that.' Jack sat at the table.

'I'll pour yer out a cuppa, lad,' said Maudie. She turned to Dolly. 'And we don't want any arguments ternight, young lady, cos it's Alice's birfday, and yer knows how I like birfdays.'

Hannah smiled. The table had been nicely set, lit with four candles instead of the usual two and tonight there was a jelly and a small cake. Maudie did like birthdays, and although Hannah knew it was a long way off, she couldn't wait for hers in May.

Now that the nights were beginning to draw in, every evening Maudie banked up the stove and they huddled round it, reading or telling stories. The girls would do their knitting or sewing, always asking Maudie for help and advice. Candles and hurricane-lamps provided the light, and it was very warm and cosy.

The mornings were dark now, and winter was approaching. It had been raining all day, and all evening the wind had been whistling and howling round the door. Maudie made a draught-excluder out of an old stocking filled with newspaper to help keep the cold out, but the wind was gently moving it, eerily scraping the stocking along the floor when everybody was in bed.

Hannah lay on her mattress listening to the church clock strike ten. Next week she was getting a rise. She would be getting four shillings and sixpence a week. The work was still hard, running errands and keeping the women on the line happy while they worked, sweeping up, and making the men and women in the bakehouse their lemonade. But she was happy to be bringing some money in, and it had turned out to be a lot better than the brush factory.

Hannah sighed and pulled her blanket up round her ears, feeling warm and comfortable. She remembered the winters at Aunt May's, and the times she had cried herself to sleep with the pain from her chilblains. Her fingers and toes had been red and swollen, and the thought of the mornings she had to break the ice to wash sent shivers down her back. Uncle Harry always slept in the stable in winter as the blacksmith's fire never went out. Aunt May, Alice and Hannah had had to be content to cuddle up together to keep warm.

Hannah was surprised at how fondly she was thinking of the past. Even though she still felt guilty about Uncle Harry, and worried about Aunt May, the memory of those bad years was beginning to fade, and the nightmares were getting fewer and fewer. She was happy living here, living like a family. She was very careful not to ask too many questions about Jack and Bert and, though she still knew very little about Maudie, she didn't really care; they didn't seem to be too worried about her and Alice's past either.

Over the weeks since Alice's birthday, Hannah had felt very pleased with herself. She had managed to buy herself and Alice winter coats from the second-hand stall, as well as some old jumpers which they had carefully unpicked. Now Maudie had taught them to knit they had warm scarves, and mitts.

Back in September, Hannah had told Alice where the school was. She couldn't have time off from work to go with her, so she had sent her along with her penny on her own. After a few weeks, Hannah wondered why her sister never seemed to have any work to do at home. Every time Hannah broached the subject, Alice told her she was doing very well and Miss Kent said she didn't need to do homework as she was well ahead of the others.

'Has your teacher asked for the money for your slate yet?' Hannah had asked anxiously.

Alice had looked at Tom. 'No, she lets me borrow the school's – she knows we haven't got a lot of money. Or any parents.'

When Hannah had told Elsie at the factory this, she had been surprised. 'Always fought she was a money-grabbing old bitch,' she'd said. 'I'll ask me boy about it, 'e used ter be in 'er class.'

Hannah worried about the fact that Alice never mentioned school unless Hannah brought the subject up, and even then she said very little. And Alice still went with Tom to the market on Saturdays, and they always came back with plenty. As she lay staring into the dark, remembering the past, Hannah couldn't help wonder what the future would hold for her and Alice.

One Saturday morning, when Hannah was on her way to work, the street appeared even darker than usual. The wind and sleet was blowing all round her, at times snatching her breath away. She pulled her coat collar tighter at her throat, and wished she was still on her warm mattress. Hope Street only had one gas-lamp and, through the gloom, Hannah thought she saw the young girl she had often seen pushing the large bassinet. Despite the wet and the cold she wasn't wearing a coat, and appeared to be very agitated, knocking on door after door and hardly waiting for an answer before running to the next. It was as she was turning quickly away from yet another closed door that she almost bumped into Hannah.

'Oops, careful,' said Hannah, holding her arm to steady her.

'Fanks.' She looked worried.

'Are you all right?' asked Hannah.

'Yer, fanks.' She quickly looked about her and went to hurry away.

Hannah turned to carry on walking. She had only taken a few steps when the young girl ran up to her again.

''Ere, yer don't know nuffink about babies, do yer?' she asked, stamping her feet to keep warm.

'No. Why?'

'It's Brian, the kid I look after, I don't fink 'e's very well.'

'Where's your mother?'

'She's at work, but Brian ain't 'ers. Look, could yer come and look at 'im?'

'Sorry, but I'm going to work. Where's the baby's mother?'

'She's at work. Please, just come and 'ave a look at 'im.' She was shivering and wrapped her arms about herself. 'Please.'

'I don't know,' said Hannah. 'I might be late for work.' She turned to walk away.

The girl, who looked a little older than Alice, tugged at Hannah's sleeve, tears welling up in her large brown eyes. 'Just 'ave a quick look, just ter tell me if I should git a doctor. There ain't nobody else round 'ere. Most of 'em go out ter work, and them that's left wouldn't give yer the drippings from their nose.' She looked up at the window of number six. 'Bet old muvver Nosy's 'aving a good look, but yer won't come down, will yer, yer old cow?'

Hannah followed her gaze. There was a slight movement at one of the lace curtains. The girl hung on to Hannah's arm. 'Please come wiv me.'

Hannah shook the girl's arm away. 'I can't. I've got to go to work. Where's your coat? You'll freeze to death out here.'

''E keeps being ever so sick. Wot if 'e . . . Yer know?' The girl sniffed and wiped her running nose on the sleeve of her faded jumper.

'Is he that bad?'

''E looks bad.'

'Where do you live?'

'Only over there.' She waved her arm behind her and began to move away.

'What about next door?'

'Old Fred ain't much 'elp, 'e's as deaf as a post.'

'Well, I'll have to be quick. I mustn't be late.'

'Come on, then.'

Hannah followed the girl into a house whose passage was dimly lit by a hissing gas-lamp. She pushed her way past the large bassinet. A musty smell of damp washing filled the air.

''E's up 'ere.' At the top of the bare wooden stairs she pushed open a door and a horrible smell almost took Hannah's breath away.

'When did you last change his nappy?' asked Hannah.

''E ain't got one on. I've 'ad ter wash all 'is clothes. Wot d'yer fink's wrong wiv 'im?'

Hannah looked at the pale, thin baby who was only wearing a vest. He seemed very small, lying on a grubby striped mattress that filled up half the floor space. There were several other young children sitting or playing near him – one girl with fair hair was in the corner, sucking her thumb and gently rocking backwards and forwards. 'Do you look after all these?' Hannah asked in amazement.

A faint smile lifted the young girl's face. 'They're all me bruvvers and sisters. There's ten of us all tergevver.'

'Ten?' repeated Hannah. 'Where's your mum and dad?'

'Me mum's at work and me dad's left 'ome. 'E couldn't stand all the kids.'

'But . . .'

'What about little Brian 'ere?' said the girl, gently stroking the whimpering baby's face.

'Where's his mum and dad?'

''Is dad died before 'e was born, and 'is mum works in the cottage 'ospital. She works all night cos it's more money, so we 'ave the baby in wiv us. Well, it gives us a bit o' extra money.'

Suddenly the baby began to scream, drawing up his tiny blue feet in pain. Hannah could only stand and watch in silence. She bent down to comfort him. 'Does he always smell like this?'

'Na.'

'Poo,' said one of the children, holding his nose. ''E don't arf pen and ink, don't 'e?'

'I think you ought to get his mother,' said Hannah anxiously. 'Where does she live?'

'Over the road. But she ain't there. Every Sat'day morning she does a cleaning job straight from the 'ospital, and I don't know where it is. She won't be back till this afternoon; then she likes a sleep before taking 'im 'ome. She's ever so 'ard up.'

'If she's so hard up, why does she have such a big expensive pram?'

'Well, it seems 'is dad was quite well orf. 'E 'ad a good job an' all that, and when 'e knew she was 'aving a baby 'e brought 'er the pram, and now all the money's gorn she ain't got the 'eart ter part wiv it, so she told me.'

'When does she see her baby?'

'Every night 'fore she goes ter work, and she 'as 'im all Sat'day night, and Sunday.'

Hannah looked at the baby again. His face was still screwed up in pain. 'I think we should get him to the doctor.' She bit her lip anxiously.

'I ain't got the money,' said the girl.

'Well, I haven't any,' said Hannah. 'What are we going to do? He does look very ill.'

'S'pose we could take 'im ter the cottage 'ospital. If they

know 'e belongs ter Mrs Dobson, pr'aps they won't charge us.'

'I think that's a good idea. I'll call in on my way home and see how you got on.' Hannah turned.

''Ang on a minute. Could you take 'im?'

Hannah shook her head. 'I'm sorry, I told you I've got to go to work, I shall be late as it is.'

'But look, I've got all these ter look after. I daresn't leave 'em, they'll fight like cat and dog the minute I go frough the door.'

'I'm sorry.' Hannah went to walk away.

'Please 'elp me.'

Hannah was filled with guilt. What could she do? She had to get to work but the baby could die without her help! 'I don't know where the hospital is,' she said softly.

'I can show 'er, Kate,' said a little boy, jumping up. He had a mop of brown tousled hair and the corners of his watery, red-rimmed eyes were full of matter. His tattered shirt hung out of trousers tied round his waist with string.

'Tuck yer shirt in then,' said Kate. 'And go and wash yer face.' She looked at Hannah. 'I'll tidy Brian up a bit.'

Hannah fidgeted with her gloves. Every minute was making her later. 'If I can, I'll leave the baby at the hospital. Perhaps you can collect him afterwards. I'll tell your brother what's wrong with him. Are you ready?'

'Yer.' Kate picked up the baby and put him over her shoulder. He was promptly sick down her back. Hannah turned up her nose and shuddered, glad it was over Kate and not her.

Kate put the baby in the pram. 'You lives wiv that funny woman round the back of the old wash-'ouse, don't yer?'

Hannah smiled at the thought of Maudie being called a funny woman. 'Yes.'

'Fought so. Seen yer before.' Kate expertly manoeuvred the

pram through the door. She bent her head closer to Hannah.
'We've 'eard she's got lots o' kids in there, and she dopes 'em
and sends 'em out pinching.'

Hannah laughed. 'Don't believe that, I go to work, and my
sister goes to school.'

'Oh,' said Kate, obviously disappointed.

As Hannah pushed the pram along she couldn't help feeling
very grown up. It certainly was very grand. Thankfully Brian
had fallen asleep with the gentle rocking. 'Is it very far?' she
asked her escort.

'Na, only a few streets away.'

Hannah carefully lowered the bassinet down the kerbs and
over the tram-lines.

'That's it,' said the boy, pointing to a small building that
from the front didn't look much larger than a grand mansion
house.

Hannah went through the gate and knocked on the door.
The boy stood behind Hannah.

A woman wearing a navy blue dress with a spotless white
starched apron over it, and a large starched head-dress, opened
the door and stood in the doorway. 'Yes?' She had a harsh
voice.

'If you please,' stammered Hannah. 'I've brought this baby.
You see he's not very well.'

'Where's your mother?'

'Oh he's not ours,' Hannah said hastily.

'What?'

'I mean, he doesn't belong to us.'

'Well, who does he belong to?'

'Mrs Dobson, the Mrs Dobson who works here.'

A wave of pleasure washed over the nurse's face. 'Mary?
Mary Dobson who works here? What's wrong with him?' She
peered into the pram.

'I don't know,' said Hannah.

'He does look poorly. Bring him inside.'

Hannah pushed the pram through the doorway. Inside it felt warm, and smelt clean and carbolicky, the tiled walls white and shining. Hannah drank in the peace as they followed the nurse down the corridor, though the gentle swishing of her starched apron and the soft padding of her footsteps on the stone floor was drowned by the clomping of the boy's over-large boots.

'Mary went home hours ago,' said the nurse over her shoulder. 'Why hasn't she brought her baby here herself?'

'She's gone to work.'

'What, straight from here?'

Hannah nodded.

'In here. Leave this door open,' she said. They followed her into a small room where she sat at a desk.

'Nurse,' the woman called to someone as they passed the open door. A young nurse wearing a light blue uniform and apron and a smaller starched hat walked in. 'This is Nurse Dobson's baby. Take him and clean him up, and take his temperature. I'll be along shortly.'

'Yes, Sister.' With an air of quiet efficiency the nurse promptly moved the pram with the sleeping baby away.

'Now young lady, perhaps you could tell me what has led up to this?' The sister picked up a pencil and, without waiting for an answer, turned to the young boy. 'I think your eyes could do with a bathe. I'll get another nurse to have a look at you.'

'We can't afford it, Miss,' he said, nervously shifting from one foot to the other. 'I'd better go.'

'Both of you, sit down for a minute. You don't have to pay.'

Hannah couldn't help smiling. He did look a sorry sight.

'Now, young lady.' The sister turned to Hannah.

'I don't know anything about it,' she said hastily. 'Kate,

that's his sister, called me when I was on my way to work and asked me to look at the baby. I didn't think he looked very well, and Kate suggested I brought him here.'

'I see – and why didn't Kate bring him?'

'She has all her brothers and sisters to look after, and she didn't want to leave them.'

'Do they all look sickly like him?' She nodded in the boy's direction.

The boy scowled. 'I ain't sickly. It's just I 'ave trouble wiv me eyes.'

'I can see that. Ahh, here's Nurse Cook. Go along with her, young man.'

The boy obediently followed the nurse.

Hannah got to her feet. 'Look, I'm sorry, but I must go, I'm ever so late for work,' said Hannah.

'What about the boy and the baby?'

'He can take him back.'

'I think we'll be keeping the baby here for a while.'

'What's wrong with him?'

'I don't know till he's been examined, but he does look very poorly.'

Hannah looked about her anxiously.

'Look, I'll send the boy home with a note for Mary. You run along.'

'Thank you.' As Hannah hurried down the corridor, she glanced up at the large clock. 'I'll be in for it now,' she said out loud.

Chapter 9

All heads turned to look at Hannah when she walked into the factory.

'Christ, you're late,' said one of the women.

'What yer been up ter? Been out on the tiles all night?' yelled Rosie, another member of their group. She added a high-pitched laugh.

Hannah blushed and, quickly donning her overall, made her way to the cupboard to get her broom, only to find Wally standing in her tracks.

'What time do yer call this?'

'I'm very sorry. I had to take a friend's baby to the hospital.'

'Did yer now?'

Hannah nodded. She was terrified of losing her job, more so now she'd been promised a rise.

'Well, I must say that's a good excuse.' His voice was sarcastic. 'Why couldn't its mother take it? And why didn't yer wait till s'afternoon?'

'He is very ill.'

'Yer knows yer'll be stopped fer yer lost time?'

Hannah nodded again.

Wally brought his head closer. 'And yer could git the sack.' He paused threateningly. 'So don't make 'abit of it.'

Hannah kept her head down, determined he shouldn't see the tears welling up in her eyes. She desperately wanted that extra money. She was saving up to buy Alice a new frock for Christmas and perhaps, if she had enough, a pair of slippers for Maudie. This was going to be the best Christmas they'd had for years, but if she lost her job . . . She quickly began the sweeping.

That afternoon, only Maudie was in when Hannah arrived home. She sat herself wearily at the table and told her what had happened this morning.

'It's a shame when young gels falls on 'ard times,' she sighed, and slurped her tea from her china saucer. 'Yer say they all live in 'Ope Street? That the one wiv all the kids?'

'Yes. You should see their place, it's not nearly as cosy as ours and, guess what? Kate called you a funny woman, and said those in Hope Street reckon you dope kids and then send them out pinching.'

'Wot?' Maudie threw her head back and laughed so much Hannah thought she would choke. ''Ere, can yer see me doping Jack?'

Hannah too found herself laughing. And the thought of Maudie pouring some sort of potion down Jack's throat had her almost falling off her chair.

Maudie wiped her eyes. 'There's some funny buggers round in that 'Ope Street.'

'Including the battling Barkers,' said Hannah. 'Have you ever seen her hat?'

That started Maudie laughing again. 'Gawd only knows where she got it from. 'Ere, ain't it 'er old man what's always drunk?'

Hannah nodded.

'Fell over 'im once in the dark I did. There 'e was, flopped against the wall: frightened the bloody daylights out o' me, 'e did.' When Maudie calmed down she said seriously, 'Yer said the baby's mum works at the cottage 'ospital and goes out cleaning?'

'Yes, it seems her husband died. Must have been awful.'
Maudie nodded silently.

'Did you ever get married, Maudie?'

'Na, no one would 'ave me?'

'I don't believe that. I bet when you were young you had plenty of suitors.'

Maudie laughed and leaned forward. 'I was walking out with a nice young man once, but 'is family didn't like me.' She patted the back of her hair that she now wore twisted into a neat bun.

'Why was that? They couldn't have known you. We all think you're very kind. You're like a mother to us.'

With a look of surprise on her face, Maudie sat back. 'Do yer fink that?'

Hannah nodded.

'Yer really fink that? All of yer?'

Again Hannah only nodded.

'Well, I'll be buggered. D'yer know that's the nicest fing anyone's ever said ter me?'

'Why do you look after all of us?' Hannah asked quietly.

'Yer looks after yerself really, and me.' Her smile crinkled her full face. To Hannah it was a warm, tender smile, and she dearly wanted to throw her arms round Maudie's neck to thank her for what she'd done for them.

'Yer see, I know wot it's like ter be 'ungry. I was brought up in a work-'ouse. It was a bloody bad 'ome; always 'itting yer wiv a big stick, they was.' She put her elbows on the table and held her cup with both hands. Suddenly she looked sad. 'I was born in that work-'ouse, never knew me mum or dad. She run orf just after I was born, so they said. I stayed there till I was ten and then I was sent inter service. That wasn't ser bad. Good food and a warm bed, well mattress really.' She poured some more tea into her saucer.

Hannah sat in silence; she didn't want to break the spell.

'Well, when I was fifteen – about your age, I suppose – don't rightly know when me birfday is, I ain't ever 'ad one of them there cercisifetic fings. Anyway, as I was saying, I met this nice young man who lived nearby, and we started walking out tergevver. Met 'im in the park when I 'ad a Sunday morning orf. Should 'ave been in church, but I ain't that religious. We used ter sit and listen ter the band. They used ter play some nice tunes. Anyway, ter cut a long story short, 'is parents made 'im stop seeing me, and I got flung out of me job.' Maudie sat back.

'Why? Why did you lose your job?'

Bonzo jumped to his feet and began wagging his tail. 'Let 'im out fer a jimmy, there's a good gel,' Maudie said.

Hannah quickly let the dog out and hurried back to the table.

'Why did you lose your job, Maudie?' Hannah persisted.

'Cos I was in the family way.'

Hannah gasped. 'What happened to the baby?'

'I lorst it.'

'Oh Maudie, I'm so sorry.'

'I wasn't. I dunno why I'm telling yer all this.'

'What happened then?' asked Hannah eagerly.

'Well, I couldn't git a proper job, not wiv out papers – a reference is what I finks they called it – only barmaid and that sorta stuff, and well, then I met this sailor, and I fought 'e was the answer ter all me prayers. But the sod let me down.' Her voice dropped to a whisper. 'I really loved that Albert.'

Bonzo started scratching at the door and Hannah hurried to let him back in.

Maudie was fumbling in the pocket of her pinafore for her handkerchief. She blew her nose. ''Annah love. Now yer nearly a woman, I fink yer better know a few fings about men.'

'The women at work have been telling me things.' Hannah

looked down as she felt her face turn scarlet. 'I don't think I could let a boy do that to me,' she whispered.

'You will, love, when yer meets the right one and yer falls in love wiv 'im. But yer must be careful, cos it ain't easy trying ter bring up kids in this day and age. It was when I was 'aving me baby I found out 'ow bloody 'ard life was. I 'ad ter pinch fings ter live. Even after young Bert was born.'

Hannah gasped. 'You mean the Bert that comes here?'

'Yer, that's right.'

'He's your son?'

'Yer.'

'But why is he . . . ?' Hannah stopped. She had to choose her words with caution.

'Always orf?'

'Well, yes.'

''E can't bear ter be shut in. As I was saying. About a year after Bert was born I found young Jack. Crying 'e was. 'E'd been badly beaten, 'e was about two, and I couldn't part wiv 'im. I'd found a place ter stay in, so I took 'im in. Then a bit later I saw this was empty, so we moved in round the back 'ere.' A smile spread across her face.

Hannah's eyes were wide open with all these revelations. 'Why doesn't Bert stay?'

''E likes ter go orf – 'e sometimes goes ter sea like 'is dad did. Goes somewhere up norf, I fink it's up norf. Anyway, 'e's wiv the fishing boats.'

'Is that why he's got an accent?'

'Yer, been up there more than down 'ere.'

'How did he get up north?'

''Is dad found me when Bert was about five and took 'im away.'

'Why didn't Albert stay with you?'

''E didn't fink I was good enough for 'im and 'is son. Broke me 'eart, it did. Bert musta remembered livin' 'ere wiv me, cos when 'e was about eleven, or thereabouts, Albert died, and 'e managed ter find 'is way back down 'ere.' Maudie sniffed and gave a faint smile, adding softly, "E looks just like 'is dad. 'E 'ad dark curly 'air and brown eyes, but my Albert was a lot taller.'E was lovely looking. I really loved that bloke, and I reckon we could 'ave been all right tergevver if 'e'd 'ave give it 'alf a chance.' She wiped her nose. 'Bert's a clever lad.' 'E pops back now an' again, but 'e can't settle down 'ere.'

'Why doesn't Jack like him?'

'They used ter git on all right 'fore Bert went away, but when 'e came back . . . I'm not really sure, it's sumfink ter do wiv some stuff wot got pinched and Jack finks Bert told the police where it was 'id. But they don't tell me much, it's just wot I 'eard.'

'Did Jack go to prison?'

'Na, 'e's too clever. The rozzers couldn't pin nuffink on 'im.' Maudie sat back. 'I fink Jack's a bit jealous.'

'Why?'

'Well, I reckons it's because Bert's me real son, but Jack says Bert only comes 'ere when 'e's 'ard up and wants sumfink. But after all 'e *is* me son, me own flesh and blood, and I can't see 'im on 'ard times, now can I?' Maudie sniffed. 'I dunno why I'm telling yer all this.'

'Perhaps you think I'm now old enough to talk to?'

'Yer, could be.' Maudie patted her hand. 'It's nice ter 'ave someone ter talk to. D'yer know, I fink yer gonner turn out ter be all right.'

'Do the others know about you?'

'Na, only Jack o' course. Don't see the point in telling 'em. And I'd be obliged if yer didn't say too much. Yer see, I've seen plenty come and go – I don't fink young Dolly'll stay long – but you and yer sister are different, yer seem settled, and now yer got yerself a nice little job . . .'

'What about Tom?'

'Well, 'e's very fond of yer sister, and all the while she stays, so will 'e.' Maudie smiled. 'On the whole I ain't a bad judge o' character.'

'But why do you do it?'

'Do wot?'

'Take us in?'

'When times was really bad and I saw lots a kids crying wiv 'unger, I vowed when I found a place I'd always try ter 'elp any kid what was on 'ard times and wanted a bit o' 'elp. Not all of 'em stayed.'

'You've had more?'

'Yer. It's been 'ard over the years, and I've 'ad some right cow-sons, I can tell yer, but ser long as they 'elp 'emselves . . .' Maudie sniffed and got her handkerchief out again and blew her nose.

Hannah jumped up and threw her arms round Maudie's neck. 'I've wanted to do that for such a long while. I'm going to stay with you for ever and ever.'

Maudie patted her head. 'We shall see, love. We shall see. And 'Annah, don't go saying nuffink ter the ovvers, especially Jack.'

'No, no course not. Fancy Jack being with you since he was two. Maudie, can Jack read?'

'Yer. We 'ad a clever bloke stay wiv us once, and when 'e wasn't drunk 'e taught Jack ter read and write. 'E said young Jack was clever and 'e picked it up real quick. Now then, better bank up the fire, the ovvers will be in soon.'

As Hannah walked home from work on Monday evening it was misty and drizzling with rain. She had decided to call in on Kate to see how the baby was. Her head was bent against the rain and as she turned the corner, she bumped into Mrs Nosy.

'Look where yer going,' she growled, clutching the jug she was holding closer to her chest. 'Dozy cow.'

'Sorry,' said Hannah.

'Where's me purse?' she suddenly screamed. 'Yer pinched it yer little cow.'

Hannah stood dumbfounded. 'I haven't touched your . . .' Her voice drifted off as she noticed curtains beginning to move.

'I 'ad it in me 'and – now it's gorn. You lot in that place are all the same. Always out pinching.'

'I go to work,' said Hannah indignantly.

'It's about time the police locked that old witch away.'

'Maudie's not an old witch, and I haven't got your purse, you must have dropped it.'

''Allo, Gertie, everyfink all right then?' an old man called out as he shuffled towards them.

'No it ain't.'

It was Fred from number fifteen, illuminated now in the yellow glow from the gas-lamp. 'Yes, she is very nice,' he said pleasantly. ''Allo love.'

Mrs Nosy was hopping mad, the gas-light emphasizing her ferret-like features. 'She's pinched me purse!' she screamed.

Poor old Fred didn't know what was happening. 'You'll 'ave ter speak up, Gertie.' He put his hand to his ear. 'Me old ear's playing me up, so's me feet. Wish I 'ad a few bob ter go and see the doctor. Does your old man suffer wiv 'is feet?'

'Oh,' said Mrs Nosy, almost stamping up and down with temper. 'I ain't got no patience wiv you, yer silly old sod.'

Fred nodded and smiled. 'No I ain't going away for Christmas. Wot about you?'

Mrs Nosy waved her jug at him; he waved back, and continued to shuffle on his way home.

Hannah suddenly bent down. 'This belongs to you, I think.' She handed Mrs Nosy her purse.

'I bet yer just put it there, didn't yer?'

Hannah, who up to now had been amused by the incident, suddenly felt very angry. 'Now you just listen to me,' she said, taking hold of the old woman's arm. 'I didn't pinch your purse, you dropped it.' Furious, Hannah went to walk away.

'Don't you talk to me like that, yer saucy cow,' Mrs Nosy called. 'Y'er just a bit of a kid.'

Hannah turned. 'I may be just a bit of a kid, but at least I helped out when someone needed me – which is more than I can say for you.' Hannah marched off, her cheeks burning with temper – and guilt, for she had never spoken to anyone like that before.

Her heart still thumping, she banged on Kate's door.

''Allo,' said Kate on opening the door.

'Grr,' said Hannah.

'What's up?' asked Kate in alarm.

'That Mrs Nosy.'

'Wot?'

'I'll tell you another time,' said Hannah, shaking her head. She didn't want to be accused of gossiping as well as thieving – after all, she didn't know Kate very well.

'Come in,' said Kate, clearly anxious.

'No, thanks all the same, but I mustn't stop. I only popped in to see how little Brian is?'

'Not ser bad. 'E's still in 'ospital, but 'is mum says 'e's doing fine. Billy's eye's better.'

Hannah smiled. 'Oh yes, your little brother. That's good. I'll call in again later on in the week, if that's all right?'

'Yer, course it is.'

Hannah felt pleased as she walked away. The baby was being properly looked after, and she had put Mrs Nosy in her place.

111

She gave a little giggle, and hastened her step. Poor old Fred, she thought, I wonder what sort of Christmas him and all of Hope Street are going to have?

It was Christmas Eve, and Hannah felt very grown up as she took Alice to Peckham Rye to buy her a new frock. There were so many people about carrying parcels and Christmas trees and, although the evening was cold, the atmosphere was warm and friendly. The mouth-watering smell of chestnuts roasting on the open braziers filled the crisp air, and the Salvation Army singing carols on the street corner added to the festivities.

'This is a bit different to last year,' said Alice gazing at the brightly lit shop windows. Without turning to face her sister, she asked softly, 'Hannah, do you ever think of Uncle Harry?'

Hannah pulled her scarf tighter round her throat. 'Yes, sometimes,' she said quietly.

'Do you think he could have – you know?'

'I don't know.' She tried to make her voice sound firm. 'Look, Alice, that's all in the past, so let's try to forget about it.'

Alice took hold of her hand. 'I'm sorry, I shouldn't have said anything.'

Hannah put her arm round her young sister's shoulders. 'That's all right. Come on, we've got a lot of shopping to do, and I've got some money to spend! I never dreamed I'd get a Christmas bonus.'

'Yes, you told me,' laughed Alice as they walked on.

'Sorry. It's just that I'm so excited about . . . I don't know – *everything*. It's great fun living with Maudie and all of them, don't you think?'

'Yes,' said Alice absent-mindedly, more interested in pressing her nose against a large store window in which was displayed one of the new ready-to-wear frocks. It had pale blue silk hanging below the overdress of blue satin. 'I like that one.'

Hannah laughed. 'So do I, but it's not very practical. You couldn't wear that sort of frock in this weather. Besides, where would you go in a frock like that?'

'But I want something like that. Do I always have to have something practical? Can't I have something pretty for a change, that don't smell of mothballs?'

Hannah knew by her tone that her sister meant what she said. 'No, I'm sorry Alice, this has to be a warm frock that will last you all winter.'

Alice began to pout. 'It'd be nice to have something pretty for a change,' she repeated.

Hannah was beginning to get angry. Why couldn't Alice be happy with everyday things? 'I'm sorry. I can't afford silly frocks like that. Now come on, otherwise Christmas will have come and gone and we'll still be out shopping. I've got to get Maudie's slippers yet.' Hannah moved on, and Alice, mumbling to herself, reluctantly followed.

When they arrived home, Hannah sat in the corner and began wrapping all the presents she had bought in colourful paper. Tomorrow was Christmas Day, and for the first time in many years they were living somewhere that was warm and had been decorated. Jack had got a tree, and the girls, along with Freddie, had been busy making trinkets to hang on it.

Hannah was planning to go to see Kate and take them a few biscuits on Boxing Day afternoon, and she was also hoping to see Brian and his mother.

Hannah could have cried she was so happy. For the first time in what seemed years she had a family and friends at Christmas. She looked up at the paper chains they had made. She'd loved Christmas when her papa was alive, but these past years . . . She shuddered.

'Won't be long,' yelled Maudie, going out of the door. They

all laughed at the sight of Tom trotting beside her carrying a baking tin with a chicken lying on its back, its legs in the air. Maudie, who had been busy stuffing it with sage and onion, was taking the chicken along to the baker's to cook in his oven. It seemed she enjoyed Christmas as much as birthdays, and Hannah, hugging herself with silent happiness, was determined to do the same.

Chapter 10

Hannah felt elated as she walked down Hope Street. It was quiet, nobody about. Inside the houses she could imagine the women cooking yesterday's leftovers. Those whose husbands were down the pub would have the kids hanging round them waiting for their fathers to come home for their dinner. It was too early for the pubs to chuck out, and much too early for the battling Barkers to bring everybody to their windows. Hannah smiled to herself, wondering how many children in this street had real presents this year?

They'd been lucky. Christmas Day had been all that she could ever have wished for; so much fun. Everybody had been so generous with their presents, and although she knew most of them had probably been stolen, and felt a little bit guilty about it, it didn't stop her from enjoying them. She could never see herself moving away from Maudie. Today the only cloud on her horizon was Alice. She was still concerned about her, and wasn't sure if she was attending school regularly. Elsie had told her her boys thought they had seen Alice, but Hannah still had her doubts. Where did she get the money from to buy my pretty scarf? she wondered. And what about the presents she'd bought for the others? Was she using her school money, or did she steal them? And she didn't like the way Alice and Tom were always giggling together; she felt out of it. Was it because she was working and they . . . ? She quickly discarded that thought, annoyed with herself for feeling jealous.

''Allo 'Annah,' said Billy when she knocked on the door.

115

'Kate's in the kitchen, so's me mum.'

''Allo 'Annah,' said Kate coming towards her with a beaming smile. 'I likes yer 'at.'

Hannah affectionately patted her large black hat with the long pink fluffy feather. She had worried when she'd bought it that its previous owner might have had fleas, but so far she hadn't been bothered with them, and she loved the hat: it made her feel very grown up.

'Look, Mum.' Kate took Hannah's hand. 'It's 'Annah.'

''Allo, love. I've 'eard a lot about you.' Kate's mother was a thin, wiry woman. She had a kind face, and her warm smile lit up her pale blue eyes. Hannah guessed she must have been pretty when she was younger.

Hannah smiled. 'Did you have a nice Christmas?'

'Not too bad. I saves up a bit all year round, the shop round the corner, yer know, 'Ermans, well 'e runs a Christmas club, and 'e lets yer put a couple o' pence on it when yer can. It's just ter give the kids a bit of a treat.' With red, sore hands she nervously patted the back of her grey hair, which was pulled back into a bun.

'D'yer like the paper chains we made?' asked Billy.

'I think they look very nice,' Hannah said politely.

''Erman gave us 'em. I 'ad ter run a few errands for 'im,' Billy said proudly. 'And we stuck 'em tergevver wiv paste Kate made out o' flour and water.'

Hannah smiled. 'I've brought you a few biscuits.'

'Fanks, that's really kind of yer,' said Kate's mum. 'Kate, take that washing orf that chair so's 'Annah can sit down. I takes in a bit a washing after I lorst me cleaning job,' she explained. 'Well it 'elps out.'

'How's Brian?' asked Hannah.

''E's all right now,' said Kate. 'D'yer wonner go and see 'im?'

'If that's all right?'

'Yer, Mrs Dobson won't mind, in fact I bet she'll be glad of a bit o company. I'll just git me coat.'

'I'd ask 'er over 'ere,' said Kate's mum. 'But it's a bit crowded wiv my lot, and noisy.' As she spoke, Kate came clattering down the bare wooden stairs. 'Good job old Fred next door's as deaf as a post.'

Hannah chuckled to herself, remembering his encounter with Mrs Nosy.

'Ready?' asked Kate, poking her head round the door.

Hannah nodded.

'Won't be long,' yelled Kate as they left the house.

'Do you go to school?' Hannah asked the young girl as they walked down Hope Street.

'Sometimes, when me mum can afford it and I can leave the kids wiv Grace. She's me young sister, and she looks after a daft kid round the corner while 'is muvver does 'ome work – she makes matchboxes. If me old grandad comes over ter stay and gives me a couple o' pence, then I sometimes goes to school fer a week. Me grandad's ever so nice,' she added. ''E give us a cake fer Christmas.'

Hannah began comparing this family with Maudie's. These people had nothing, and yet they would rather go without than steal. Once again her conscience started to bother her.

'This is 'er 'ouse,' said Kate, knocking on a door at the far end of the street.

Hannah was surprised at the clean curtains and front doorstep.

Kate noticed Hannah's reaction. 'She keeps it nice, don't she?'

'Yes, yes she does.'

The door opened and Hannah was taken aback to see such a slim young woman. She'd expected someone older.

'Hello, Kate. Come in, and bring your friend.'

'This is 'Annah. Yer know, the one I told yer about.'

'Oh yes. Come in, Hannah.' She closed the door behind them. 'Thank you for taking Brian to the hospital that morning. I was very grateful. In here,' she said over her shoulder as they followed her down the passage. 'Brian's in there, he's still asleep.' She nodded towards a closed door.

Hannah was still amazed at the difference between Kate's house and this one. Although there wasn't a lot of furniture in either of them, this one was neat and tidy. The kitchen range, well polished with blacklead, shone, and the whitestone hearth and its small brass fender were gleaming.

'Sit down. Would you like a cup of tea?' Mrs Dobson asked.

Hannah nodded. 'Yes please.' She glanced, surprised, at the few decorations and small Christmas tree.

Mrs Dobson picked the black kettle from off the range and shook it. 'I'll just put a drop more water in this. Where do you work?' She called from the scullery.

'The biscuit factory.'

'Oh yes, I know it.' She entered the kitchen again and stood the kettle on the stove. 'It won't take long. When I was on days we had some girls come in with burns from the ovens – they can be very nasty.'

The bobbing of the kettle's lid brought Mrs Dobson to her feet. She took the kettle and hurried into the scullery, returning almost immediately carrying a tray with a teapot, and a plateful of small cakes, neatly arranged. 'It's nice to do a bit of entertaining. Don't see many round here, only Kate and her family.' She began taking cups and saucers from off the dresser that filled the recess at the side of the range. It wasn't well stocked, but everything looked nice and clean.

'What was wrong with Brian?' asked Hannah.

'We don't really know, but once he started keeping his food

118

down, he soon got better. Must have been something he ate. Sugar?'

Hannah nodded. 'Please. Do you live here alone?'

'Yes. I expect Kate told you my husband died a while back.'

'Yes, she did.'

'I was very fortunate that they let me keep my job. I'm trying to keep the house on.' She smiled, but the expression in her eyes was serious. 'It's a bit of a struggle. That's why I have to do a cleaning job as well. I'm afraid we don't get paid that much at the hospital.'

'Are you a nurse?' asked Hannah.

'Well, I'm not so much of a nurse, more of a skivvy really.'

'Couldn't you find somewhere else to live so you could have more time with Brian?'

Mrs Dobson looked sad. 'No, not really. You see, I don't want to leave this house, it has so many good memories for me, and I want Brian to share those with me as he gets older.'

Hannah swallowed hard. 'Yes, I understand.' She stirred her tea.

'Besides, I'll still have to find somewhere to live, and the rent might be almost the same and the place not as nice. Help yourself to a cake, Kate.'

'Ta.' Kate quickly took one.

'I have thought of letting the rooms upstairs, but with so many people out of work it could be hard to find a good tenant, and of course it would have to be a young lady, or a business woman. Where do you live, Hannah?'

'Just round the back of the wash-house.'

Mary Dobson must have thought she meant the road round the back as she didn't query it. 'Do you live with your family.'

'Yes.' Hannah smiled. Maudie's was indeed one big happy family, but she wasn't going to tell them they were a lot of tea-leafs, as the law would call them.

When they finished their tea, Hannah said she had to go.

'Did you want to take a peep at Brian?'

'Yes, please.' Hannah followed Mrs Dobson into the front room. It was almost devoid of furniture, no three-piece, or rugs on the bare lino, and it felt cold and damp. The only bright thing in the room was a beautifully embroidered firescreen standing in the empty grate. 'That's lovely. Did you do that?' asked Hannah.

Mrs Dobson nodded as she leant over the large pram and carefully pulled the covers from Brian's face.

'He looks a lot better now,' said Hannah, gazing down on the contented baby with his tufts of brown hair neatly combed into a sausage-like curl. 'How old is he?'

Mrs Dobson smiled and gently ran the back of her fingers over his cheek. 'He's ten months,' she whispered. 'This is his first Christmas.'

''E can't 'alf yell,' said Kate from the doorway.

Hannah wondered why Mrs Dobson, who clearly cared desperately for Brian, left her baby to someone as young as Kate to look after.

As they moved away from the pram, Mrs Dobson answered the unasked question. 'I'm very lucky to have Kate to look after Brian. It's very hard to find someone who will have him all night. I don't know what I'm going to do when he gets too big to sleep in his pram. They haven't the room for his cot.' She quietly closed the door. 'It's been nice meeting you, Hannah. Pop in one Sunday afternoon. I'm at home then.'

'I'd like that,' said Hannah. 'I'll come round next Sunday after dinner.'

'She's nice, ain't she?' Kate said as they crossed the road.

Hannah nodded. 'Yes, she is.'

'D'yer know she made all of us gloves fer Christmas?'

Hannah was impressed. How did the poor woman find the

time, with two jobs, and Brian? 'That was kind of her,' she said. 'Thanks for taking me to see her.'

''Sall right. Yer going 'ome now?'

Hannah nodded. 'Yes, I must. Bye.' She pulled her scarf tighter. It was beginning to get dark, and she hurried home, home to the warm fire and her family. Once again, she thought how lucky she was.

As 1911 opened, life went on very much the same for Hannah and Maudie's family. Hannah's work was still very hard, but with the extra money she had been getting she had bought Alice some more clothes from the second-hand stall, and her knitting and sewing was improving, thanks to Maudie. Although most of the time Hannah was happy, she was growing increasingly upset over Alice. Her sister was becoming more and more difficult, arguing over anything, always insisting on having the last word. Hannah knew for sure now she wasn't attending school regularly – Hannah couldn't help but over-hear Alice's whispered tales to the others of what she'd got up to – and her speech was getting more and more slovenly. If Hannah ever brought up the subject of Alice's behaviour when they were at home, the household all took Alice's part, for her young sister knew how to twist them all round her little finger. They were drifting apart and it made Hannah very unhappy.

In the long evenings of May, they all sat outside. It was Hannah's birthday next week. It was a year ago that . . . She shuddered when she remembered the events of a year ago, determinedly dismissing them from her mind. It would be her first birthday at Maudie's, and she wondered what would be in store for her; she had made a bit of a show for Alice's and Dolly's.

A lot had happened since they'd moved here, Hannah

reflected. Tom was getting on very well with his reading and writing though Bert hadn't been back, and nobody mentioned him. Today Jack had been telling them about the suffragettes he'd seen marching and waving their banners. 'I tell yer, fings a gitting pretty bad over the water. Gawd only knows 'ow many of 'em are gitting arrested.'

'It's all that force-feeding wot'd git me,' said Maudie. 'It's all very well fighting fer rights, but I wouldn't do it.'

'Yer quiet ternight, gel,' said Jack to Hannah. 'I fought you might 'ave 'ad sumfink ter say about it.'

Hannah was about to speak when Dolly interrupted. 'Well, I wouldn't git meself arrested just ter git a vote,' she said.

'What's a v-v-vote?' asked Freddie.

'Oh, you wouldn't know even if I told yer,' said Dolly, quickly dismissing him.

Freddie walked over to Alice, who was as usual playing with the dog. 'I reckon our Hannah will be a suffragette one day,' said Alice without looking up.

'Why do you say that?' asked Hannah.

'Well, you like to be in charge, and don't like to be bossed about.'

Hannah felt hurt. Was she bossy with Alice?

'It says 'ere about the coronation,' said Tom, looking up from the newspaper he'd found. 'Cor, I'd like ter go and see that.'

'Does it say what day?' asked Jack.

'Friday the twenty-fird of June,' answered Tom.

'I'll tell yer what, why don't we all make a day of it?' said Jack. 'Let's all go up west. What d'yer say?'

'Cor that'd be smashing,' said Alice. 'What about you, Hannah, you 'aving the day off?'

Hannah shrugged her shoulders. 'I don't know.'

'Tell yer what, they'll be plenty of 'andbags and pockets ter dip inter if yer gits in the right place. I can show yer where ter stand,' said Jack.

Hannah looked away. She didn't want them to see the look of disapproval on her face.

Alice giggled. 'It sounds ever so exciting.'

'I don't fink I'll come wiv yer,' said Maudie. 'Can't stand all the crowds pushing and shoving. 'Sides, someone might pick me pocket.'

They all fell about laughing at that.

Every fourth Sunday, Hannah now had tea with Mary Dobson. They found they could laugh and talk together, and Hannah was surprised to find out Mary was just twenty. She had been married at seventeen, her husband had been a lot older, and he had died just after she found out she was having a baby. He had been a clerk in the City. She said he was a real city gentleman, and when he had had the heart attack she had been devastated. Mary often said how much she missed him, and was determined to keep his memory alive for Brian. He'd liked to buy her nice things, including the large pram, but he hadn't left her very much money. Hannah admired the way Mary was trying to be independent, to live by her own means. And she was pleased she had found a friend with whom she could share her fears about Alice.

Now it was spring, they'd take Brian out in his big pram for walks in the park.

'I think I'll have to give up working nights soon,' said Mary as she pushed him along one day.

'Why? How will you manage?'

'I don't know. Brian's getting too big to sleep in his pram, and I can't let him sleep on the floor with all Kate's brothers and sisters. Oh, don't get me wrong,' Mary added hastily, 'I've been very grateful to them for looking after him, but I think the time has come when I'll have to try and rearrange my life.'

'Will Kate still have Brian if you go on days?' asked Hannah as they sat on a seat.

'I don't know. She's getting older and she said the other day she was thinking of trying to find some work soon, and the next sister, Grace, is much too young to look after him.' Mary sighed. 'I'll have to find someone.'

Hannah knew all about Grace. She was only seven, and she already helped a woman to look after her son. 'What about letting your upstairs rooms – that would be a help.'

'Funny you should say that. I was going to ask at the hospital. I was told a new nurse is starting soon, and she might want to live near the hospital. I'll still have to find someone to look after Brian through the day though.'

Suddenly Hannah laughed. 'What if I ask Maudie to look after him?'

Mary too laughed. Hannah had told her all about Maudie and her waifs and strays and how they lived. 'Just as long as she doesn't teach him to pick pockets.'

Hannah laughed. 'I don't think she'll do that.' Mary had accepted the way they lived: she didn't approve, but said that was Maudie's business.

'Do you think she would look after him?' Mary asked. 'I'd pay her, and deliver him and pick him up.'

'I'll ask her when I get back. She might if she thought she'd get paid.'

Brian, who was sitting up, also laughed. He was a healthy-looking lad now, the image of his dad, so Mary had proudly told Hannah.

'It's your birthday next week, isn't it?' asked Mary.

'Yes, yes it is, on Friday.'

'Well, happy sixteenth.' Mary handed Hannah a little neat parcel.

'This for me?'

Mary nodded. 'You can open it now if you want to.'

'Can I? Thank you.' Hannah carefully unwrapped the packet and was surprised to find an embroidered handkerchief inside. 'Oh, thank you.' She kissed Mary's cheek. 'It's very pretty. Did you do all these stitches yourself?'

'Yes, I love sewing and knitting at night when it's quiet. I won't have time when I'm on days though.'

'This is very nice. Thank you. You are very clever.' Hannah looked up at the church clock. 'I must be off, I'll let you know about Maudie.'

All the way home the thought of Maudie looking after Brian made Hannah smile.

'Maudie, how would you like to look after a baby all day?' asked Hannah when she walked in.

Maudie turned to look at her, her little eyes bright with interest 'Whose?'

'Mary's Brian.'

'Dunno. Wot about the gel what looks after 'im now?'

'Well, she's going to try and get a job.' Hannah shot a look at Alice. 'You could look after him if you didn't go to school.'

Alice walked away without answering.

'I wouldn't mind,' said Maudie. 'How much will I git?'

'I don't know. Mary's hoping to go on days, so her money will be a lot less, and she'll have to give up her cleaning job. I'll find out.'

Maudie smiled. 'It'd be nice 'aving a little 'en round the place again.'

Hannah noticed Dolly and Alice whispering together, and they both screwed up their noses. They didn't want to know anything about babies or, she thought, about earning an honest living.

* * *

It was Friday, Hannah's birthday, and eager to see what the others had got her, she'd rushed home from work. Now she stood and looked at the table in amazement. There was the usual birthday jelly, and even a small cake.

''Appy birfday, 'Annah,' said Maudie, beaming.

'Maudie, how . . . ? Where . . . ?'

'It don't do ter ask too many questions, gel,' said Maudie. 'Take yer 'at and coat orf and come and sit down.'

Alice rushed up to her and hugged her. 'Happy birthday,' she said, thrusting a brown paper bag in to her sister's hand. 'Look at what I got you first.'

Hannah tore at the paper. 'Alice – they're lovely, where did you get them from?' She carefully slipped her hand into one of the soft black leather gloves.

'Do they fit?' inquired Alice excitedly.

'Yes, yes they do.' Hannah held up her hand, twisting it back and forth to admire the shiny leather. Suddenly her face changed.

'Before you say anything,' interrupted Alice. 'I didn't pinch 'em, I bought 'em.'

'Them, Alice. Them.' Alice was beginning to talk more and more like the others. 'Where did you get the money from?' she asked.

Alice turned to Tom. 'See, what did I tell you? If she's not telling me off for not talking proper, she finds something else to nag about.' Her mouth turned down into a pout as she plonked herself at the table. 'You won't believe me even if I told you, so what's the point of telling you?'

'Look what I got yer, 'Annah,' said Tom quickly. 'Go on, smell it.'

Hannah put the lavender bag to her nose. 'It's lovely. Thank you, Tom.'

'You feel it, it's all lovely and scrunchy,' he said, giving it a squeeze.

'See, she didn't ask you where you got that from, did she?' Alice pointed to the lavender bag.

At that moment, Dolly came in from outside with Freddie at her heels. ''Allo 'Annah. 'Appy birfday.' She pushed Freddie towards her. 'Give 'er the present then.'

''Appy b-b-birfday, 'Annah.' Freddie almost threw the paper bag at her, and then ran and hid behind Dolly.

'Thank you Freddie, and you, Dolly.' Eagerly Hannah opened the bag. Inside was a bar of soap. Hannah sniffed it. 'It smells nice.'

'Lavender,' volunteered Dolly.

'I fought yer'd like one of me little ornaments,' said Maudie, putting a small glass dog on the table. 'D'yer like it?'

'It's lovely, Maudie, thank you.' She kissed her cheek. 'But I thought this was one of your favourites.'

'It is, but I got plenty.' She winked at Hannah, who smiled back broadly. They'd grown so much closer since their little talk.

'Is Jack home yet?' she asked, looking around.

'Na, not yet. Don't fink we'll 'ang about waiting fer 'im. Never know when 'e's gonner show up.'

They sat down to the birthday tea and, although there was plenty of laughing and chatter, Hannah was a little sad that Jack wasn't there to share it with her.

Two days later, Jack came home. 'Sorry I missed yer birfday, gel, but there was all this trouble wiv those suffragettes again. Yer always gits a good crowd round 'em, so I decided ter 'ang around. I didn't fergit yer, though. And, 'fore yer says anyfink, I bought this.' He handed her a small paper bag. 'It ain't real, and it might turn yer finger green, but I fought it looked pretty.'

'Oh Jack, it's lovely, really lovely.' She quickly found a finger the ring fitted and turned her hand this way and that so the diamond-shaped glass caught the light.

'Let's 'ave a look,' said Dolly.

Hannah thrust her hand under Dolly's nose.

'Humm, very nice. Don't know wot yer got ter git nice fings from 'im. Come on, Freddie, let's git ready fer bed.'

Alice giggled. 'Looks like you've upset her again. Can I try it on, Hannah?'

Hannah passed the ring to her, and then turned to Jack. 'Thank you. You are very kind.'

Jack took a cigarette from a packet and lit it. 'Don't git too excited, gel, it only cost a couple o' pence.' He blew smoke into the air. 'And I told yer, it could turn yer finger green.'

Hannah laughed. 'I still think it's very nice.'

128

Chapter 11

Everybody was up very early on the morning of Friday 23 June, and they were buzzing with excitement at going over the water to see the coronation of King George and Queen Mary.

Hannah was pleased she had the day off, and was looking forward to the trip out with all of them.

'It's very warm out,' said Hannah.

'That's good, wouldn't like ter see it rain on 'em,' said Maudie.

'Are you sure you wouldn't like to come with us?' asked Hannah.

'Na, me old feet're playing up sumfink rotten, and I couldn't stand around fer hours just ter git a quick glimpse of 'em. Tell yer what, you bring me in a paper; that'll 'ave all the pictures in it.'

'Do you want me to stay with you?' asked Hannah.

'Na, course not. You go orf and enjoy yerself. 'Sides, yer've been busy sprucing yerself up fer terday.'

Maudie had found an old flat iron last week on a pile of rubbish in the next street, and Tom had polished the rust off it. Hannah had been making full use of it.

She quickly kissed Maudie's cheek, and ran out to catch the others up. She was glad Jack had waited for her, and, in her new felt hat, and with her handbag tucked under her arm, she trotted beside him, feeling very grown up. Jack was wearing his best suit, his brown trilby set at a very jaunty angle, and he looked very smart. Hannah felt herself blush when he smiled at her. He was so good looking, far better than some of the delivery boys who whistled and shouted after her at the factory.

When they caught the others up, Jack called out, 'Now kids, remember, if yer gits inter any trouble, yer on yer own.'

'What trouble are you expecting?' asked Hannah a little apprehensively.

'Well, yer never know. Best ter let 'em know yer not gonner 'ang around if fings go wrong.'

'What can go wrong?' Hannah wasn't quite sure what he meant – they were going out to have a good time, not to . . . She quickly dismissed that thought.

'Don't worry about it, gel.'

They walked to the underground; although Hannah had passed the station many times, she'd never been on an underground train. Outside, the pavement was packed with people pushing and shoving. Men dressed in their best clothes looked very dapper, and most of them were carrying great hampers of food. Children were running about shouting and screaming, and women were trying to walk sedately in their fashionable long, tight skirts. Some were twittering and giggling, afraid of getting them caught. Bewildered, Hannah stood at the entrance, holding on to her hat, grateful to Maudie for lending her some extra hat-pins.

'Come on, gel,' said Jack. 'It ain't gonner bite yer.'

Alice was giggling and hanging on to Tom. 'I'm ever so excited.' She moved closer to Hannah. 'I reckon I'll pick up a few bob here and there,' she said cockily.

Hannah looked shocked. 'Alice, what do you mean?'

Alice smiled and moved on, quickly lost in the crowd as they collected their tickets. She didn't seem to be at all afraid.

Dolly was holding on to Freddie's hand. ''E's always scared stiff of falling down 'ere,' she said, dragging him towards the steep steps.

Hannah was also scared stiff, but tried hard not to show it. 'You've been down here before?' she asked.

'Yer, only a couple of times when it was pouring wiv rain and we'd 'ad a good day.' Dolly, who was also wearing her best coat and hat, looked very confident as she walked on.

Hannah was almost afraid to breathe as her eyes took in her surroundings. Slowly pushed along with the crowd, she descended into the gleaming, white-tiled, secret tunnel, far below. The bright electric lights lit everything up – there were coloured posters telling her about cough medicine and cigarettes, but the ones that intrigued her most were those showing which artistes were appearing at the music hall. Gradually excitement began to replace her fear. It was wonderful to think you were under the ground, under London. It was Queen Victoria who'd done all this, she remembered her father saying. She'd been a wonderful queen.

When they got to the platform, the sight of so many people made her very nervous again, and she found she was gripping Jack's hand tightly. He looked down and smiled, but said nothing. Then the sound of the train rushing from the dark end of the tunnel made her jump.

'Relax,' said Jack. 'Ain't yer been down 'ere before?' he shouted.

Hannah shook her head.

'It's a bit frightening at first, but it ain't nuffink ter worry about.' He ushered her to the train. 'We don't go very far.'

Hannah smiled as Jack pointed out the stations on the map above their heads, pleased he was with her on her first trip in the underground. She could never have done anything like this on her own.

When they emerged out into the bright sunlight, Hannah gasped at all the thick ropes of bunting and decorations that hung from every building. Every shop window was full of pictures of the king and queen. Flags, and red, white and blue ribbons were everywhere. She turned this way and that, like a small child trying to take it all in. 'I didn't think it would be like this,' she shouted, trying to make herself heard above the din that was all round them.

'Not bad, is it?' said Jack, pulling her along. ''Ang on, else yer gonner git lorst.'

'Where's Alice?' she said anxiously, looking behind her.

'Don't worry about 'er, young Tom's keeping an eye on 'er. 'E knows 'is way round 'ere.'

'Look, there she is. Alice.' Hannah shouted and waved, and Alice waved back, a great grin on her face.

'Looks like she's enjoying 'erself,' said Jack. 'We'll make our way up ter the abbey – should git a good viewing place there. I told Tom and Dolly where ter go, so don't worry about 'em.'

'Look, look up there.' Hannah was pointing to a huge flag.

Jack laughed. 'Yer just a big kid at 'eart, ain't yer? I ought ter take yer out more often, I didn't know yer'd be this excited.'

Thrilled at Jack's talk about taking her out, Hannah held on to his hand. This was the best day of her life. She smiled up at him. 'I'd like that,' she said.

They managed to get a good spot near the abbey, and all morning they watched the comings and goings of important people. Every now and again a great roaring cheer would go up, and Hannah would stand on tiptoe trying to see over the sea of heads and large hats. She oohed and aahed along with the rest of them, waving her handkerchief at the loud brass bands, and at the coaches pulled by horses with bobbing heads. Many of the men wore shining medals that glinted in the sunlight.

To her relief, Alice was at her side most of the time, waving and cheering. Hannah felt so happy to be with the two people she loved, enjoying a wonderful day out. Suddenly another huge roar went up, and they caught sight of the sun dancing on the guards' gleaming helmets, their white plumes swaying gently back and forth as they sat very upright on their horses. Then came the beautiful golden coach. Hannah was speechless – it was like something out of a fairy-tale. She couldn't see it when it stopped, nor could she catch sight of the king and queen when they entered the abbey, but like everyone else she joined in the cheers and sang the National Anthem with great gusto.

'D'yer know, 'e's gonner be in there fer about seven hours?' said Jack as slowly the crowd began to disperse.

'*How* long?' asked Hannah, incredulous.

'About seven hours.'

'How do you know?' asked Hannah.

'Read about it, didn't I?'

'Look, we're gonner go orf.' Tom gave Jack a wink and took hold of Alice's hand.

'Yer, but remember wot I told yer,' said Jack.

'Alice,' called Hannah. 'Where're you going?'

She grinned. 'Don't worry, we're all right. See yer back here in a couple of hours.'

'But Alice,' said Hannah. 'I thought we'd spend the day together.'

'I told you, I'll be all right – don't worry.' With that she turned and disappeared into the crowd.

'What're they up to?' asked Hannah. 'She's not . . . ?' She went to move after her, but Jack pulled her back.

'Leave 'er be. She won't fank yer fer stopping 'er doing what she wants ter.'

Hannah looked at the ground. 'Jack, do you think I'm too bossy?'

'Na. Look, let's go and find sumfink ter eat. I reckon we

could be up 'ere till late ternight. Gonner be a lot of bonfires later.'

'All right.' Suddenly Hannah was feeling very low. How could Alice go off like that? Why didn't she want them all to stay together? And what was she going to get up to that she didn't want her with her? Hannah caught a brief glimpse of Alice picking her way through the horse dung as she and Tom crossed the road. Hannah called her name, but with all the noise going on Alice didn't hear her or, if she did, she didn't turn round.

'I told yer, leave 'er be,' said Jack.

Hannah turned on him. 'I don't like her going through these crowds on her own.'

'She ain't on 'er own. You worry about 'er too much. She'll be all right, she's wiv Tom.'

When Hannah looked back, Tom and Alice had disappeared once more into the milling throng. Dolly and Freddie had also moved on.

'Come on, gel, let's go ter St James's Park. We might git a cuppa there.'

'Jack,' Hannah hesitated. 'Are you going to . . . ? You know?'

He grinned, a broad grin that crinkled his blue eyes. He pushed his trilby back. 'Don't worry about it, gel.'

As they were being jostled and pushed by the crowds, Hannah tried hard to keep her eye on Jack's hands, but it was impossible. Many times he put his hands out to steady himself, but she couldn't see if he put them into someone's pocket.

When they finally reached the park they made their way to the lake where a number of stalls had been set up.

'Give us two mugs o' tea, mate,' said Jack, marching up to one of them. 'D'yer fancy a sandwich?' he asked Hannah.

She nodded. 'Yes, please.'

'Only got cheese left,' said the stall-holder.

'That'll do,' said Jack, and to her surprise he gave the man half a crown. Hannah couldn't think where he'd got the money from: she hadn't seen him do anything.

''Ere are, gel,' he said, handing her a steaming mug of tea.

They sat on the grass, and Hannah, who hadn't realized how hungry she was, sank her teeth into the thick doorstep of a sandwich, telling herself not to let her worries spoil their day.

After a while they got to their feet and began moving about with the crowd once more.

'We'd better go back and see if the others are waiting for us,' said Hannah.

'Yer, then I fink we'll start ter make our way 'ome. Should be able ter see some of the bonfires from the roof of the old wash-'ouse.'

Hannah was very cross when they arrived back at the pre-arranged meeting place and there was no sign of the others. She stood on tiptoe looking this way and that over the heads of the crowd, hoping to catch sight of her sister.

'There ain't no sign of 'em,' said Jack, also straining to see above the crowds. 'They could be on their way 'ome. I fink we should be making a move in that direction as well – we might 'ave a bit of a job gitting on a train.'

All the way home, Hannah felt herself growing more and more angry with Alice. If she was at home she was going to give her a piece of her mind.

As soon as Hannah pushed the door open, she could hear Maudie laughing.

Maudie looked up. 'Young Dolly 'ere's been telling me all about it. Sounds smashing.'

'Is Alice home yet?' asked Hannah.

'No, ain't she wiv you?'

'No, we haven't seen her or Tom all day.'

'I bet the poor little cow's fair worn out tramping round all day. Did yer 'ave a good day, Jack?'

Jack began to empty his pockets.

'Cor, look at this lot,' said Maudie.

Jack smiled.

Hannah stood open-mouthed at the money and the watch he threw on the table. 'When? How?' she gasped.

Jack laughed. 'See, I told yer I was good, didn't I?'

She slowly nodded. 'But you've been with me all day, and I didn't see . . .' Her voice trailed off.

'I 'ad a good day as well, didn't I, Maudie?'

'You certainly did, Dolly,' said Maudie, nodding in agreement. 'Did yer git me paper, Jack?'

'Yer, 'ere are. There's some smashing pictures of the procession – pity you can't see the colours.'

Maudie picked up the paper and glanced at the front page. 'Yer, that'd've bin really nice. Well, I fink I'll be orf now and 'ave a nice read in bed. Make yerself a cuppa. Come on, Bonzo, move yer lazy self.'

Slowly the dog got to his feet and stretched first his front legs then his back ones, both movements accompanied by a series of loud cracks. His long floppy tail slowly wagging back and forth, he followed Maudie into her bedroom.

'D'yer wonner come on the roof?' asked Jack.

'Maudie said we mustn't cos that ladder's dangerous,' said Dolly.

'Please yerself,' said Jack. 'Wot about you gel?'

'I'd rather not,' said Hannah.

'Yer, well, I don't suppose we'll see much anyway, not wiv all the new buildings going up round 'ere.'

Dolly began to get ready for bed whilst Hannah sat at the table, restless.

'Jack, do you think Alice is all right?'

'Do stop going on about 'er. I'm gonner git some shut-eye and I suggest you do the same.'

'Yer, keep the noise down 'Annah,' said Dolly from her corner.

Hannah watched Jack drag his mattress to his special place. She discreetly turned her head when he took his trousers off and threw them over a chair. When she heard him strike a match she knew he was lying on his back smoking a cigarette. She was still sitting with her elbows on the table, resting her chin on her hands, when her head fell forward. The jolting woke her up and made her jump. It was dark and the church clock was chiming. Quietly she went to her corner and looked at her clock, her prized possession. In the glow of a far away street-lamp she could just make out the hands, which pointed to midnight. Wherever was Alice?

Jack's hushed voice came from the corner of the room. 'Why don't yer git ter bed, gel? Remember yer gotter git ter work in the morning.'

'Yes, yes,' whispered Hannah. 'I was just going.' Hannah dragged her mattress to her spot and settled down. For a long while she lay on her back and gazed at the ceiling. She knew Jack was awake, smoking. What was he thinking about? Today had been such an exciting day. All day she had been with Jack. He had held her hand, pointing out London's landmarks, looking after her – she had been so happy. Why did Alice have to go and spoil it for her? Why couldn't she come back home like the rest of them?

Chapter 12

Hannah woke with a start. The church clock was chiming. She reached over to touch Alice. The space was empty. Where was she? How dare she stay out all night? Panic gripped her. What if something had happened to her? How would Alice let her know? Hannah raised her head and looked at the place where Tom usually slept. There was nothing – his mattress wasn't there. They must be out together. She sat up angrily.

In the early morning glow she could see Jack pushing wood into the stove. 'I've got the kettle on,' he whispered, looking in her direction. 'Looks like yer sister and Tom got caught up in the crowds.'

Hannah quickly dressed herself and went out to the washhouse. All the while she was getting ready for work she felt fear building up inside her. Surely Alice wouldn't stay out all night, not without letting her know; she knew how much she'd worry. What if she'd had an accident? What if she'd . . . ? No, Tom would have come home and told them if something was wrong. The last thing Hannah wanted to do was to go to work. She wanted to go looking for Alice, but where? Where would she start? And if she didn't go to work, she wouldn't get paid.

When at last the one o'clock hooter went, Hannah hurriedly left the factory. Anxious to get home, she wouldn't call in on Kate as she normally did on a Saturday.

Maudie, Jack and Tom were sitting at the table when she

walked in. 'Hello, Jack, didn't you go out today? Where's Alice?' she asked.

Nobody spoke.

'Isn't she back yet?' she asked, frantically looking around.

Again silence.

'What is it?' she cried out, suddenly realizing they were all looking very serious.

'Sit down, gel,' said Jack softly.

She did as she was told.

'I'll make yer a cuppa,' said Maudie.

Tom, so far, had kept his head down.

Panic filled Hannah and she jumped to her feet. 'What's happened to her?' Her worst fears – that Alice was dead, in hospital, ill – rushed through her mind. 'Where is she?' she whispered as tears stung her eyes.

Jack came and gently pushed her back down into a chair. Her heart was pounding, filling her ears: Hannah could feel the air heavy with anxiety and tension.

Jack pulled his chair closer and sat next to her. 'Alice got caught pinching some woman's 'andbag last night,' he whispered.

Hannah gasped and quickly put her hand to her mouth. 'No.' Then with her eyes blazing she turned on Tom. 'Where were you? You were supposed to be looking after her. Why didn't you get caught? Is she in prison?'

''Ang on, gel. Give Tom a chance ter answer one question at a time,' said Jack.

Tears began streaming down Hannah's face.

Tom looked very uneasy. 'I'm sorry, 'Annah – Alice was being silly, and all cocky-like. She wasn't being careful enough.' He wiped the beads of sweat from his top lip with the back of his hand. 'She was just dipping inter this woman's bag when 'er bloke caught 'old of 'er 'and . . .' He stopped as Maudie

140

put the teapot on the table. 'I didn't know wot ter do. Be now a crowd was beginning to get round 'em – there was a lot o' people shouting and shoving and pulling at Alice. I just stood there . . . At first I fought I'd try and pull 'er away, but this bloke was 'anging on ter Alice's arm real tight. 'E was shouting and shaking 'er, and the woman was yelling and gitting all hysterical-like. I fought the rozzers would 'ear 'em.'

Hannah brushed the tears from her cheeks. 'Did the police take her away?' Her soft voice cracked with emotion.

'Na. Yer see be now Alice was crying and she made 'er limp look even worse – yer knows 'ow she does when she wants 'er own way. Well, the woman, who was ever so well dressed, calmed down and she said sumfink ter 'er bloke. Well, 'e then put 'is arm round Alice's shoulders and they moved on.'

'How do you know he wasn't taking her to the police station?'

'I followed 'em, didn't I? I pushed me way frew the crowd and when Alice saw me she shook 'er 'ead at me. She wanted me ter go away.'

Fear was beginning to rise like bile in Hannah's throat. 'Why would she do that?' Her head was swimming. Her father's voice as he lay dying was going over and over in her head. 'You will look after Alice when I've gone, won't you? Promise me that, Hannah.' She remembered how the tears had spilled from her eyes as she'd promised to do as he said, just as they were doing now. She'd let Papa, and Alice, down.

Maudie handed her a cup of tea. ''Ere are, love, git this down yer. I've put lots o' sugar in it.'

'Tom, do you know where they took her?' sobbed Hannah.

He shook his head. 'I followed 'em – they musta been well orf cos they got inter ever such a posh motor car.'

'And they took Alice with them?'

Tom nodded.

'If they didn't take her to the police station, where did they take her?'

''Annah, I don't fink they'll do 'er any 'arm, cos be the time they got ter the car she was laughing.'

'What?' It was like an explosion. 'She was laughing?'

'Yer. I fought it funny. One minute they're all shouting and yelling and she's crying, then a bit later on as she limped along, she's làughing.'

Hannah was speechless.

'I'm sure she'll be 'ome soon, gel, then she'll be able ter tell yer all about it 'erself,' said Jack.

Maudie smiled. 'Always said that gel's gonner make a bloody good actress one day – you mark my words. Drink yer tea up love, 'fore it gits cold.'

Angrily Hannah turned on Maudie. 'It's all your fault. You made her steal.' Tears ran down her face.

'Now 'ang about, gel,' said Jack. 'Nobody forced yer ter stay 'ere.'

'Leave 'er be, Jack, she's upset,' said Maudie.

'Yer I know, but she shouldn't . . .'

Maudie shook her head at him, then put her arm round Hannah's shoulders. 'Sit yerself down, love, and drink yer tea – we'll try and sort sumfink out.'

Hannah put her elbows on the table and, lifting the cup shakily to her lips, began sipping the hot sweet brown liquid. She didn't notice that Maudie had given her her best bone-china cup to drink out of. All she could think about was what she was going to do. What was Alice up to now? 'D'you realize that if she has been taken to a police station, they could come here looking for me?' She said suddenly.

'Don't say that, love,' said Maudie, anxiously glancing round.

'Don't see why they should,' said Jack. 'Not if they only

wonner make sure she's got a sister.'

'Yer said some posh woman took 'er, Tom?' It was clear from Maudie's tone that she was worried by Hannah's remark.

Tom nodded.

'Don't suppose yer noticed anyfink about the car?' asked Jack.

Tom shook his head this time.

Hannah looked up hopelessly. 'What's the point of this conversation? She's been taken away, and we don't know where to start to find her.' Hannah played with the spoon. 'She can't even write to me,' she said softly. 'This place hasn't got an address.' Choking back her sobs, she pushed her chair back and ran outside. With tears streaming down her face, she sat on the wall and buried her head in her hands. Suddenly she felt all the pent-up anger, fear and unhappiness she'd known during the past years begin to overwhelm her. 'Please Alice, come back,' she whispered.

All Sunday morning, Hannah moped around, and after dinner she hurried round to see Mary. As soon as she sat down in her friend's kitchen, the story of how Alice had gone missing spilled out. Mary sat very quietly listening. When at last Hannah finished her crying, Mary suggested she make a cup of tea.

'Hannah, I'd think that if she had been arrested they would have let her off by now,' she said, returning to the kitchen with the tea-tray.

'Why ? Why do you say that?'

'They must have caught a lot of hardened pickpockets up there, and I'd think that they'd let a small crippled girl off. Would she have any money to get home?'

Hannah's expression changed. 'I don't know.' She smiled. 'Do you really think that? Do you think that could have happened?'

It was Mary's turn to smile. 'I wouldn't mind betting that, when you get home, she's busy relating all her experiences to the others.'

'If she is, I'll make sure she goes to school and forgets all about this way of earning a living.'

'Now drink your tea,' said Mary. 'And we'll take Brian out for a little while. Oh, by the way, I've got a lodger – she starts at the hospital next month and she's going to rent one of the bedrooms. We're going to share the cooking and kitchen, so that's one of my problems out of the way, and if Maudie will have Brian, Matron said I could go back on days.'

Hannah felt cheered by her friend's good news. 'I'm so pleased for you; at least you'll have more time with Brian. I did ask Maudie, and she seemed very interested.' Hannah laughed. 'She wanted to know what you'll pay her. I'll ask her again when I get home – but with this thing about Alice . . .'

'Don't worry about it, we've got a few weeks yet.'

'Mary, do you like working at the hospital?'

'Oh yes. I would love to have been properly trained, but there you go, it wasn't to be. I've been very lucky that Matron kept me on even when I had Brian. Some places make you leave when you get married, you know, let alone start a family.'

'She must feel your worth it.'

'No, I don't think so. I think it's more of a case that she can ask me to do anything, and a new person might not, especially one of these women who go to the suffragette meetings.'

'Jack said he went out with one of those women once. She was from the hospital.'

Mary nodded. 'That could have been young Barbara North. She left.'

'Was she nice?'

'Yes, but she had very strong views.'

'Do you believe in women voting?' asked Hannah curiously.

'Yes, I do, but I'm not in a position to rock the boat with my beliefs.' Mary put Brian in his pram.

'They don't do operations and that at your hospital, do they?' asked Hannah, screwing up her nose.

Mary laughed. 'No, only the very small ones, those that can be done under a local anaesthetic. It's mostly dressing people's wounds after they've had accidents, or operations, or seeing to children like Kate's brother.'

'Oh,' said Hannah thoughtfully.

Ten minutes later, Hannah left her friend's house feeling cheered and confident her sister would be waiting at Maudie's. But when Hannah got home, to her great disappointment, Alice still hadn't returned.

Summer had come and gone, and for Hannah it had been miserable: there was no news of Alice. Life in Maudie's continued just the same for all the others. Mary's lodger, a Miss King, a lady older than Mary, arrived and Mary went on day work. Hannah still went round there most Sundays, but it wasn't the same with a stranger in the house. She and Mary didn't seem to laugh and giggle like they used to. But perhaps, Hannah thought, it was her own fault. She found it difficult to be cheerful nowadays. Or maybe she was just growing up?

As Kate had now found work in the pickle factory, Maudie was looking after Brian.

One Sunday morning, Maudie was bustling around. 'Yer knows, I miss having little Brian round here. You should see 'is face when I finish giving 'im 'is egg and fingers. 'E's a good little lad and no mistake.'

'I'm glad 'e's gorn be the time we gits in,' said Dolly. 'Can't stand screaming kids.'

'He doesn't scream,' said Hannah, getting up from the table.

'Look at you, up on yer 'igh 'orse again,' said Dolly

following her. 'Yer know, you ain't 'arf gitting ter be a misery.'

'So would you be if Freddie was missing.'

'Well 'e ain't, and yer sister wouldn't be if she'd been a bit more careful.'

'So you think it's clever then, stealing, do you?'

'Well, I ain't got caught yet.' Dolly tossed her head in the air.

'Don't be so cocky,' Hannah said grimly. 'You could be heading for a fall.'

'There ain't nuffink I couldn't pinch if I puts me mind to it, and I wouldn't git caught,' said Dolly proudly. 'So there.'

'You wait, you won't always be so sure of yourself.'

'Shut it you two,' said Jack wearily from the table.

'She started it,' said Hannah.

'Yer, well, give it a rest.'

'I'm going out.' Tears were stinging Hannah's eyes. She was so angry and unhappy. If only Alice would come back, things could go back to normal again.

As she walked through the wash-house gate, Hannah's thoughts were full. Last week had been Alice's birthday. In the cupboard was the tortoiseshell hairbrush Hannah had bought her. Would she ever get to give it to her? Alice had been gone for over three months now. Tears trickled down Hannah's face. Where was she? What had those people in the car done to her? If she was safe why hadn't she got in touch?

Hope Street was full of noisy kids shouting and playing games. Kate's brothers gave her a wave as they spun round the lamp-post on a rope. There were the usual women chatting on their doorsteps; a few had brought out their chairs as the sky held the promise of another warm autumn day. Over the months she recognized some of them, and they gave her a friendly nod. She was pleased Mrs Nosy wasn't around to make some of her cutting remarks. Hannah thought about Maudie's. Now

Alice had gone she would like to get away from them all, find somewhere new to live. But where could she go on her wages? Besides, deep down, she knew she really couldn't leave Maudie, or Jack, and what if Alice came back?

She arrived home from work one evening to find, much to her surprise, Bert sitting at the table.

''Allo love,' said Maudie with a big grin on her face. 'Look who's turned up.'

'Hello, Bert.' She thought of him differently now she knew he was Maudie's son. 'You've not been round here for a long while.'

'Na, been too busy.' He smiled, his white teeth contrasting with his tanned, weather-beaten face. 'You're still working then?'

'Yes.' Hannah was nervous – what did he want? And if Jack came in would there be a row? 'Are you staying here for very long?' she asked casually.

'A couple o' nights, that's if the bold Jack don't mind.' He ran his fingers through his thick black hair.

'I fink 'e's away fer a few days, ain't that right, 'Annah?' said Maudie, putting the teapot on the table.

'Yes, he did say that.'

'Maudie 'ere was telling me about your sister,' Bert said. 'She's gone missing then?'

Hannah looked down. 'Yes, she has.'

'That's a shame.' He leaned forward. 'Maudie don't reckon she's been picked up be the rozzers, though. Still, I bet yer really worried about 'er.'

Hannah quickly glanced up, taken by surprise. He sounded as if he genuinely cared. 'Yes, I am.' Her conversation was stilted.

At that moment Tom came racing in and stopped dead.

'It's all right, son, I ain't gonner eat yer.'

Hannah laughed, and was immediately aware her laugh sounded false. 'Maudie, do you want me to take Bonzo out for a while?' she said quickly.

'Yer, yer could do. Dinner ain't ready yet. 'E ain't 'ad a good run since Alice went.'

'If that dog started running I reckon 'e'd drop dead,' laughed Bert. 'I'll come with you, gel. Can't stand being cooped up in 'ere for long.'

'You coming Tom?' Hannah's look was pleading. She didn't want to be alone with Bert – she wouldn't know what to talk to him about.

'I can't, I promised the bloke round the news-stand I'd 'elp 'im.'

Hannah couldn't argue, it was her who'd got him the job.

Maudie looked worried. ''Annah, 'as it stopped raining?' she said suddenly.

Hannah shrugged. 'I don't know.'

'Could I 'ave a quick word?' Maudie whispered, taking hold of Hannah's arm and half dragging her outside.

'What is it?' Hannah asked. She could guess what was coming and it made her angry. 'What's he done this time? Has he asked you for money again?'

'Na, it ain't nuffink like that. In fact 'e's give me some,' she smiled.

That would give Jack something else to have a go about, Hannah thought. He'd like the idea of Bert giving Maudie money even less than him taking it from her.

'Na, it's just that I don't want yer ter tell 'im about . . . Yer know?' She looked over her shoulder. 'Me telling yer 'e's me son.'

Hannah looked surprised. 'He doesn't know?'

'Yes, course 'e does, but I don't want 'im ter fink I've been talking about 'im.'

Hannah smiled, 'Course I won't. See you later. Come on, Bonzo. Ready, Bert?' She called.

The dog walked beside them very slowly. It was still very wet underfoot, and the street was quiet. Most of the kids who usually filled the road didn't have decent boots, so wet weather drove them inside. She was pleased most of the front doors were shut. She didn't want too many comments about her and Bert. Quickly she glanced at him. He had pushed most of his unruly black hair under his cap – he was quite good looking in a dark, rugged way, she thought. They walked along in silence.

'Bonzo must be ever so old,' said Hannah, waiting for the dog to finish sniffing the lamp-post. Finally he cocked his leg, and then moved on. She didn't know what else to talk about.

'Bonzo's been 'ere ever since I can remember.' Bert stopped and looked back. 'Bit like this street, I suppose; it ain't changed either. Mind you some of the places look a bit cleaner. I'm always surprised someone ain't come and turned Maudie out of that old wash-house.'

Hannah too stood and stared at the large red building that dominated the end of the street. 'Could they?'

'Well, she don't pay no rent, and it must belong ter someone.'

'That would be awful, she's been there years.'

'I know. I expect a lot of the old dears down 'ere thinks she pays rent, otherwise I reckon they would 'ave shopped 'er.'

'Especially Mrs Nosy.'

'She still 'ere?' Bert grinned. 'She was 'ere when I was a kid. Always chasing me and Jack when we used to 'ave fights with 'er boy and the other kids round 'ere. Funny old dear.'

'She's got a son?'

'Yer, 'e's 'bout the same age as me and Jack.'

'I've never seen him.'

'I wonder where 'e's finished up. He was a funny little bloke, wore glasses. 'E had 'em on a piece of string that went round the back of his head.' He laughed. 'I remember we used to pull it.'

'That was cruel.'

'Yer, I suppose it was.'

'I'll ask Kate about him, she might know. I bet you and Jack used to get up to some things.'

'Yer,' he smiled. 'I remember when the local bobby chased us fer pinching an apple. Me and Jack were like a couple of runner beans – talk about skinny. But we couldn't 'alf move. He never did catch us, but I tell yer gel I was scared stiff. It was just after that Albert came and asked me to go away with 'im.'

'Albert?' queried Hannah, making sure not to let on she knew who he was.

'Yer, seems he knew Maudie from way back. He was a nice bloke.'

She wanted to tell him she knew he was his father, but remembered her promise to Maudie. And *did* he know Albert was his father, she wondered suddenly.

'Me and Jack used to be good mates.'

'What went wrong?' Hannah asked gently.

'It's a long story, I'll tell yer about it one day.' Bert thrust his hands deep in his pockets and moved on.

She could see she wasn't going to get any more answers today. 'My friend lives here,' she said as they passed the last house in the street.'

'Is that Kate?'

'No, Mary.'

'She got many kids?'

'No, only Brian, the one Maudie looks after, you saw him.'

'Oh yer. His mum seems nice, well spoken.'

'She works at the cottage hospital, her husband's dead.'

'She on 'er own?'

Hannah nodded. 'She's got a lodger. I would have liked to

move in with her, but I don't earn enough to pay rent, and I really wouldn't want to leave Maudie. She's been good to us.'

Bert glanced at her. 'D'yer know Maudie thinks a lot of you. You're the first one to 'old down a steady job, and stay. Shame about your sister getting caught, though. I don't go along with 'em pinching. Said all along it's a mug's game.'

'They've got to eat, and you used to do it.' Hannah was surprised to find herself defending thieving.

'To eat, yer, but not pinch all the stuff Jack does.'

Hannah felt her temper rise. How dare he say things about Jack? Even if she did agree with him. 'We'd better get back,' she said curtly.

'I like you,' Bert said out of the blue. 'You're a nice-looking kid, and I reckon you've got your 'ead screwed on. Don't reckon I'll leave it so long next time to come and see Maudie.'

'Come on, Bonzo, let's go home,' said Hannah, blushing.

The following evening Hannah rushed home from work. To her delight Jack was home, but Bert had gone. Part of her felt quite disappointed.

''Allo, gel.' Jack was scowling.

Maudie was grinning. ''E's upset 'e missed Bert.'

Like Maudie, Hannah was pleased he'd missed Bert: she didn't want them to argue. She was fond of them both now.

This was going to be Hannah's second Christmas with Maudie, and she knew it was going to be difficult without Alice. Her sister had been gone for so long now, she'd given up imagining all the things that could have happened to her – murdered; taken away to some far-off city by the couple in the car; Rosie at work had even muttered about men who kidnapped young girls for wicked purposes. Hannah didn't think about any of these any more – she just felt an awful emptiness. She lay on her mattress thinking of Alice, and how every time she went out she looked for her, hoping. Mary had been to the police station but they knew nothing about her.

'Merry Christmas, 'Annah,' said Tom. 'Come on, git up, lazy bones.'

She smiled – she mustn't spoil their day as everyone at Maudie's seemed determined to cheer her up for Christmas. The place looked very festive with more than the usual candles on the table, and Dolly and Tom had made some paper chains and decorated the sideboard with them. They eagerly filled their plates with chicken: Maudie had cooked a chicken in the baker's oven like last year.

'Got a nice bit a dripping so yer can 'ave dripping toast fer tea. That's if yer sits and make it yerself,' said Maudie, her cheeks rosy from the stove. She was wearing the new pinny Hannah had bought her.

Hannah sat quietly, half listening to the conversation: it seemed everybody was talking at once.

Dolly nudged Hannah. 'Fanks fer me book about the animals. The pictures are really smashing, and I can read it a bit.' She sat back and played with her hair. It was long and dark, and today she wore it tied back with a new ribbon. Her dark eyes sparkled: she was pale and thin, but she was a pretty young girl, Hannah thought. She wondered if Alice had changed much. 'I'd like ter go ter the country,' Dolly went on. 'It must be really lovely wiv all them trees and green fields; much better than the park.'

'I-I-It's a lot b-b-bigger,' said Freddie.

Hannah smiled, Freddie was the image of his sister, with his dark hair and big brown eyes. He was talking a little more now, thank goodness, but was still very shy.

'And there's cows,' said Tom. Tom looked very smart today. Bob, the paper-man, had given him one of his son's suits, and Maudie had cut his hair. They had laughed when he sat with the pudding basin on his head, but Maudie had insisted she needed a guide, otherwise he could finish up bald.

'Dunno if I'd like ter see a cow close up,' said Maudie, shuddering in mock-horror. All evening everyone was laughing and telling stories, but although they tried hard to make Hannah happy, her thoughts kept going back to Alice. If she was alive, why hadn't she tried to get in touch? What kind of a Christmas was she having? Was she thinking about Hannah like Hannah was thinking about her?

'Say, how d'yer fancy coming out wiv me next Sat'day, gel?' asked Jack. 'That'll buck yer up.'

Hannah smiled. 'That would be nice. Where would we go?'

'We could go to the music 'all, that's if yer fancy it.'

'You mean like we saw on the posters that time?' Hannah was smiling.

'Yer, mind, it'll only be up in the gods.'

'Gods?'

'Yer, the cheapest seats.'

'I'd like ter go and see that,' said Dolly.

'Well, I ain't asking you.'

'Didn't fink yer would. Come on, Freddie, you can 'ave a look at me new book wiv me.'

'Well, gel, what d'yer fink?'

'It would be nice.' Hannah sat on the chair beside him. 'You wouldn't, you know . . . ?'

He laughed. 'Can't promise yer that. Yer see, if a big fat wallet's 'anging out o some bloke's pocket, well . . .'

'No thank you, Jack,' she said furiously. She walked to the other side of the room and began fingering the paper chains.

'Please yerself,' he called after her.

'I wouldn't mind going ter see the music 'all, 'Annah,' said Tom. 'When we see it on the posters, it looked ever so good.'

'Well you go with Jack, and you can both pick some poor

devil's pocket.' She stormed out of the door.

Dolly laughed. 'Cor, 'ark at Miss 'igh and mighty,' she yelled after her.

Once more Hannah felt like an outsider. Did she really fit in here now Alice had gone?

On Saturday, when Jack and Tom were getting ready to go to the music hall, Hannah dearly wanted to climb down and ask them to take her with them, but she didn't want to lose face.

'Sure yer won't change yer mind, gel?' said Jack, brushing imaginary dirt from his trilby.

'No, I told you how I feel about stealing.'

'Well, please yerself. See yer later,' said Jack, going out of the door.

'I fink yer daft not going wiv 'em,' said Maudie, puffing on her clay pipe. 'It's Alice, ain't it?'

Hannah nodded. 'I don't feel I should be out enjoying myself while she's missing. And I don't like the thought of Jack stealing while he's out with me either.'

'Yer ain't gonner stop 'im doing that. Bin doing it all 'is life.'

'Look,' said Dolly, 'why don't yer git yer mate Mary ter try and find out if the rozzers . . . You know? Took Alice.'

'She did, but they don't know anything. I'll take Bonzo for a walk.'

'Wrap up, love,' said Maudie caringly. 'It's perishing out.'

Hannah wandered along, not sure of where she was going. All kinds of thoughts were filling her mind, but the main one was that she wished she'd gone with Jack and Tom tonight.

Hannah was in a deep sleep, but suddenly she was being shaken.

''Annah, quick, 'Annah, wake up.'

She sat up. 'What is it? Oh, it's you Tom.' Her voice thick

with sleep. 'What's wrong? What's the matter?' She was disorientated.

Jack and Tom were kneeling beside her.

Dolly was sitting up. 'What's all the row about?'

'It's Alice,' said Tom excitedly.

'Alice,' yelled Hannah, scrambling to her feet. 'Alice is here?'

'No, she ain't 'ere. But we seen the woman.' Tom was almost jumping up and down.

Jack had moved over to the table. He lit a candle, and was now lighting a cigarette.

'What d'you mean, you've seen the woman?'

'Come over 'ere and sit down,' said Jack casually.

Hannah sat at the table.

'Well, you know we went to the Empire?'

'Yes, yes,' she said eagerly.

'Well, according ter Tom 'ere, one of the tarts on the stage was the one what took Alice.'

'She couldn't 'alf sing and dance, 'Annah,' said Tom.

Hannah was crying, she didn't know why.

'Anyway,' Jack tapped the end of his cigarette into the ashtray. 'When it finished, we went round the back ter 'ave a word wiv 'er.'

Hannah was shaking with excitement and fear. 'And was it her? What did she say?'

Jack drew heavily on his cigarette. 'We missed 'er.'

Hannah felt as if all the breath had been forced out of her body. She could have crumpled into a heap. 'So why are you telling me all this?' she sobbed.

'Look.' Jack quickly glanced at Maudie's door and lowered his voice. 'As termorrer's Sunday, the Empire ain't open, so we fought we'd go on Monday night ter see if we can see 'er then. Yer'd better come wiv us.'

155

Unthinking, Hannah threw her arms round Jack's neck and kissed his cheek.

''Ere, steady on, gel.' He pushed her away.

Hannah blushed.

'Can we all go back ter sleep now?' asked Dolly from her corner.

'Yer, I fink so,' said Jack.

'I'm sorry 'Annah,' said Tom.

'Are you sure it was the woman?'

'I fink so. But we was up in the gods, and it's a bit 'ard ter tell stuck right up there.'

'Better git some shut-eye, ovverwise we'll 'ave Maudie coming out shouting the odds.' Jack blew out the candle.

Hannah lay on her back. She knew she wouldn't be able to sleep, and Monday night seemed a lifetime away.

Chapter 13

Sunday dragged, and Hannah couldn't wait for the afternoon to tell Mary, who became almost as excited as Hannah at her good news.

The following day, Hannah was on edge. What if the woman wasn't on the stage tonight? What if Jack didn't get back in time?

'Yer got a lot ter look forward to ternight then,' said Elsie when Hannah told her at lunch-time, 'I ain't never been ter the music 'all.' She bent her head closer. 'I've 'eard that some of the women don't wear any clothes.'

'Don't give us that,' laughed Rosie, one of the group of women who sat together for lunch. 'I've been and it's good, got lots o' singing and dancing. You'll enjoy it, gel. Wait till yer sees their frocks.'

Elsie sat back. 'Wot about when the tarts do the can-can then? I've 'eard they ain't got no drawers on.'

'They wouldn't be allowed to . . . Would they?' asked Hannah, wide-eyed.

'Don't listen to 'er,' said Rosie.

'Don't 'old wiv women flaunting 'emselves. 'Ere, wot if this tart says she don't know nuffink about yer sister?'

'I don't know, I hadn't thought of that.'

'Give it a rest, Els,' said Rosie. 'Give the poor cow time ter get over one shock 'fore yer starts giving 'er anovver.'

When the hooter went at six, Hannah was first out of the door, and she ran all the way home.

''Ere are, love,' said Maudie. 'I've made yer a sandwich, yer ain't got time fer dinner. Jack and Tom's all ready, they're waiting outside.'

'Thanks, Maudie.' Hannah took the thick plum-jam sandwich but knew she wouldn't be able to eat it. She was far too excited to worry about food, her stomach churning. She hoped she wasn't going to be sick.

'All right then, gel?' Jack grinned.

Hannah nodded, and smiled. This might just be the happiest day of her life – she could be seeing Alice in a few hours' time.

'Shouldn't we wait for her outside?' asked Hannah looking round the elaborately embellished foyer of the New Cross Empire.

'Na,' said Jack. 'We might as well see the show first.'

Hannah was concerned. 'But what if we miss her again?'

'Na, we won't, we'll come out before the end.'

'That way,' said Tom, 'if she is on the stage, I'll be able ter point 'er out to yer.'

Hannah was worried. Again that thought went through her mind that she might not be on tonight. She pulled on Jack's arm. 'Do you think she'll be here?'

'Dunno, they change the acts every now and again.'

Once more fear gripped Hannah. What if . . . ? She must be here. They climbed the steep steps to the seats in the upper circle. Hannah, afraid they would tumble down on to the people below, held on to the sides of her seat. She looked cautiously around: they were so high up she felt she could almost touch the richly painted ceiling.

The lights were dimmed. Hannah felt her palms sweating. Suddenly, as the music started, the curtain began, very slowly, to rise. Hannah knew her mouth had fallen open: she was in awe at the bright, beautiful spectacle before them; she had never seen anything like this before. Tom was tugging at her arm.

'That's 'er,' he whispered loudly. 'The one wiv the fair 'air – next ter the end.'

The woman was in line with five other girls who were in long white frocks and large white hats. They all carried a parasol and were dancing very elegantly. They looked beautiful, and when they sang – a very saucy song – everybody laughed and joined in the chorus. When they finished, Hannah clapped till her hands stung.

One after another, different people came out on the stage; they sang, told jokes, juggled and danced. The curtain came down and the lights went up.

'Quick, quick, we'll miss her,' cried Hannah, leaping up. 'You said we'd go before the end.'

'Sit down, gel. This ain't the end, it's the interval. There's a lot more ter see yet.'

Sheepishly, Hannah sat down again.

Tom leaned over to her. 'Don't worry, I went an' did the same fing.'

'Well, gel, d'yer like it?' asked Jack.

'Oh yes, it's wonderful. Thank you for bringing me.' Hannah smiled. She was glad she was with Jack. She felt safe with him, even if he was a thief, and likely to get into the same kind of trouble as Alice one day. But he knew how to look after himself and he certainly knew his way around. And he knew how to enjoy himself too. She eagerly watched for the curtain to go up on the second half, then sat back to enjoy it.

Finally, everybody came out on the stage and took a bow. 'Come on gel,' Jack said. 'It's the end.'

As they raced down the concrete steps, the sound of the National Anthem drifted towards them. When they reached the foyer the large doors were flung wide open and, as the people spilled out, they were laughing and talking at the top of their voices.

'It's round 'ere,' said Jack.

Tom and Hannah were close on his heels as they pushed their way through the crowd. Outside, they turned the corner and went down a dingy alley. Hannah hesitated. It was smelly, and the dustbins were overflowing.

'In 'ere.' Jack pushed open a door with a small light over.

The heat and bright lights were such a contrast to the dark outside; Hannah hung back.

'Yer, wotcher want?' A man with his shirtsleeves rolled up and a cigarette dangling from his thick lips blocked Jack's path.

'We've come ter see one of the gels. She's in the chorus,' said Jack confidently.

'Oh yer,' the man flicked back his trilby. 'We don't want any stage-door Johnnies round 'ere, so sling yer 'ook.'

'I ain't a stage-door Johnnie, I've got me gel 'ere, ain' I? 'Annah, come and show yer face.'

Hannah slowly walked forward. Jack had called her by her name, and he said she was his girl!

'Yer, well, wotcher want then?'

'Please,' said Hannah. 'Could I speak to her?'

'Why?'

'You see, I'm hoping . . .' Hannah gave a nervous cough. 'I'm hoping she'll be able to give me some news about my sister.'

'Now wot would she know about yer sister?'

Hannah looked at Jack. What could she say?

''Er sister's run away, and we fink she might 'ave . . .'

The man in the shirtsleeves laughed. 'I can't see any of that lot – ' he jerked his thumb over his shoulder 'looking after any waifs or strays. But I'll tell yer wot, yer can stand 'ere and wait and see if she comes out. But don't git in the way.'

'No, no we won't – thank you,' gushed Hannah.

They stood to one side as the performers came streaming out, laughing and chatting.

'Cor, look at that right load o' iron-hoofs,' said Jack to Tom. 'How can those blokes stand 'aving all that muck on their faces? Yer'd fink they'd wash it orf 'fore they come out.'

Hannah pulled at Jack's arm. 'Shh, they'll hear you. Keep your eyes on them, Tom.'

'There she is, that's the one, the one wiv the big 'at.' Tom pointed to a well-made-up young woman, whose wisps of fair hair were peeping out from under a large black hat.

At first Hannah could only stare at this woman. She was wearing the fanciest clothes Hannah had ever seen. Her tight black skirt had buttons all the way down one side, and she had left three of the bottom ones undone, but she still had to take very tiny steps, revealing her high buttoned black boots. Jack jogged her arm, and Hannah pushed her way over to her. 'Excuse me,' said Hannah tentatively.

'Yer, wot d'yer want?' She turned to her friend. 'It ain't me autograph.' They both laughed.

'Can I talk to you?'

'Well, 'urry up, me young man's waiting outside in 'is car.' She pulled her fur stole round her shoulders.

'It's Alice, my sister.'

'Alice?' She looked at Hannah, her face suddenly full of concentration. 'Alice? With fair 'air and a limp?'

Hannah nodded excitedly.

'She's yer sister?'

Hannah's lip trembled. 'D'you know where she is?'

The woman took hold of Hannah's arm and pulled her to one side. Her scent was very overpowering. 'She didn't say she 'ad a sister. She always said she was an orphan.'

'Oh, she is, our parents are dead. Please, tell me where she is?'

'She might not wonner see yer,' the woman said suspiciously. 'After all, she ain't said nothink about yer.'

Tears filled Hannah's eyes. 'I've been so worried about her,' she sniffed.

'Look, don't stand 'ere snivelling,' the woman said hastily.

'Do you know where . . . ?' Hannah wiped her eyes.

'Well.' She interrupted and pulled at her fur. 'I dunno, she's never said . . .'

'Lady, d'yer knows where is she now?' asked Jack angrily.

'She's at 'ome. She's looking after me boy.'

'Please, could I see her?' Hannah's head began reeling. Why hadn't Alice tried to get in touch with her? Why hadn't she told this woman she had a sister?

'I don't think so.'

'Why not, Missis?' said Jack. 'She's really upset.'

'I ain't a Missis, and if Alice don't want nothink to do with 'er, well, that's 'er affair.' She went to move away.

Jack held on to her arm.

'Watch it, sonny,' she said, brushing his arm away. 'Or I'll call Dan.'

Hannah began crying. 'Is she all right?'

'Yer, course she is.'

'She's not . . . ? You're not keeping . . . ?' Rosie's muttering about kidnapping rushed back to her. Hannah couldn't finish the sentence.

'Yer not keeping 'er against 'er will, are yer?' asked Jack.

She laughed. 'No, I ain't.'

'Well then?'

'I don't want the likes of you lot tramping all round me 'ouse: you might all be robbers.'

'Please, can I have your address, then I can write to her.'

'S'pose that'll be all right. I don't know if she'll want ter see yer, though – she's been with me a long while now.'

'Six months,' sobbed Hannah.

'Everyfink all right, Bet?' asked the doorman.

'Yer, thanks Dan. Look, we can't stand around 'ere arguing.'

Hannah began crying again. 'Please. You will tell her I love her and miss her, and perhaps I could meet her somewhere.'

'Yer, course.' Her face broke into a smile.

'You won't forget, will you?'

'Na. 'Ere, yer looks a nice kid, and I've always been a soft one for tears. I'll tell yer what,' she said softly, 'why don't I take yer 'ome with us – me bloke's outside, we can all get in 'is car – then yer can see for yerself she's all right.'

'Thank you, oh thank you so much.' Hannah was crying and laughing together. She was going to see Alice. Once again her stomach lurched. Why hadn't Alice mentioned her? Had she disowned her?

Jack took Hannah's arm protectively. 'Come on, gel.'

The rush of fresh air cleared Hannah's head. 'Is it far?' she croaked.

'No, we live over Fulham way.'

Hannah thought she was going to pass out. 'Fulham?' she repeated weakly.

'Yer. 'Ere we are, Ricky darling.' They walked up to a black car and a tall man wearing a long black coat and homburg jumped out.

'Who have we got here then?' he asked. He was very well spoken.

'Ricky, darling, you are never going to guess?' She went on tiptoes to kiss his cheek. 'This is Alice's big sister. The little cow never told us she had a sister, now did she?'

'Well, I never, and who's the rest of the motley crowd?'

Hannah stepped forward. She didn't like anyone calling her

sister a cow. 'These are my friends. Miss . . .' She turned inquiringly to face the woman.

'Kelly,' came back the answer.

'Miss Kelly said Alice was at her house,' Hannah concluded.

'*Ours*, darling,' she said to Hannah. '*Our* house.' Her tone and her voice had changed. She was speaking very differently in front of her friend. 'I said we'd take them to see her. Is that all right with you, my love?'

Rick smiled and patted her hand. 'Of course, anything you want. Her sister, eh? I say, this is going to give her a bit of a shock – what?'

Hannah noticed Tom and Jack were standing back, and she could tell by their shaking shoulders they were trying hard not to laugh out loud.

When the three of them were settled in the back of the car, Hannah wanted to ask a lot of questions, but Miss Kelly and her friend completely ignored them. She talked continually about the girls she worked with, and some of the main performers. She didn't seem to have a good word to say about any of them, and all he did was guffaw at her every sentence; every other word was 'darling'.

Tom nudged Hannah and grinned at her like a Cheshire cat. 'Cor, I never fought I'd git a ride in a car like this,' he whispered.

'This is great,' said Jack as he gazed out of the window. 'Like the car Rick,' he said confidently.

'It's not bad,' Rick shouted over his shoulder.

Hannah, sitting in the middle, was in awe. So much was happening in one day that she couldn't take it all in. It was almost like a dream. She tried to see where they were going, but she didn't know the area. It didn't look familiar from their days with Uncle Harry.

Finally Rick brought the car to a standstill outside a large terraced house. Hannah gave a sigh of relief, it wasn't anywhere near where they used to live. She was shaking with excitement and trepidation. What would Alice look like? Had they been treating her all right? And why hadn't she got in touch with her? What if she was happy? Would she be cross with Hannah for turning up out of the blue? Hannah's head was full of questions. She looked up. The house had three storeys, and appeared to have lights in every window. Miss Kelly lifted her long tight black skirt way above her ankles, and very carefully mounted the stone steps. Her black buttoned boots were like the ones Hannah had been admiring in the shop window for months; they were very expensive. Hannah looked over the iron railings to the dark basement below.

'Come on,' Miss Kelly called over her shoulder when she reached the wide front door. 'Nobody lives down there.'

Hannah, Jack and Tom shuffled in behind them. Inside, Tom quickly snatched his cap from his head, and Jack took off his trilby. Hannah hung back.

'This way,' said Miss Kelly. 'By the way, how comes yer found out she was with me?'

'Tom here saw you take Alice, and then he saw you on the stage.'

'So yer knows all about what happened then, don't you? And how she came to be living here?'

Hannah didn't answer. They followed her up the stairs. There were ornamental glass shades on the gas-lamps, which burned brightly all the way up, and, impressed, Hannah realized they were treading on carpet.

Miss Kelly pushed open a door and marched in. 'Alice, you didn't tell me you had a sister.'

Hannah stood in the doorway of a well-lit, lavishly furnished room. A warm and inviting fire blazed in a wide brick fireplace. Alice, who was curled up in a large red velvet armchair reading a book, looked up. The colour drained from her face. Hannah, with arms outstretched, ran towards her. She fell to her knees and threw her arms round her sister's neck, letting her tears run unchecked. Alice remained quite still. She appeared to be in shock.

'Well now, young lady, what have you got to say for yourself?' Peeling off her long black gloves, Miss Kelly moved across the room and stood in front of a very large ornamental mirror. She removed the hatpins from her big black hat, threw it on a chair and patted the neat blond chignon at the back of her head. Licking her fingers, she twirled the stray strands of hair which fell into pretty corkscrew curls round her face.

'How did you find me?' whispered Alice.

Hannah wiped her eyes with her handkerchief. 'It's a long story. Why didn't you write, or come and tell us you were all right? All this time I've been worried sick about you.' Her voice came out in broken sobs.

'Yer should 'ave let yer sister know,' said Jack from the other side of the room.

'Hello Jack, Tom.' Alice gave them a slight nod.

'Get us a drink then, Alice,' said Miss Kelly, who was now lolling on the plush red velvet sofa.

Alice, who was visibly shaken, struggled out of the large armchair. She limped across the room and, standing behind a counter, poured out two amber-coloured drinks. She handed one to the man and the other to Miss Kelly, who immediately took a large gulp.

'Betty, would you mind if I took my sister in the other room so we can talk?' Alice said.

'Oh, so you admit she's yer sister then? Oh, go on, but git me another whisky first. What about you, Ricky darling?' she asked, handing Alice her empty glass.

'I'm all right, thank you darling.'

'How's my little John been tonight?' she asked Alice.

A faint smile lifted Alice's worried face. 'Good, as usual.'

'She's got a way with kids,' said Betty Kelly, waving her glass in Alice's direction, not talking to anyone in particular.

Hannah wondered disbelievingly at Miss Kelly's remark as she followed Alice into another room. As soon as she shut the door, Alice turned on her. 'What're you doing here?'

'What?' Hannah was taken aback. She quickly pulled herself together. 'Alice, I've been almost out of my mind wondering what had happened to you. Wondering if you were in prison, had been kidnapped, or even murdered . . .'

Alice laughed.

'Don't you laugh at me.' Hannah was angry, and tears ran down her cheeks.

'I'm sorry.'

Hannah's voice softened. 'Why didn't you get in touch?'

Alice sat in a chair. 'I'll tell you why. I don't want you to take me back to Maudie's.'

'But . . .'

'I expect Tom told you I got caught pinching her purse?'

Hannah nodded.

'Well, I managed to convince her I was an orphan, and didn't have any family.'

'You disowned me,' whispered Hannah, sinking into a chair opposite Alice.

'Yes, well, not really. You see, when I first came here, I thought it best to say nothing about you. They were going to turn me in, but then, when I told them about myself and I started to limp, they felt sorry for me and decided to bring me here to discuss what to do. When I found out she was on the stage, and I saw how they lived, I thought this was the life for me, and I convinced them to let me stay.'

'Without any thoughts about me?'

'Hannah, for the first time in my life I have a bedroom of my own, and I have a real bed to sleep in, and some decent clothes. You don't begrudge me that, do you?'

Hannah shook her head.

'I bet you would have stayed if it had been you.' Alice was pouting.

Hannah couldn't answer that. She knew she'd have been in touch with her sister, though. 'You should have let me know,' she said. 'Anyway, why did she let you stay here and not tell the police?'

'I told them it was the first time I'd done anything like that, and she believed me. She's a bit, well, loud, but she's ever so nice – a bit like Maudie, I suppose. By the way, don't say anything about you all living at Maudie's, and them all being tea-leafs.'

'But what if she asks where we've come from?'

'Just say you live with her, and Tom and Jack are friends who live in the same road.'

'Will she believe that?'

'I don't think Betty's interested in where I came from – well, not now. Anyway, I was telling you, her nanny was going to leave, and when she heard how well I spoke, she thought I'd be good for John, and when the nanny left – I stepped into her shoes. We didn't get on, anyway, she tried to boss me around.'

'And that's something you could never stand,' Hannah said wryly. She looked at her sister. 'Weren't you ever going to get in touch with me again?' She twisted her handkerchief into a knot.

'Of course I was. I thought when I was really settled and she couldn't do without me, then I'd tell her I'd found my long-lost sister.'

'I can't believe this.' Hannah stood up and walked to the fireplace. She ran her fingers over the rich green cloth elegantly draped along the mantelpiece. 'I can't believe what I'm hearing. After all we've been through together.' She quickly turned her back on Alice as her tears began to fall again.

'I'm sorry, Hannah. I didn't think you'd be this upset.'

Hannah spun round. 'What?' she sobbed. 'You didn't think I'd be this upset? You were always selfish, but this – this is the limit. Well, at least I won't have to worry about you now.' Hannah moved towards the door.

'Hannah, please, wait a minute. It was a shock seeing you. Please, sit down.'

'Why? What's the point?'

Alice jumped up and threw her arms round Hannah's neck. Now it was Hannah's turn to be aloof and offhand. 'I've wanted to tell you I was all right. I know I should have written, but we didn't have a proper address.'

'You could have sent it to Mary, you know where she lives.'

'I didn't think of that,' said Alice, sinking back into the chair again.

'Well, you wouldn't, would you, not if you were all right? Living here in the lap of luxury . . . I bet if she hadn't been well off you would have come back quickly enough, wouldn't you?'

Alice nodded very gently.

'Well, there's not a lot left to say, is there?'

'Hannah, I'm sorry. I should have tried to get in touch.'

Hannah wiped her eyes. 'Well, it doesn't matter now. Will you write from time to time, just to let me know how you are? You can send it to Mary's, she won't mind.' She gave her sister a long look. 'She lives at number forty.'

Alice nodded. 'I know that. You will come to see me again, won't you?'

'I don't know.' Hannah walked to the door. As she reached out for the handle she felt herself softening. After all, Alice was safe. 'That's a nice frock,' she said.

'Betty has a lot of friends, and sometimes they have things they don't want. I only have to alter them a bit.'

'Good job Maudie taught you to sew. By the way, did you have a nice birthday?'

'Yes, yes I did. They were really wonderful, and I had lots and lots of really lovely presents at Christmas.' Alice waved her arms in a very theatrical way. 'When you come here again I'll show you them, and my room.'

Hannah knew that the hairbrush she had bought her would look very cheap now.

'Betty and Rick are very good to me.' Alice added quickly. 'I have to work though. I look after Betty's baby while she sleeps in.'

Hannah had gathered as much, but she still found it hard to believe. 'What, you looking after a baby?'

'Well, he's not really a baby, he's going on four. Besides, I'm thirteen now, and a lot of girls my age are out to work.'

'Thirteen going on thirty, more like it,' Hannah sniffed.

'I have to make sure everything is all right for Betty, lay her clothes out and all that,' Alice went on.

'Do you have to do the cooking and cleaning?' Despite herself, Hannah was intrigued – she knew Alice didn't like housework.

'No, a woman – Mrs Main – comes in and does that.'

'It's a big house?'

'Yes. It belongs to Rick. He lets some of their friends stay here.' Alice half laughed. 'It can be very noisy at times, and some of them are very weird people: dancers and actors.'

Hannah felt guilty. How could she blame Alice for not wanting to move away from all this? 'I'm still amazed that they didn't take you to the police station.'

'Well, the old limp comes in handy,' she smiled. Hannah

had forgotten how innocent and pretty she could look when her dimples deepened. 'When I snivelled and told them I was an orphan, and hungry – and spoke in a very posh voice, they knew I must have hit rock bottom. And I don't think Betty's life's been all roses, so she felt sorry for me. Anyway, they brought me here and, well, you know the rest now.'

Hannah could almost hear Maudie saying that Alice would make a good actress one day. 'You want to stay?'

'Yes, yes Hannah, I do.' Alice rushed to Hannah and threw her arms round her. 'I'm so sorry, so very sorry. You will come and see me again, won't you?'

'I'll try.' Hannah stood back. 'Alice, be careful.'

'What d'you mean?'

'Well, all these funny theatre people.'

'Don't worry about them, they're all right, and Betty does look after me. You will come here again?'

'I don't know.' Hannah hesitated. 'I don't know about coming over to Fulham. Don't you ever worry about meeting . . . You know?'

'No, we live a long way away from Uncle Harry's place. I'm not likely to meet anyone who knew him.'

For a few moments they stood in silence. Hannah was thinking about the past, and looking at Alice she realized how she had grown in just six short months. She was so much better dressed, and seemed more self-assured. 'Look, I must go. Give me your address and I'll write.'

'Rick 'ere said 'e'll take us 'ome in 'is motor,' said Jack when they walked into the other room.

'That's very kind of you.'

'This is our address,' said Alice, handing Hannah a piece of paper.

'Thanks. Bye Miss Kelly, and thank you,' said Hannah as they got into the car.

'For what?'

'Looking after my sister.'

'Don't know what I'd do without her now.' She smiled and put her arm round Alice's shoulders. 'Come and see 'er any time.'

Hannah was jealous. Alice had found a home, and was happy. Hannah looked out of the back window at Alice waving as they drove away. She was hurt. Alice hadn't worried about her. She didn't even ask her what sort of Christmas she had had. Alice had found what she wanted. Tears rolled down Hannah's cheek. Would she ever find what *she* really wanted, and did she even know what it was? She looked at the back of Jack's head. At this moment she knew she wanted love and affection more than anything else in the world.

Chapter 14

All the way home, Tom twisted this way and that, still excited at being in the car. 'Cor, 'Annah, when I saw 'em take Alice away in this I never fought I'd be sitting in 'ere.' He gently stroked the soft tan leather seat.

Hannah too should have been over the moon at riding in a motor car, but it was Alice who filled her thoughts.

'And wot about Alice?' Tom whispered. 'She didn't 'arf look posh in that frock, and 'er 'air looked real nice.'

Hannah nodded, but didn't answer. Alice did look wonderful; even her soft leather shoes looked expensive and made her tiny feet look very dainty. She'd been wearing her hair coiled into a neat chignon, which made her look very grown up. Alice made Hannah feel scruffy even though she'd worn the best clothes she had to go out with Jack. She was quiet all the way home, staring through the window, but seeing nothing. Once or twice, Tom tried to make conversation, but Hannah wasn't listening, so he gave up. Jack was sitting in the front, busy chatting to Rick, and occasionally their loud laughter invaded her thoughts.

Hannah still couldn't believe Alice would want to disown her. They only had each other. How could she? But could she blame her for not wanting to leave such a lovely house – a house that was full of light and comforts. How would she feel if it had been her and not Alice? Hannah let the silent tears fall.

They stopped at the top of Hope Street and they clambered out.

'See yer sometime, Rick old boy,' called Jack, closing the car door behind him.

A couple of drunks were helping each other along the road and one of them pulled himself up and leant against the wall. ''Ere, look at this posh car. Gis a lift, mate.'

As the car pulled away, Hannah recognized Mr Barker, and guessed there would be another row when he got home.

'Why? Where're yer going then, George?' asked his friend. 'Yer lives 'ere, don't yer?' He held on to the lamp-post and, with great difficulty, looked around. ''Ere, ain't this 'Ope Street then?'

'Yer,' said George. 'Mind you, yer bloody well need more than a bit o' 'ope living round 'ere.' He walked on, leaving his friend, who very slowly slid down the lamp-post and lay slumped on the ground.

'That man lives in number twelve,' whispered Hannah, pointing to the drunk weaving his way along the street. 'I don't know who this is,' she said as they stepped over the one on the ground.

Jack laughed. 'I bet there'll be a few choice words from 'is Missis when 'e gits in.'

As they walked on, the long, deep, throaty noise of a ship's foghorn floated on the cold night air.

''Urry up, you two,' said Tom, blowing on his hands. His breath formed small clouds in front of him. 'It's ever so late, better not make too much noise.'

When they were inside, Tom dragged his mattress across the room. 'Night 'Annah,' he whispered.

'You all right gel?' Jack's voice came from out of the darkness – he didn't wait for an answer and added, 'Been quite a night.'

'Yes, it has.' Hannah too pulled her bed into her space and settled down, but she knew sleep wouldn't come easily, and she let her thoughts drift. Alice was back in Fulham. What if she ever bumped into Aunt May? Did she know it was her and Alice who'd killed Uncle Harry? Would they go to prison? Could they be hung? Hannah shuddered. What would Betty Kelly say if she knew about their past? Hannah tossed and turned, drifting into a fitful sleep. She was being chased. She screamed out when someone caught hold of her.

'Shh, gel.' Jack was gently shaking her. 'Yer 'aving a nightmare again.'

Hannah threw her arms round his neck and cried.

'Yer shivering.' He held her close and tenderly stroked her hair. She put her wet face up to his and he softly kissed her lips. Hannah closed her eyes. She didn't want this wonderful moment to end; she wasn't even sure she wasn't dreaming. Jack was holding her, kissing her. She wanted to be held tight, to be loved and, above all, to be wanted. She put her arms round his neck and kissed him.

He pulled away. 'Sorry, gel,' he whispered, moving back. 'Got a bit carried away.'

'It's all right,' said Hannah, pushing her troublesome hair away from her face. She wanted him to hold her close. She wanted him to love her and care for her.

'No it ain't, yer still a kid. 'Sides, I should know better.' It was a loud whisper full of anger. 'Maudie'll 'ave me guts fer garters if she ever found us . . .' He stopped and cocked his head to one side. 'Shh, listen.'

Hannah strained her ears. 'I can't hear anything.'

'Fought I 'eard young Dolly,' he whispered. 'You all right now, gel?'

'Yes, thank you. And Jack . . .'

He began moving away. 'Yer?'

'Nothing.' She wanted to tell him she loved him, but it would sound silly. She wanted to shout out, tell everyone. She desperately needed him to hold her, comfort her and love her, but to him she was still a kid. Did he just think of her as a sister?

'Git back ter sleep, gel. See yer in the morning.'

It wasn't till she got home the following evening that she saw Maudie.

'Yer found 'er then? Wot a night yer 'ad? Tom 'ere's been telling me all about it, and what did yer fink of the music 'all? Cor, it sounded real good, and 'e's full of that car. Fancy 'aving a ride in a car!'

Hannah smiled.

Maudie was still talking about Tom's experiences. 'And fancy Alice finishing up in some toff's 'ouse. Tom said it was ever so posh, and over Fulham way. Ain't that where yer used ter live?'

'Yes, it was.' Hannah didn't want to be reminded of the past. Even though Hannah knew all about Maudie's secret, and over the years they had become very close, she still hadn't told her the truth as to why they had been running away. 'Maudie, Alice won't be coming back here to live,' she said quietly.

'So Tom said. Still, I'm glad she's safe. I didn't like ter say too much before. I was dead worried sumfink might 'ave 'appened to 'er. I'll miss 'er, you know.' Maudie paused, and Hannah suddenly realized that she hadn't even thought about how she might feel about losing her favourite, Alice. 'But I still fink she should 'ave let yer know,' Maudie went on. 'Then again, I s'pose yer can't blame 'er. It must be nice ter live in a big 'ouse. I still say it was a bit orf 'er not telling 'em she 'ad a sister.'

Hannah shrugged, trying not to look hurt. 'Yes, but then you know Alice.'

'Yer.' Maudie left the table.

'Wot you gonner do now?' Dolly asked Hannah.

'Nothing.'

'Ain't yer gonner try and git in wiv 'em?'

'No.'

'Fought yer would 'ave.'

'No, Alice is quite happy without me.' Hannah pushed her chair back. 'I'm going round to Mary's.'

Mary was pleased when Hannah called on her, and delighted with her news. 'You found Alice then?'

Hannah nodded.

'Sit down and tell me all about it.'

Hannah told the whole tale of the previous evening without any interruptions from Mary. 'I don't know what I'm going to do without her to worry about,' Hannah said finally.

'Well, you could start by thinking about yourself for a change.'

Hannah gazed at her. 'But I've always had Alice to worry about.'

'That's what I mean.'

It wasn't until March that Hannah received her first letter from Alice; it was in reply to the one she had written soon after their meeting. Hannah smiled at the scrawly handwriting as Mary handed it over.

My dear sister Hannah

I'm sorry I wasn't that pleased to see you at first, that night you found me, but now I know you are not going to take me away from Betty I feel a lot happier. It's really lovely living here. We have a lot of parties and her little boy is very good – I bet you never thought I'd be looking after a kid. By the way, Rick is not his dad, but nobody seems to worry about that. We have a lot of people from the music hall come here, some of them are a bit strange. Did you like the music hall? Betty took me backstage once. It was wonderful. I wish I could sing and dance like her but I couldn't, not with my leg. Betty said you can come over any time. She likes you. She thinks you are very pretty. So do I.

All my love,
Alice.
xxx

Hannah could have cried. It was such a funny, stilted letter. And she knew Alice would never return now – had they really drifted apart for ever?

One Saturday evening, a few weeks after Hannah had received the letter, she was telling Maudie's 'family' that she was thinking of going to see her sister. She'd decided that if she wasn't going to lose touch with her altogether, she'd have to be the one to make the effort. And she still worried about Alice.

'I miss Alice too,' said Tom, clearing the tea things away.

'So does old Bonzo,' said Jack. 'Look at the scruffy bugger, all 'e ever does now is mope about.'

'Shall we take him out?' suggested Hannah. She was looking for an excuse to be alone with Jack. She was growing more and more desperate to find out how he felt about her. In all the months that had followed, he had never spoken about the night he'd kissed her, or asked to take her out again.

'Na,' Jack said, turning back to his paper.

Half an hour later, Jack suddenly asked her, 'What yer doing termorrer?'

Hannah looked up from her book, surprised. 'I don't know. Going round to Mary's, I expect. Why?'

'How about going over ter yer sister's?'

'Why?' she eagerly inquired. 'Do you want to come with me?'

'Yer, I fink I will. I reckon that Rick bloke knows a fing or two.'

Hannah turned on him. 'You're not just coming with me to find out what you can steal, are you?'

''Ere, 'old on, gel. Don't you start gitting on yer 'igh 'orse wiv me.'

She bit her lip, regretting her hasty words. 'Sorry. It's just that I don't want Alice to get into any trouble.'

Jack smiled and his blue eyes sparkled. He leaned back in his chair and Hannah weakened. He was so manly, she wanted to throw her arms round his neck and smother his face in kisses. He was so good-looking, and she knew she loved him.

'Now would I do a fing like that? Yer knows me. Me, the height of discretion.' He put his head in the air and puffed on his cigarette.

Maudie screamed out laughing. ''Ere, 'ark at you using bloody long words. See, wot did I tell yer? It's all your fault, 'Annah, yer turning us all inter a lot of inter, interlec . . .'

'Interlectuals,' said Jack.

Hannah laughed. 'Now Tom works on the paper-stall, we're getting ideas from all the papers we get to read.'

'All right if I come wiv yer ter see Alice an' all?' asked Tom.

Hannah was a little put out. She wanted to be alone with Jack.

'Yer, why not?' said Jack. 'Young Alice'll be pleased ter see yer.'

The following day, Jack, Tom and Hannah made their way back to Fulham. Hannah was very apprehensive and, when they got off the tram, she looked about her continually.

'It didn't take ser long in the car,' said Tom as they walked up the road.

'D'yer know, I fancy gitting a car one of these days,' Jack remarked.

'You'd soon get caught driving off in a car,' said Hannah.

'Yer got a sharp tongue in yer 'ead, gel. I didn't mean pinch it.'

'Well I can't see you buying one.'

Jack ignored her remark, and when they turned the corner said, 'This is it.'

They stopped in front of the tall house again.

'I'll go and knock and see if they're in,' said Hannah, tentatively mounting the stairs.

The look of surprise on Alice's face was a picture. She hugged Hannah so hard she thought they might topple over.

'Hello, Jack. Tom,' she said over Hannah's shoulder. 'Come on in.'

'Well, this is a better welcome than the last time,' said Hannah.

Alice smiled. 'It's so good to see you all again. Come on up. Did you get my letter, Hannah?'

'Yes, did you get mine?'

'Yes,' said Alice as they walked up the stairs.

Once again they entered the luxurious room.

'Where's Miss Kelly?' asked Hannah looking around.

'She's out. They won't be back till late tonight. I've just put John down, so we won't be disturbed, unless some of the others come back.'

'How many live 'ere then?' asked Jack.

'Don't really know; there's always someone coming and going. You must admit, it's a good place to live.'

'I should say so,' said Tom, wandering around. 'She's got some smashing fings. Cor, wouldn't old Maudie like ter feast 'er eyes on some o' this?'

'Yes, but Tom, don't touch anything, in case you break it,' said Hannah, anxiously watching him.

'It's not Betty's house,' said Alice. 'Well, in some ways it is, but I think Rick owns it. Come along to the kitchen and I'll make a cup of tea.'

'You make tea?' said Hannah, raising her eyebrows.

'You'll be surprised at what I can do now.'

When Hannah saw Alice's bedroom, she was filled with envy.

'This is lovely,' she said, running her hands over the white folkweave bedspread. 'And look at your cupboard, and your clothes.' Hannah picked up a shoe. 'These are nice.'

'I told you they were good to me.'

'But why? Why?'

'Cos they like me, that's why.'

'But Alice, are they . . . ? Are you sure they . . . ?' Hannah was groping for words. She didn't want Alice to know how jealous she felt, but she was worried they might have other ideas for her.

'Well, go on then, spit it out.'

'There must be a reason.'

'There is. I look after John.'

'And they give you all this for that? But you're only a child.'

Alice looked irritated. 'The nanny had all this, and I just stepped into her shoes. That's all, there's nothing sinister about it. I happen to speak well, and that's what Betty wants for John, and she doesn't have to pay out wages now.' She paused angrily. 'So, is there anything else you want to know?'

Hannah shook her head. 'I'm sorry – it's just that I worry about you. I don't want anything to happen to you.'

'Don't worry, it won't,' she said flippantly. 'Now, come on, let's go back into the drawing room before Tom and Jack pinch half the house.'

181

Hannah followed her back to the other room. Even if there was anything to worry about, there was no way Alice was going to give all this up.

All afternoon they laughed and talked. When John woke, Hannah was amazed at the way Alice looked after him. He was a lovely little lad.

They all looked up when the door was pushed open. A tall thin young man came in, wearing a long black overcoat even though the weather was warm. The white silk scarf draped round his neck dangled down almost to the floor. He had to lift his head to peer under the wide brim of his black hat which was pulled down over his eyes. 'Alice, my little love. What time are you expecting Betty back?'

'Don't know.'

'Well, tell them both I'll meet them at the club later. Bye, darling.' With that he left.

Hannah laughed. 'Who was that?'

'Don't know his real name, everybody calls him Sally.'

'Sally! Bloody 'ell, what is 'e?' asked Jack.

'He's a dancer.'

'Look's a right ponce ter me.'

'D'you know, I don't think he even noticed us,' said Hannah.

'He probably did,' said Alice. 'But they don't bother about who's here.'

Jack was laughing. 'Are they all nutters like 'im?'

'Most of them,' agreed Alice.

When the time came, Hannah was reluctant to leave. 'You will write, won't you?' she whispered, hugging Alice goodbye.

'Of course I will.'

'Come on you two,' yelled Jack.

Alice stood at the top of the steps and waved.

'She looks ever so grown up,' said Tom wistfully.

'She's certainly living the life of old Riley, ain't she?' said Jack as they walked away.

'Yes, yes, she is,' said Hannah thoughtfully.

'Let's 'ope it lasts, fer 'er sake,' said Jack.

Hannah didn't answer. She also hoped for Alice's sake it would last.

The following month the papers were full of the tragic sinking of the *Titanic*. Every day Hannah read the papers to Maudie. It was a great shock to all of them, even those who couldn't begin to imagine the size of such a liner.

Maudie was particularly worried. 'If a big ship like that can sink, what about little boats like wot Bert goes in?' she asked.

'I'm sure they are safe,' said Hannah, but she was concerned for his safety as well.

'Do they go near these 'ere icebergs?' asked Maudie as she studied the pictures.

'I shouldn't think so.'

'I wish 'e'd come and see us again.'

Hannah was thoughtful. It had been a while since Bert had been here, and she also wished he'd come to see them again, if only to make Maudie happy. She also wondered, now that things were settling down, whether she could perhaps help heal the breach between Bert and Jack the next time Bert came back. She quickly dismissed that thought, as Jack would accuse her of interfering.

For the rest of the summer, life remained the same, and Hannah guessed the people in Hope Street were still having their ups and downs. Every evening on her way home from work, Hannah would nod and quickly pass the time of day with those that were seated outside, always hoping to avoid Mrs Nosy. Hannah had been intrigued when she had asked Kate about Mrs Nosy's son. Kate had told her she could just about remember him. It seemed his older sister was always arguing with her mother, sometimes even having stand-up fights in the street. The sister had got married years ago, and taken the boy with her. Kate didn't think they had ever been back.

Hannah was very lonely. She saw less of Kate now as Kate was busy working in the onion factory. There was no one of her age at the biscuit factory who she could really talk to; even the boys were silly. The memory of the day Ginger Wright had grabbed her behind the ovens still made her cringe. He had bright ginger hair and squinty pale watery eyes and a spotty face. He had tried to kiss her, and she'd hated it: his breath smelled and his face was all stubbly. After a great struggle she'd managed to push him away. Hannah had felt so miserable. She knew for her there couldn't be anyone like Jack.

Although Mary always made her welcome, her lodger Miss King was usually hovering around, and Hannah never felt really at ease with the upright, matronly older woman. Mary had told Hannah that nursing was all she was interested in.

Even Dolly had a friend now. She had met a girl at the market and was always full of what Violet said and did. It seemed her parents had a fruit and veg stall, and somehow Dolly had won their trust.

Hannah and Alice exchanged letters, but Hannah was very disappointed when her seventeenth birthday came and went, and Alice didn't mention it, or invite her to go and see her.

It wasn't until September, and the Saturday following Alice's fourteenth birthday, that Hannah suddenly decided to take Alice her present. On the journey she became very apprehensive at going to see her alone. Would she be home? Would she be pleased to see her? When Alice opened the door, Hannah was a little put out when she didn't greet her as before.

'Hannah, what are you doing here?'

'I've brought your birthday present. Can I come in?'

'You should have told me you were coming.'

'Why? Are you going out?'

'No.'

Hannah followed Alice into a house that seemed to be full of people.

'I'm a bit busy. You'd better sit yourself down.'

Hannah did as she was told. She watched Alice pour out drinks, feeling ill at ease. All the rooms were full of people coming and going, and everybody seemed in a rush. Alice briefly told Hannah that Betty was at the theatre. Finally, when most of them had left, Hannah got round to giving Alice her present. Alice thanked her, then took her to her room and showed Hannah all the other lovely things people had bought her. Hannah's scarf looked very insignificant beside the bracelet, gloves, brooch and powder bowl. Alice was full of the grand tea they had had, and Hannah couldn't help feeling upset that she hadn't been invited. She said as much but Alice just shrugged her off.

'Well, you were at work,' she said dismissively, and that was the end of that.

All the way home, Hannah was deep in thought. Why was Alice so offhand? Why hadn't she told anyone at the house who Hannah was? Was she ashamed of her? The answer, she knew, was yes.

Christmas was almost on them once more. It was going to be another sad one for Hannah with Alice away. She was always hoping for an invitation to go and stay with Alice, but none ever came. Hannah hadn't gone to see her: she didn't want to be rejected again. She had another rise, and had been promoted to working on the bench. It was boring work, but it was clean, and she resigned herself to it. She was spending more on her clothes from the second-hand barrow in Jamaica Road market. She could walk round there with a clear conscience, more so now the old woman from whom she'd stolen the pinafore years ago had gone. Her rise didn't allow her to get many new things, but she was saving up for a pair of high button boots, like the ones Betty Kelly wore. On the face of it, everybody seemed to be carrying on just the same.

Dolly was still full of her friend Violet, and had been showing Hannah the Christmas present she was making her. She had cut the lace off an old handkerchief and made a doll out of the handkerchief itself, dressing it in the lace. It looked very pretty. Hannah had spoken to Violet, and she seemed a nice girl. The family must have been very taken with Dolly because, for weeks now, at the end of the day, they'd given her a lot of the veg that was on the turn.

'Guess wot,' said Dolly, bursting in one evening. Her face was glowing through cold and excitement. 'Violet's gran's gonner take me and Freddie 'opping next summer.'

'Where's that?' asked Tom.

'In Kent, silly. Violet said it's all green fields and trees – it's just like the pictures in that book yer got me, 'Annah.'

'But yer 'as ter work,' said Maudie.

'Yer I know, yer 'as ter pull all these 'op fings orf these 'igh poles, but yer gits paid.' She sighed. 'But just fink, we'll be going on a train, and we'll be gitting money and 'aving a good time. Violet says we have sing-songs round a camp fire.'

'Where're yer gonner git the money ter git on a train from?' asked Tom.

'Don't worry.' A determined look came into her eyes. 'I'll git it somehow.'

'You be careful you don't finish up in prison before you get a chance to go away,' said Hannah, determined to have her say.

'Yer, well, we're not all as daft as yer sister.'

Hannah bristled. 'She's certainly not daft. Look where she's finished up.'

Dolly laughed. 'Well, yer. She was lucky.'

'I'm surprised the family let Violet talk to you,' Hannah remarked haughtily.

'They ain't stuck up like you. They know we was left and we got beaten. They fill sorry for us, that's why they lets us go round and play wiv Violet.'

'Even when they know you're a, a . . .'

'Tea-leaf – go on, say it, go on.'

'That's enough of it, you two. Tea's ready, so sit down and shut up.' Maudie made sure she had the last word.

As the evening drifted on, Dolly seemed restless. Hannah, with her elbows on the table, was sitting quietly drinking a cup of tea and Maudie had gone out to find the bookies' runner: now they had the papers regularly, Maudie had been having the odd sixpence each way on any horse she fancied the name of – not that she ever won very much. Tom was also out: he'd gone to see Bob round his paper-stall. Hannah was miles away when Dolly came and sat next to her.

'Penny fer 'em,' said Dolly.

'What?' Hannah smiled. 'I wasn't really thinking about anything.'

'Yer know, it's a shame Alice don't come ter see yer.'

Hannah started to bristle. She didn't like anyone talking about Alice, even if she did agree with them. 'Well, she has a lot to do, and I don't suppose she would even now how to get here now.'

'Yer musta 'ad a rough time before yer came ter stay wiv Maudie.'

'Well, yes, but that was a long while ago. Why do you ask?'

'Yer still 'as nightmares though, don't yer?'

Hannah jerked her head up. 'I didn't think . . . Have I kept you awake?'

'Na. I've 'eard yer shouting and calling out a couple o' times.' Dolly moved closer. 'I used ter 'ave 'em when we first come 'ere . . . 'Annah, now yer at work wiv boys . . .'

Hannah looked at her.

'Freddie, go outside, sling yer 'ook fer five minutes.'

Freddie did as he was told without a word.

''Annah. Would yer let them boys at work do rude fings ter yer?'

'Like what?'

'Yer know. Touch yer private parts.'

'No. No, I wouldn't.' Hannah's face flushed. She was embarrassed, and said angrily, 'Why do you ask?'

'Well, before we run away, me uncle used ter, ter me. And 'it us. Well, 'e wasn't our uncle, really, just Mum's friend, and when I told me mate Violet, she told 'er mum, and that's why she took a liking to us. She says it's ever so wrong for men ter do that.'

Hannah was shocked. 'Didn't your mum ever stop him?'

'Na, didn't tell 'er, did I? 'E used ter beat 'er up as it was, and I fought me telling 'er would only make it worse fer 'er. Then, yer never guess, she run orf wiv anuver bloke and left us wiv 'im. So it just goes ter show, don't it?'

Hannah sat and looked at Dolly in astonishment. All these years, and she hadn't known what they'd been through. 'I thought Maudie said you were running away from the police,' she whispered.

'We was. We set light ter the 'ouse and made out we was still in it. Well, nobody was gonner make a fuss over us if we was still in it.'

'Was he in it?'

'Na, 'e was out. We stood and watched the neighbours crying

over us, then someone spotted us and they chased us.'

Hannah felt sad, wanting to hold and comfort her. If only she had known. 'Dolly, why are you telling me all this?'

'Well, Violet reckons you should tell the truf, and I've always liked yer, and I fought we could be friends.'

Hannah hugged her. 'We are, and to me you're just like a sister. Me and Alice used to have rows, and then make it up, like you and me.'

Dolly smiled. 'I've always wanted a sister. Violet's like a sister, she's a real good mate.'

Hannah looked at Dolly, she too was growing up. Perhaps like Hannah the hurt and the fear of her past was beginning to fade.

One cold, winter Saturday afternoon Hannah and Maudie were sitting in front of the fire. They often had a quiet talk together like this.

'Can see young Dolly going orf fer good come summer,' said Maudie, holding up the frock she was altering for her.

'That's pretty. Did Violet give her that?' Hannah asked.

'Yer.'

'You always said she wouldn't stay for ever.'

'Yer. What about you? When yer going to see Alice again?'

'Don't know. I've only had one letter since I saw her last.' Hannah sighed.

'I was surprised she didn't ask yer over at Christmas.'

'I read you that letter, the one full of what they were going to do over Christmas and the New Year.' Hannah sighed.

'She'll be popping back, you mark my words. Bit like young Bert, I reckon.'

'We haven't seen Bert for ages now,' said Hannah, changing the subject: it was still painful for her to talk about Alice.

'It's mostly when the wevver gits bad, and 'e's a bit short.'

189

'There's been a lot of changes since we moved in here. Tom seems happy enough working with Bob on the newspaper-stand.'

'I was talking to old Bob the other day when I took Brian fer a walk – I like 'aving that big pram ter 'old on ter. 'E was saying young Tom's a godsend. Bob's chest is playing 'im up sumfink rotten, and 'e knows 'e can leave the stand in Tom's 'ands. 'E's turned out ter be a good lad and 'e's much 'appier doing that than pinching. 'Ere, yer seems ter be reforming all me waifs,' Maudie threw her head back and laughed. ''Ere, 'ark at me using long words. It's all your fault.'

Hannah laughed too.

'Yer've even got *me* earning a couple a bob a week. Still it's nice ter 'ave a bit coming in regular-like. Mind you, yer ain't 'ad much luck wiv trying ter change Jack, though, 'ave yer?'

Hannah looked away. She desperately wished Jack would give up stealing. What if he got caught? They had had so many arguments over it, and although she hated having to say no she refused to go out with him if the trip was just an excuse to go dipping. 'Is he coming home tonight?' she asked casually.

''E didn't say. Wouldn't be surprised if 'e ain't got a lady friend,' said Maudie.

Hannah's head shot up. She was shaken at Maudie's words, and tried to keep her voice steady. 'Did he say who it is?'

'Na. I'm only guessing. Jack's a good-looking lad. I'm surprised 'e's stayed wiv me fer so long, I'd a fought 'e'd 'ave found 'isself a wife be now.'

Hannah's heart was thumping. Could he have a woman friend? She would be desperate if he went and left her, like Alice. But perhaps she was being silly, trying to force others to do what she wanted. After all, she'd lost Alice through being bossy, could she lose Jack as well? Night after night she'd lain in bed listening to his deep regular breathing and thought of the night he had kissed her. He never woke her up now when she had a bad dream, it was the others who mentioned it. She was seventeen now, and a lot of girls got married at her age. Would *she* ever get married? A couple of the boys at the factory had asked her out but she didn't like any of them, especially after Ginger Wright had caught her alone round the back of the factory a few months ago. He'd tried to kiss her and touch her private places. She hadn't told anyone what had happened, not even Dolly who would have understood. She knew Jack would never do such a thing.

Maudie's voice broke into her thoughts. ''Ere, I nearly forgot ter tell yer, there was a right old bust up in 'Ope Street this morning. Seems the one in number four . . .'

'I don't know her,' interrupted Hannah. 'Well not to talk to.'

'Na, I don't know 'er name eivver. She's a quiet little fing, got a couple o' boys. Well, it seems one of 'em chucked a ball frew Mrs Barker's winder. You should 'ave 'eard the rumpus! I fought the little woman in number four was gonner bash old Barker – yer see she'd caught 'er hitting one of 'er kids and she flew at 'er like a tiger. So yer don't wonner go upsetting that one,' she chuckled. 'Fill the kettle up, love.'

Hannah put the kettle on the stove and sat down.

'You all right, gel?' asked Maudie. 'You was miles away then.'

'Yes, just thinking. I might go and see Alice sometime. After all, she's not going to come back here, and we mustn't lose touch.'

'Na, course not. 'Sides, that'll be nice for yer. I'll make the tea.'

191

Chapter 15

Although 1913 had started like any other year, this winter was proving to be long and bitterly cold. The newspapers Tom brought home were full of stories about people dying from the cold. Most nights they managed to keep the fire well stoked up so that it would last throughout the night: Maudie spent most of her day collecting firewood and, if she was quick enough, any old piece of coal that fell from the cart. Mary wouldn't have been all that pleased if she had seen her pram piled up with wood, but little Brian loved it, and Maudie always made sure it was clean when Mary collected him.

The papers also told of the suffragettes and how their movement was getting stronger, their rallies and marches causing a great deal of concern. They had started damaging shop windows and disrupting meetings. Many had been arrested, sent to prison and force-fed. To Hannah's annoyance, Jack always went to their meetings, and she wondered if he was seeing that suffragette nurse again, the one who'd worked with Mary. She'd asked Mary about her but Mary said no one had had any news of her. Then again Jack always went anywhere he knew a well-off crowd would gather. But that was bad enough! She couldn't see how he'd ever change . . .

The days were short, and it was dark as Hannah hurried to and from work, so she saw very little of Kate's brothers playing in the street, or Kate herself. Some Saturday afternoons, if Kate was home, she would have a quick word with her, but with the run-up to Christmas, there had been plenty of overtime for Kate in the pickle factory and she needed the money. Skinning onions was dirty, smelly work, but it paid better than Hannah's biscuit factory and, with her help, the family were a little better off now. Hannah saw Mary most Sundays, despite Miss King. Hannah couldn't help but admire Mary's lodger: she seemed to be happy to devote her life to nursing, untroubled by her lack of a husband or family.

With her scarf wound tightly round her throat, and her hands thrust deep in her pockets, Hannah hurried home one Saturday afternoon. The sleet stung her eyes and Hope Street was quiet. She felt guilty at not popping into Kate's, but today she really didn't want to stop.

She pushed open the door and was taken aback when she saw, seated in an armchair, Bert.

Maudie was beaming. 'This is a nice surprise, ain't it, 'Annah?'

Hannah nodded. For once she was pleased Jack was away for the weekend; he'd said he was going to a big rally tomorrow. This time Hannah asked him outright if he had a lady friend he met at these rallies but he'd just laughed and told her it was none of her business.

But she was thankful for small mercies: at least he and Bert wouldn't meet and argue.

'How long you here for?' she casually asked Bert, while smoothing down her hair.

'Why's that? Wonner get rid of me quick-like, gel?' He sat forward. 'Maudie here was telling me you found yer sister all right, then?'

'Yes, she's doing very well.' She didn't know why, but something about Bert always kept her on her guard. She felt uneasy when he leaned back in the chair and she felt his dark eyes studying her.

'She was saying what an influence you've had on 'er little flock; even got Maudie earning a honest bob or two. Seems you've reformed all of 'em except our Jack.' He laughed. 'I think you've got a job on with that one, gel.'

Hannah bristled angrily. How dare he talk about her Jack like that? 'Any tea?' she asked, picking up the teapot and shaking it.

'Just made it,' said Maudie.

Although Hannah hadn't found it difficult to talk to Bert the last time he was here, his presence seemed to put up a barrier in the household, and she resented him spoiling the one afternoon in the week she had alone with Maudie. She was pleased when Dolly and Freddie walked in – it eased the tension.

All evening they sat round the stove and chatted and, much to Hannah's surprise, when Bert started to tell them about his life on a boat, it was very interesting. He was a good story-teller and had Freddie and Tom hanging on his every word. Hannah was still mystified as to why Jack was so against him, and why he'd been so much trouble. One day she would find out exactly. Maudie had said she'd thought it was over Bert's telling the police where Jack had hidden something he'd stolen. But he didn't seem like he'd do anything so spiteful now: he seemed nice. Hannah looked at him leaning forward telling Freddie about some of the fish he'd caught. He was smiling, and he looked happy, at home. Like them all, he'd had a difficult life.

When it was time for bed, they all settled down, Hannah still busy with her thoughts. She thought Bert was all right, she decided, and he did have a nice smile. And, like her, he believed in people earning a living and not pinching.

The following morning was bright, the threatened snow had

held off, and Hannah was going to take Bonzo out. She was taken aback when Bert asked her if he could go with her. Apprehensively she remembered the last time – they hadn't had a lot to say then – but she could hardly refuse.

'Yer could git some shrimps and winkles while yer out,' said Maudie. 'Just a minute, 'Annah.' She looked round, checking the others were busy. 'Don't go saying anyfink ter Bert about . . . you know? 'Im being me son. Will yer?' she whispered.

'No, of course not. You asked me that before.'

Maudie smiled. 'Well, just fought I'd mention it in case yer forgot.'

Hannah would never forget that sort of information. She was still puzzled as to whether Bert really knew that Albert was his father.

'Ready gel?' called Bert from the doorway.

He looked very mannish in his navy blue reefer jacket and soft cap. As they walked along, Hannah realized he was much taller than her, a real man. She knew some of the curtains in Hope Street were being ruffled, could feel several pairs of eyes on them. She felt very grown up, being out with a sailor and gave Mrs Nosy's house a smile. She would be dying to know all about him. What would she say if she knew he was Maudie's son?

'Why do you live up north?' she asked as they made their way to the park.

'It ain't up north really, it's Lowestoft, in Suffolk.'

'But Maudie said . . .' Hannah quickly checked herself – he mustn't know she knew all about him.

'Well, Maudie thinks anywhere north of the Thames is up in Scotland,' Bert chuckled.

Hannah laughed nervously.

'Many years ago Albert took me up there, didn't I tell yer this before?'

196

Hannah nodded. 'Only that someone called Albert took you away.'

'Well, he got a job as a fisherman, and 'e used to take me on his boat in the school holidays.'

'You've been to school?' asked Hannah, intrigued that he never said it was his father.

'Of course. We ain't all backward, you know!'

'Where's Albert now?' asked Hannah, knowing the answer to her question.

'He died a good many years back. Poor old Maudie. I 'ated 'aving ter tell 'er. She was very fond of him. That didn't please Jack, me upsetting Maudie.'

Fascinated, Hannah took in this new bit of information. 'What's it like being at sea?' she asked.

'Can be a bit rough at times, but it's a good, honest life.'

'I've never seen the sea,' she said wistfully.

'It's very big, and can be very wild at times.'

'It must be exciting. All those waves and seagulls.'

Bert glanced at her, amused. 'You're a funny kid.'

'No I'm not, why did you say that?'

'Dunno. Maybe I could see you standing on a cliff with your hair blowing in the wind, listening to the seagulls and watching the waves break over the shore.'

She smiled. She too could picture that. 'I'd like to live near the sea,' she said almost to herself.

'You can always come up to see me.'

She laughed. 'Oh, I'm sure my foreman would let me go off just like that.' She moved on.

'Where're we off to?' he asked.

'Just a quick walk round the park, it's a bit too cold to stay out long.'

Bert laughed. 'Don't call this cold, do you? You want to be out in a boat when the nets freeze.'

Hannah shuddered. 'I don't think I'd like that. Come on, Bonzo, let's get back.'

The dog ambled towards them. Hannah bent down to pat his head – and Bert did the same. Their hands touched.

'You are cold. Where're your gloves?' He took her hand and gently rubbed it.

'In my pocket.'

'Well, they won't keep you warm in there.' He put her hand to his lips and blew on it. 'Put your glove on quick.'

Hannah smiled and did as she was told. He was kind, and she realized she felt excited. No one had ever touched her so tenderly before. Bert smiled, and Hannah felt all her remaining fears and anxieties about him disappear.

'Will you be away for very long?' she croaked.

'I don't know, Hannah.' He kicked his boot along the ground embarrassedly.

Hannah couldn't believe he had called her by her name; the Bert everybody feared, the Bert that Jack hated. Maudie was right, he did have a nice side to him.

'Hannah,' he repeated. 'That's a pretty name.'

She could feel her face flush.

'It suits you.'

'Come on, Bonzo, let's get back.' Hannah went to walk on.

Bert held her arm. 'When I come here again, could I take you out?'

'I don't know. Jack always says you only come here when you want money.'

'Jack.' He almost spat the word out. 'Well, 'e would say that, now wouldn't 'e?'

Hannah still knew she had to defend her Jack. 'But what about when you took that watch?'

'I didn't take it. Maudie gave it to me.'

'But you knew it was stolen. You say you hate stealing.'

'Yes, yes I did know. And I admit I did need the money then.'

'So you just told me a lie. You do only come here when you want money.' She began to march on.

'Hannah, you've got it all wrong. I did need the money then, to repair our boat.'

She stopped. 'Our boat? But last night you said you worked for someone, what was his name?'

'Ernie.'

'So what's all this, "our" then?'

'I don't know why I'm bothering to tell you all this.' Bert's voice was sulky.

'Neither do I.' Hannah walked quickly away. Why was she talking like this? She knew he'd given Maudie money. Why had she mentioned the damn watch? They had been getting on so well. She was cross with herself. When would she learn not to poke her nose into other people's affairs!

Bert caught her up and swung her round. 'I will bloody well tell you. I want you to know the truth.'

'Why?'

'I don't know – yes I do. I like you, Hannah, and I know you and I feel the same way about certain things, and I don't want you to think I'm a liar.'

She looked into his deep brown eyes. His thick brows had lost their scowl. Her thoughts were racing . . . he likes me, he likes me.

Bert was still talking. 'Ernie 'as two little kids, nice little 'ens, they are. Well, without the boat 'e can't work, and they wouldn't pinch a fing – even if they was starving. Yer don't find many like that.'

Hannah didn't speak; she knew people like that. Kate and her family, for one.

'Well, you see, I know Maudie's always got a few bob, and I fought if I could borrow it, just till things got better . . . besides, I've paid it back now.' He stopped and looked at Hannah. 'Oh, what's the point. Come on, let's get back. Come on Bonzo.'

Hannah wanted to stop and talk. 'I know what you're saying,' she called after him. 'Just a . . .' But Bert had walked on. Why had he stopped himself? Was he afraid of showing his feelings? Did he have to be tough all the time? She was so annoyed with herself for bringing up that damn watch again. When would she learn?

Ten minutes later she got back to find Bert and Bonzo had arrived before her. Luckily Maudie was in her room and didn't see they'd come home separately. That evening was very different to Saturday. Bert sat at the table scowling and everybody left him alone.

Hannah wasn't surprised to see he had already gone when she got up for work the next day. Maudie told her later that day that he always tried to catch a milk train back.

Early in the year, the topic on everybody's lips was the cause of the suffragettes. Every day Hannah would spend hours poring over the newspapers Tom brought in, reading out loud parts that Maudie didn't quite understand. Many women had been sent to prison, and Hannah was worried that, with all those police about, Jack might get caught.

In May Hannah began to plan to visit Alice, but Jack told her not to go as there was a lot of uneasiness. Most of the dockers were on strike, and he reckoned that when other unions joined them, it could get very nasty.

It was after the Derby in June that the newspapers reported the death of Emily Davison. She had thrown herself under the king's horse, creating a lot of sympathy for the women who were willing to die for their cause. There was a huge following at her funeral, including Jack, but Hannah knew he wasn't going for the same reason as all the rest. She just wondered whether it was pinching or a girl that was uppermost in his mind.

It was just after that that Hannah finally got to see Alice from whom she still had the occasional letter. Although Alice made her welcome at the house, Hannah felt in the way and ill at ease, and the conversation always seemed stilted. At times it was almost like being with a stranger. All the way home, Hannah thought about Alice. She knew her sister would never come back to Hope Street, but what else did Hannah herself have? And did she still want to keep going to see Alice, just to feel rejected?

It was a warm, still day, and Hannah was planning to call in on Kate on her way home from work. As she turned into Hope Street, many of the women were sitting outside their front doors, the kids screaming and yelling, playing games and swinging round the lamp-posts.

'All right then, gel,' called Mrs Brown at number three, sitting on her doorstep.

'Yes thank you,' she said, knocking on Kate's open door.

'She don't 'arf talk nice, don't she?' Mrs Brown called to Mrs Nosy across the road who was nagging some of the kids for chalking outside her door.

Mrs Nosy stopped and looked up. 'Don't know why she 'as ter live wiv that one.' She jerked her head towards the end of the street. 'And I don't know why that there Mrs D. lets 'er kid be looked after by that old woman. D'yer know, I swears she's a witch.'

'Don't start on that again, Gertie. She ain't, is she love?'

Hannah smiled at Mrs Brown. 'Course not.'

'Don't see that little crippled kid now, do we?' Mrs Nosy folded her arms. 'Wot's old Maudie done wiv 'er? That's sumfink I'd like ter know.'

Hannah held her tongue and banged on Kate's door. She wasn't going to get into another row with Mrs Nosy, or give her the satisfaction of knowing Alice was her sister and had moved away.

''Annah,' said Kate, holding her tight. 'We ain't seen yer fer ages.'

Hannah stood back and screwed up her nose.

'Yer I know. The bloody onions don't 'arf stink, don't they?' she laughed. 'Look at me 'ands.'

Hannah looked down at her bright yellow hands. 'Can't you get it off?'

'Na, still, not ter worry. Can't see any bloke wanting ter 'old me 'and, though, can you?'

Hannah laughed. 'They will one day. How is everybody?' She asked as they made their way down the overcrowded passage.

'OK. That's Billy's,' said Kate, proudly stepping over a wooden cart that had two large pram wheels at the back. 'Made it 'isself, 'e did. Yer knows 'e works fer the greengrocer now?'

'Yes, he told me.'

'That's where 'e got the wood.'

''Allo, 'Annah,' said Mrs Linton, wiping her wet hands on the bottom of her pinny. 'Sit yerself down, love.' Mrs Linton looked thinner than ever. Her greying hair, pulled back into an untidy bun at the nape of her neck, emphasized her pale, drawn face. ''Ow's yer sister? Kate told me yer'd bin to see 'er.'

'Fine, thank you,' said Hannah, not wanting to say any more. 'How're all the little Lintons?'

'We're all right. It's good now Kate works, and Billy brings in a few pence and a bit a veg, so fings ain't ser bad.'

'We even gits a bit o' fruit sometimes,' said Kate. 'Our Grace was poorly a while back, but Mrs D. gave 'er some medicine. She's all right now.'

'What about you 'Annah? Yer looking well, filling out a bit now.'

Hannah blushed and pulled her coat round her. She was still very conscious of her small breasts, and had to take a lot of ribbing from the women at work. When she took her coat off, she couldn't get her overall on quick enough.

They sat and talked for a while, till it was time for Hannah to leave.

Kate walked to the door with her. Looking out, she started to giggle. 'D'yer know, we still 'ave ter laugh when we fink about you 'aving a go at old Mrs Nosy.'

'That was ages ago. She really got on my nerves that day, said I pinched her purse – me, I ask you. She's always going on about poor old Maudie, always making snide remarks about her. Now she wants to know where Alice is – she thinks Maudie's sold her.' Hannah smiled. 'By the way, does anyone round here know her real name?'

Kate laughed. 'Don't fink so – everybody calls 'er Nosy. I fink even she's forgotten 'er real name!'

When Hannah arrived home, Maudie was sitting in her arm-chair, crying.

Hannah rushed over to her. 'What is it? What's wrong?'

Maudie blew her nose. 'It's Bonzo. 'E's dead.'

Hannah sat on the chair. 'No. He can't be. He was all right this morning. How . . . ? When did it happen?'

''Smorning, after you all left 'e went outside. I fought 'e'd just gorn for a jimmy – 'e didn't come in when I called 'im so

I left 'im. Well, yer know what a cantankerous bugger 'e can be?'

Hannah nodded.

'Well, when I went out looking for 'im . . .' She stopped to blow her nose again. 'When I went out, 'e'd gorn right ter the end of the yard – he was all stiff.'

'Oh, Maudie, I'm so sorry.'

'I've 'ad that dog fer years, I 'ave.'

'He was very old.'

'Yer, I know.'

Hannah looked round apprehensively. 'Is he still outside?'

'Na, I went round ter Bob, and 'e sent young Tom back with a wheelbarrer, and they took 'im away. I 'ad ter cover 'im up; couldn't bear ter look at 'im all stiff-like.' Maudie sniffed. 'I ain't 'alf gonner miss 'im.'

'Would you like me to get you another dog?'

'Na, fanks all the same – but there won't be anovver like 'im.'

'Alice will be very upset when she hears about it, she was very fond of Bonzo. She always asks after him.'

'Does she?'

Hannah nodded.

'Why didn't she come back 'ere again? Seems everyone I likes goes orf.' Maudie sniffed even louder.

'I'm still here.' Hannah was a little put out at Maudie's remark.

'I knows that love, don't I, and I'm really grateful,' Maudie said quickly. 'When yer gonner see 'er again?' She asked, wiping her nose.

'I don't know.' Hannah sat at the table. 'I'm surprised Mrs Nosy didn't say anything about Tom taking poor Bonzo off.'

'Didn't see 'er, she must a bin out shopping. Christ that would 'ave started 'er going on again.'

Hannah smiled. 'I reckon she would have tried to see under the cover in case it was Alice. She still thinks you've done something to her.'

Maudie wiped her eyes and gave Hannah a weak smile. 'That wouldn't 'alf 'ave caused a rumpus, I can tell yer, if she'd 'ad touched 'im.'

Hannah too smiled at the thought of Maudie and Mrs Nosy, pulling and fighting over a cover, Mrs Nosy trying to see what was underneath it.

Dolly and Freddie were also upset over the news about Bonzo, and when Jack got in even he said he was sad about it.

A few weeks later, Hannah received a letter from Alice.

My dear Hannah

It was so good to see you. Sorry I've been so long before writing but not a lot happens – well, it does, but you wouldn't be interested.

We were out the other day, that's Betty and me, we were looking for some new shoes for me. We had to walk round a pub's cellar doors that were up as they were delivering the beer. And guess who popped his head up just as we got level? Alf. Do you remember, he was the boy that used to come in Uncle Harry's yard. Well he saw me and said hello, I could have died, and quickly walked on. Betty asked me who he was, and I just said someone I used to know, but she wanted to know how he knew my name. I didn't know what to say, so I told her he once lived at Maudie's. So if she asks you, would you please say the same. I know he wanted to talk to me, but I just hurried on.

Hannah stared at the letter. Alice had seen Alf! Fear and panic gripped her. Did he know about what they'd done to Uncle

Harry? Would he be able to find out where Alice lived? She had to go and see her, and it had to be alone. All these years they had kept their past a secret, and Hannah wasn't prepared to have the truth tumble out into the open now.

On the following Saturday afternoon, Hannah went to see Alice, having told Maudie she was going shopping. Alice looked surprised when she opened the door.

'Alice, I've been so worried about you.'

'Why? I'm all right.'

'But in your letter . . .'

'Oh, that. Not to worry.'

'But you said you'd seen Alf.'

'Yes, we did, but that was weeks ago, and Betty hasn't said any more about it. Just so long as you say he lived at Maudie's a long while ago – that's of course if she asks. That's all I was really concerned about. I don't suppose she will; she's probably forgotten all about it by now.'

Hannah sat in the large red velvet chair. 'And I've been worrying about you, wondering if he found out where you lived.'

'Why? Why would he do that?'

'I don't know. What if he knew about Uncle Harry?'

'I don't know. Besides, he wouldn't know if we were there when he died, now would he?'

'I don't know. Alice, what if he found out where you lived?'

She waved her hand dismissively. 'Course he won't.'

'Well, I'm worried about it.'

Alice shrugged her shoulders. 'Well, I'm not.'

Hannah stiffened. 'No, I didn't think you would be.'

'I'll make some tea.' Alice said, closing the subject.

As Hannah made her way home half an hour later, Alice

was still on her mind. Would she ever be free from worrying about her? And did Alice ever worry over her? Hannah didn't think so.

Chapter 16

It was August, and Dolly and Freddie, along with Violet and her grandmother, were going hopping in Kent. She was so happy and excited as she kissed and hugged Hannah goodbye.

'Fanks fer 'elping us out wiv the money for our train fare,' she said gratefully.

Hannah swallowed hard. 'Well, I didn't want you to get caught pinching it, and being put away before you got there.'

'Yer a good mate, I'm gonner miss yer.' Dolly then turned to Maudie.

Although Hannah and Dolly had had their differences over the years, they still thought a lot of each other, more so since their little chat when Dolly had told Hannah what she'd gone through. Hannah felt a little sad at Dolly's leaving, and wished her and Alice were still together.

Maudie and Hannah stood at the gate and waved. When they disappeared round the corner, Maudie turned to Hannah and said. 'D'yer know, I reckon that's the last we're gonner see of 'em.'

'Why? What makes you say that?'

'Dunno, just a feeling I got. First it was Alice, then Bonzo.' She sighed. 'The place'll seem empty wivout 'em. Not that Freddie said a lot, poor little devil. Still,' she added with a smile, 'Dolly made up for 'im.'

'You've still got me and Tom.'

'Yer. Mind you, I can see Tom going soon.'

'Mrs Nosy's right, you are an old witch – have you got a crystal ball you look into?'

Maudie smiled. 'Saucy cow. Na. I don't like all these changes – must be gitting old. Come on gel, let's 'ave a cuppa.'

Hannah put her arm round Maudie's shoulders. 'You'll never be old. They'll be back, you wait and see.' As Maudie nestled into the crook of her arm, Hannah suddenly realized how small she was getting. Or was it that Hannah herself was now taller, growing up?

Since Alice left, and now that she no longer had to pay out for her clothes, Hannah took a great deal of trouble with her appearance, proud of how she managed to make her second-hand clothes fit. She pored over the adverts in the papers which showed the latest fashions, but her real weakness was hats. She loved them, and Maudie had given her a cupboard to keep them in ever since Bonzo had grabbed one and ran off with it. When she'd finally got it back it had been dirty and torn, and Hannah had cried for days. Poor old Bonzo, Hannah thought, as they made their way indoors. Perhaps Maudie was right; he and Alice certainly weren't coming back. Maybe Dolly wouldn't either.

At the end of September, Violet came and confirmed that Dolly wouldn't be returning to London. She had got herself a job on a farm, and she loved it.

'Told yer, didn't I?' said Maudie smugly.

'Dolly on a farm, I can't imagine that, can you?' asked Hannah.

'Can yer see 'er mucking out pigs, or milking a cow? I reckon she'd run a mile if one turned round and looked at 'er.' Maudie laughed, but Hannah knew she was upset.

During this past year, Hannah had only seen Alice now and again, and every time their meetings and conversations had been getting harder and harder. Alice was always full of the people that came to the house and the good time she was having. She was now fifteen, and looked very grown up. Her hair was always neat and well groomed, and her clothes were all she'd ever wanted – there was nothing practical about them now, and no matter how Hannah tried, Alice always made her feel dowdy and discontented.

Once again, as the nights began to draw in, the year drew to an end too. Alice had told Hannah that Betty Kelly would be working away over Christmas, and they would all be going with her. Hannah was feeling very low. She only had Mary and Kate to talk to, and Kate was busy at work at this time of year as there was a lot of overtime. What's more, she was walking out with a young lad from the pickle factory.

It was when Hannah was sitting telling Maudie about it that Jack asked her to go to the music hall again. In the past, and as much as she'd wanted to go out with him, she had declined, as he wouldn't promise not to pick any pockets.

'Go on, gel, it'll do yer good,' said Maudie. 'Yer always moping about now.'

Hannah smiled. What was the point in being so angry with him when deep down she knew she loved him. He had never kissed her again since that night, and sometimes she longed for him to hold her, but she knew he just looked on her as a sister. She still worried when he went off for days in case it was with a woman friend, and she also worried that he might get picked up by the police. Was she being silly? And could she end up being an old maid? She thought of Miss King, Mary's lodger. 'Oh, all right then,' she said at last.

'Good, we'll go Sat'day night.'

'Well I'm orf ter bed,' said Maudie.

'And me,' said Tom. 'Don't make too much noise, you two. Remember, I 'ave ter git up early ter git the papers out.'

'You certainly got 'im sorted out all right,' said Jack, lighting a cigarette.

'He likes it. You're the only one I haven't reformed. If only you would get a job,' she said. 'Why won't you, Jack?'

'Fer Christ's sake, gel, don't start on that again. You've seen how many blokes are out o' work, and yer've seen 'em on strike fer more money.' He looked angry. 'Listen, gel, I tell yer fings could get pretty nasty, and I fer one don't want any part of it.'

Hannah didn't say any more, for they had been over this argument many times before.

On Saturday, Hannah felt very smart in her new hat, and gently ran her fingers over the shiny brown fox-fur she had bought from the market. It was a bit thin and mangy-looking, and only had one eye, but she put it carefully round her shoulders and, opening the clasp, popped his tail into his mouth. When she turned her head quickly, the smell of mothballs wafted up, but she didn't care and, as she walked down Hope Street holding Jack's arm, she wanted everybody to see them. It was a pity it was a dark, cold evening, with snow threatening.

They went to the New Cross Empire, and Hannah looked out for Betty Kelly. At first she was disappointed when she saw Betty wasn't in the chorus, but then Hannah sat back and enjoyed the show. She had forgotten what a good time she had had before, and now she laughed and clapped, and got cross with herself for not letting Jack take her out more often. From now on, she thought as they walked out of the Empire, I'll go out with him whenever he asks me. She shivered with delight when she remembered what had happened when they'd got home the last time they were out together – could that happen again? Could she make it happen again?

'Wot's 'appened ter that tart Alice lives wiv?' asked Jack as they walked home.

'I don't know. Alice said they were going away for Christmas – they must have gone already.'

'Bit early, ain't it? They got anuvver week yet 'fore Christmas.'

'It's going to be very dead again this year. There'll only be the four of us.'

'Yer, yer going round ter yer mate?'

'I expect I'll see Mary sometime over Christmas. Are you staying at home?' She had to know the answer; she didn't want him to go away.

'Don't rightly know.' They turned into Hope Street and he stopped under the gas-lamp. ''Annah.' He took her arm. 'We've known each ovver a long while, ain't we?'

She nodded. He'd called her Hannah, and he was holding her arm. As she looked into his blue eyes she thought her heart would stop. She wanted to throw her arms round his neck and kiss him and kiss him, but she knew she must never do that, it wouldn't be proper – not in the street. As Elsie at work would say, she'd be behaving like a hussy.

'I knows yer don't like me nicking fings,' Jack said gently, 'but it's the way I am, and it's the way I'll always be. I like you, and I would a liked us ter walk out tergevver.'

Hannah thought she'd faint. He *didn't* just think of her as a sister.

'But I knows how yer feels about what I do, so I'm finking of going away.'

'What?' Panic gripped her. Her head was reeling. He was going away. Everybody she loved wanted to get away from her. What could she say? 'Why? Is it this woman friend you've got?'

He laughed. 'I ain't got no woman friend.'

'But I thought . . .'

He kicked his boot against the lamp-post. 'I only let yer

213

fink that cos – I don't fink I can trust meself. Yer see, at night, when I sees yer lying there, wiv yer 'air all down and over the piller, well . . .'

She put her finger on his lips. 'Don't Jack. Please, don't go away.'

'I fink I must. 'Sides, I promised Maudie I'd never touch yer.'

'You promised Maudie . . . When?' She was stunned.

'Yer knows that night I kissed yer; well, it was Maudie what I 'eard, she saw us, and she fretened ter frow me out if I did . . . Yer know.'

Hannah pulled herself up, furious. 'What right has Maudie to interfere? What if I had wanted you to . . . ?' She stopped. What was she saying; she was almost inviting him to make love to her! But she didn't care.

'Well, Maudie's very fond of yer, yer know. She finks of yer as a daughter, and she's frightened yer'll finish up in the family way.'

Hannah turned her head; she didn't want Jack to see her blush. 'I can do what I like, I don't have to ask Maudie. She doesn't own me.' She knew she was pouting.

'I do like yer, 'Annah.' He grabbed her arms and kissed her mouth long and hard.

When he let her go, her legs felt weak and she almost fell backwards.

'I fink the world of Maudie, and I wouldn't do anyfink ter upset 'er – yer see, I owe 'er a lot.'

Hannah's head was in a whirl. 'So what you're trying to tell me is that you think more of Maudie than me?'

'No, I didn't say that. It's just that . . . Well. Oh, I dunno. Yer can never say the right fing ter women. Come on, let's git back home, it's cold out 'ere, it's started ter snow, and yer shivering.'

Hannah wasn't shivering with the cold, it was with anger – and pleasure. She was angry with Maudie for interfering in her life, but she was shivering with pleasure at Jack's kissing and holding her. She hadn't even noticed the snow gently falling. It was settling on Jack's hat, she realized. She brushed it from her eyelashes and looked up at the sky. In the pale yellow gas-light, it looked pretty and unreal, almost magical, just like the pictures in the books. She didn't want to go home, she wanted Jack to kiss her and hold her, but he took hold of her arm and hurried her along.

When they reached the old wash-house, they quietly closed the door, careful not to wake Tom. The church clock struck midnight.

An hour later Hannah still lay wide awake. In the far corner she could see the end of Jack's cigarette glowing in the dark. She wanted to go over to him. She wanted him to caress her, smother her with kisses and, she knew, make love to her. She had never felt like this before. She was a woman now and had strong feelings. She could have cried, she hurt for his love and affection so much.

All over Christmas, she tried to get Maudie alone to tell her to mind her own business, that she wanted Jack. She also tried to get Jack on his own. She was going to tell him she loved him and would do anything to keep him there, but she never got a chance. The week after Christmas, Jack casually announced he was going away.

'How long for?' she asked apprehensively, gazing at him across the table.

'Dunno, could be fer a long while.'

'Wot? Yer don't mean fer good, do yer?' asked Maudie.

'Dunno. Could be.' Jack looked at Hannah.

'Not anuvver one?' said Maudie, storming out of the room.

'Why?' asked Hannah, as soon as Maudie went outside and they were alone.

'I told yer last week.'

'You can't go.'

'Oh yes I can.'

'But what about Maudie? You said you owed her a lot.'

'Yer, I do, but I fink it's time I moved on. I wonner live me own life.'

'Well, I'm coming with you.'

'Wot? Don't talk daft gel.'

'Is it because you want to . . . ? You know? That you're . . . tempted?'

'Yer, partly.'

'Why are you so much of a gentleman?'

He laughed. 'I ain't no gentleman, as you call it, I've 'ad me fair share. Na, I just feel it's time ter move on.' He grinned. 'And I might tell yer I've 'ad some right little darlings in me time.'

Hannah stiffened. She knew the girls at the factory let their fellers do what they wanted. She hated the idea of Jack doing the same with other women. 'And I thought you would have made your own mind up,' she went on, 'not be told what to do by Maudie.'

'Yer, well, I might be a tea-leaf, and I know yer won't believe this, but I 'ave got some . . .'

'Morals, is the word you're looking for, I think.'

He laughed. 'Yer, that's right. Yer see I respect yer, 'Annah.'

Hannah was trembling. She didn't want him to go away, she didn't want him to respect her, and she knew if she wanted him to stay she had to think of something quickly. 'Well then, let's get married.'

'What?' Jack almost spat his tea over her.

'I'll be nineteen in May, and I don't have anyone to look

after me, so why not?' She couldn't believe what she was saying, and almost wanted to laugh at the expression on his face. 'My friend Mary got married when she was seventeen, and she was happy.'

He grinned. 'Well, I never fought I'd 'ear you propose.'

Hannah blushed. Was she being too pushy? 'I love you, Jack,' she whispered.

He looked uneasy. 'You've been going on at me ever since yer got 'ere ter pack up pinching, now yer reckon yer wants ter marry me and live orf me ill-gotten gains.' He stood up. 'Well, I ain't gonner 'ave you nag me fer the rest of me natural.'

'Who's nagging who?' asked Maudie as she walked in.

''Er.' Jack picked up his cigarette. 'I'm going ter the bog.'

'What yer bin saying to 'im?'

'Nothing, only the usual about getting a job.'

'Yer know, I reckon it's your fault 'e's going.' Maudie looked angry. 'Yer gonner chase 'im away fer good, keeping on at 'im. And I 'appen ter know 'e's very fond of yer.'

'Well, he's got a funny way of showing it,' Hannah said angrily. 'Besides, what about you?'

'Now wot 'ave I done?'

'I know you told him not to . . . to . . . You know?' Hannah blushed, embarrassed.

'Oh, so that's wot this is all about? I fink wot yer trying to say is, just cos I wouldn't let 'im 'ave a poke at yer, yer fink it's my fault 'e's going?'

Hannah was upset. Maudie made it sound dirty and wrong.

'Well, yer can't expect everyone ter do as yer want, now can yer?'

Hannah looked down at the table, suddenly deflated. 'No, I suppose not.'

'First yer sister, then Dolly; they've all gorn.'

'That's not my fault.'

'Yer always keeping on at Jack.' Maudie thumped the table, making Hannah jump.

'Don't start nagging me,' she snapped, 'or I'll be the next.'

'That's it, git rid of all the ovvers, then you bugger orf. Nobody finks about me. It's a bloody good start ter the New Year.' Maudie fished in her pinafore pocket for her handkerchief.

Hannah's feelings were in turmoil. She loved Jack, but he didn't want her. Alice had gone. She only had Maudie now. Suddenly she felt a rush of affection for the old woman. 'I'm sorry, Maudie. I'll never leave you. I promise.'

Then Hannah thought of Mary in her own house. What wouldn't she give to live in a house, to cook on a stove, to sleep in a proper bed and keep a house clean? She knew she must try one more time to make Jack stay, make him see things her way. That way they could all be happy.

But it was in vain. When she got home from work the following evening, Jack had gone. He told Maudie he was shacking up with some bird he'd met some time back. Had he just told Maudie that, or was it true? Shocked, Hannah didn't know what to think, but for weeks the atmosphere between her and Maudie was very strained.

It wasn't till the end of February that Hannah got to see Alice. On the way home again she wondered why she'd bothered. Alice had been full of what she had done over Christmas and the New Year. She wasn't at all interested in the fact that Dolly, Freddie, and now Jack, had gone. She'd been more upset over Bonzo dying. Hannah had left her early, and was deep in thought as she waited for her tram. Suddenly she was aware of her name being called, and looked up. To her horror she saw Alf sitting driving a brewer's dray loaded with large wooden beer barrels. He called her name again and, bringing the heavy shire-horse to a standstill, jumped down and walked towards her.

'Well, well, well. If it ain't 'Annah Miller.' He peered under the brim of her hat. 'This is a surprise. Fought it was you. Saw young Alice a while back. You two living round this way then?'

'Hello, Alf. See you're in charge of your own cart now.'

'Yer. I must say yer both turned out ter be a nice-looking pair. Did she tell yer I saw 'er wiv some posh tart.'

'Yes, yes she did.'

His greedy eyes were looking her up and down. 'Looks like yer both doing all right fer yerselves. Yer look real lady-like. She was dressed up ter the nines as well.'

'We manage.' Hannah pulled at her fox-fur.

'I was doing a delivery, so I didn't git a chance ter talk to 'er. Look, I've finished fer the day and there's a pub round the corner: fancy a drink?'

'No, thank you.'

'Come on, just fer old times' sake. It must be – wot – all a four years since yer went.'

'I'm sorry, Alf, but I must get home.'

'Oh yer, and where's 'ome then?'

'Not round here.'

'That's a pity. Got a lot ter tell yer. Yer aunt said she ain't seen yer for years. She's bin worried about yer, fought yer might a got in touch.'

Hannah looked nervously about her. 'How is Aunt May?' she asked hesitantly.

'Not ser bad, considering.' Alf slowly pushed his cap back. 'I knows I don't look all that smart, but I fink it'll be worf yer while ter come and 'ave a drink wiv me after all this time. Yer see, I've got a lot ter tell yer.' He grinned, a sly, evil grin.

Hannah was frightened – what was he going to tell her? 'Is Uncle Harry all right?' Her voice was high and unnatural, she was beginning to panic. She had to behave as if she thought her uncle was still alive.

He leaned forward, putting his face close to hers. 'Now wouldn't yer like ter know? Yer see, I knows a lot more than yer fink.' He touched the side of his nose. 'And it don't do ter stand out 'ere in the cold talking about it, now does it?'

She stood back and shook her head. She didn't have any choice.

Alf took the horse's reins and it walked slowly beside him. The gentle clip-clopping of its hooves on the tarry block road was the only sound between them.

When they reached the pub he took his leather apron off and tucked it under the seat. He put a nose-bag on the horse then, taking Hannah's arm, led her into the pub. 'We'll go in the snug.'

It was warm and smoky. A huge fire was roaring in the grate, and although it was still quite early, there were a number of men sitting about smoking and playing cards. Hannah felt totally out of place.

'Sit over there, 'Annah.' Alf pointed to a corner seat under the window. The deep red velvet cloth of the high-backed buttoned seat was torn and dirty, half its buttons missing.

Hannah brushed at it with her gloved hand.

'Watcher 'aving?'

'I don't know.'

'I'll git yer a port an' lemon.'

Hannah tentatively sat and watched him. He was deep in conversation with the barman. Every now and again they would both laugh very loudly, and look over in her direction. She wanted to run away, but she knew she had to brave it out.

'This is nice,' he said, placing the glasses on the table and sitting opposite her. 'Cor, never fought I'd ever see yer again, let alone be 'aving a drink wiv yer. D'yer remember 'ow I used ter slope orf ter the Red Lion ter git a quick one in, and you'd be round there gitting a jugful fer old 'Arry?'

Hannah nodded. She removed her glove and toyed with her glass. What could she say?

'What about when yer worked at the brush factory?' He grabbed her hand. 'Looks a lot better now. Wot yer doing now then?'

She pulled her hand away.

Without waiting for an answer, Alf continued. 'I was dead pleased when I got me own cart. Me old mate Charlie put in a good word for me when 'e 'ad ter retire.'

Hannah kept her head down. She wanted to scream. She wasn't interested in any of this.

'Yer working then?' He took a swig of beer and wiped the froth from his mouth with the back of his hand.

'Yes,' she croaked.

'Yer sister looked real smart – 'ardly recognized 'er. Mind you, you look very nice an' all.'

'Alf. What do you want?'

'Oh yer. Well.' He bent his head nearer. 'Yer remember that day that cart knocked yer aunt down? By the way, she's all right – just a few bruises, nuffink ter worry about. Oh yer, where was I?'

Hannah felt like shaking him.

'Well.' He sat back in his chair. 'When I came in the yard looking for yer, ter ask about yer aunt, I sees yer running from the smiffy, so I fought I'd 'ave a nose ter see wot yer was running away from. I tell yer, yer both looked scared ter deaf.'

Hannah sat back, stunned. He'd seen them. It was his boots they had heard on the cobblestones. He knew they'd killed their uncle. She felt the colour drain from her face.

'Well, yer could 'ave knocked me down wiv a fevver when I walked in there.' He took his tobacco tin from his pocket and slowly began rolling a cigarette. 'There was yer poor old uncle, 'is face all covered wiv dirt and stuff, fighting fer 'is breaf. Well, I fought at the time, that ain't very nice of them gels, running orf like that.' He licked the cigarette paper, looked at it, and struck a match. 'Come on, 'Annah git yer drink down yer. I'm gonner git anuvver.'

Hannah put her hand on his arm.

''Allo, wot's this then? A little fond touch?' He laughed very loudly. Over the years he had lost a couple of teeth, and those that were left had become more yellow.

She quickly pulled it back. She knew he was deliberately playing with her. He was enjoying watching her tremble, he was waiting for her to admit to something; but she too could play this cat-and-mouse game. She sat upright. 'Yes, we did leave him. He was always wicked to us and that was the only way we could get away. I'm going. You can have my drink.' She stood up.

'Yer better sit down, 'Annah.' His face took on a scowl. 'Yer see, it ain't as cut-an'-dried as all that.'

She slumped on to the seat.

'Yer see . . .' He looked round and bent his head nearer. His voice dropped to a whisper. 'When I got all the muck out of 'is mouf, 'e started ranting and raging, and 'e told me yer'd tried to kill 'im wiv a 'ammer, and 'e reckons that if 'e ever found out where yer was, 'e'd kill yer 'imself, or git yer chucked in clink fer the rest of yer natural.'

Her throat went dry. She felt sick. Her head was swimming. He was alive. All these years of nightmares and bad dreams could now be over.

'Now, if I tell 'im I'd seen yer both, 'e'd probably pay quite 'andsome for that bit of information.'

'You don't know where we live.' Hannah tried to sound uninterested.

Alf sat back. 'It shouldn't be too 'ard ter find out, now should it?'

'I don't live anywhere near here.' She was determined to brazen this out.

'So, what yer doing round this way then. Could it be yer was visiting Alice?'

'No, no, I wasn't. I was shopping.'

'Oh yer.' He looked on the floor. 'Ain't got much, 'ave yer?'

'I'm going.' Hannah stood up. She suddenly felt very confident and, leaning on the table, looked him straight in the eye and said, 'And Alf, don't try to follow me, because you can't take your horse and cart down the underground.' She pulled her gloves on with such gusto she heard the stitching break and, tucking her handbag under her arm, turned away.

Alf jumped up and stood in front of her. 'Cocky little cow, ain't yer? Well, we'll see about that. I found yer once, so it won't be that 'ard ter do it again.'

She pushed past him without a word. Outside it was dark. She leant against the wall, her heart pounding. She realized she was shaking with fear, and with the realization her tears began to fall. What if he did tell Uncle Harry, and he did find them? She had to tell Alice to be on her guard. This was all her fault. If she hadn't got caught stealing, they would never have been round this way. Hannah dabbed at her eyes, and looked at Alf's horse. I'd better not go to her now, she thought, just in case he follows me. Quickly she headed off towards the underground.

Chapter 17

Hannah hurried home, desperate to tell someone about her encounter with Alf. As soon as she walked in she sat and told Maudie everything.

Without her usual comments and interruptions, Maudie listened wide eyed and open mouthed. 'Well, I'll be buggered,' she whispered when Hannah finished. 'All these years and yer ain't said a dicky bird. Mind you, I always fought you two 'ad sumfink ter 'ide, but I didn't fink it would be sumfink like that, and I didn't like ter ask too many questions. Still, fank gawd the old bloke's alive.' Maudie started laughing.

'What is it? What's so funny?'

'I was just finking about Jack. Yer've always led orf alarming about 'im pinching fings, and all the time yer fought yer'd done yer old uncle in. I tell yer what, 'e'd be livid if 'e knew.'

Hannah caught her breath. 'Don't ever tell him, will you?'

'Na, course not. Wot yer gonner do about this Alf bloke then?'

'I don't know. Tomorrow I'll go over and see Alice and put her on her guard. What if Uncle Harry does find out where she lives?'

'I dunno, love.'

'What can we do?'

Maudie shrugged. 'Dunno. Mind you, it's only 'is word against yours.'

'Yes, I know. But we're only girls.'

'Yer, that's true enough. Look, don't worry too much about

225

it. After all, 'e's gotter find yer first.'

That night, Hannah lay for a long while reflecting on the past. So Uncle Harry was still alive – and what about Aunt May? She would dearly love to see her again, but she knew that would be impossible. What would everybody say if they knew about her past? Would they be angry? For so long she'd felt accepted as part of Maudie's family, and she thought they all respected her. What would they think of her for keeping her past such a secret? They all seemed to have a purpose in life now. Tom was happy selling his papers. Maudie was content looking after Brian. Jack was still away, and she missed him. Dolly was now on a farm and, according to Violet, who had had a letter from her, she loved it. She'd told Violet how good their lives were now, and how much fatter she was getting. Hannah smiled. She could never imagine Dolly fat: her stick arms were the thinnest she'd ever seen. And Alice was with the kind of people she liked, who were free with money and hell-bent on enjoying themselves. She was the only one who didn't seem to have much of a future. And what about her duty to look after Alice? *Her* happiness could be ruined if Alf found out where she lived . . . Hannah drifted into a deep sleep.

The look of surprise on Alice's face when she opened the front door the following morning made Hannah smile.

'Hannah? What're you doing here? What's wrong?' Alice hustled her in. 'Don't make too much noise, Betty's still in bed. You was only over here yesterday,' she whispered over her shoulder as they mounted the stairs.

Hannah removed her hat and gloves and sat on the red plush chair. 'Alice, last night when I left here, I saw Alf.'

'So? I told you I saw him . . .'

'Alice.' Hannah's voice was firm. 'Just sit down and listen.'

Alice slowly sank in the chair. 'Did you talk to him?'

Hannah nodded. 'He took me to a pub.'

'What?'

'Now calm down and shut up, and listen very carefully.'

As Hannah began relating the conversation that had taken place with Alf the previous evening, the colour drained from Alice's face leaving bright red patches of rouge on her cheeks that made her look like a clown. For once Alice didn't interrupt.

'So, you've got to be on your guard when you go out, and if you ever see him, don't talk to him, and make sure he doesn't follow you home.'

Alice shook her head. 'But what if Uncle Harry comes looking for us?' Her voice was unsteady.

'I don't think he will. Don't forget he's never been on a tram, and I can't see him changing his habits now.'

'But what if . . . ?'

'I don't know,' snapped Hannah. 'You must be extremely careful, that's all I can say. Unless . . .' Hannah said the word slowly. She stood up and walked calmly to the window. Here was the chance she had been waiting for.

'What, Hannah?' Alice sat forward and clasped her hands. 'I'll do anything rather than face Uncle Harry.'

'Unless you come back to Maudie's.'

Alice sank back in the chair, staring at Hannah wide eyed. Slowly tears trickled down her face. 'But Hannah, I don't want to leave here.'

Hannah felt guilty. Was she being wicked to even suggest such a thing when she knew how much living here with Betty meant to Alice? 'Well, that's up to you.'

Alice's mood quickly changed. 'It's your fault,' she said angrily. 'You hit him. I wanted to help him.'

'Then what would have happened?' Hannah demanded.

'I don't know,' she paused. 'What if I do stay here?'

Hannah moved back to the chair and picked up her gloves. 'Well, you know the consequences if they ever find you.'

'But he knows it wasn't me,' whined Alice.

'Do you think that would make any difference to Uncle Harry?'

'Hannah, I don't want to go back to Maudie's.'

Hannah pulled on her gloves, her hands trembling. She knew she was being selfish, but she wanted Alice back with her. 'Well, please yourself,' she repeated. Hannah opened the door. She too had tears in her eyes. Suddenly she turned and hugged Alice. 'Take care, and write and let me know if you see him.' She held Alice tight.

That same afternoon, Hannah went to see Mary and told her the full story.

When she too recovered from the shock, Mary agreed with Maudie that Uncle Harry had to find them first, but she also agreed with Hannah that it would have been better for Alice if she had moved back here to Hope Street.

Then having unburdened herself about one trouble, she told Mary how much she missed Jack.

Mary nodded understandingly. 'I know Jack was nice, but I don't approve of what he does, and I'm sure you would never have been happy married to him. You would always be wondering if he had been picked up by the police.'

Hannah sighed. 'If only he would find a job.'

'Well, you mustn't spend your life worrying about him. You're a nice-looking young lady, so go out and find yourself a nice, hard-working young man. I see Kate's walking out with a young man.'

Hannah smiled. 'Chance would be a fine thing. There aren't many nice ones at our factory. Besides, I'm getting fed up there as well, doing the same thing day after day. I wish I could get away from everything.'

'You wouldn't leave Maudie, now would you?'

Hannah shook her head. 'I can't. I'm all she's got left now. Mary, what can I do?' Tears began to slowly trickle down her cheek.

'My oh my, we are in a sad state. It must be the time of year.'

'Don't you ever get fed up with your job?' Hannah asked, dabbing at her eyes.

'No. I get a bit cross with Matron sometimes, but that's only when she makes me do something over again. But you see, every day is different.'

Hannah played with the spoon in her saucer. Suddenly all her misery welled up inside her. 'I feel so unhappy,' she sobbed.

Mary put her arm round Hannah's shoulder. 'There, there. Don't cry. I think you're still suffering from the shock of seeing Alf. I'm sure everything will work out for the best.'

'I wish Jack and Alice would come back. Even Tom spends all his time round at Bob's. He only seems to come home to sleep, and that's not every night.' She slapped her hands in her lap. 'Even Bert would help break the monotony,' she cried.

'And if wishes were horses, beggars would ride, so the saying goes. I'm sure they'll be back one day. Now come on, cheer up. Besides, what would Maudie do without you?'

'I don't know. It's probably my fault they've all gone.'

'Now you can't say that.'

Hannah stood up. 'Well, at least Jack would still be here.'

Life carried on the same but, a few weeks later, one of Hannah's wishes did come to fruition when Bert walked through the door.

Both Hannah and Maudie were overjoyed to see him. Maudie threw her arms round his neck.

'It's good ter see yer.' She laughed. 'We needed someone ter cheer us up, didn't we 'Annah?'

Hannah nodded.

'How long yer 'ere fer?' beamed Maudie.

'Only a few days. Ernie 'ad to bring 'is wife and boy down to go to 'is grandmother's funeral, so we thought we'd 'ave a few days off.'

'That's sad,' said Maudie.

'They didn't really know her. Where's the dog?'

''E's gorn,' said Maudie. 'And Dolly and Freddie, and Jack.'

'What? What's been going on?'

Maudie sat and told Bert what had happened since he was here last.

'So Jack's gone?' Bert looked at Hannah.

She quickly turned away. She didn't want him to see the tears welling in her eyes. Wouldn't anybody she loved stay with her? If only she had a room of her own, a room she could run and hide in, she thought desperately. She didn't allow her eyes to travel back to Bert. She mustn't be alone with him. She liked him, but at the moment she was far too vulnerable to talk to him on her own.

Throughout the two days Bert was around, Hannah made sure Maudie was there when she got home from work. In the evenings they laughed and talked together. When he asked her to go out, she declined – he had no dog to give him an excuse. At night she pulled a chair close to her mattress so she would hear him if he came near to her.

On the third evening of his visit, they were finishing tea when Bert announced, 'I'll be off in the morning.' He leaned back in his chair.

'That's a shame, ain't it, 'Annah? We've really enjoyed yer being 'ere.'

'Have you, Hannah?' he asked her directly.

Hannah blushed. 'Course.'

'Just gonner 'ave a jimmy,' said Maudie.

As soon as Maudie left the room, Bert leaned forward and pulled her hand. 'Why didn't you want to come out for a walk with me last night?'

'No reason. It's cold and when I get in I'm too tired.'

'You've been avoiding being alone with me – why?'

'Have I?' Hannah hesitated, she knew she was being evasive, but how could she tell him of her mixed-up feelings, feelings she didn't understand herself. She loved Jack, but knew that was pointless. Maybe she was silly not going out with Bert? Could he make her happy? Could this be the change she needed? But would she want to move away from Maudie and Alice?

'Hannah, I wanted to have a quiet word with you.' Bert's voice was low. 'You know what I'm . . .'

Hannah quickly interrupted. 'Bert. I like you, but . . .'

'But what?'

She looked into his deep brown eyes. They were soft and kind. 'I'm afraid.'

He laughed. 'What, of me?'

She nodded.

He was still holding her hand. 'Hannah. There's something I want to ask you.'

'Cor, that's better,' said Maudie, bursting in.

Hannah quickly pulled her hand back. Bert took a cigarette from the packet on the table.

'I'll make a cuppa,' said Maudie, looking quizzically from one to the other.

Hannah jumped up. 'I'll do it.' She looked questioningly at Bert. What was it he'd wanted to ask her? It was too late to go out now. He'd probably be gone by the time she got up tomorrow. Would he come to her tonight? Tom hadn't come home. Would they be alone? Could she trust herself? She remembered the way he'd rubbed her hands last time she'd been home. She trembled with apprehension, a tingling feeling rushing all through her.

Maudie looked at her watch when the church clock struck ten. 'Tom must be staying the night wiv Bob again. I'll just fill me 'ot-water bottle, then I'll be orf. 'Annah, I fink yer better come inter my room ternight.'

'What?'

'Don't mean no disrespect, Bert, but I don't wonner be responsible fer what might 'appen between you two if yer left on yer own.'

'What?' It was Hannah asking this time.

'I see the way 'e looks at yer, and yer a pretty gel.' She held up her hand to silence them both. 'I fill sorta, well, a bit like yer muvver. I worry about yer, and I don't wont yer ter finish up like I did.'

'Maudie!' shouted Bert, jumping to his feet.

'It's all right, son, she knows about me and Albert.' She fixed him with a long, firm gaze.

He slumped in the chair and looked sheepishly at Hannah. 'I found out too late 'e was me father,' he said quietly. 'You knows I don't like talking about it, Maudie.'

Hannah wanted to hold and comfort him, he looked so hurt and vulnerable.

Maudie ignored him. 'So yer see, I don't want anyfink ter 'appen between yer. Now come on, gel, let's git ter bed.' Maudie walked off, cackling to herself.

Hannah suddenly thought of Mrs Nosy. At this moment Maudie did seem like an old witch, and she certainly sounded like one.

'I'm sorry, Hannah,' Bert said quietly. 'I don't like talking about this Albert thing. And I think she's right about us. I'm very fond of you.'

'Come on, 'Annah,' shouted Maudie from the bedroom.

'I'm coming. And Bert, I'm quite fond of you.' She quickly kissed his cheek and hurried in and shut the door. She didn't have much choice.

Maudie was propped up in bed. 'I'm sorry, gel. But yer see, I gotter look after yer.'

Hannah turned her back to her, pretending to get undressed. She couldn't let Maudie see the tears that were slowly trickling down her cheeks. What could she do? She knew Maudie meant well, but it was her life. She'd wanted to try and sort her feelings for Bert out for herself. 'Why?' she asked, angrily pulling her stockings off. 'Why can't you leave me alone?'

'You're all I got now.' Maudie put her head on her pillow.

'First you warn off Jack, now Bert. I want a life of my own. I want to get married.'

'Yer will one day; yer got plenty a time fer that. 'Sides, I don't wonner be left on me own. I'm too old ter start looking fer new kids now, and I don't fink I could cope wiv a lotta little buggers. Na, fings is good as they are.' Maudie turned over and plumped up her pillow. 'Come on, git in. You can 'ave me bottle.'

Hannah felt trapped. There was no point in arguing. Why couldn't she be strong and tell Maudie to mind her own business? She didn't know why. What was she afraid of? She crept in beside Maudie, and feeling for the stone ginger-beer bottle, cuddled it next to her. At least she had the luxury of sleeping in a bed, she thought, trying to look on the bright side.

Hannah lay listening to Maudie grunting and snoring. Should she go into Bert? She longed to be hugged and held by someone. She turned over and Maudie shouted.

'What is it? What's up?'

Hannah soothed her back to sleep, and gave up the idea of sneaking off.

The first light of dawn was slowly lighting the room when Hannah opened her eyes. Panic filled her. What was the time? Would she be late for work? She hurried into the other room, and wasn't surprised to see Bert had left. There was a note on the table addressed to her.

My dear Hannah,

Maudie was right. I do have very strong feelings for you, and she told me Jack also feels the same way. I don't want to come between you two, but what if Jack is going to be away for ever? Do you think there could be a chance for me? I will write from time to time.

Love Bert,

xxx

Hannah looked at the clear writing and held the small piece of paper to her cheek. Tears filled her eyes. Why did Maudie have to tell him about Jack? What if Bert was right and Jack never came back? Hannah wanted to run away. Run away from all the heartache that seemed to be all round her. She looked at her clock. All the running she would have to do today would be to work – otherwise she'd be late, and that would be another problem to cope with.

Chapter 18

That evening, as soon as she walked in, Hannah threw Bert's letter on to the table. The black clouds and driving rain that had mingled with her tears as she hurried from work made her even more miserable. All the way home she had been planning what to say to Maudie. She wasn't going to be trapped any longer. She was going, leaving her. Her face was burning with temper.

'No good yer chucking it at me, yer knows I can't read,' said Maudie, looking up at Hannah. 'Git yer wet fings orf, 'fore yer catches yer deaf.'

Hannah's hands were still trembling. Without even taking her hat off, she picked up the letter and read part of it out loud, leaving out the bit about, 'could there be a chance for me, and I will write from time to time'. 'So you see,' she said aggressively, 'once again you've just ruined my chance of some happiness.'

'Did 'e say where 'e lived?'

'No, he didn't.'

'So yer can't answer it then, can yer? 'E would 'ave give yer 'is address if 'e wanted yer ter write to 'im,' said Maudie smugly.

That had occurred to Hannah, but she had chosen to ignore it. 'First you warn Jack off, now Bert. They've been the only two men in my life and look what you've done – you've put an end to my chances of getting away from here.' She waved her arm round the room. 'Away from all this.' Hannah took her hat and coat off and threw them on the chair.

Maudie laughed. 'Come on love, sit down, and stop being so dramatic. Yer gitting like yer sister. I've just made a pot o' tea. Yer just a bit upset, must be a touch o' spring fever – gels git funny ideas this time o' year. Yer'll git over it. Yer'd better git yer wet stockings orf.'

Hannah sat down and did as she was told. 'You're not listening, are you? I said I'm going. I'm going to get away from all this. I mean it, you know,' she said, raising her voice angrily as she draped her stockings over the back of the chair.

Maudie looked shocked. 'Wot d'yer wonner go away fer?'

Hannah leant on the table, her clenched knuckles white, tears running down her face. 'I want to have a decent room, and a home, a proper home, not live in a hovel round the back of a wash-house.'

'It ain't a 'ovel, it's me 'ome. Yer was fankful enough ter live 'ere when yer was on the run.' Maudie was upset.

'I was just a kid then.'

'Yer could 'ave gorn when Alice left, so why all of a sudden this, "I wonner go" lark?'

Hannah couldn't answer; she didn't know herself.

'So where're yer finking of going then? Mary's?'

'She hasn't got the room,' Hannah pouted.

'What about yer mate Kate's then?' Maudie's voice rose angrily. 'If yer've made up yer mind ter go, then go. See if I care.'

Hannah looked at Maudie. 'You want me to go, don't you? Who's going to help feed you? You don't get enough from Mary to keep yourself.' Hannah knew it was an unkind thing to say, but she couldn't help herself.

Maudie stood up and grabbed up the empty teapot to her chest. 'I still got Tom 'ere.'

'What if he goes?'

'I ain't gonner sit 'ere and listen ter all this drivel. I fought I was doing the right fing. Just cos I stopped yer carrying on like a couple o' alley cats.'

'You make it sound cheap and nasty.'

'Huuh! Life ain't like all that stuff yer read in them books, yer know. What if yer finish up in the pudding club – wot then?'

Hannah hung her head. 'Bert would have married me,' she whispered.

'Would 'e? How d'yer know? 'E didn't even tell yer where 'e lived, so 'ow would yer be able ter find 'im? I tell yer gel, it's bloody 'ard bringing up a kid wiv no farver – I should know, so don't start going orf at me. I fought I was doing the right fing, seems I was wrong.' Maudie banged the teapot back on the table, making Hannah jump. 'Yer've been dying ter git away ever since Alice went. Well go on then, bugger orf. I managed 'fore yer come 'ere, and I daresay I'll manage wivout yer.' At the door of her bedroom she turned and, wagging her finger, said, 'If it 'adn't been fer you and yer keeping on, Jack might still be 'ere and I wouldn't 'ave ter bovver about keeping meself then. And, if either of 'em wanted yer, really wanted yer, they wouldn't 'ave let me interfere, so don't kid yourself!' She went inside and slammed the door.

Hannah sat and stared at the door. Could Maudie be right? If they did love her, why didn't they tell Maudie to mind her own business. But did they love her? Jack had laughed when she'd mentioned marriage. Was she fooling herself, trying to make her life sound like a silly romance? Tears ran down her face. Could she leave Maudie? It would be almost like leaving a mother. She loved Maudie, but she needed to be loved, loved by a man, loved by Jack or Bert. But at the moment she didn't know which one would bring her happiness. Perhaps neither. She put her head in her hands and wept.

* * *

The following day she called in on Mary on her way home.

'I heard all about yesterday when I collected Brian,' said Mary as she got Brian ready for bed. 'Maudie is very upset.'

'So am I,' said Hannah petulantly. 'D'you know, I wish Bert had taken me with him. I think he would have done if I'd had the opportunity to ask him, but no, Maudie has to stick her nose in.'

'Can you really be sure of that? Be fair, Hannah, she thought she was doing the right thing. She loves you, you know?'

'Well, she's got a funny way of showing it. Why couldn't she let me make up my own mind?'

'She was only trying to protect you.'

'Well, I don't need her protection. I've made up my mind, I'm definitely leaving her.'

'Where are you going?'

'I don't know. It's a pity Miss King lives here, otherwise I could have come here.'

Mary looked up. 'Well, yes. I suppose you could. But what about Maudie? I don't give her enough to live on, how would she manage?'

'I don't know.'

Mary looked a little put out. 'Why don't you go and have a word with Alice, she might be of some help. She might suggest you stay at her house, even if it's only for a weekend, it would be a break.'

Hannah nodded thoughtfully. 'That's a good idea. I could go and see her on Saturday.'

Mary gathered Brian up in her arms. 'Say good-night to Hannah.' She held Brian close to Hannah's face for a kiss.

'Good-night,' Hannah smiled, and gently touched his face which made him giggle.

'I'll just put him down. You can put the kettle on if you like.' At the door, Brian squirmed in Mary's arms and, looking over his mother's shoulder, waved.

Hannah looked around her. She wanted a house of her own so much. Then she'd be happy.

All week, Hannah moped around, the atmosphere between Maudie and her very strained. They only spoke when it was necessary, and they were both glad when Tom walked in to relieve the tension.

'I'm going to see Alice tomorrow, so don't bother about getting me any tea,' said Hannah on Friday night as Maudie stood up to go to bed.

Maudie didn't answer.

When Hannah arrived at Alice's house the following afternoon, she was surprised to see her dressed in a really smart outdoor outfit, obviously ready to go out. She looked far older than her fifteen years.

Alice ushered her inside. 'I didn't expect to see you today,' hissed Alice, looking far from pleased.

'Where're you off to?' asked Hannah.

'We're going shopping.'

'With Betty?'

'No, she's out.'

'Oh. I was hoping we could have a little chat.'

Alice was clearly agitated. 'What about?'

Hannah sat down. 'About all sorts of things. Alice, I've got to talk to someone, I don't get much chance to talk . . .'

'I'm sorry Hannah,' interrupted Alice, 'But I must . . .'

'Hello, who have we here?' A tall, good-looking young man came into the room.

'This is my sister, Hannah,' said Alice, smiling. She tilted her head and looked coy, and her dimples deepened.

He politely shook Hannah's hand. 'Alice is always talking about you.'

'Is she? Nice things, I hope.' Hannah felt awkward, and although she didn't know why, she was trying to make a good impression. But beside Alice, she felt dowdy, young and silly.

'Hannah, this is Roy, he lives here,' Alice added quickly.

'Me and dozens of others. But it's only temporary. Say, why don't you come out with us? We're going on for a meal after Madam here has finished her shopping, then we're going on to the music hall. How about it?'

'Hannah has to get back,' said Alice quickly. 'Besides, she hasn't really come dressed up to go out, have you?'

Hannah could have died, she was wearing her best hat and fox-fur, and Alice was ashamed of her. Once again, Hannah felt she was being rejected. 'No, no thank you. That's very kind of you,' she said softly. 'Who's looking after John?'

'He's with Betty; they've gone to look at a boarding school.'

'For John?'

Alice nodded.

'But he's only small,' said Hannah.

'That's what I said, but Betty insisted.'

'What about you? What will happen to your job?'

Alice looked angry. 'It won't be for a while yet. Besides, I still have to see that things go smoothly for Betty in the house.'

'But that's only till she goes off somewhere,' said Roy.

'Betty's going away?' asked Hannah.

'We don't know.' Alice was pouting. 'Come on, Roy. Sorry about this, Hannah. I'll write and let you know if I go too.' She ushered Hannah out of the room.

Outside, Alice waved goodbye, and she and Roy strolled off in the opposite direction to the one Hannah was going to take. Hannah could have cried, she felt so unhappy. She wanted to talk to her sister. She needed her. Why did Alice always have to have her own way? Why did she always get what she wanted?

Any idea Hannah might have had of moving in with her had been well and truly quashed.

Although Hannah was unhappy with her situation, she knew she had to live with it. Things did not get any easier between her and Maudie throughout the spring of 1914. The one letter she had from Alice was full of the usual comments about the people who lived in the house, and the fact that John wouldn't be going to a boarding school after all for many years yet. Tom was staying with Bob more and more, and when he brought in any papers, Hannah read with interest about the trouble the suffragettes were causing. There were even times she thought of going to one of their meetings in the hope of seeing Jack.

It was May, and today was her birthday, but as usual she wandered home without much enthusiasm. As she turned into Hope Street she bumped into Mary.

'Hello, Mary. Don't often see you out this time of day.' Hannah peered into the large pram. 'And how's our Brian today?'

He smiled and banged his wooden spoon on the side of his pram.

'I'm just popping along to Herman's. I was hoping I'd see you, I've got a letter for you.'

'I expect it's from Alice.'

'It's not her writing.'

Hannah was intrigued. 'Nobody else knows your address.'

'Well, let me get it for you.' Mary pushed the pram the few yards to her front door. She was out again in an instant, and handed the letter to Hannah.

Hannah gasped when she read the address, aware of her face flushing.

'You all right?' asked Mary.

'Yes, yes thank you. It's from Bert,' she said huskily. 'It's

241

his handwriting.' She turned the envelope over. She had re-read his first note so many times that she instantly recognized it.

'Well, I'll be off. By the way, Happy Birthday.'

Beaming, she clutched the letter. 'My birthday? Fancy you remembering.'

'I must confess I didn't – it was Maudie who told me.'

'Maudie?' said Hannah. 'But I deliberately didn't remind her.'

'Well, she obviously didn't need reminding. I'll see you later, bye.'

'Bye,' said Hannah, adding softly to herself. 'Fancy Maudie remembering, and why did she tell Mary?'

''Allo gel,' said Mrs Warren, who lived opposite Mary. She was sitting on a chair outside her front door. ''Er little 'en's getting on a real treat, ain't 'e? Should see 'im up at the window.'

Hannah nodded. She didn't really want to stop and talk, but Mrs Warren was a big, friendly woman who hadn't lived in the street very long. Mary always had a good word to say about her, not like some of the neighbours.

'I'm waiting fer young Ted,' Mrs Warren panted. Because of her weight, she had a lot of difficulty breathing. ''E's gorn ter git a job.' Her face broke into a smile and her eyes disappeared into the folds of her flesh.

Hannah was dying to open her letter, but she forced herself to be polite. 'Where's he gone?'

'Over the tanneries – 'e's gonner be apprenticed,' she said proudly. 'Mind you, I dunno 'ow 'e's gonner stand it. It stinks ter 'igh 'eaven over there, but I told 'im, beggars can't be choosers, now can they?'

Hannah smiled. 'No. How old is Ted now?'

'Just gorn sixteen, this'll be 'is first job. Well, first proper job anyway.' With the bottom of her apron she dabbed at the beads of perspiration glistening on her face.

'I wish him good luck.'

'Fanks, gel.'

Hannah walked on. Summer would soon be here, she thought, and everybody would be sitting outside, kids shouting and running about, all the gossips waiting to jump on any morsel they could chew over. Maudie didn't provide very much now. Walking through the gate of the high railings that surrounded the wash-house, Hannah stopped and sat on the wall in the courtyard and excitedly opened her letter. It was from Bert, just one page. He had bothered to write after all and this time there was an address for her to reply to. Tears filled her eyes. He had remembered Mary's address.

> My dear Hannah,
>
> I was hoping I would be able to get down to see you some time, but at this time of the year we are very busy. We never had any time alone together. I suppose that was my fault, I should have told you how I felt, but I was concerned as I know how you feel about Jack, and if he is back I'll understand if you don't write.

He went on to tell her about his mate Ernie and the kids. As she finished his quietly respectful letter, for the first time in months Hannah felt happy. It was her birthday, and she'd had a letter from Bert. She quickly put it in her handbag. She wouldn't tell Maudie – there wasn't any point.

Chapter 19

Hannah was taken by surprise when, as soon as she walked in, Maudie said cheerfully, ''Appy Birfday, 'Annah.'

The table was set out for a birthday tea. The extra candles were in place and there was a small cake and sandwiches. Hannah stood and looked at it, then she turned her gaze towards Maudie, who was grinning from ear to ear. For the first time Hannah realized how frail Maudie was beginning to look, how much she had changed in the past four years. Four years, thought Hannah as she sat at the table, so much had changed. Alice and Dolly had gone, and her past life hardly entered her head now, more so since she knew she hadn't killed Uncle Harry, and she'd stopped having those bad dreams. She smiled at Maudie, who now wasn't quite the little round person with the ginger hair who had found them. Maudie's hair, which she wore in a bun on top of her head, now had a generous sprinkling of white. Her overall was always clean and white, but she still shuffled around in old shoes that were split at the sides to make room for her bunions.

'Can't fergit yer birfday, now can I? 'Sides, yer knows how I like birfdays, even if it's only the two of us. Got yer a little present, though – go on, open it.'

Hannah picked up the small parcel, and eagerly tore it open. 'What can I say?' she whispered.

'Yer could try fanks,' Maudie laughed. 'Been saving up fer it.'

Hannah found she had tears rolling down her face. Maudie had remembered her birthday, she was the only one. She looked down at the tortoiseshell button-hook in her hands.

'I've seen the time it takes yer ter do up the buttons on those new boots of yours, so I fought I get yer one o' them.' Maudie looked embarrassed.

Hannah couldn't contain herself any longer. She jumped up and threw her arms round Maudie and hugged her close.

''Ere, come on, love, can't 'ave yer crying on yer birfday, now can we?' Maudie patted her back in a comforting way. 'Yer knows wot they say? Cry on yer birfday, and yer'll be crying all the year round.'

Hannah tried to smile. 'Oh Maudie, you're the only one to remember,' she sobbed. 'I didn't even get a letter from Alice. I'm sorry. I've been so rotten to you, but . . .' She couldn't speak, and her tears continued to fall.

'Sit yerself down, tea's made. Tom said 'e'll pop in later, when 'e's finished – 'e ain't forgotten yer, I fink 'e's got yer a little sumfink.'

Hannah sat down. Just as Maudie was pouring out the tea, Mary walked in.

'Mary, what are you doing here? And where's Brian?' asked Hannah.

'Yer just in time fer a cuppa,' said Maudie.

Mary looked at Hannah. 'Maudie asked me round for tea. Mrs Warren's keeping an eye on Brian. Besides, I had to bring you round your present.'

Once more Hannah was tearing at a brown paper parcel, and this time she had a pair of white crocheted gloves. 'Did you make these?' She asked, touched.

Mary nodded.

'They are lovely. Thank you.' She kissed Mary's cheek.

'So you see,' laughed Mary. 'It hasn't turned out to be a bad day after all. First you had your letter from Bert, then Maudie gave you this little surprise.'

'Yer got a letter from Bert?' said Maudie quickly. 'Yer didn't tell me.'

Hannah was flustered. 'I didn't get a chance. I'll show you later.'

To her relief, Maudie seemed quite satisfied with that.

It was well after Mary had left and they were sitting quietly when Maudie asked, 'What did Bert 'ave ter say, then?'

'Not a lot, really, just that they are very busy at this time of the year.'

'Did 'e give yer 'is address?'

'Yes, yes he did.'

'Yer gonner write to 'im then?'

'Yes, I expect I will.'

Maudie smiled. 'That'll be nice fer 'im.'

It was then that Tom came home with her present, one of the latest magazines for women. Hannah was thrilled; she and Maudie pored over every page, laughing at some of the outrageous fashions.

''Ere, could yer see me in that?' Maudie was pointing at a picture of the new hobble skirts. 'Can't say I'd wonner show me ankles like she is.'

'Yer wouldn't 'alf look a right one bringing 'ome some firewood in that,' laughed Tom. 'That'd give old Ma Nosy sumfink ter go on about.'

Hannah was laughing too. 'Mind you, that's the sort of thing that Betty wears.'

'That the woman Alice lives wiv?' asked Maudie.

Hannah nodded.

'What about Alice, d'yer fink she'd wear it?' asked Tom, looking over their shoulders.

'I expect she will one day.'

247

'I miss 'er, yer know.'

'We all do, son,' said Maudie sadly as she fished for her handkerchief. 'And Dolly and Freddie.'

'D'yer fink Jack'll come back?' asked Tom.

'Dunno.' Maudie blew her nose.

'He's been gone quite a while now,' said Hannah softly.

'Yer. Still, I expect 'e'll be back.'

Hannah looked at Maudie, and her heart was once more full of love for her. She was the one person in the world she could depend on to really care about her. How could she ever have thought of leaving her?

It was as though everything in Hannah's life was settling down again. Perhaps Maudie had been right and she had been suffering from spring fever; even the weather was settling down now, and May was proving to be long and hot. Alice had written and apologized for forgetting her birthday, but most of the letter was full of what Roy had bought her, and their visit to the music hall. Hannah answered Bert's letter, telling him about her birthday tea, and she even confessed that she missed him, and would be looking forward to his reply. Many nights, as she lay on the floor listening to Maudie snoring, she tried to compare Bert with Jack. She was now sleeping in Maudie's room since the Bert affair. She was quite happy about that: it meant she didn't have to drag her mattress out every night, and when Tom slept away she was nervous of being in the large room on her own, as many a time she heard the scurry of mice now Bonzo had gone. Maudie was also letting her use her cupboard for her clothes.

The following week, on a warm, pleasant evening, Hannah decided to call in on Kate on her way home from work.

''Annah. Come on in. We ain't seen yer fer weeks.' Kate looked very happy, Hannah noticed.

'Well, you're always working,' she said as she picked her way down the dark, overcrowded passage.

Kate turned and smiled. 'Yer, got ter grab all the overtime I can git.' Kate pushed open the kitchen door. 'Look, Mum, it's 'Annah.'

Mrs Linton was just as pleased as Kate to see her, and Hannah felt guilty at not calling on them before.

They sat outside in the corner of the tiny yard that was criss-crossed with lines full of lethargic wet washing, and caught up with what little news they had. Grace was working, and so was Billy, and Sally, the youngest girl, was now going round to help the lady who made the matchboxes.

'So yer see, 'Annah, fings is looking good. Got a few bob coming in now,' whispered Mrs Linton, looking over her shoulder at the brick wall as if to catch someone peering over. 'Just ser long as that old man o' mine don't find out, ovverwise 'e'll be back.'

'Yer, well, if 'e does my Charlie'll frow 'im out,' said Kate aggressively.

'Is Charlie your young man?' asked Hannah.

Kate's face lit up. 'Yer. 'E's nice, ain't 'e, Mum?'

Mrs Linton too smiled. 'Yer. 'E's a good lad.'

'On August Bank 'Oliday Monday 'e's taking me ter Soufend. The firm's got a charabang outing and we've bin putting away tuppence a week ter pay for it. Should be ever ser good. I ain't 'arf looking forward to it. Ain't ever been ter the seaside before, or bin on a chara. Just fink, I'll be sitting wiv Charlie, and the wind'll be blowing me 'air.'

'Let's 'ope it don't rain,' said Mrs Linton.

'Oh, Mum, don't say fings like that.'

Hannah laughed. 'It should be lovely. I've never seen the sea. Our firm went there last year.'

'Did they 'ave a chara?'

Hannah nodded.

'Why didn't yer go?'

'I didn't have anyone to go with. Besides, they're all a lot older than me, and well, I don't know. I suppose I would have felt a bit out of place.'

'Yer daft 'aporth.'

'That's what Maudie said.'

'I dunno why yer stays there if yer not 'appy. We 'ave a lotta laughs at our place. Why don't yer give it a try? Did they enjoy 'emselves on the outing?'

'I think so, although most of them got so drunk they didn't know what they got up to – and d'you know?' She bent her head closer. 'One of them finished up in the family way.'

Mrs Linton laughed. 'See. I told our Kate. Yer gotter be careful wiv all that booze about. All sorts a fings can 'appen.'

'Yer, well, I'll be wiv Charlie. Where're your lot going this year?'

'To Margate.'

'Is that at the seaside?'

'Yes.'

'Don't yer wish yer was going wiv 'em?'

'Yes, I do in some ways,' Hannah said a little wistfully.

They laughed and talked and, after a while, Hannah said her goodbyes and left. She shuddered at the thought of working in the pickle factory. Kate meant well, but that wasn't for her. But she envied her the trip. She was going on an open-top chara – with her new young man.

After Hannah's birthday, things seemed to get better bit by bit. First there was the letter from Bert. Then, a week after seeing Kate, Jack walked in.

''Allo, gel. Bit 'ot, ain't it?' he said, casually throwing his trilby on the chair as if he'd only been away for a few days. He undid his tie.

'Jack,' was all Hannah could utter, trying to hold back her tears of happiness.

'Where's Maudie?'

'She's sitting outside.'

'She still smoking that bloody old pipe o' 'ers?'

Hannah nodded. Why didn't he kiss her? Why didn't he say he missed her? 'Are you staying long?' she croaked.

'A while. I'll just pop out ter Maudie.'

When Maudie clapped her eyes on him, she jumped up and screamed with delight. 'Jack, me boy. How are yer?' She gathered him in her arms.

'Not ser bad,' he gasped when she let him go.

'It's bin a long while. Yer staying long?'

'Yer, I fink so.'

Hannah followed him out. She too wanted to throw her arms round him. He was going to stay.

'Yer bin gorn quite a while this time,' said Maudie.

'Almost five months,' said Hannah.

'Didn't it work out wiv yer lady friend then?'

Hannah shuddered, her heart beating very fast, pounding in her head while she waited for the answer.

'I told yer before, Maudie, I wasn't wiv a woman.' He sat on the wall and lit a cigarette. He glanced at Hannah. 'If yer must know, yer nosy pair o' cows, I've bin in the nick.'

Hannah's mouth dropped open, and Maudie let out a moan.

Jack jumped up and pointed his finger at Hannah. ''Fore yer say anyfink, I didn't git nicked fer pinching. I got twenty-eight days fer being in a ruckus.'

''Ow long yer bin out?' asked Maudie.

'A couple a weeks.'

'So where yer bin all this time?'

'Well, when I first left, I fought I'd go over an' see Rick.'

'What, the Rick who Alice lives with?' yelled Hannah. 'You

went to see Alice? She didn't tell me . . .'

'I didn't go ter see Alice. 'Sides, she was out – and I went ter see Rick. I fought he might know a fing or two 'bout places to live, seeing as how 'e's got that big 'ouse an' all sorts seem to come and go there.'

'You went over there to stay?' asked Hannah, almost in disbelief.

'Na, course not. But I fought I'd make inquiries, just the same.'

Hannah looked at him suspiciously.

He grinned at her. 'Well, Rick told me about a mate of 'is over in Befnel Green. 'E 'as a lot a blokes what's down on their luck living there. That Rick's a nice bloke, 'e even took me over there in 'is car. D'yer know, 'e was showing me 'ow ter drive. I tell yer, I wouldn't mind 'aving a go at that. Well, anyway, I only stayed wiv 'em for a couple o' weeks – I swear they're all daft, those featre lot, bloody mad 'as 'atters, they are. Got a bit tired o' it after a while. I left there and started sleeping rough.' He drew long and hard on his cigarette, then, with the toe of his boot, he ground the butt into the ground. 'I was finking of coming back 'ere, but then I went ter one o' them suffragette meetings. I'd only just got there and the ruckus started. The rozzers picked me up, but they didn't find nuffink on me, so they could only do me for fighting.'

Hannah sat on the wall. 'You went to prison? Was it very awful in there?'

'Can't say I'd like ter make an 'abit of it,' he said light-heartedly.

Hannah wanted to smile and say, I told you so, but the expression on Jack's face made her think better of it.

'Well, wot's being going on 'ere since I've been away?'

'Not a lot really. Yer know Dolly didn't come back?'

Jack nodded.

'Bert's bin back, though – 'e's writing ter 'Annah.'

'What? What did 'e want this time?'

'Nuffink. In fact, 'e give me a couple of pounds,' said Maudie smugly.

'Did 'e now? Wonder where 'e got that from?'

'I didn't ask – I expect 'e worked fer it.'

'O yer, I forgot 'e's turned honest.'

Hannah also looked astonished. She didn't know Bert had given Maudie that much.

Jack turned to Hannah. 'So 'e writes ter yer now? What does 'e 'ave ter say, then?'

'I've only had the one letter so far, and he really didn't say much at all.'

'Yer staying 'ere now then, Jack?' asked Maudie.

'Yer, might as well,' he said casually.

Maudie stood up. 'Well, please yer bloody self, I ain't gitting on me knees ter ask yer to stop 'ere.'

Hannah looked at him. He appeared to be thinner, his clothes didn't look so smart, but he was still good-looking, and *she* would willingly have gone down on her knees to beg him to stay. 'You've been gone a long while,' she said softly.

'Yer, it's bin a while. D'yer see anyfink of Alice these days?'

'Yes, sometimes.'

'I could murder a cuppa,' he said, his eyes twinkling.

'I'll make it,' said Hannah, hoping he would follow her and she'd have him all to herself.

'I'll 'ave a chat ter me old mate Maudie.' He grinned at the old lady who beamed back at him.

Disappointed, Hannah walked inside. He didn't want to see her on his own. Was he telling the truth about going to prison just for fighting?

Later that evening, when Tom came home, he too was pleased to see Jack and eager to tell him about Bob, and how much he enjoyed working for him.

When it was time for bed, Hannah made her way as usual to Maudie's room. She lay thinking about Jack and comparing him with Bert. Bert was honest and hard-working, but deep down she knew he could never have a place in her heart like Jack.

The long hot summer days were drifting on. Hannah was upset that Jack didn't ask her out, and he had gone back to his old ways. Night after night she lay restless in Maudie's room, longing to go and talk to him, just to find out his true feelings, but he never let the opportunity arise.

One warm evening near the end of July, she turned listlessly into Hope Street. The road teemed with children playing with buckets of water, laughing and splashing, the girls screaming. All day it had been stifling hot in the factory, and Hannah had been thankful when six o'clock came. Next Monday was the Bank Holiday and, as she passed Kate's house, she thought of her going to Southend, seeing the sea, standing and letting the water trickle over her bare feet. She was sorry she wasn't going to Margate, getting away from all the smoke and heat. She ran her hand round the back of her wet neck. Perhaps she could talk Jack into taking her out for the day. She hastened her step, and smiled, nodding politely to her neighbours sitting outside their front doors.

As she walked in, Hannah put her hat on the chair. 'It's warm out there.'

'Fings are 'ottin' up in Europe too,' said Jack, his nose in the newspaper. 'Don't like the look of what's 'appening over in Germany.'

'Yer don't fink there'll be a war, do yer son?' Maudie sounded distressed.

'Wouldn't like ter say.'

Hannah sat at the table. 'Will it affect us?'

'Dunno. They says 'ere it depends if the Germans go inter Belgium.'

Hannah too had been concerned about the news lately, but hadn't said too much to Maudie. She didn't see the point. 'Jack, shall we go out for the day on Monday?' she suddenly asked.

He looked up from the newspaper. 'Dunno. Where're yer finking of going then – over ter see Alice?'

'No, I expect she's going out. Kate's going on the firm's outing to Southend.'

'I told yer yer should 'ave gorn wiv yer firm last year. Where're they orf to this time then?' asked Maudie.

'Margate.'

'Where's that?'

'In Kent.'

'Is it near Dolly?'

'Shouldn't think so. Kent's a big place.'

'Sounds posh.'

Hannah laughed. 'I bet it's a lot cooler.'

'Can't yer go wiv 'em?' asked Maudie.

'No, the chara's full.'

'That's a shame.'

'So, where d'yer reckon on going then, gel?' asked Jack as he folded the newspaper.

'Oh, not as far as Southend, or Margate. What about just going into the country, or what about a boat trip up the river? Elsie at work did that, she said it was ever so good.'

Jack smiled. 'S'pose that's one way of keeping me out of somebody's pocket.'

'That's not the reason. I didn't mean . . . I didn't even think of that.'

'Yer gotter 'and it to 'er, son, she's clever,' laughed Maudie. 'She's got it all worked out.'

'No, I haven't,' said Hannah angrily. 'I told you, I didn't even think of that.' She stormed outside and sat on the wall.

Jack followed her out. 'Sorry, gel, I didn't mean ter upset yer.'

Hannah turned her back on him despite the fact every muscle in her body wanted to hold him close.

He sat next to her and gently turned her to face him. 'I'm sorry, gel. Course I'll take yer out – take yer anywhere yer like.'

'Jack,' she said quietly. 'Do you still like me?'

'Course I do.'

'But you haven't asked me out and, since you came back, we haven't had a chance to talk.'

He stood up and, with his hands thrust deep in his pockets, he kicked the wall. 'Yer still writing ter Bert?'

She nodded.

'Yer, well. Yer see, I've bin finking a lot about what yer said before, before I went away.' He turned and looked at her. 'Yer know, yer a nice-looking kid.'

Hannah could have cried, he still looked on her as a kid sister. She stood up. What was the point? But she had to ask him. 'So, what have you been thinking about?'

He looked embarrassed. 'Yer know? What yer said about us gitting . . .'

Hannah gazed at him, astonished. Surely he wasn't going to propose?

He sat down again. 'If yer don't keep on about me wicked ways . . .' He laughed nervously. 'I reckon you and me could make a go of it.'

Hannah couldn't believe her ears. 'What you mean . . . ? You mean, get married?'

'Well, yer, I suppose so. Yer, why not?'

Hannah gasped. 'You mean it? Really mean it?'

'Course.'

She threw her arms round his neck and smothered his face with kisses.

''Ere, steady on, gel.'

'We must go and tell Maudie.'

'Yer, well, 'ang on a mo,' he protested, 'I only said . . .' but Hannah wasn't listening.

'Come on, quick.' She grabbed his hand and dragged him inside.

'Maudie, Maudie,' she screamed. 'Me and Jack's going to get married.'

Maudie sat in her armchair. 'Well, I'll be buggered. What brought this on?'

Hannah looked at Jack, waiting for him to speak, but he said nothing.

Maudie looked from one to the other. 'It's a bit sudden, ain't it?'

'Aren't you pleased?' asked Hannah, slightly deflated.

'Yer, course I am, love.' But her tone was indifferent.

Hannah was disappointed at her reaction. She had expected her to be more excited.

'When yer finking of tying the knot, then?'

'Dunno,' said Jack. 'Give us a chance, only just mentioned it, and she drags me in 'ere.'

'I'll make a cup of tea,' said Hannah, all her dreams of everyone laughing and throwing their arms round them both, sharing their joy, quickly fading.

'Where're yer gonner live?' asked Maudie.

'Dunno,' said Jack. ''Ere, I s'pose. Ain't really fought about it, she ain't give me time.'

Hannah quickly glanced across at him. She didn't want to live here. She wanted a house.

'I ain't giving up me room,' said Maudie. 'So you'll 'ave ter tell Tom ter move out.'

'Couldn't we find a house?' asked Hannah.

'Na, where would I git the money from ter pay the rent?'

'Yer, and what would 'appen ter me, I ain't got enough ter live on,' said Maudie.

Hannah couldn't believe that the thing she wanted most – to marry Jack – was beginning to cause so many problems so quickly. 'I'll have to write and tell Alice,' she said.

'We could go over and see 'er, if yer like,' said Jack.

'Yes, that would be nice. We'll go after the holiday.'

Hannah began to wonder what difference being married to Jack would make? At the moment, and as far as she could see, it would only mean sharing his mattress. She wanted more. She wanted a home, a proper home, and children. They hadn't discussed children, in fact they hadn't discussed anything. He hadn't even said he loved her. She sat at the table and studied him, and once more fear gripped her. What if he got caught by the police, and was put in prison? What sort of a husband would he be then? Suddenly Hannah's feelings were in a turmoil. She loved him, but was this what she really wanted? To stay here and live like this?

When Tom came home he was more enthusiastic over the forthcoming marriage than Maudie. He nudged Hannah. 'Yer knows why 'e's asked yer, don't yer?'

She shook her head.

''E's frightened yer gonner run orf wiv someone else.' He glanced mischievously at Jack.

She laughed, 'Chance would be a fine thing.'

'I reckon 'e's worried about Bert. Cor, that wouldn't 'alf be a turn-up fer the book, you going orf wiv 'im.'

Hannah was embarrassed. 'Don't talk silly, Tom.'

'Yer still gonner live 'ere then, 'Annah? Yer not gonner move away?' said Tom.

'Na,' said Jack. 'Ain't a lotta point. 'Sides, I ain't gotter a lotta money fer furniture and stuff.'

'That's good,' said Tom. 'I've bin finking of moving in wiv Bob, but I didn't want ter leave Maudie, I knows she likes my little bit coming in every week, but now you two are gonner live 'ere I fink I'll go wiv Bob. 'Sides, yer don't want me looking over yer shoulder every night.'

Hannah blushed. She and Jack would have had no privacy with Tom in the room.

'Well, they ain't 'aving my bed,' said Maudie.

'Don't you want me to get married?' asked Hannah. 'I thought you would have been pleased.'

'I am. But I don't want it upsetting me ways. I'm orf now. Come on, 'Annah, remember yer got ter git up fer work in the morning. Just cos yer getting married, don't mean ter say yer gonner be a lady of leisure.'

Jack didn't suggest they went outside to talk, he just kissed her cheek, wished her good-night, and Hannah reluctantly followed Maudie.

Hannah lay thinking about her wedding. They hadn't talked about a date, or whether it would be in a church. Would Alice be pleased? Would Alice even come? This wasn't how she had imagined it would be, not a bit like it was in the books. What would she wear? Hannah sighed. She wouldn't say anything to anyone else at the moment, she decided. She was beginning to wonder if Jack had really meant it. Had he asked her just because he was jealous of Bert? Was it her fault? Had she been too quick, pushing him into this corner?

Chapter 20

As Hannah made her way to work the following morning, the heat of the day was beginning to rise. Windows were being flung open to catch even the smallest breeze, and although snatches of loud conversation drifted through the open doors, she wasn't really aware of them. Her thoughts were on last night. She hadn't slept very well, and this morning Jack had left before she was up. To get away from her and her questions?

All day her mind had drifted from her work as she thought about Jack and whether he really wanted to marry her.

''Ere, wot's up wiv you?' asked Rosie as they filed out at lunch-time. 'Yer've looked right fed up all morning.' She gave Hannah a nudge. 'Yer feeling all right?'

'Yes, I'm all right,' said Hannah.

'It's like a bloody sweat-shop in there,' said Rosie, wiping a grey piece of rag round her face. She sat on the wall and pulled her thick black skirt way up over her knees.

'Put yer skirt down, Rosie,' said Elsie, looking over her shoulder. 'Yer showing yer drawers and yer stocking-tops.'

'I don't care. If I 'ad me way I'd be working in just me chemise and me drawers.' Rosie threw her head back and laughed.

Elsie laughed with her. 'I bet old Wally would like ter see that! Yer a dirty cow.'

'I suppose you're looking forward to going to Margate on Monday,' said Hannah.

'Yer, not 'arf. They've got gawd knows 'ow many crates o'

beer in. Looks like we're gonner 'ave a real good time. Let's 'ope it stays fine.'

'That shouldn't worry you,' said Elsie.

'I still wonner paddle.'

'Why's that, so yer can lift yer skirts?'

'Don't keep on about me. Wot about some of the ovvers? At least I ain't got no old man ter worry about.'

'It must be nice to paddle in the sea,' said Hannah. 'I've never seen the sea.'

'That's a shame. I told yer yer should come wiv us. 'Ere, yer not 'aving second foughts about the outing, are yer, 'Annah?' asked Elsie.

'No.' Hannah's reply sounded very half-hearted.

'Cos if yer are, I reckon I could git yer on our chara.'

'No, no thank you. That's very kind of you but I'm going up the Thames.'

'D'yer know, I like it when yer talks, yer always sound ser nice. I'm always surprised old Wally ain't got yer a job in the office.'

Hannah smiled at Elsie. She knew why she hadn't got a job in the office. It was because she didn't let him get too close to her and allow him to touch her, like a lot of them did.

''Ere, who yer going up the river wiv then, gel – yer boyfriend?' asked Rosie.

Hannah blushed. 'Just someone I know.'

'Wot yer blushing fer? Is 'e nice?' Rosie swung her legs over the edge of the wall and pulled down her skirt.

Hannah wasn't going to tell them it was her future husband. Well, not just yet.

'I went up-river once,' said Elsie.

'Yer, so yer told us.' Rosie lifted her eyes to the sky. 'Kept on about it fer weeks, yer did.'

Elsie shot her a glance of disapproval. 'Well, let's face it, I don't git many days out. You'll like it,' she said to Hannah.

Her voice was drowned by the lunch-time hooter calling them back to work. Hannah felt relieved she didn't have to answer any more questions.

Jack wasn't home when Hannah walked in that evening.

'Tea's made,' said Maudie.

Hannah took off her hat. 'It's been warm again today.' She paused. 'Maudie, are you pleased about me and Jack?'

'Yer, course I am.' She had her back to Hannah so she couldn't see her face. 'When yer finking of doing it then?' she asked.

'Don't know, we haven't really discussed it.'

Maudie turned. 'Yer sure yer doing the right fing, love?' Her voice was full of concern.

'Why? Why do you ask?'

'Well, the way yer carry on about 'im nicking fings.'

Hannah had no answer.

''E ain't gonner stop, yer know.' Maudie looked at her long and hard. 'Yer sure it's not just an excuse to git away?'

Hannah shrugged her shoulders. 'But I'm not going to get away, am I? Jack wants to stay here, so things won't be any different, will they?'

'No, s'pose not.'

An hour later, Jack walked in, and all her doubts seemed to disappear the minute she saw his smile.

Hannah followed him outside and sat and watched him prepare to wash at the tap. He rolled up his sleeves, pulled down his braces, and splashed water over his face. She handed him a towel, longing to hold him and kiss him.

'That's better.' He handed her back the towel. 'I've bin finking, gel, we could go over and see yer sister termorrer if yer like.'

'That would be nice, and what about Monday? I would like to go up the river.'

'Yer, well, let's git one day over at a time. Fancy a stroll later on?'

She smiled. 'That would be lovely.'

As they walked round the park, the band was playing. They sat on a seat and Hannah's heart was full. She was sitting here with Jack listening to the music, and she was going to marry him. 'Jack, have you thought any more about what you said about us getting married?'

'Can't say I 'ave, why?'

'I thought we could work out a date, then we can tell Alice tomorrow.'

'I fink we should wait a bit.'

'But why? Why can't I tell Alice?'

'Give it time, we ain't in no 'urry. 'Sides, I don't know what yer 'ave ter do.'

'I could ask Mary on Sunday.'

'Yer, OK, but only 'er – let's keep it to ourselves fer the time being.'

'Why?'

'Don't like ter rush fings.' He patted the back of her hand.

She was upset. Why had he bothered to ask her if he wasn't ready? She paused, summoning her courage. 'Jack, do you really want to marry me?'

'Yer, course I do.'

'You don't seem to be . . . I don't know.'

'Look, 'Annah. I told yer I want to, so let's leave it at that, shall we? By the way, I don't wonner do it in church.'

Hannah was stunned. She'd always wanted to get married in church, it was the right and proper thing to do it like that. But if Jack was so adamant . . . 'All right, if that's what you want,' she whispered meekly.

All the way home they avoided any more talk of the wedding. When they reached the door, Hannah was longing for him to kiss her, to hold her, to whisper that he loved her. He hadn't ever told her that he loved her.

Suddenly he took her in his arms and all her fears melted. His kisses were hard and forceful; she felt she was being swept away. What would it be like being married? To have his body next to hers? She hoped she didn't have to wait too long to find out.

On Saturday afternoon, Hannah ran laughing up the steps to Alice's front door. She was so happy as she banged on the knocker. She turned and looked around at Jack standing on the bottom step. There was no reply. She banged harder, and the door was opened by a stranger.

'Hello,' she said. 'Is my sister in?'

'And who is your sister, pray?'

'Alice.'

The man looked over Hannah's shoulder. 'I'm afraid our blessed little Alice is out. I'll tell her you called.'

'Will she be out long?'

'Can't say, dear.'

Hannah was very disappointed. 'You won't forget, will you?'

'Course not, dear. Bye.' He closed the door.

Hannah made her way back down the steps. 'She's out,' she said angrily. 'She always seems to go out on a Saturday afternoon. D'you think she does it on purpose, just in case I come over?'

'I shouldn't fink so.' Jack took hold of her arm. 'Not to worry, come on, let's get the tram back.'

As they walked on, a brewer's dray ambled along beside them. Hannah hung back, turning her head away from the road.

Jack stopped. 'What's up? 'Ere, you all right? Yer gorn as white as a ghost.'

'Nothing. I was just a bit upset at not seeing Alice.'

'Yer be'aved like yer wanted to avoid that bloke,' he nodded towards the back of the cart, 'be the way yer were lookin'.'

'What bloke?' asked Hannah, trying to look relaxed. To her relief it hadn't been Alf, after all. She walked on normally. Should she tell Jack about Uncle Harry? What would he say about that, and would he be angry with her for always going on about him stealing when what she had done had been just as wicked? And would she always have this fear of bumping into Alf again?

'Come on, let's git 'ome,' said Jack, shaking his head in puzzlement.

On Sunday afternoon, Hannah went to see Mary. 'Jack has asked me to marry him,' she announced out of the blue.

Mary put Brian on the floor. 'Hannah, I'm so pleased for you!' she exclaimed, giving her a hug. 'When's the great day going to be?'

'I don't know. Jack hasn't said.'

'Where are you going to live?'

'Still at Maudie's.'

Mary sat down. 'Is this what you want?'

'I don't know. I want to marry Jack, but I also want a home, a proper home.'

'And he doesn't?'

'He said he can't afford rent or furniture.'

'Why? Is he going to give up stealing?'

Hannah shook her head.

'Hannah, you must be sure this is what you really want. Remember, it's for the rest of your life.'

'I know. Mary, I do want to marry him. What do we have to do to get married?'

'You have to go to church to put up the banns. They have to

be read out three weeks before the wedding.'

Hannah bit her lip anxiously. 'Jack doesn't want to get married in church.'

'Oh dear. I think you have to go along to the town hall, then. They'll tell you all about it, and what you have to do. I expect Alice will be pleased for you.'

'We went to see her yesterday, but she was out. Jack doesn't want me to tell her yet.'

'Why's that?'

'I don't know.'

'He must have his reasons.' Mary picked up Brian. 'Have you heard the news? I do so hope we don't have to go to war.'

'So do I,' Hannah whispered.

On the way home, Hannah knew Mary was right. Jack must have his reasons: if only he would tell her what they were.

She was up early on Monday. Today they were going on a boat up the Thames. When they arrived at Tower Bridge, Hannah was surprised to see so many people. They were all dressed in their Sunday best, and everybody was laughing and chatting as they pushed and jostled, waiting to board the steamer. Hannah had done up a picnic, and at first she tried hard to keep her eyes on Jack's hands. Was this going to happen every time they were out together? She quickly gave up worrying about that; today she was out to enjoy herself.

All day the sun shone, and they wandered about on the boat, watching all the action on the Thames. Everything seemed so normal, it was hard to believe that if the Germans walked into Belgium, they could be at war.

'Jack, do you think there will be a war?'

'Dunno. 'Annah . . . If there is, I've bin finking, I reckon I might 'ave ter join up.'

Hannah laughed. 'What, you join the army?'

'Yer. So yer see, I fink we ought ter wait a while 'fore we git 'itched.'

Hannah was taken aback. 'I can't see you taking orders from someone. I thought that was one of the reasons you've never been to work.'

'Don't start on that again. This is different. If they need me I've got ter be ready to serve me king and country. I'm able-bodied, and I ain't got no ties.'

'But what about me?'

'Yer, I fought about that, and I do wonner marry yer, but . . .'

'But what?' Hannah was angry. 'You should have thought about that before you asked me.'

'Well, let's face it, gel, yer didn't give me much of a chance, now did yer? No sooner 'ad I said than yer rushed me in ter Maudie.'

She looked over the side of the boat. She couldn't answer. Once more her happiness was slipping away.

Jack continued. 'Well, I fink we should wait and see what 'appens.'

Hannah could have screamed. How dare her happiness depend on some man walking into another country? 'I . . . What . . .? If there is a war, couldn't we get married before you went?'

'Let's wait and see.'

For Hannah the rest of the day was spoiled, and she made her way home with a heavy heart.

Hannah sat up, disorientated. What was happening? She could hear Tom shouting and charging round the other room. It was five in the morning.

'It's 'appened,' she heard him shout at Jack. 'We're at war.'

Hannah quickly began dressing herself.

'Wot the bloody 'ell's going on out there?' said Maudie,

her voice thick with sleep. She sat up in bed and blinked at the early morning light.

'It's Tom,' said Hannah, slipping her skirt over her head. 'The war, it's started.'

'Well, it can carry on wivout me,' she snorted and, plumping up her pillow, laid down.

'Maudie, the country's at war,' said Hannah earnestly.

'So, wot d'yer want me ter do?'

Hannah looked at her. 'Nothing, I suppose.'

Twisting her long dark hair into a bun, Hannah walked into the main room. 'Hello, Tom.'

''Annah, 'ere, look at the papers,' he said excitedly. 'They've just come, so I fought I'd bring yer one round quick, 'fore I open up.'

Jack was sitting at the table, a cigarette dangling from his lips as he studied the paper. 'Sez 'ere, everybody was going mad outside Buckingham Palace last night.'

Hannah scanned the papers. It was true. The country was at war with Germany. She wanted to cry. What was going to happen to them now?

'Bob reckons it'll all be over be Christmas,' said Tom.

'Let's hope he's right,' said Hannah. She looked across at Jack. She didn't want him to go away.

Chapter 21

That morning, Hannah left home early so she could call in on Mary on her way to work to tell her the news. 'What are we going to do?' Hannah asked, as she followed Mary inside.

'There's not a lot we can do. We'll just have to carry on as normal and pray that it will be over soon.' Mary cuddled her son to her. 'Thank God you're not old enough to go to war,' she whispered to him.

'Tom was saying that Bob reckons it will all be finished by Christmas.'

'Let's hope he's right.'

'Jack reckons he's going in the army.'

'What? When?'

'I don't know.'

'I wouldn't have thought he would have been eager to go . . . I'm sorry Hannah. It's just that I can't imagine him taking orders.'

'That's what I said when he told me. I must be off.' Hannah opened the front door. 'Here's the postman,' she called over her shoulder.

'I never get any letters,' said Mary. 'It must be for you.'

The postman handed Hannah the letter. Mary was right: it had her name on it, with Mary's address. It was from Bert. She tore open the envelope.

My dear Hannah,
Many thanks for your most welcome letter. I'm glad

you had a nice birthday. I didn't know it was in May, you'll have to tell me the date. I was so pleased to hear you missed me. This is our busy time, and I can't get down to see you, but I would really like it if you could come up here. As you know, I live with Ernie and his family, and I have told them all about you, and Sarah, Ernie's wife, knows of a cottage near here. It's only small but the rent is very cheap, I know you will love it. It's on a cliff and the views are much better than what you've got now, and I know you'll be happy here. I also know how much you think of Maudie, and may have doubts about leaving her, but I do feel you should live your own life which, perhaps, I could be part of one day.

> Yours,
> Bert.

Hannah was taken aback. She didn't know what to think.

'What is it?' asked Mary.

Hannah handed her the letter.

'Are you sure you want me to read this?'

Hannah nodded.

Mary put her hand to her mouth. 'Oh, this can't be an easy decision to make. What are you going to do?'

'I don't know.'

'Do you love him?'

'No. I'm very fond of him.'

'Being fond isn't the same as love.'

'No, I know, but he's offering me a home. Jack can't. Or won't.'

'Is that what you want, a home?'

'Yes, I mean no. Oh, I don't know. Why can't it be Jack?'

'You must give it a lot of thought before you make up your mind. Remember, if you marry Bert, it's for life.'

'I hadn't thought about marrying him.'

'Well, he clearly has!'

'But I love Jack.'

Mary anxiously glanced at the clock. 'Look, Hannah, I'm sorry, but I must get to work.'

'Yes,' said Hannah. 'So must I. You won't tell Maudie about this, will you?'

'Of course not. The war's all anyone will be able to talk about for the next few days.'

'The war! Bert hasn't mentioned the war!'

'Well, the letter was posted before we knew, and I daresay he's got enough to keep him busy with bringing in the fish. Now I must go. Call in tonight!'

'Bye, Mary.' Hannah hurried to work. This was certainly going to be a strange day.

It seemed hardly anyone was at the factory. Rosie and some of the girls who worked on the bench and ovens hadn't turned up.

'Where are they?' Hannah asked Elsie as they made their way inside the factory to clock on.

'Ain't it awful,' said Elsie above the buzz of voices, her face full of worry. 'Us going ter war? I dunno wot's gonner 'appen to us. I said ter my old man, "Yer'd better not be finking of going in the army!" Mind you, you won't see some o' the blokes' arses fer dust. All some of 'em need is a good excuse ter git away from their old women.'

'But where is Rosie and . . . ?' Hannah looked around her.

'I fink some of the young lads 'ere 'ave gorn and joined the army.'

'What, already?'

'So I 'eard. But most of the ovvers got 'emselves in a right old state yesterday. You should 'ave seen Rosie – she was sick all the way 'ome. She looked a right mess, I can tell yer.' Elsie looked around, then bent her head closer. 'Someone caught 'er round the back of the chara. She was on the floor wiv one of the bakers, who's married. They said 'er skirts were right over 'er 'ead.'

Hannah laughed. 'So how did they know it was Rosie?'

'They knew it was 'er, all right.' With a grim expression on her face, Elsie straightened her shoulders. 'Good job only us lot could go on the outing, ovverwise 'is Missis would 'ave given 'im what for.'

'Still, if the family had been there it wouldn't have happened.'

'Don't you believe it, gel. It caused a right rumpus, I can tell yer. Did you 'ave a good day?'

'Yes, thank you.' When the biscuits arrived they didn't have time for idle chatter, and Hannah's thoughts went to Bert's letter. A small cottage on a cliff. She had never dared even to dream about anything so wonderful. She sighed. If only her life could be straightforward. She liked Bert, and he was offering her a home, and he was honest. But she loved Jack, even though he wasn't going to change, and with him neither would her life. Could she be happy with Bert? She really didn't know a lot about him, only that he was a fisherman and Maudie's son. Could she learn to love him?

After the first few days of non-stop chatter about the war, things gradually returned to normal.

On Saturday Hannah went alone to see Alice: Jack had said he wouldn't go with her as he had to meet someone. She didn't ask who – she knew he would tell her if he wanted to.

As she walked to catch her tram, Hannah was amazed at the long line of young men waiting to join up. Recruiting offices had been hastily set up in the town hall, and in any disused shops. The men seemed full of high spirits as she passed them patiently waiting in line. She felt exhilarated at the eagerness of all these men, and blushed at some of their comments.

When she finally arrived at Alice's, she was surprised at her welcome. Alice was just like her old self again, almost childlike. She eagerly hugged Hannah and jumped up and down.

'What are you so happy about?' asked Hannah.

'The war. Come on upstairs.'

'The war? But why?'

'Oh it's so exciting. We . . .'

'Who's we?' interrupted Hannah, feeling herself growing cross with Alice. How could anyone be pleased that there was a war?

'Me, Roy, Sally – you remember Sally, he came here once – well, we went up to Buckingham Palace on Monday night. And we all stood shouting for the king to come out on his balcony.'

'Did he?'

She started to pout. 'Please. Let me finish. It was so exciting, the atmosphere was wonderful. You could hardly move in the crush, people were laughing and singing, even dancing. Can you imagine, dancing in the street? It was like being at a huge party.' Alice's blue eyes were wide open and sparkling, and her cheeks, which this afternoon were devoid of rouge, flushed to a pretty pink. 'Then, Hannah . . .' she put her hands together as if saying a prayer, 'suddenly – it must have been as eleven o'clock struck – everybody went quiet. Oh Hannah, I was all goose-bumps, it was marvellous, then one man started to sing, "God Save Our King". It rippled round the crowd. Oh Hannah, I cried and cried, I felt so proud to be British. We sang all the patriotic songs, and danced till it was almost light. On the way home, Roy and Sally said they were joining the army right away. Aren't they brave? I wish

I was a man, I'd willingly go and fight the Germans.'

Hannah laughed. 'You fight? You'd get your gloves dirty.'

Alice limped across the room. 'That's not very nice. Do you know, Hannah Miller, you can be so hurtful at times.' She plonked herself in the chair.

'Where is everybody?' asked Hannah.

Rick has gone to join the army as well. Betty's furious with him.'

'Why?'

'She's worried about who will pay the rent. This is a big house, and if they all go off, well, heaven only knows how we'll manage.'

'You'll have to get yourself a job,' Hannah said curtly.

'And who will look after John?'

Hannah shrugged her shoulders. 'Who had him on Monday?'

'Betty and Rick took him out in the car somewhere.'

Hannah sat back. 'Jack said he might join the army.'

'Good for him, I always knew he was very brave.'

Hannah smiled. 'Well, I'll believe it when I see it.'

After a while, Alice calmed down, though by then Hannah had to leave. She desperately wanted to tell her that she was going to marry Jack, but didn't want to break her promise to him. Besides, what could she tell her when they hadn't set a date yet?

It wasn't till the end of the month, and after the terrible news of the battle at Mons, that people began to realize the true implications of Britain's involvement in the war. The newspapers reported on the number of young men injured and killed. Posters of Lord Kitchener pointing, urging young men to fight, appeared everywhere. One evening, when Hannah arrived home from work, she found Maudie sitting in her armchair crying.

'What is it, Maudie?' Hannah asked, quietly dropping to her knees beside her.

'It's Jack. 'E said e's gorn and joined the army.'

Hannah flushed with fury. Although he had talked about it at the beginning of the war, deep down she hadn't really thought he would go – she just couldn't imagine him taking orders. But why didn't he tell her he was going? Why'd he told Maudie first? Hannah sat at the table, dry eyed. But, she thought bleakly, what difference would it have made? After all, it didn't seem to matter what she said: he would always do what he wanted.

'Ain't yer upset?' sniffed Maudie, peering cautiously at her. Hannah nodded.

'I would 'ave fought yer'd 'ave tried to stop 'im.'

'Do you honestly think that anything I said would have changed his mind?'

Maudie shook her head. 'Na, s'pose not.' She wiped her eyes on the bottom of her apron. 'Well, let's 'ope Bob's right and it is all over be Christmas.'

A few weeks later, Jack got the letter Hannah had been dreading. When the time came for him to go, he took Hannah in his arms and she held her face up for his kisses. Her tears gently fell.

'I s'pose I should 'ave waited till after we got 'itched but, I dunno, I saw all these blokes in a line, and they was all going on about gitting the bastards, and the next fing I knew I was in this place, signing me name on the dotted line. I'm sorry, gel. Still, there's one good fing that'll please yer.'

'What's that?'

He pulled her close. 'I'll be earning a honest living for the first time in me life, and I got the king's shilling – look.'

Despite the tears running down her face, Hannah laughed.

''Ere, you take it, keep it fer good luck.' He placed the bright silver coin in her hand.

She clutched it tight. She loved him so much, but it had taken a war to make him go straight. 'You will write when you get time, won't you?' she croaked.

'Course I will. I s'pect it'll all be over in no time now I've joined up. We'll get those Germans on the run, just yer wait and see. Then we'll all be dancing and singing in the streets.'

Hannah held him tight. 'I do love you, Jack.'

He kissed her lips long and hard. 'Look after yerself, gel.' He picked up his brown paper parcel containing his shaving things and clean socks and underwear, and left.

Hannah stood at the iron gates quietly watching him go, wondering when she would see him again.

Over the next few weeks, one by one most of the young men they knew eagerly signed up to go and fight. After Jack went Kate's Charlie, and next was Mrs Warren's young son, Ted, who had lied about his age so that he could join. Kate told Hannah his mother had taken to her bed, she was so distressed.

A few weeks later, Alice wrote and told Hannah she was secretly pleased that Sally and Roy hadn't passed their medical, because if they had gone she wouldn't have had anyone to take her out. Rick had gone, and Betty was going to try and keep the house on, so things for Alice seemed to be going well, as usual.

One Sunday afternoon, Hannah and Mary were discussing the war.

'They say there have been hundreds of casualties in France,' said Mary. 'We've had a letter round asking for volunteers to go to some of the hospitals near Dover, and over in France. I think Miss King is thinking of going.'

'What will you do without her money coming in?' asked Hannah.

'I don't know. I'll have to try and manage. By the way, have you answered Bert's letter yet?'

Hannah shook her head.

'Are you going to see him?'

'No. Even if it is just to be friendly, what about Jack? He'll want me to be here when he comes back. And how can I leave Maudie? She's only got me now. How's Mrs Warren, by the way?'

'She's a little better, poor thing. Ted's her only one. She was telling me she waited years for him, he's the apple of his father's eye.'

'She's not very well, is she?' said Hannah.

'No, she suffers with her chest.'

Hannah thought of Ted. He was a good lad, and in the short while they had lived in Hope Street, everybody got on with him.

'He is such a nice boy,' said Mary.

'Humm,' nodded Hannah thoughtfully.

The war in Europe was steadily getting worse, and didn't look as if it would be over by Christmas as everyone had predicted.

One cold, damp Saturday afternoon, Kate was standing at the window when Hannah walked past. Kate beckoned for her to come in. 'Kate, I haven't seen you for weeks, how are you?' Hannah cried.

Kate smiled. 'We're all right. Come on in fer a tick.'

Hannah followed Kate into the kitchen. 'Hello, how are you, Mrs Linton?'

'Fine, fanks.' She moved the pile of damp washing off the chair. 'Sit yerself down. I'll just move the clothes-'orse, then yer can see the fire. Got time fer a cuppa?'

'Yes, why not?'

'Won't be seeing ser much of yer now,' said Kate cheerfully. 'Got meself a new job.'

'Where's that?'

'In the munition factory. I'm gonner make shells.'

Hannah was taken back. 'Is it dangerous?'

'Dunno. I don't fink so.'

'Well, I'm not very 'appy about it,' said Mrs Linton.

'Yer, but Mum, the money's ever so good. D'yer know, 'Annah, I'll be getting firty bob a week ter start. Just fink: *firty* bob.'

'That's very good money, Kate,' said Hannah, aware of the fifteen shillings a week she got now. 'When do you start?'

'Next week. It's long hours, but still I'll be able ter save a bit fer me wedding.'

'You're getting married. When?'

Kate looked at her mother and smiled broadly, her dark eyes flashing with happiness. 'When Charlie gits some leave. 'E reckons we should.'

Hannah threw her arms round Kate's neck. 'Oh Kate, I'm so pleased for you. You must let me know. Can I come to see you get married?'

'Yer, course yer can! Don't know when it'll be mind,' she added truthfully.

Hannah could hardly believe that Kate, little Kate, was getting married. How the years had sped by since she moved in with Maudie! 'Does Mary know?'

'Na, don't see a lot of 'er now. You can tell 'er if yer like.'

'She'll be really pleased for you.'

As Hannah continued on her way home, she pulled up her coat collar. The days had a bite to them now, winter was on its way. Her thoughts went to Jack. Where was he? She had only had one letter so far, and, as with Bert's, she had been surprised at Jack's neat and tidy writing. It had only been a few lines really, written just after he'd left. He said the training was a lot harder than he thought it would be, and he didn't care much for the sergeant. Hannah had smiled at the thought of him taking orders. She answered it straight away, but he could have been moved on by now. She shuddered at the thought of him in some cold trench in France. Perhaps they could get married when he came home on leave?

Hannah still hadn't answered Bert's letter. She knew she had to give some kind of reply but something was holding her back. Many times she had begun her letter, telling him she wouldn't be leaving Maudie now the war had started, but she couldn't finish it. Was it because she didn't want to make it sound too final? She also knew she had to tell him she was going to marry Jack when he was on leave. The trouble was, she didn't know whether to believe it herself.

Chapter 22

Everyone now knew that, despite the politicians' early optimism, this was going to be a long and bloody war. Every day the news was getting worse, and Hannah, who had still had only one letter from Jack, prayed he was safe, and not sitting in some cold, wet fox-hole somewhere in France.

Christmas was in two weeks' time and, until last week, it had looked as if it was going to be another dismal affair for Hannah and Maudie; so when Mary asked them to join her, Hannah was delighted. Maudie said she would be happy to do the cooking for them on Mary's range, and got Hannah to make a list of things they would need. Miss King was going to spend Christmas at the hospital.

As Hannah, hurrying home from work, turned into Hope Street, she was surprised to see Mary, a worried look on her face, banging on her front room window and beckoning for Hannah to come in. Hannah rarely called on Mary in the week as she knew her friend was always in a hurry to get Brian's tea and get him ready for bed where she could spend some time with him, playing and reading him a story.

Mary flung open the front door. 'I'm glad I caught you, quick, come in – it's Maudie.'

'Maudie? What's happened? Is she ill? Where is she?'

'She's in the kitchen.'

Hannah raced past Mary and along the passage, pushing open the kitchen door. Maudie was sitting at the table, her eyes red from crying. She looked at Hannah, and the tears began to fall again. She rubbed her eyes with her handkerchief. 'Oh, 'Annah. The wicked lot o' buggers.'

'What's happened? What's the matter?' Hannah caught her breath and sat down. 'Is it Jack?' she said slowly.

Maudie looked up. 'Na,' she sobbed. 'It's Louis.'

'Louis?' questioned Hannah. She cast her eyes towards Mary who just shrugged her shoulders. 'Who are you talking about, Maudie? What's happened?'

Maudie blew her nose loudly. 'Well, yer see,' she sobbed. 'Round the grocer's, yer know, old 'Erman's, bin there fer years 'e 'as. Well, the kids all started calling out, "Old 'Erman the German", and it seems fings got a bit out o' 'and.' She stopped and blew her nose again. 'Then they started frowing stones at 'im and 'is lad – yer know, 'e 'elps 'is dad. I was scared stiff, I can tell yer. I couldn't git past 'em, they seem ter come from everywhere. I was worried ter deaf about young Brian.'

'Is he all right?' asked Hannah anxiously.

Mary nodded.

'I tell yer, 'Annah, I was really scared stiff. All that glass crashing round us. D'yer know, someone got a 'ammer and started smashing down 'is wall and frowing great big lumps at 'em.'

'Why would they do that?'

'Cos they're Germans.'

'But, as you say, they've been there for years,' said Hannah. 'Everybody knows them.'

Maudie shook her head bitterly. 'Don't seem ter make much difference. You should 'ave seen old Nosy: she was jumping up and down and laughing 'er 'ead orf. When I fink of the times old 'Erman's let 'er 'ave sumfink on the slate, it makes me blood boil.'

'People are very angry about the war though, Maudie,' said Mary gently.

'Yer, I knows, but yer don't 'ave ter start carrying on like that, now do yer?' she sniffed. 'It's poor Louis I feel sorry fer. Born 'ere, 'e was; now 'e's finished up round the 'ospital.'

'Why? What happened?' asked Mary, her voice full of concern.

'When they finished breaking up the wall and all the shop winders, yer should 'ave seen the blood – everywhere, it was. 'Erman, 'is Missis and 'is boy, was all trying ter stop 'em rushing in and pinching all 'is stuff. Then some big bloke, I ain't never seen 'im before, 'e chucked the 'ammer at Louis and knocked 'im out.'

'Where was the policeman?' asked Hannah.

'Old Ron? Wasn't anywhere ter be seen, that was till they all started ter kick the poor lad, then 'e came out o' nowhere. 'E musta bin 'iding, crafty sod.'

'What's going to happen to their place?' asked Hannah.

'Wouldn't like ter say. Shouldn't fink they'll be much left after they've all bin in and 'elped 'emselves.'

'That's awful,' said Hannah.

'Here's your tea, Maudie,' said Mary, pushing a cup and saucer towards her. 'Here's yours, Hannah.'

Maudie poured the tea into the saucer and slurped loudly.

'What's this war doing to people?' asked Hannah. Her elbows on the table, she picked up her cup and stared sadly into space.

'I don't know,' said Mary.

They finished their tea in silence, and made their way home. Maudie, holding tightly to Hannah's arm, was pleased to see Mrs Nosy's front door was firmly shut. Otherwise there could have been more trouble.

Tom came round that night and told them that the police had taken Herman and his family away for their own protection. He also broke the news that Bob was worried about staying on his own after his son had joined the army. Tom would be moving in with him.

For a few days after the Herman incident, Maudie was upset and reluctant to go out. Hannah thought about Bert's offer of the cottage, and wondered if this would be a good time to say something. Perhaps getting away would do them both good, but would Maudie go with her? Hannah didn't think so, and at this moment she wouldn't leave her. More and more Hannah felt she needed to hear something of Jack, to know how he really felt.

Hannah had decided to go to see Alice on Saturday afternoon; there were so many things she wanted to talk over with her. To her surprise, her sister was home, and for once she was alone.

'Hannah,' Alice's face broke into a smile. 'I'm so glad to see you, this place is like a morgue.'

'It is quiet here today. Where is everybody?' asked Hannah as she made her way up the stairs.

'Betty's got a rehearsal with Roy and Sally. They're doing a new show, something to do with the war, I think.'

Hannah paused. 'Alice, I've a lot to tell you.'

Alice looked alarmed. 'What? What's happened? Have you seen Alf again?'

'No,' answered Hannah as they entered the large room.

'What is it then? Take your hat off,' said Alice, fussing round her, 'and come and sit down.'

Hannah did as she was told. 'Alice,' she said quietly, 'Jack asked me to marry him before he went in the army.'

Alice sat back in the chair and giggled. 'And what did you tell him?'

'I said I would.'

Alice's face suddenly grew serious. 'Oh, Hannah. No, not Jack. I don't think that's very wise, do you?'

Hannah was taken back at that remark. 'Don't you like Jack?'

'Of course I do, but I can't imagine you being married to him.' Alice looked over her shoulder at the door, almost as if expecting someone to come in. She leaned forward and said in a loud whisper, 'What if he carries on pinching? You've always been so against that.'

'Yes, I know.' Hannah began to play with her gloves, scrunching them up, straightening them out, then smoothing them nervously on her lap. 'Alice. Bert has also asked me to go to Lowestoft.'

Alice laughed. 'Who's Bert?' She suddenly stopped laughing. 'Not the Bert at Maudie's?'

'Yes.'

Alice looked shocked. 'He's asked you to go away with him?'

'Yes.'

'But I thought you just said . . . What about Jack?'

Hannah sat forward. 'Jack has asked me to marry him, but I can't help thinking my life would just go on the same with him.'

'And would it with Bert?'

'Well, at least I'd get away from London.'

'Is that what you want?'

Hannah shook her head. 'I don't know.'

'So, lucky you,' Alice said gaily, 'you've got two beaux?'

Hannah didn't answer.

'So what are you going to do? Where is this Lowestoft, anyway?'

'In Suffolk.'

Alice blinked. 'I'm none the wiser.'

Hannah looked at her little sister, sitting there so grown up and full of confidence. Nowadays it seemed almost impossible to really get through to her. 'It doesn't matter,' she said quietly.

Alice was laughing again. 'You and Bert? You certainly

are a dark horse. Does Bert want to marry you?'

'I think so.'

'You only think so. Didn't he ask you?'

'Not in so many words, but he has found a cottage for me to stay in.'

'A cottage? Is that so he can have his wicked way?' Alice was smiling broadly but she put her hand to her mouth to hide it.

'Don't talk nonsense,' Hannah snapped.

'Is it nice?'

'I think so.'

'Well, that's going to put the cat amongst the pigeons between Jack and Bert, good and proper. They've always been at each other's throats, and this is really going to stir it up.'

Hannah chewed her lip. 'I must admit I'm worried about that.'

'Did you ever find out what the trouble was between them?'

Hannah shook her head.

'So what're you going to do?' Alice laughed again. 'You've always wanted to get away from Maudie, this could be your big chance. Have you been out with Bert?'

'Only a few times.'

'You didn't tell me!'

'Well, you're usually so full of what you've been doing that I don't get a chance.'

Alice pouted. 'What's Bert like? Really like – everybody used to be scared stiff of him.'

'He's very nice when you get to know him.'

'What does he do? Is he honest?'

'Yes, yes he is.' Hannah smiled. 'He's a fisherman.'

Alice screwed up her nose. 'A fisherman? I don't think I'd fancy that. What does Maudie have to say about all this?'

'I haven't told her.'

'What, not even about Jack wanting to marry you?'

'Well, I told her that.'

'And?'

'She's not sure I'll be doing the right thing. Alice . . .'

Alice looked puzzled at Hannah's sudden change of tone.

'Bert is Maudie's son.'

Alice caught her breath. 'What? How do you know that?'

'Maudie told me ages ago.'

'And you've never said anything?'

'Didn't see the point.'

'Well, you might have told me.' There was a look of anger on Alice's face. 'What other little secrets have you got?'

'I haven't got any. It was just important to Maudie that nobody should know.'

'So what about Jack? Is he Maudie's son as well?'

'No.'

'Well, who does he belong to? He must have a mother.'

'Maudie's looked after him since he was two. I think that's the reason they didn't get on. Jack was jealous. And when Bert went off with Albert, I think he felt even more jealous.'

'Does he still live with this Albert?'

'No, he died years ago.'

'And you've kept all this to yourself?'

Hannah nodded.

'But what about Bert?' Alice's face broke into a broad grin. 'If you marry him, Maudie will be your mother-in-law.'

'Yes, but I don't think I want to marry him. Oh Alice, I'm in such a . . .' She looked about her and threw her hands in the air. 'What can I do?' Tears welled up in her eyes.

Alice suddenly grew serious. She came across the room and sat on the arm of Hannah's chair. Leaning over, she put her arm round Hannah's shoulder. 'I don't think you'll be doing the right thing marrying Jack. He'll never change his ways, and you'll be worried about him. And I don't think going to Bert's will be the answer. Hannah, you're pretty, and I'm sure you'll find someone to really love one of these days.'

Hannah took her handkerchief from her handbag and dabbed at her eyes. She couldn't tell Alice that she'd never love anyone else but Jack. She tried to pull herself together. 'I'm very worried about Maudie, and don't want to leave her, more so now Tom's staying with Bob. She got ever so upset the other day when some people stoned the grocer and his son.'

'What?'

'The grocer round the corner, you know, the German family. A gang set on them, and Maudie was there.'

'That must have been awful. Poor old Maudie.'

'I was thinking of asking her to come to the cottage with me.'

'What to Lowestoft?'

Hannah nodded.

'I bet she won't go. She wouldn't leave London.'

'Oh Alice, it sounds wonderful.'

Her sister was silent. 'I'll make some tea,' she said eventually.

Hannah followed her into the kitchen. 'Alice, what do you think I should do?'

'Don't ask me.' Alice's tone was one of indifference.

'Alice, have you got anyone here?'

Alice laughed, and her face flushed. 'Most of them are spoken for. Besides – ' Alice looked embarrassed – 'I don't think I could let any man do those sort of things to me.'

'What sort of things?' It suddenly occurred to Hannah that Alice might not know about the facts of life. 'Alice? Has Betty ever told you about men?'

'Course she has, and you should hear what some of the girls who come here talk about, and some of the men.'

'Has any of them tried to . . . You know?'

Alice laughed. 'No. They look on me as a kind of lucky mascot. You see, ever since I've been here, all their shows have been good. Besides, Betty thinks of me as one of the family.'

'What about Roy?' asked Hannah. 'I thought you liked him.'

'Oh, I do, but he's not interested in girls in that way. He's good fun to be with, and great to take shopping. He's very well off.'

'Is that all you think about?'

'I think John's awake.' Alice glanced at the door. 'Watch the kettle while I go and get him.'

Hannah stood gazing out of the window at the street below. Alice was certainly worldly wise now. How would she have turned out if they had still been in Richmond, leading the sheltered life their parents must have hoped for them. But what if they had still been with Uncle Harry? Alice would have been out to work in some smelly factory, and they could both have been trying to find someone to marry them to get away from him. Maybe things hadn't worked out so badly after all. The late afternoon's watery sun trickled through the window. What sort of view would she have from the kitchen window of the cottage? Would she see the sea, and hear the seagulls overhead?

Alice came in with John over her shoulder, interrupting her daydreams.

'Hannah, you're supposed to be watching the kettle.'

'Sorry, I was miles away. Hello young feller,' she said, holding John's hand.

'I'll do the tea, you take him into the drawing room.'

Alice put John on the floor and Hannah, taking his hand, led him away.

While they were having their tea, Hannah told Alice that she and Maudie would be spending Christmas day with Mary.

'That'll be nice for you,' Alice said. 'I expect we shall have a houseful, as usual.'

Hannah was disappointed her sister didn't suggest seeing her over the holiday, but she went on to tell her about Kate and her young man, how she was going into a munitions factory, and about Mary's lodger, Miss King, who might be going to France to help nurse the wounded. 'That must be really worthwhile, doing a real job like that,' Hannah concluded.

'I wouldn't go into a munitions factory, but I'd love to go to France,' Alice agreed longingly. 'Just imagine going to gay Paree. Going up the Eiffel Tower, the Moulin Rouge and the Follies; and what about all those wonderful shops? And sitting outside a café sipping coffee, and wearing the latest fashions.'

'I don't think Miss King will be doing any of that,' Hannah said. 'She'll be far too busy, up to her knees in mud, caring for the wounded, I shouldn't wonder.'

'Uggh, I'd hate that, all that blood and . . .' Alice shuddered. 'No, thank you. I'll stay in Paris.'

Hannah looked at her and smiled. Alice would never change.

On the way home, Hannah resolved to ask Maudie to come to Lowestoft with her. Maudie might like the idea of living with her son, and maybe going there would help her make up her own mind, once and for all. After Christmas would be a good time for them to make a move. She would write to Bert, and tell Jack she was going. Maybe that way he'd make up his mind too.

'Alice all right then, gel?' asked Maudie when Hannah walked in.

'Yes, yes, she is. We had a long talk today.' Hannah took off her hat. 'Maudie,' she said eagerly, sitting down next to her. 'Would you like to move away from here?'

'Na.'

'Not even to a nice little cottage somewhere?'

'Na. 'Sides, who's got a cottage? Alice going orf somewhere then? Na, I'm too settled in me ways.' She stood up and pushed some more wood into the fire.

Hannah was beginning to get agitated. 'Don't you want to hear about it?'

'Na.'

'Maudie, please, just sit down and listen.' Hannah's voice was loud and harsh.

''Ere, who yer shouting at?'

'I'm sorry. It's just that Bert has written and told me he's found me a cottage and wants me to go up there with him.'

'What?' Maudie sat down with a rush. 'I fought yer was going ter marry Jack; now yer talking about marrying Bert. Wot's the matter wiv yer, can't yer make up yer bleeding mind?'

'I am going to marry Jack, but that doesn't mean to say we can't go and live somewhere nice.' Hannah bit her lip. She couldn't tell Maudie what had been going through her mind.

'Well, Jack won't stand fer it.'

'But it will only be till the war's over. Then perhaps Jack could get a job, and we could come back.'

Maudie laughed. 'I gotter 'and it ter yer, gel, yer don't ever give up, do yer? Yer still trying ter git 'im a job.'

'But wouldn't you like to get away from here? We could have a nice room with a fireplace, and you could have a proper oven to cook in.'

'I've managed all me life living like this, and I ain't gonner start ter change now.'

'I can't believe this!' Hannah cried, appalled that all her plans were going to be frustrated.

''Sides,' said Maudie smugly, 'who'll pay the rent? Yer can't expect Bert to fork out if yer ain't gonna marry 'im.'

Hannah was taken aback. She hadn't thought about that.

'I'll get a job,' she blurted out confidently. 'There must be work for women up there.'

'Well please yerself,' said Maudie. 'If yer wonner go, then go. Don't worry about me.'

'But I do worry about you! We've got another winter in front of us, and this place is too big to keep warm.' Hannah was starting to get angry.

'Well, I ain't moving, so there, and I can't see Jack wanting ter move away, so yer better make up yer mind what yer want.'

Hannah wanted to cry. She knew exactly what she wanted. She wanted Jack *and* a new, decent life.

Chapter 23

Hannah had made up her mind, and that evening she wrote and told Bert that, in the New Year, when the weather got a little better, she would like to come up and see the cottage. She tried to keep the letter lighthearted and not commit herself and she felt guilty at not telling him about Jack's proposal. She would be as honest as she could be about the situation when the time came but felt it would be better to tell him to his face rather than try to explain in a letter. She also wrote a loving letter to Jack telling him how much she missed him, but she didn't see the point of telling him she was thinking of moving away, not till she was sure herself.

Christmas Day was quiet, even with Brian around. It was so very different to the noisy ones they had had when everybody was at Maudie's. But Mary, who was always trim and smart, looked relaxed in her brown skirt and pink, pin-tucked blouse, very different from her navy blue uniform. Today, her long dark hair – which she normally wore in a bun, tucked out of sight under her white starched cap – was loose and tied back with a pink bow, made from material she had left over from her blouse.

Hannah could see Maudie was in her element as, red faced, she bustled round the scullery, making a big fuss about cooking on the kitchen range with the proper oven. After dinner they settled down in front of the open fire and played with Brian.

The church clock was chiming ten as they wandered back to the wash-house, Maudie hanging on to Hannah's arm. She felt Maudie shudder as she walked inside, for the fire had gone out and the room looked and felt bleak and cold.

'That was kind of Mary to invite us today, wasn't it? Did you enjoy yourself?'

'Yer. Push some paper in that stove ter git it going again.'

'Did you like sitting in her nice warm kitchen?'

'Yer know I did,' Maudie said gruffly, 'now don't keep on. I'm going out ter git some wood.'

Hannah, behind Maudie's back, smiled. This was a good time to try and wear her down.

When Maudie rushed back in, an icy blast came through the door with her. 'Christ, this wood's frozen solid.' She said, throwing it to the floor and blowing on her hands.

'Now, if we had a proper place to keep the wood and coal . . .' said Hannah, smiling.

'Don't start on that again,' Maudie shouted. 'I told yer I ain't moving, so that's that. I can't git this wet wood ter light, so let's git ter bed.' She threw the few sticks down and stormed off to her bedroom.

Hannah sat at the table. Today had been lovely. If only Maudie would . . . But she was doing it again, making other people's minds up for them. She let her thoughts wander to Jack. What kind of Christmas had he had? Perhaps next year the war would be over, and they would be together, and married. She missed him, and the good times they had all had here together. She suddenly thought about Dolly. She would be in some warm farmhouse, the table laden with food. Hannah smiled. She hoped she was happy. Every time Hannah went to the market, she always asked Violet about her. Violet said she didn't write very often, and she had a job to read Dolly's writing, but she seemed very content. Hannah sighed. Lucky Dolly. Somehow Hannah had to get away too, to make something of her life. Eagerly she awaited Bert's letter.

* * *

It was in the middle of January that the newspapers reported a new menace. The Germans had sent over Zeppelins, and they had bombed the east coast at Great Yarmouth.

'This is awful news,' said Mary as she took in the headlines.

'Do you think they could come here, to London?'

'I don't know. Yarmouth is a long way away. Look, it's near Lowestoft,' said Mary as they spread the newspaper over the table.

Hannah and Mary traced their fingers over the map.

'I wonder if it's anywhere near Bert's?' Mary said.

'I don't know.'

'Has he answered your letter?'

'No, not yet.'

'Do you think it would be very wise to go there now?'

Hannah shook her head. 'I don't know what to do.'

Mary sat back. 'Well, I don't think you should go, but then it's not really any of my business.'

'But what else can I do? Every time I make up my mind to do something, something else crops up.' Hannah sighed.

'Hannah . . .' Mary paused. 'Now I'm going to put the cat amongst the pigeons. You see, I've got a proposition for you.'

Hannah looked up.

'Miss King is going to France. She's leaving at the end of the month, and I was wondering if you and Maudie would like to move in here with me. I won't ask for a lot of rent, and perhaps if . . .'

Hannah's mouth fell open. She leapt to her feet and threw her arms round Mary's neck.

'You and Maudie will have to share the bedroom,' gasped Mary.

'We can live here?'

Mary nodded. 'Do you think you would be able to persuade Maudie to come here?'

Hannah sat down. 'Stay here in Hope Street. Well, that's up to her, but I can tell you that I'd like to live here, and if she doesn't, well, that's up to her.' Hannah was smiling so much her jaw ached. 'This is the best news I've had for ages.' Tears ran down her face.

'What about Bert?'

'I'll write and tell him,' sniffed Hannah. Suddenly she felt life would be bearable. What would happen with Jack, she didn't know, but at least she was changing things for the better. 'Just think, a proper bedroom.' She threw her arms round Mary's neck again. 'You wait till I tell Alice.'

'She wouldn't want to come here, would she?' asked Mary in alarm.

'No. Nothing would get her away from Betty. Don't worry about that,' said Hannah, grinning at her good fortune.

All the way back to the wash-house, Hannah felt like singing. The cold wind and rain blowing in her face, or even Maudie, couldn't dampen her spirits today.

Maudie was sitting crouched in front of the stove.

'Guess what?' shouted Hannah as she walked in.

Maudie looked up. 'Well?'

Hannah pulled a chair close to her. 'Maudie. Mary wants us to go and live at her house.'

'What?'

'Mary wants . . .'

'Yer, yer, I 'eard.'

'Well?'

'Why?'

'Miss King is going to France at the end of the month, and she wants us to help pay the rent, and she likes your cooking.' Hannah was trying to keep calm, but she really wanted to run round the room shouting with excitement.

'Oh.'

'Well?' Hannah was getting a little angry. 'Yes or no?'

'I dunno. I'm a bit set in me ways.' Maudie hunched grumpily into her chair.

Hannah stood up. 'You've only got to go up the street. I'm not asking you to go to the end of the earth.' She glared at the glowering old lady. 'You make me so bloody angry.'

Maudie's head shot up.

'Yes, I said bloody, and I'll say it again and again.'

Suddenly Maudie burst out laughing. 'Well, I never fought I'd 'ear you carrying on like this.'

'Well, I've never been so determined about anything in my life as this, and I'll tell you now, I'm going, and I mean it this time. So you can please yourself.' She took off her hat and threw it across the room.

'It would be nice ter 'ave a warm place.' Maudie rubbed her hands together and held them out in front of the stove. 'And Mary wouldn't 'ave ter bring Brian round 'ere. And I could git 'er tea all ready fer 'er when she gits in: she'd like that.' Maudie sat back and grinned. 'Yer, I reckon it'd be a bit of all right. Yer, why not?'

Hannah grabbed hold of her and, pulling her to her feet, hugged her, dancing her round the room.

''Ere, 'old on, mind me poor old dogs!' squeaked Maudie.

Hannah had tears rolling down her face. 'I can't believe it, a house, we're going to live in a house!'

'Well, it's a good way ter start the New Year, ain't it?'

'It couldn't be better.' She plonked a loud, resounding kiss on Maudie's cheek.

Maudie rubbed her cheek. 'Yer a daft 'apporf, and no mistake.'

That evening Hannah sat and wrote to Jack and Alice, telling them the good news.

* * *

In the two weeks that followed, Hannah and Maudie were busy packing the few bits they had. Tom was thrilled at the move and promised he would get a barrow to take their things to Mary's. Hannah said she could hardly wait till the Sunday, when Miss King would be going.

Miss King was leaving early in the morning, and Hannah was up and dressed, ready to start moving long before Maudie had opened her eyes.

'Wot time is it?' she asked when Hannah took her in a cup of tea.

'Eight o'clock.'

'It's a bit dark.'

'And cold, it's been snowing. So wrap up.'

'Wot time we gotter git going?'

'Miss King is leaving about ten, so we've got a couple of hours yet. Besides, Tom won't be bringing the barrow round till he's finished for the day.'

'Our little Tom. 'E's growing up, ain't 'e?'

Hannah nodded.

Maudie patted the bed. 'Sit 'ere fer a tick, love. D'yer know, I was dead pleased when 'e didn't pass 'is medical. I would 'ate ter fink of 'im fighting. It ain't in 'is nature.'

'Bob was pleased as well,' said Hannah. 'But I was surprised it was his flat feet that stopped him.'

Maudie laughed. 'Well, one good fing, they'll never take me wiv my plates o' meat. Right, come on, we've got a lot ter do.'

Hannah too was laughing.

For the next hour, Maudie laid out all her precious things on the big table. 'Gis a 'and wiv this mattress, gel,' she called from her room.

Hannah walked in and stopped at the door. 'You're not going to take that? Mary would go mad with that in her house.'

'Why, it ain't got no bugs in it.' Maudie looked hurt. 'Sides, I gotter 'ave a bed.'

Hannah was worried. Mary hadn't said if there would be any furniture in the room, but surely Miss King must have had a bed; she wasn't the type to sleep on the floor. 'Well, I'm not so sure. We'll ask her first.' Hannah turned away. She couldn't let Maudie see she was grinning. What would Mary say?

Finally it was time for them to go. Carrying their bags, they slipped and slid over the slushy pavements. Mary greeted them warmly, and they made their way up to the bedroom.

'I've never been up here,' whispered Hannah to Maudie.

'Can't say I fancy keep climbing these stairs. Ain't used ter stairs,' puffed Maudie.

'This is your room,' Mary said. 'What time did you say Tom was coming over?' She opened one of the two doors at the top of the stairs. 'You're at the front.'

'About two o'clock, he hopes,' said Hannah, walking into the room. She stopped when Mary touched her arm.

'I was wondering . . . We didn't say anything . . .' Mary was floundering for words. 'I sleep in the other room with Brian at the moment, and I was wondering if Tom could help me down the stairs with this bed. You see, later on, when Brian gets a little older, I'm hoping he can sleep downstairs in the front room. There isn't much furniture in there now. I had to sell a lot of it after . . .' Mary was clearly worried about there only being one bed.

'I reckon me and you could do that now,' said Hannah, quickly interrupting. She smiled when she looked at the single bed; there was no way her and Maudie could sleep in that. 'Maudie was wondering about her bed.' Hannah turned to Maudie. 'See, I told you not to worry; now that problem's solved.'

'Wot about me dressing table?'

'You can bring whatever you like, just as long as we can fit it in,' said Mary.

At two Tom came with the barrow, and he and Hannah took the first load. Laughing and giggling, they trundled down Hope Street, quickly grabbing anything that began to slide off. They could see Mrs Nosy at her window after they'd passed, she flung the upstairs casement window right up. 'She'll fall out if she's not careful!' Hannah laughed, turning back to watch her. 'Look, she's hanging right out. I bet she's dying to know where we're going.'

Tom smiled. 'She'll find out soon enough.'

'I shall be glad when this is finished and I don't have to pass her door any more,' said Hannah.

The last load was finally unloaded, many hands making light work of getting everything in place. Hannah stood at the bedroom window. Hope Street looked very different from up here. She sighed, she was happy and felt at ease for the first time in years. But now she had to tell Bert.

That evening she wrote him a long letter, explaining that she wouldn't be coming to the cottage just yet, as she was frightened of the Zeppelin raids over the east coast. She also told him how Mary had offered her and Maudie a home with her now her lodger had gone. Hannah was very careful not to say she would never go and see him. After all, who knew exactly what the future would hold?

The weeks drifted into months, and everything in number forty Hope Street was working out just fine. Mary was happy with the arrangements, and so was Maudie. When Hannah received a card from Jack telling her he was in France she was very upset, for it was just after Mary had had a letter from Miss King telling her about the conditions they had to work in. She prayed Jack would be safe, and couldn't help wishing he'd said something a little more affectionate in his card. But she was beginning to see that maybe reassuring her about her place in his life was the least of his worries.

'Yer don't wonner worry too much about Jack,' said Maudie when Hannah read the card to her. ''E's a born survivor.'

Hannah smiled, she hoped she was right.

Hannah also had a letter from Bert in which he said he could understand her anxiety, but the Zeppelin raid was miles away from them. He told her the offer was always open. He was also pleased to hear they were now living with Mary, and was surprised that Jack had joined the army. He said that, when it was possible, he would come down to see them.

When Hannah went to see Alice, she was pleased Hannah had moved in with Mary too. 'Now perhaps you'll be able to settle down and stop moping. You've been looking such a misery lately.' Alice held Hannah tight. 'I'm really glad you're not going to move all that way away,' she whispered shyly.

Hannah was very touched at that.

Alice then went on to tell her about the sewing circle she and Betty went to.

'What? You sewing?' said Hannah.

'Well, I look after John, really, but it's lovely. We go to this big hotel and have tea and dainty cakes, and sit and chat. I do a little bit now and again. I feel it's right to try and help the war effort.'

Hannah wanted to laugh at her sister's remark: the government was urging women to go out to work, and even do men's jobs, and Alice was so proud of her sewing! The thought of Alice doing any kind of dirty job made her burst out laughing.

It was after the terrible battle at Ypres and the horror of the troops being gassed that the Germans sunk the passenger ship, the *Lusitania*.

'D'yer fink they'll go fer the little ships?' asked Maudie.

'No, course not,' said Hannah, keeping her fingers firmly crossed. 'They only want the big ships.'

Hannah was pleased Maudie accepted that statement, for she too had fears for Bert's safety. She was also very worried about Jack. She had written many letters to him, but since he had been in France she had only received four cards from him, which she had stuck round the edge of the mirror. She would read them over and over again.

Night after night, Hannah and Mary would sit studying the newspapers, reading out loud some of the dreadful things that were happening in France. But it was Jack who constantly filled her thoughts. What if he got injured? Or even . . . She wouldn't let her mind dwell on any worse possibilities, and prayed for his safe return.

For weeks Maudie had been moaning about certain goods disappearing from the shops, and one evening she was telling them that she'd had a row with the coalman when he only let her have a small bag of coal. ''Ad the bloody cheek ter tell me there was a war on,' she said angrily. 'And me been tramping round the shops all day fer a bit a sugar. Gawd only knows where it's all gorn.'

However, it was only in May 1915, just after Hannah's twentieth birthday, that the war came right to the people of Hope Street. On that day the first Zeppelin flew silently over London.

Hannah was at work when someone ran in shouting that a Zeppelin was overhead, dropping bombs. Everybody stopped work and rushed into the yard. They all looked up at the large silver cigar-shaped object as it slowly drifted across the sky. Nobody spoke, the only sound a peculiar whirling noise. They stood transfixed, like statues. Someone pointed in the direction of the Thames.

'Look!'

They all followed his line of gaze. A small column of black smoke was gently drifting upwards into the cloudless blue sky.

'The bastards,' said Wally. His tone was full of hatred.

'That's it,' said Rosie. 'That's made up me mind. I'm gonner 'elp git the bastards.'

'Wot d'yer fink you're gonner do?' shouted one of the other women.

'Go in the munitions factory, been finking about it fer weeks.'

'I've 'eard they git good money,' said Elsie.

'Yer, it's well over two quid a week now,' said Rosie.

There was a slight muttering among the women.

'It's gotter be better than biscuits. But it ain't only the money,' There was no stopping Rosie now she knew she had a captive audience. 'I fink I should do me bit ter try and end the war. I'll be helping make shells ter blast them buggers out the sky.'

A great cheer went up and, despite the fear Hannah knew they must all have been feeling, they laughed.

'Good fer you, Rosie,' someone shouted out.

Hannah looked again at the pall of thick black smoke hanging in the sky. She didn't find the thought of work in the munitions factory very attractive, but she was beginning to feel, like Rosie, that she should now do something positive to help the war effort.

Chapter 24

There wasn't a lot of work done after the bomb, despite Wally's constant shouting for everyone to get back down to it. Everybody was worried about where it had dropped, even though most of them were from close-knit families who didn't have relatives living that far away.

Hannah was worried about Alice and rushed home from work that evening, hoping someone would have more news.

'Oh 'Annah, ain't it awful?' said Maudie as soon as she walked in. She was flustered and flapped her hands. 'Did yer see it, bloody great fing 'anging in the sky like that. Ain't ever seen nuffink like it before. Fought it was gonner take the chimney tops orf. It ain't natural, only birds were meant ter fly – shouldn't be allowed. I tell yer it frightened the bloody daylights out o' me, fought it would fall out the sky on top o' us.'

Mary gave a slight cough.

'Sorry, ducks, I knows I shouldn't swear in front o' Brian, but it just makes me blood boil when I finks of all the poor . . .' she hesitated, 'devils what musta got killed when the bomb dropped. Wicked bug . . .'

'Did many get killed?' asked Hannah quickly.

'Dunno.'

'Do you know where it fell?'

'Down-river somewhere, so old Ron told me.'

'How does he know?' asked Hannah.

'Seems they can find out these fings at the nick.'

'They've got a telephone,' volunteered Mary.

'I hope it wasn't anywhere near Alice,' Hannah said anxiously.

'I shouldn't think so,' said Mary. 'And I think only the one came over.'

'And that's one too many,' said Maudie. 'Bombing women and children. That's a coward's way ter win a war. Shouldn't be allowed.' She shook her head in disgust. 'I've made a pot o' tea, gels, so sit yerselves down.'

Hannah and Mary did as they were told.

'I'll have to go over to see Alice on Saturday, just to make sure she's all right.' Hannah was very concerned.

'It's the injured I feel sorry for,' said Mary. 'I hope we don't have a lot of those beastly things coming over.'

'Would they take them to the cottage hospital?' asked Hannah.

'Yes, I expect so, if things got really bad. Not that we've got a lot of room, it's only a small place after all. In fact there's talk of them bringing in some of the wounded soldiers.'

'But we're a long way from any ports.'

'I think it would only be a last resort, before they were moved on to a convalescent home.'

Maudie was clearly growing uncomfortable with all this talk of injuries and wounded soldiers and, much to Brian's delight, she stuck the neatly crocheted tea cosy with multi-coloured flowers all over it on his head. He giggled and threw it to the floor. They all laughed, and the mood was suddenly lifted.

The following Saturday afternoon, Hannah went over to Fulham to see Alice. To Hannah's relief, her sister was fine, and their first topic of conversation was Monday's raid.

'I tell you, Hannah, I was so excited when I first saw it; it looked so elegant floating through the sky, like a great big silver cigar. But when we heard the loud bangs of the bombs, my heart went in my mouth, I was so frightened. I think it's very wicked of the kaiser to send over things like that.'

Hannah almost smiled. The war was still a game to Alice.

'Oh, by the way, Rick is coming home on embarkation leave soon. He's going to France to fight the hun. Isn't he brave?'

'How is he?' asked Hannah, wondering why Jack didn't get leave before he went to France.

'He's an officer. I bet he looks very smart in his uniform.' She bent her head closer. 'And I wouldn't be at all surprised if he and Betty didn't get married.'

'Why? What makes you say that?'

'Well, it seems then she'd get an allowance for being his wife, so Betty was saying, and having that would help pay the rent on this place.'

Hannah sat back. Why hadn't Jack thought like that? If they had been married she too could have had an allowance, and she could be saving it towards their future home.

'What about the others who live here?'

'They all help, but you never know when they're going off.'

They were having a cup of tea when suddenly they heard whistles blowing and people shouting. Hannah and Alice hurried to the open window. A policeman was racing up and down the road on his bicycle, his face red with the effort of riding and blowing his whistle as hard as he could, a cardboard notice slung round his neck telling everyone to take cover as an air-raid was in progress.

'What are we going to do?' shouted Alice hysterically.

'I don't know. What did you do the last time?'

'We went outside and watched till the bomb fell, then we all rushed inside. Hannah, I'm frightened!'

'Well, calm down. Go and get John, quickly,' said Hannah. 'We'll go downstairs. Can we get into the basement?'

'Well, yes, but it's ever so creepy down there. I don't want to go down there.'

'We've got to,' Hannah insisted.

'But it's dark . . .'

'That doesn't matter. Alice, stop being so stupid. Now go on, go and get John.'

Alice returned very quickly with a sleepy John over her shoulder, and they made their way down the stairs.

'Are there gas-lamps down there?' asked Hannah.

'Don't know.'

'Well, have you got a candle?'

'There's some in the kitchen. You hold John while I go and get them.'

'Don't forget the matches,' Hannah called after her.

John started to get a little restless, so Hannah tried to soothe him. He was getting a big lad, and difficult to hold, and Hannah was pleased when Alice returned.

At the bottom of the stairs they went along a dark passage.

'It's through this door,' Alice said.

Hannah lit the candle, and tried to protect the flame with her hand. They slowly inched their way into the room which felt cold and smelt of damp. The candle flickered, and John began to whimper.

'Shh,' said Alice comfortingly. 'Alice has got you. Don't be afraid – we're going to play hide and seek.'

Hannah marvelled at her sister for, despite her own fear, she had pulled herself together, comforting the little lad. She certainly had a way with him. As they slowly walked in, Hannah shut her eyes tight, trying to get them adjusted to the light. Hannah hesitated. What if there were mice, or even rats . . . ?

'I've never been down here,' whispered Alice, looking around. 'I only poked my head round the door once. Look,

look over there, there's a gas-light. I don't think the mantle looks too good.'

'I'll see if I can light it,' said Hannah, her footsteps echoing on the bare floorboards as she walked across the room.

After a lot of popping and hissing, she finally got the mantle to light, its yellow glow warm and comforting. The large room was completely empty, with large patches of damp on the walls.

'I'm surprised Betty hasn't done up this room and let it,' said Hannah.

'It probably costs too much to keep warm. And it's a bit creepy with the windows boarded up. I wonder how long we've got to wait down here? I hope they don't drop any more bombs.'

At that moment there was a dull thud, and the house gently rocked.

Alice shuddered, and her voice rose in fear. 'I'm scared, Hannah! I don't want to die,' she cried hysterically.

Hannah put her arm round her shoulders. 'There, there. Shh, Alice, you're upsetting John. None of us wants to die.'

With John in her arms, Alice hugged Hannah close. They were a tight little bunch. Only the sound of their breathing filled their ears as they stood quietly waiting.

After what seemed a lifetime, they heard the whistles telling them the raid was over. They ran up the stairs and threw open the front door. People were dashing about but, unlike the last time, there was no smoke rising behind the tall buildings.

'What happened?' Hannah called to a woman hurrying down the road.

'The bomb knocked down some 'ouses over the West End, so the bobby said. Me sister lives over that way, got ter see if she's all right.' The woman had hardly stopped for breath.

'I must get back to Maudie,' said Hannah.

'What about me? You're not going to leave me?' gasped Alice.

'You're all right, it's all over now.'

'But what if they come back? I'm all on my own.' Alice's voice trembled with fear.

'They won't be back now.'

'How do you know?' asked Alice.

Hannah couldn't answer that. 'Perhaps Betty will be home soon.'

'What if she's been killed or injured.' Tears filled her eyes. 'She could be lying buried in some awful dark hole, crying out in pain.'

Hannah looked at Alice. 'Don't be so dramatic. I'm sure she's perfectly safe.'

'Well, I'm not so sure.'

'You'd better come home with me then.' Hannah said curtly.

Alice turned and marched up the steps, dragging John with her. She pushed open the front door. 'You'd better get your hat and bag,' she said, disappearing inside.

Hannah followed her. 'Look, Alice,' she said more gently, 'I'm sure Betty will be here as soon as she can.'

'Hannah, can't you stay, just till she gets home? I'm very frightened.'

Hannah for once felt wanted.

'All right,' she said graciously. 'I'll stay for a little while.'

It was an hour later when Betty came rushing in crying. 'My baby, my baby. I was so worried about you.' She swept John up in her arms and hugged him close. 'Are you all right? Where did you go?' she asked Alice. 'This is it, we're not going to stay in London, we've got to get away.'

'But Betty,' said Alice. 'We're fine. We went down to the basement.'

'Ugh, you went down there?'

'We thought it would be the safest place,' said Hannah.

'Yer, well, I suppose it is. Can't say I'd want to make a 'abit of it though.'

'They may not come over again,' said Alice.

'Don't you believe it. I reckon 'e's out ter break us now, the wicked bugger. No, we've got ter get away.'

'Where would you go?' asked Hannah.

'Don't know, I'll 'ave ter find out from me friends what shows are on in the provinces.'

Alice turned up her nose. 'I wouldn't have thought you'd be happy playing out of London. Look at that time we went away and you did the show that Christmas.'

Betty smiled. 'Yer, it was pretty lousy. She don't forget, does she?' Betty turned to Alice. 'Get me a drink, love, I need something to settle me nerves.'

'I'll be off now,' said Hannah.

At the door, Alice held her sister tight. 'Thanks for staying.'

Hannah hurried down the road, her thoughts full of bombs. She wished she knew where they had dropped. The woman said the West End, which meant over the water, a long way from Rotherhithe. She hoped she was right. Although everybody was full of what they were doing when the Zeppelin came over, she saw nothing unusual on the tram home.

When she turned into Hope Street, she almost cried with relief. It looked like any other warm Saturday afternoon, with everybody at their door, gossiping. Maudie was talking to Mrs Warren, and her face lit up when Hannah came up to them.

''Allo there, gel. Fank God yer 'ome,' said Maudie. 'You all right? I've been worried sick about yer. The bloody Zeps been over again. Did it drop its bombs over your way?'

'No, some woman told us it was the West End.'

'Poor buggers,' said Maudie.

''Allo there, 'Annah. All right then, gel?' said Mrs Warren.

'Yes, thank you. Are you feeling a bit better now?' inquired Hannah.

'Yes fanks. My Ted's coming 'ome soon.' Her face was wreathed in smiles.

'How's he getting on?'

''E don't say a lot, but I fink 'e's finding it 'ard. Silly little bugger, putting 'is age up ter git in. I'll give 'im wot for when 'e gits 'ome.'

Hannah smiled, and thought about poor Ted having to face his mother's wrath after weeks of being bullied by a sergeant. She turned to Maudie. 'I'll go on in.'

'Make a pot o' tea, there's a love. Mary should be back soon.'

'Where's she gone?'

'Someone from the 'ospital come and asked 'er ter go back ter work.'

'Why?'

'She didn't say, she just put 'er coat on and went.'

Hannah was deep in thought as she crossed the road. Were the injured being moved to her hospital, as they'd thought?

The house was quiet. Hannah was still sitting in the kitchen. She'd been reading but had dozed off, and her book dropping to the floor startled her. She looked at the clock: it was almost midnight. She heard the key being pulled through the letter-box. She quickly jumped up and opened the kitchen door.

'Hannah, you're still up?' said Mary. She looked tired and drawn.

'Yes, I thought I'd wait up for you. Would you like a cup of tea?'

'Yes, please. That's very kind of you.' She sat on the chair and, kicking her shoes off, gently rubbed her toes. 'It's been a long day, changing beds and moving them around, trying to get more and more injured in. Thank goodness I've got you

314

and Maudie here so I don't have to worry about Brian.'

'Was the raid awful? Were many people hurt?' Hannah asked softly.

'I don't know. It's not been the injured from the raid we've had; we've had a lot of soldiers brought in from other hospitals. It seems they were short of beds. Anyway, we're going to keep them now. Hopefully this will be their last move before going home. Some of them have had appalling wounds – and they're so very young.' Tears began to slowly trickle down Mary's cheek. She quickly brushed them aside. 'I'm sorry, that's not very professional of me.'

Hannah swallowed hard, and reached over and gently touched her hand. 'You're tired, it's been a long day for you. You go on up and I'll bring you your tea in bed. You can have a lie-in in the morning. I'll see to Brian.'

'Hannah. They've asked me to go in tomorrow.'

'Oh, that's all right, don't worry about Brian.'

She sighed. 'Thanks. We'll have to have more staff. None of us will be able to keep this pace up.'

'You go on up, the kettle's almost boiled.'

Hannah stood, slowly stirring the tea round and round in the pot. What Mary was doing was really worthwhile. If they needed more staff, would they want trained ones, or . . . ? For the first time in her life, Hannah knew what she wanted. She wanted to help the injured soldiers.

She carried the tea up to Mary, and gently pushed open her door. Mary was lying on top of the bed, fast asleep. She hadn't even bothered to take her uniform off. Hannah smiled as she quietly closed the door and made her way to her own room. Maudie was on her back, snoring. Hannah crept in beside her, but sleep wouldn't come. Her mind was racing. Tomorrow she would go to the hospital and find out if she could work there.

She suddenly felt happy. She had a home and, if she could do an interesting, worthwhile job, then her life would have a purpose.

Chapter 25

Hannah could hear Mary moving about as dawn began to lighten the sky. Hannah slid out of bed and padded out of the room.

Mary's bedroom door was open. 'I'm sorry, Hannah, did I wake you?' Mary was dressed and looked refreshed after her night's sleep. She was holding Brian.

'No. What time have you got to go?'

'As soon as I can.' She sat on the bed. 'Come on, my lad, let me take you down for your breakfast.'

'Don't worry about Brian,' Hannah said. 'I'll see to his breakfast.' She hesitated. 'Mary, last night you said they may want more staff at the hospital. Would they have to be trained?'

Mary's head shot up. 'No, it's not necessary, not to do the cleaning and that kind of work. Why?'

'I think I'd like to work there.'

Mary looked surprised. 'It's not always pleasant.'

'But I'd be doing something worthwhile.' Hannah sat on the bed next to her, her enthusiasm bubbling under the surface.

'You wouldn't get as much money.'

'I don't care. I just won't buy so many clothes.'

Mary shrugged. 'I don't know what to say.'

'Couldn't you find out for me?'

'Would you really be interested?'

'Yes. Yes, I would.'

'Well. Look, why don't you come round this morning? I could have a word with Sister, just to try and find out more, and that will give you a chance to look round, and perhaps

317

help you make up your mind. Matron won't be in today, but Sister will be able to give me all the details.'

Mary had barely finished when Hannah threw her arms round her neck and hugged her.

'Thank you, thank you.'

'Hold on! I haven't done anything yet.'

'No, but you've certainly got me thinking. What time shall I come?'

'About ten, we should get a break then. Now I must get going.' She kissed Brian and settled him back in the bed.

'I'll see you about ten then, Hannah.'

Hannah was still standing in the bedroom when Mary quietly closed the front door. She wanted to run into Maudie to tell her her news, but knew she wouldn't be welcome at this time of the morning, so she went downstairs to make herself a cup of tea. Ten o'clock couldn't come soon enough for Hannah.

There was a spring in Hannah's step this warm, sunny June morning. She smiled to herself when she recalled the look of horror on Maudie's face when earlier she had told her where she was going, and why.

'Yer must be bloody mad. Yer wouldn't catch me doing a job like that – all the blood and gore.'

Hannah felt guilty at being so happy when she remembered the war, and the young men in the hospital. She wondered how many people were lying injured or dead after the Zeppelin raid yesterday. The thought made her hasten her step.

As she walked through the gate of the cottage hospital, she suddenly felt nervous. Hannah remembered the last time she was here. Kate had been looking after Brian, and young Billy had brought her here. Such a lot had happened since then. Hannah shuddered. Mary had told her it wasn't the same Sister she'd seen that time. At least that was something. She rang the bell and waited. She was taken aback when a good-looking young man with deep-set brown eyes and a pale face, wearing the blue uniform of the injured, peered round the door.

'Hello,' he said smiling. 'Another pretty girl. Who have you come to see?'

Hannah blushed. 'Sister,' she stammered.

'Come on in.' He held the door wide open and Hannah walked past him. She turned and was surprised to see he was on crutches, and that his left leg finished just below the knee. She went to close the door. 'That's all right, I can manage. I'm one of the walking wounded.' He moved along the corridor with ease. 'She's not the dragon everyone says she is, is she? Oh, you're not related? You didn't mean *that* kind of sister?'

'No,' laughed Hannah.

'That's her office.' He waved a crutch at an open door.

'Thank you,' she said, grateful that his cheerfulness had made her feel relaxed.

Sister was sitting at her desk. She looked up when Hannah gently knocked on the door. 'Come in. You must be Hannah Miller. Close the door and sit down.'

Hannah did as she was told.

'Now, Nurse Dobson has told me all about you. She said you've been working at the biscuit factory.'

Hannah nodded. 'I still am, at the moment.'

'What makes you think you will be suitable here?'

'I don't know. I just want to do something useful, and Mary – er, Nurse Dobson – said you might want more staff.'

'Yes, we do, but you haven't had any training.'

'But I'm a very quick learner. Please, give me a chance.'

'I understand that you can read and write.'

'Yes, yes I can.'

'You will be expected to make tea, wash floors, and carry out general cleaning work. Nurse Dobson speaks very highly of you. Do you think you'll be interested in doing these sort of menial tasks?'

Hannah nodded. She'd been hoping for something more responsible, but this was at least a start.

A smile slowly spread across Sister's face. 'Well, I think we can find something for you here. It won't always be pleasant work, I warn you, and sometimes your feet will feel they are about to drop off, and your back will be breaking, and you'll be at everyone's beck and call; but if you stick at it, I'm sure you will get a great deal of satisfaction from your new post. When can you start?'

'I can give my notice in tomorrow.'

'Good. Now remember you won't get as much money as in a factory, and the hours will be a lot longer. There's no going home when the hooter sounds, and if a patient needs you then you stay till the crisis is over: their recovery would be your reward. Do you understand?'

Hannah nodded. She didn't like to ask how much money she'd be getting.

'Good,' Sister said again. 'Come back and see me as soon as possible. I'm sure Matron will approve of you.' She stood up and Hannah jumped to her feet. 'I'll find Nurse Dobson to show you round.' She rustled out of the room, with Hannah quickly following close behind.

Mary was with another nurse in a very small room full of cupboards.

'Take this young lady round,' said Sister. 'But don't be too long. Remember you have a lot of work to do.'

'Yes, Sister,' said Mary in a very subdued voice.

As soon as Sister walked away, Mary hugged Hannah. 'You've got the job then?'

'I think so,' said Hannah, totally bemused. 'It's all happened so fast.'

'Well, we've got more than enough work, and I think Matron has said recruit anyone who can read and write. By the way, this is Vera, Nurse Moore.'

'Hello,' said Hannah, holding out her hand.

'Welcome to the madhouse,' said Vera.

'And this is the linen room,' said Mary. 'Right, follow me.' She swished out of the room, and once again Hannah found herself following someone. 'This is one of the wards. We only have two.' Mary bent her head closer. 'These poor lads are the worst.'

At first, as they stood in the doorway, Hannah could only see a sea of beds with men in them. She quickly noted that eight beds had been crammed into this small room. There was just enough room for the men to get in and out; not that any of the young men were moving very much, most of them lay back with their eyes closed. They had lost their colour, and they all seemed to have the same grey look. Two had hands and arms missing; their stumps were swathed in bandages. Another young man had bandages round his head, another two were just lying very still, while the bedclothes of the other three were flat: Hannah realized they had no legs. It was a very sorry sight and she could have cried for them. They looked so lost and abandoned.

When they walked away, Hannah whispered, 'I didn't think there would be any really badly injured ones here.'

'I know it's hard to believe, but these are getting better. It was the disruption of being driven here yesterday that has upset them. You mark my words, most of them will be up and running in a few days' time.'

Hannah found that impossible to believe.

'This is the day room,' said Mary, pushing open a door.

This room was very different. Men were sitting in chairs laughing and talking, the air full of cigarette smoke. Some were playing cards and a couple looked up when Hannah and Mary entered the room.

'Look who's here. It's our little Mary.' A thick-set man with a mop of black hair began chanting. "Mary, Mary, quite contrary, how does your garden grow?" '

'Now, Private Brown, behave, or I'll make you go back to bed.'

'I'm in love with you, Mary. Say you'll marry me. I'd get down on me knees, but I'd fall over.' He threw his head back and laughed. It was then that Hannah noticed that he didn't have any legs.

'Now that's quite enough of that,' said Mary sternly, but her face had flushed to a pretty pink.

'I'm ever so sorry, Nurse,' he said in a soft, whimpering tone, which caused everybody to laugh.

'Who's yer pretty mate then?' called out another.

This time it was Hannah's turn to blush.

'This is Miss Miller, she's going to work here.'

'Whoopee,' shouted someone else. 'We could do with a few pretty girls round here.'

'Come on, Hannah, I'll show you the rest of the place.'

Outside, Mary smiled. 'They're a good bunch of lads. They've been through a lot, so don't worry about the things they say.'

Hannah was secretly feeling very pleased. It had been a long time since anyone had called her pretty and this was the second time in a morning!

'Come on, I'll show you where the kitchen is. We have a cook who comes in to do the dinners, but we have to do all the breakfasts, and make all the teas and sandwiches throughout the day. That's the treatment room. We have a doctor who comes here most days.' She waved her hand at a closed door.

'I don't think I'll remember where everything is.'

'I'm sure you will. That's the bathroom, and the next one is the lavatory. There's another round the corner, and two more upstairs.' Hannah was almost running to keep up with her as she seemed to glide effortlessly along the corridor. 'Right, that seems to be all for now. There are some other small rooms upstairs that the lads in the day room are in, but you'll soon find your way round. We're back at the front door now. I'll be able to tell Sister when you're going to start. Well, what do you think?'

'I think it'll be wonderful, helping.'

'Yes, but don't forget, your job will be a lot of clearing up and making tea. We can talk about it tonight – I must dash, see you later. Tell Maudie I hope to be home about four.' She turned and walked away, leaving Hannah breathless. There were so many things she wanted to ask her but, as Mary said, they would have to wait till later.

Outside, Hannah slowly walked to the gate. Mary seemed so impressive at work, efficient and disciplined; but then when Hannah thought about it, she was like that at home as well. Hannah felt happy as she stepped out into the warm sunshine.

'Hello.' The young man who had opened the door to her was sitting on a wooden bench. 'Did you see her?'

'Yes,' said Hannah.

'Have you got a few minutes?'

'Yes.'

'Come and sit down.' He patted the empty space next to him. 'I could do with someone to talk to. Do you live near here?'

'Yes, as a matter of fact, I live with Mary, Nurse Dobson.'

'Oh, do you now? She's very nice and very gentle. We only got here yesterday but, d'you know, she's been wonderful to some of the poor lads. Some of them are only boys.'

Hannah looked at him, guessing he wasn't much older than

her. 'I'm hoping to work here,' she said tentatively.

'You are? When?'

'In a week or so. I've got to give in my notice at the biscuit factory first.'

He laughed. 'The biscuit factory?'

She nodded.

'This is going to be a lot different,' he suggested. 'I always thought nurses had to have training.'

'Oh, I'm not going to be a nurse, I'm just going to help out.'

'That'll be nice. By the way the name's Jeff, Private Jeff Owen.' He held out his hand.

'I'm Hannah, Hannah Miller.'

'Pleased to meet you, Hannah Miller.'

She smiled. 'And I'm pleased to meet you.'

They both fell silent, then said together, 'Are you married?' They laughed.

'Sorry,' he said. 'Well, are you?'

'No, not yet. I hope to when my young man comes home on leave.'

'Oh, where is he?'

'In France.'

Jeff's happy expression changed. 'It's pretty bad over there. Do you know where he is?'

'No. Are you married?' Hannah quickly asked, keen to change the subject. She didn't want to think that Jack could end up like some of these men.

'Yes. When you come again I'll show you a picture of my wife and little girl. Her name's Rene.'

'That's nice, how old is she?'

His face was beaming with pride. 'She'll be two next month. She's got a mop of fair curls and she's very pretty.'

'She sounds lovely. I'd like to see her picture.' The church clock began striking. 'I must go,' said Hannah. 'Perhaps I'll see you when I start work.'

'I wouldn't be at all surprised.' He went to stand up.

'No, please don't get up.' Hannah gently pushed him back down. 'Bye.'

She smiled as she walked away, a definite bounce in her step. Jeff Owen was nice, and he was clearly so proud of his family. It made Hannah wonder if Jack talked about her like that?

'Well, 'ow did yer git on?' asked Maudie.

'I've got the job. I can start as soon as I like. I'm going to ask Wally if I have to work out a full week's notice.' Hannah plonked herself down in the chair. 'Oh, Maudie, you should see some of those poor fellows. Some have got no arms, and others have lost their legs.' Suddenly the enthusiasm of the day disappeared, and tears filled her eyes. 'I'm so glad I'll be able to help a bit,' she croaked.

Maudie swallowed hard. 'I'll make yer a cup o' tea. Did Mary say what time she'd be 'ome?'

Hannah nodded and wiped her eyes. 'About four, she hopes.'

'Now, come on, pull yerself tergevver. Yer gonner see a lot of 'orrible sights, and if yer don't fink yer can take it, well then, don't go.'

'I'm going to go, whatever happens.' Hannah knew there would be times when she would be upset, but also that it mustn't stop her from doing the best she could.

Wally wasn't very happy at losing another experienced hand, but he said she could go on Saturday. Elsie was also very upset about Hannah's decision, and couldn't wait for lunch-time to come to let her feelings be known.

'First Rosie, now you. Won't be anybody left 'ere soon.

325

Biscuits are still very important, yer know. A lotta stuff goes to our soldiers in France.'

'Yes, I know, Elsie. But I have to do something that really makes me feel I'm helping the war effort, and I didn't fancy going in the munitions factory.'

'I've 'eard they're talking about getting women ter go on the trams – they want 'em ter be conductors.'

'What? I can't see that.'

Elsie straightened her shoulders. Hannah knew that meant she had something to say. 'Well, that's wot I 'eard, and if it's so, then I fink I'll apply.' She grinned. 'Could be a bit of a laugh. 'Ere, I bet old Rosie would like ter do that, chatting up all the blokes.'

'Have you seen anything of Rosie?' Hannah asked.

'Na. Fink she's too busy earning plenty a dough. Yer gonner git much?'

'No. They don't pay that well.'

''Ow much yer gonner git then?'

Hannah blushed. She felt silly saying she didn't know. 'Someone came in and the sister forgot to tell me.' She knew it was a little white lie, but she didn't want Elsie to know the truth.

Elsie seemed satisfied with that answer and went on, 'Well, yer wouldn't catch me working there. D'yer 'ave ter put the bandages on 'em?'

'I shouldn't think so, but I'll have to make them a cup of tea,' laughed Hannah.

Elsie looked about her. 'And wot about when they wonner, yer know . . .' She bent her head closer. 'Yer know? 'Ave a jimmy. D'yer 'ave ter 'elp 'em if they're in bed?'

'I shouldn't think so,' she said hastily. 'That would be a nurse's job.' Hannah suddenly thought about the lads without arms.

'Oh,' said Elsie as, to Hannah's relief, the hooter went, calling them back to work. She wouldn't have to answer any more questions today, and hopefully by tomorrow, there would be some other topic of more interest.

When Saturday came, Hannah was upset that everybody rushed off at one o'clock without saying a word. Only Elsie said goodbye and wished her luck. She sighed and made her way home.

'I'm going over to see Alice this afternoon. I may not get another chance for a while,' said Hannah as she walked in.

'OK, love. Give 'er me love. Guess wot? Tom popped in 'ere this morning. Seems old Bob ain't none too well. 'Is son got injured in France, and 'e's in a 'ome down Kent way.'

'I am sorry. Was he badly injured?'

'Bob don't know, 'e's 'oping ter go down there next weekend.'

'Will he be all right, going all that way on his own?'

'Tom seems ter fink so.'

'Pity Tom couldn't go with him.'

'Yer, but 'e's gotter git the papers out.'

Hannah sat back. Everybody had a job to do. Should she offer to go to Kent with Bob? 'Maudie, when I get a day off, do you think Bob would like me to go with him?'

'That's real kind of yer. D'yer know, I reckon 'e'd be tickled pink. I'll pop round later and tell 'im.'

'But I don't know when, tell him.'

'Yer, yer, course I will. Yer a good gel, and no mistake.'

Hannah felt warmed by Maudie's praise. It was nice to do things for other people, she decided.

Hannah could hear music as she walked towards the house where Alice lived. All the windows had been flung open, and loud music and laughter drifted into the street below. Hannah tentatively knocked on the door. There was no answer. She knocked again, this time much harder. The door was flung open by a young man she had seen once before.

'Hello, come on in.'

'Is Alice in?' she asked.

'Course. Alice,' he yelled up the stairs. 'You'd better come in, she may not be able to hear you with all this din going on.'

'What's happened?' asked Hannah.

'Rick's home. You better go on up.'

At the top of the stairs, Hannah stood in the doorway. The room was full of people, smoke and noise. The women were all dressed in the latest fashion, and some of the men in army officers' uniform looked very smart; others looked like dandies.

'Hannah,' called Alice. 'What are you doing here?'

Hannah looked at Alice in amazement. Her hair was piled up on her head, and she had a long pink feather wafting about at the back of it. Her face was painted, and she was wearing a long slinky pink dress that clung to her slight figure, showing off her tiny waist and small breasts.

'Look at you,' gasped Hannah.

'D'you like it?' Alice smiled and twirled round.

'No, I don't,' said Hannah crossly. 'You look cheap.'

'Well, thank you very much. Is that what you've come all the way over here to tell me?' She pushed Hannah along the corridor away from the doorway. 'I happen to be enjoying myself, and I wear what I like. You always were dowdy, always on about wearing practical clothes. Well, I can do what I like here, and if you don't like it, then don't bother to come.' Alice began to walk away.

Hannah put her hand out to stop her. 'I'm sorry. It's the shock of seeing . . . Well, I didn't expect to . . . That young man said Rick was home.'

'Yes, he is, and if you must know, he and Betty are getting married on Monday. Now, what did you want to see me about?'

Hannah wanted to shake her. How dare she speak to her like this? But she held her tongue. 'I've just come over to tell you I'm going to work with Mary at the cottage hospital, and I don't know when I'll be able to see you again.' Hannah knew Alice wasn't really listening; her foot was tapping in time to the music. 'Alice, did you hear what I said?'

'Yes, of course.'

'Well, what do you say?'

'It's up to you what you do.'

'Is that it?'

Alice looked towards the door. 'Well, come over when you can.'

'I don't believe this,' said Hannah angrily. 'The last time I was here you didn't want me to go, you were frightened – now you can't get rid of me quickly enough! Well, if you can find the time, could you drop me a line now and again? I'm sorry I've interrupted your little party.' Hannah stormed off down the stairs. At the bottom she turned, half expecting Alice to be behind her, but she wasn't.

Hannah was furious. Alice had called her dowdy. And she always acted offhandedly when the others were around. She was ashamed of her; didn't want the others to see her.

Tears filled Hannah's eyes as she made her way home. What was Alice doing to help the war effort? Sitting in some posh hotel sewing and drinking tea hardly qualified.

Chapter 26

Over the weekend, Hannah had asked Mary dozens of questions. Mary had given her clear, patient answers, but Hannah was still apprehensive.

'I told you, don't worry, you'll soon get the hang of things,' said Mary as they made their way to the hospital on Monday morning.

Hannah had been up early, and as she walked along with Mary, felt very nervous. 'D'you think Sister will like me?'

'As long as you do your work as well as you can, she'll be fine.'

'What about Matron?'

'She'll be the same. You may not see her for days, even weeks. She's very elusive, and it's best to keep out of her way.'

That statement didn't help calm Hannah's fears.

Once inside, Sister gave instructions for Mary to give Hannah an overall and show her where everything of importance was in the kitchen. After she had finished the huge pile of breakfast washing-up, she made tea, then did more washing-up and cleaning. It was hot and her hair stuck to the back of her neck. When it was time for a short lunch-break she took a cup of tea and staggered out into the warm sunshine. She plonked herself down on the nearest seat, kicked her shoes off, and lay back with her eyes closed.

'Hello there, Hannah Miller.'

Hannah looked up at Jeff Owen, who was standing over her. 'Hello,' she answered. 'How are you today?'

'I'm fine, but I must say you don't look as fresh and happy as you did last week.'

Hannah smiled. 'I don't feel it.'

'Can I sit with you?'

'Course, but only for a while, I have to get back to all the washing-up.'

Jeff smiled and, to Hannah's surprise, took her hand. He turned it over. 'Take care of these, otherwise they'll end up sore. Make sure you rub some cream in them: Fuller's Earth is very good.'

Hannah blushed and quickly pulled her hand away. 'Thank you, I'll remember that. I don't know why they bothered asking me if I could read and write, not if I'm going to spend all my time in the sink.'

'Perhaps they have better things in store for you.'

Hannah laughed. 'I hope so.' She stood up. 'I must be getting back.'

'See you around, Hannah Miller.'

Inside, the cook, a large woman with huge wet patches under her armpits, stopped slopping the mashed potatoes on the plates and wiped her wet forehead on the bottom of her apron. Hannah looked at the pile of dirty dishes and pans, and her heart sank. This wasn't how she'd hoped to help the soldiers. She wanted to be part of the hospital. Part of the healing.

'You'd better get started,' said the cook. 'Don't let Sister see 'em all piled up.'

Hannah didn't answer, but she donned her sacking apron and thrust her hands into the hot soda water again.

At last it was time to leave.

'Well? How did you enjoy your first day?' Mary asked on the way home.

'I'm very tired.'

'After tea we'll get the bath in and you can have a nice soak.'

'That would be heaven. I'm not used to being on my feet like that, running around all day. Look at them, they look like Maudie's!' Laughing, Hannah held on to Mary and lifted her swollen foot up. 'They feel like great blobs of raw meat.'

'Just so long as you don't have to start cutting the sides of your shoes out like she has to,' laughed Mary. 'Come on, let's get home and have a nice cup of tea.' She took hold of Hannah's arm and tucked it under hers.

'Well, gel, 'ow d'yer git on?' asked Maudie as soon as they walked in.

'Not bad,' said Hannah, sinking into the armchair.

'Did yer git ter do any operations?' laughed Maudie.

'No, not today, been too busy washing up.'

'Maudie, after tea, Hannah would like a bath,' said Mary.

'Why? It ain't Friday.'

'No, I know, but it'll help ease her aches and pains.'

'Well, please yerself. It'll take a while ter boil up a few saucepans.'

'That's all right, I'll give you a hand.'

'I managed ter git yer a nice kipper fer tea. 'Ad ter queue up fer it, mind. 'Annah, wot d'yer . . .'

But Hannah wasn't listening. She had fallen fast asleep.

She woke with a start when Mary gently shook her arm. 'Hannah, Hannah,' she whispered. 'Your bath's ready.'

Hannah opened her eyes. 'How long have I been asleep?'

'Not too long. Me and Maudie are going in the front room so you can have your bath in peace.'

When the kitchen door closed, Hannah took off her clothes and gently sank into the tin bath. The warm water was only a few inches deep, and with her knees almost under her chin, she lay back as best she could. She felt relaxed. Today had been hard, but she felt content and, hopefully, one day she'd get out of the kitchen. She let her mind drift to the men in the hospital. At least more of them seemed to be walking about than before, but some of them were so young . . . Her thoughts went to Ted across the road. He was going to fight soon. She prayed he wouldn't finish up like some of those in the hospital. But they were the lucky ones; they were alive. What about Jack? She had written to tell him about her new job, but she hadn't had a card from him for weeks, and the four she had had were very vague. If she mentioned to Maudie how worried she was, she would always say no news was good news, but was it?

A gentle knocking on the door brought her back to number forty, Hope Street.

'Are you all right?' inquired Mary.

'Yes, thank you, I've almost finished,' said Hannah, scrambling out of the bath. She quickly dried herself on the rough towel and, pulling on her chemise and petticoat, opened the door.

'We were getting worried about you, we thought you'd fallen asleep again. Get the bucket and I'll start emptying the water out,' said Mary.

When the last bucket of water was taken away, they carried the bath outside into the tiny yard and hung it on the large hook that stuck out from the closet wall. It would stay there till Friday.

'I'm going to bed now,' said Hannah. 'See you both in the morning.'

'Good-night, love,' said Maudie, her eyes twinkling with kindness.

'Good-night, Hannah. Perhaps tomorrow might not be quite so hard,' said Mary.

But it was, and so were the next three weeks.

* * *

It was the start of Hannah's fourth week, at the end of which she would get her first pay-packet. She knew now it would only be half what she had been getting at the factory, but she didn't mind.

There had been some changes in the hospital; some of the men had gone home, and new ones had quickly taken their place. Every lunch-break Hannah tried to sit with Jeff Owen for a short while. He was friendly and she was fond of him. Over the past few weeks – and rather to Hannah's relief – he had shown her pictures of his wife and little girl. In fact, he talked about them non-stop. He told her he lived in North London, and had worked in the City before the war.

'Hannah, guess what?' he called excitedly as soon as she walked to their seat. 'Marie and Rene are coming to see me.'

She sat beside him. 'Oh Jeff, I'm so pleased for you. When?'

'Next week, Sunday. I must get a hair-cut, I don't look too ill, do I?'

'No, of course not. Sitting here in the sun has done wonders for you.' Hannah paused. 'Jeff,' she said softly. 'You have told your wife about your injuries?'

He threw his head back and laughed, crinkling his brown eyes. 'You mean this?' He pulled at the empty flap of blue trouser leg that was pinned half-way up his leg.

Hannah nodded.

'Course, but she told me not to worry about it. It won't make any difference. She's a wonderful girl, Hannah. Will you be here on Sunday?'

'No, that's my day off, unless they need me to come in.'

'That's a pity, I'd like you to meet Marie.'

'And I'd like to have met her. I must go, otherwise I'll be in trouble.' Hannah patted his shoulder as she walked away. What would his wife's reaction be when she saw him, she wondered anxiously. Over these past three weeks she had seen many wives, sisters and mothers. Some had coped, but others had just sat dumbfounded, unable to speak. Many had cried, struggling to come to terms with the dreadful injuries their husbands and sons had suffered. The shell-shocked victims stared into space. Some had lost the power of speech; their wives and mothers just sat silently with them. It was the mothers of young lads that upset her the most, the way they cried and held on to their sons. Hannah sometimes wondered what it was all about, this war? Was this terrible pain and loss of life worth it? Hannah didn't think so.

Maudie was beaming like a Cheshire cat when Mary and Hannah walked in.

'Yer got a letter,' she said, handing a grubby envelope to Hannah. 'I fink it's from Jack.'

Hannah grinned in delight. 'Yes, it's his writing.' She tore open the envelope. Slowly tears began to run down her cheeks.

'What is it?' asked Mary. 'Is he all right?'

Hannah nodded, smiling despite the tears. 'Guess what? He's learnt to drive. He's been driving the Red Cross lorries. He said it's better than being at the Front, although it can get a bit hairy at times.' She turned the page over. 'This next bit has been blacked out by the censor. But he goes on to say.' She stopped. 'It's a bit personal.' She felt embarrassed and silly when she felt a red flush creeping up from her collar. 'But he does say we should get married when he gets home.'

'Oh, 'Annah, that's good.'

'And Maudie, he's put you down as his next-of-kin for now.'

'Wot's 'e done that for?'

'He says if anything should happen to him –' Hannah's voice became very low – 'without a next-of-kin, we wouldn't know.'

'Oh,' said Maudie solemnly.

'He's being practical,' said Mary gently.

Hannah folded the letter and wiped her eyes. 'Still, at least we know he's safe,' she smiled. 'Fancy him learning to drive! He always said he wanted a car after he went in Rick's.'

'That's going to stand him in good stead when the war's over,' said Mary. 'He could get a job anywhere.'

'That would be nice.'

'Well, gel, it looks like everyfink could turn out real good for yer. Now come on, tea's ready. 'Ad ter queue up fer bread terday. I tell yer, fings ain't gitting any better.'

'I don't know what we'd do without you to look after us,' said Mary, putting her arm round the little old woman.

Maudie smiled. 'Yer. Well. It's nice ter be 'ere.'

Hannah was still thinking about Jack's letter. For the first time he had said he missed her and loved her. She couldn't believe it: he *did* want to marry her. Tears were stinging her eyes; she wanted to cry she was so happy. He was a driver, so perhaps when this war was over he would get a job and, like Mary said, go straight. Then all her dreams would come true. She said a silent prayer: please Lord, don't take all this away from me.

Jeff Owen was at the gate to meet Hannah and Mary on Monday morning. He didn't look his usual chirpy self, but old and drawn.

'Hello Jeff, what you doing here?' Hannah asked.

'Thought I'd come to meet you.'

'How was your wife, and little Rene?' she asked as they slowly made their way down the gravel path.

'Rene was lovely, you should see how much she has grown. She's a real little princess.' He paused. 'Hannah. Could I have a word with you later?'

'If I get time.'

'I'll go on,' said Mary.

'It's very important,' said Jeff.

Hannah looked at him, she could see he was troubled. 'Is it to do with your wife?' she whispered.

He quickly bent his head and nodded.

Hannah looked anxiously around. 'Look, give me a moment. Mary!' She called after her friend.

Mary stopped and Hannah caught up with her.

'Jeff wants a word with me. I think it's his wife – do you think Sister would mind?'

'Go and have a word with her. She pretends she doesn't like us listening to their problems, but we all know it helps.'

Hannah hurried along to Sister's room and knocked on the door.

'Come in. Ah, Miss Miller, I was going to speak to you later today.'

'Please,' interrupted Hannah nervously.

'Well, what can I do for you?'

'It's Jeff Owen.'

'Private Owen? What about him? You know Matron doesn't like the staff fraternizing with the patients.'

'We only talk. He tells me about his wife.'

Sister looked stern. 'You could lose your job over this, young lady.'

'But I haven't done anything wrong,' Hannah protested.

'So, what is this all about?'

'He wants to talk to me. His wife came to see him yesterday, and I think she was unhappy about his leg.'

'Well, I'm afraid that's something she will have to learn to live with.'

'Is it all right if I have a word with him. I'll stay later.'

'Oh, very well then, but be quick, then report back here.'

'Yes, Sister.' Hannah quickly left the room and hurried outside. Jeff was sitting on their bench.

'Oh, good, you've been able to come, then. I hope you didn't get into any trouble.'

'No,' said Hannah, thinking: well, not yet. 'Now, what's this all about?'

'I don't think my wife will be able to accept this.' He pulled at his trouser leg.

'Give her time. It's a great shock at first. I'm sure she will eventually.'

'I don't think so. Yesterday she hardly said a word, she just sat looking at my leg or, should I say, the place that was my leg. Hannah, I'm worried.'

'But why?'

'What about when she sees my stump?'

'I'm sure she'll accept it, you must give her time.'

Jeff looked doubtful. 'It's not a pretty sight.'

'Now, come on, you mustn't dwell on it. After all, it's just your first meeting. When you get home, things will be different.'

He tapped his crutch on the ground. 'I don't think so. You see, she doesn't think I'll be able to get a job.'

'But there are plenty of jobs you can do. You could go back into your office. Besides, the government will have to find jobs for people like you. After all *you* didn't pick the fight with Germany.'

Jeff smiled. 'For a young girl you've certainly got an old head on your shoulders. Have you had a hard life, Hannah?'

She blushed. 'No, not really. Look, I've got to go and see Sister. I'll see you at lunch-time, and stop worrying.'

He went to stand, but Hannah gently pushed him back down.

'I hope I haven't got you into any trouble.'

'No. But I must go.' As she hurried away, she too hoped he hadn't got her into any trouble.

'Miss Miller,' called Sister. 'We have a new girl in the kitchens, so you're cleaning the wards. But mind, I don't want to see you standing around chatting all day.'

'No, Sister.'

'Go and get an overall, you know the ones.'

'Yes, Sister.' Hannah could have kissed her – this meant she had been promoted!

The new men in the ward were very quiet, and Hannah went about her business silently and efficiently. Mary gave her a wink when she saw her with her mop and bucket.

That evening, when they walked home together, Hannah told her about Jeff Owen.

'Be careful,' said Mary. 'Don't get too involved with him. I've seen it before, it'll only bring you heartache.'

Hannah laughed. 'I'm not going to get involved with him. He's very nice to talk to, and I feel sorry for him. But it's no more than that. Besides, he's married, and so will I be when Jack comes home.'

That night Tom came round. As soon as Hannah saw him, she knew he had bad news. She was right. Bob's son had died. Hannah felt upset. Even though she hadn't promised him, she felt guilty at not having got round to going to Kent with Bob as she'd intended. Then she thought back to poor Jeff. Every day this war seemed to bring some new hurt to someone's life. She prayed Jack was safe.

Chapter 27

On 12 October 1915, Britain and her Allies were shocked when Nurse Edith Cavell was executed by the Germans for helping young French and British soldiers to escape across the Dutch border.

Staff and patients alike in the small cottage hospital where Mary and Hannah worked were sickened at the news, and all the staff wore black armbands as a mark of respect.

'I can't believe they would do a thing like that,' said Hannah as they read the newspaper's account.

'Just goes ter show what a wicked lot o' . . .' Maudie quickly looked at Mary, who was trying to put food into Brian's firmly closed mouth.

'I often wonder how Miss King is,' said Mary.

'I don't suppose she gets time to write,' said Hannah. 'I'm very worried about Jack, I haven't heard from him for ages.'

'Yer, well,' said Maudie. 'I expect we'd 'ear soon enough if anyfink . . .' She suddenly stopped and began clearing the table quickly. She looked across at Mary. 'I don't fink Brian wants any more,' she said hurriedly. 'Come on, let me take yer out ter the scullery and wash yer dirty face.'

Brian held up his arms to Maudie.

Hannah smiled as they left the kitchen. 'I can't believe the way she looks after him.'

'She must have been like an angel from heaven to those children she took in,' said Mary. She looked towards the scullery door and lowered her voice. 'Even if she did teach them to steal.'

'Well, at least they didn't get beaten, or go hungry,' said Hannah. 'And all those we know about have turned out fine.' She thought about Jack – the only one who hadn't give up stealing. Maybe in his own way he'd turn out fine too.

A week later, the girl from the kitchen was given Hannah's cleaning job, and Hannah was asked to help on the wards. She quickly learnt how to take temperatures, lay out the trolleys for the next lot of dressings, feed those that were unable to do it for themselves and how to roll bandages and empty bedpans. When the men called her Nurse she was thrilled, and sometimes she was asked to write a letter to their wives or mothers. She was surprised at how cheerful they kept their news, not revealing their terrible injuries. It made her wonder how much Jack had been keeping a stiff upper lip in the last letter she'd received. She hadn't heard from him for some time now, and was beginning to grow a little worried.

Many times she got very upset when the men called out in pain, and the smell of gangrene turned her stomach, but so far she had managed to keep her feelings under control. She comforted herself with the thought that now at last she was doing something really worthwhile. Her job meant everything to her as she proudly swished about in her stiff white apron. And now Hannah was working closer to Mary she was even more in awe of her and the efficient way she helped Doctor James when there was an emergency. She felt she'd learnt a lot in the last few months.

She hadn't been to see Alice since she began working at the hospital, but the odd letter she did receive told Hannah she was well and happy; Hannah knew she didn't have to worry about her. Bert had also written a short letter to say he was pleased she was now living with Mary, and that her new job was keeping her busy. He also said he was very busy, and disappointed Hannah wasn't coming to see him. It was a very formal note – had he guessed about Jack, Hannah wondered, relieved at least that he hadn't got the wrong idea about her intentions.

Since her new job had started, she didn't see a lot of the inhabitants of Hope Street, and most evenings she and Mary would sit listening to Maudie, who kept them up to date with all the street's latest gossip. It seemed Mrs Nosy had been very quiet lately. Her son had come back to live with her and Maudie was annoyed that she couldn't find out why he was back. She wondered if his sister had thrown the boy out since Mrs Nosy had told her a while ago that her son-in-law had joined the army.

A few of the young men Hannah knew just by sight had gone into the army, and the battling Barkers were still at it, according to Maudie: George still came home drunk with his mate every Saturday. Now the weather had turned, Mrs Warren's chest was playing her up again. Maudie said at least all this queuing gave them time to chew things over, and she was always amazed at some of the jobs women were doing now. The day she saw a woman delivering coal it seemed the whole street had heard about it!

Hannah hadn't seen anything of Kate for months, and Maudie told her she was working seven days a week now. Mrs Linton had said she was hoping Charlie would be coming home on leave soon, and they hoped to get married.

One cold, grey misty Sunday evening in late October, the sort of day that never really got light, they were startled by someone banging on the front door.

'I'll go,' said Hannah. 'Kate!' she yelled in amazement, throwing open the door and hugging her close. 'What a lovely surprise. Come on in. I was only saying to Maudie last week

343

that I haven't seen you for ages. How are you?' Hannah followed Kate swiftly down the passage. 'At least you don't stink of onions now. Look who's come to see us,' she announced, eagerly pushing open the kitchen door.

Hannah caught sight of a surprised look on Maudie's face as she turned towards Kate, who still had her back to Hannah.

'My God, gel, wot's 'appened ter yer?'

'It's the gunpowder,' said Kate.

Hannah gasped when, in the kitchen's light, she too saw Kate's yellow face.

'D'yer know what they call us?'

Hannah slowly shook her head.

'Canaries, cos we're all yeller,' she laughed.

'Can't you get it off?' asked Mary.

'Na. Scrubbed meself raw, I 'ave.' She grinned. 'Anyway, I come ter tell yer I'm gitting married. Charlie's coming 'ome next week, and we're tying the knot on Tuesday at eleven o'clock. 'E's only 'ere fer forty-eight 'ours, then 'e's orf ter France. 'E's been lucky so far, been stuck in some godfersaken place up north all this time. This is the first time 'e's 'ad any leave.'

'I'm really pleased for you, Kate,' said Hannah, kissing her cheek.

'Mind you, I don't know wot 'e'll 'ave ter say when he sees this lot.' She pushed up the sleeve of her jumper.

'Are you that colour all over?' asked Mary.

Kate nodded. 'It gits right inter yer skin. Anyway, I've gotter go. I knows yer'll all be working, but I fought I'd just let yer know.'

'Thanks. We'll be thinking of you,' said Hannah. She closed the front door behind Kate and leant against it for a minute or two. Little Kate getting married. One day soon it might be her turn.

* * *

Now the weather had become miserable and cold, Hannah didn't sit outside, and she didn't see so much of Jeff Owen, other than in the ward. He didn't seem to want to talk, had lost his mischievous sparkle, and kept his head buried in a book whenever Hannah was around. She noticed he was beginning to look very grey and downcast. Mary had told her his stump wasn't responding to treatment, and Doctor James was worried at how much pain he was in. Hannah knew his wife hadn't been back to see him, and she was concerned for him.

Today was Kate's wedding day. Mary, Maudie and Hannah had bought her a cut-glass vase. Strange that food and essentials were getting very scarce, but you could still buy luxuries, Hannah reflected. Maudie had said she would go along to give Kate a wave, and take her her present. Hannah was upset that she couldn't go and see her get married. As the morning wore on, Hannah glanced at the clock. Eleven: Kate would be saying her vows now.

Suddenly there was great commotion coming from the corridor. Someone was shouting. Vera Moore and Mary were hurrying towards the noise.

Sister threw open her door. 'Nurse. What is going on?' she demanded. 'Nurse, don't run!'

For once Mary seemed to take no notice of Sister and Hannah quickly followed her friend.

Sister stood in her doorway. 'Miss Miller, I asked what all the noise is about. Remember this is a hospital.'

The yelling from the lavatory was louder, a man's voice Hannah realized, screaming out for a nurse.

'We don't know, Sister,' said Hannah, hurrying past her.

'Well, tell him to be quiet, he's disturbing the other patients.'

Men were beginning to crowd into the corridor making it difficult to get past them.

'Hannah, Hannah. Quick, bring a chair,' yelled Mary. Her voice came from the lavatory.

Someone passed Hannah a chair and she pushed her way through the men crowding and blocking her way, terrified she would knock those on crutches over.

'Quick,' said Mary, grabbing the chair.

Hannah could see Vera Moore bending over. When she pushed her way in, one man was sitting on the floor shaking, his head resting on his knees. His loud sobs were heart-breaking. Out of the corner of her eye she could see someone hanging from the doorway. Vera was trying to take his weight on her back. Hannah gasped and put her hand to her mouth as she watched Mary scramble on to the chair and hack away with her small scissors at the rope that was tight round his neck.

Jeff Owen's crutches were on the floor. Hannah wanted to cry as she looked up. His eyes were closed, his face blue and contorted with pain.

'Don't just stand there!' shouted Mary. 'Get me a knife from the kitchen.'

Just as Hannah turned, someone pushed a knife into her hand. Sister was close behind.

When the rope was cut, they gently lowered Jeff to the floor. Mary put her head on his chest. Sitting back on her haunches she slowly shook her head.

'I couldn't believe it,' said the soldier who had been yelling. 'There 'e was, just 'anging there. Silly sod.' Tears rolled down his face. 'I couldn't 'elp 'im, not wiv this.' He waved his right arm at Hannah. His hand was missing. 'It was 'is wife, yer know.'

'Right, come along men.' Sister clapped her hands. 'Back to your rooms. Miss Miller, take Private Harris back, and then make all the men some tea.'

Hannah put her arm round Private Harris.

'If I'd 'a been a bit quicker, I might 'ave saved 'im,' he whispered.

'You mustn't reproach yourself. Or his wife.'

'Yer, but . . .' His voice drifted off into a low-pitched sob.

She gently but firmly moved him away. This was all wrong. Jeff had come through a horrible and wicked war, only to die by his own hand. What would his wife say? In the kitchen, Hannah filled the kettles in a state of shock. If only she could have talked to him more – perhaps she could have written to his wife. What about his lovely Rene? What was going to happen to her? Hannah banged the enamel teapot hard on the table. She wanted to cry, but knew it would be wrong to show her feelings. Why did men have to fight?

'Doctor James is going to be very upset over this,' said Mary quietly as they walked home that evening, 'but I was very proud of you.' But Hannah didn't feel she had much to be proud of.

When they pushed open the kitchen door, they were both astonished to see Maudie looking very smart. Her eyes were sparkling and her face flushed.

''Allo, gels,' she said, smiling. ''Ad a good day then?'

Hannah suddenly remembered it was Kate's wedding day. 'Did you see Kate?' she asked.

'Yer, she looked really smashing, 'ad a real nice 'at on. Pity she's ser yeller. 'E's a nice bloke. D'yer know, they invited me in fer a drink.'

Mary smiled. 'I thought so.'

''Ere, I ain't drunk, just 'ad the one, or was it two? Anyway, Brian enjoyed 'imself wiv all the kids. She liked 'er present. 'Er Grandad's a nice old bloke, d'yer know 'e got 'er a cake, got a bit fer yer both. Anyway, 'ow was your day?'

Hannah looked at Mary. 'About the same.' She didn't see any point in upsetting Maudie.

* * *

The second Christmas of the war was very quiet: food, or the lack of it, was beginning to be the main topic of Maudie's conversation. Things in Europe were not improving, and at the beginning of the New Year, conscription for all unmarried men became compulsory.

January was cold, with snow falling on and off throughout, making the pavements treacherous. Most nights Mary and Hannah came home with freezing, wet feet. Although the war news wasn't good, so far Hope Street had been spared any bombs, and the sight everybody dreaded even more than the Zeppelins: the telegram boy. He hadn't cycled down their street yet, but everybody knew of someone he'd called on. Hannah often thought about Bob's son, and of Jeff Owen's wife who was now a widow.

Hannah was idly gazing out of the bedroom window on Sunday morning. It was now late February, and still very cold; she watched the snowflakes flurrying all around, always in such a hurry, but going nowhere. She looked at the gas-lamp, reminded of the night she and Jack had stood under it on the way home from the Empire. It had been snowing that night, and he'd told her he was fond of her, and that he was going away. She sighed, it seemed an age ago; they had wasted so much time. She thought of all she could have done with him if she hadn't been so silly. She let a slight smile lift her face. At least he didn't have any pockets to pick where he was now. Silent tears ran down her cheek. Still, she knew he loved her, he had said so in his letter. Where are you, Jack? she whispered to herself. Please come back to me soon. Her eyes settled on a small box on the dressing table. In it was the ring he had given her many years ago – she didn't wear it as it turned her finger green as he'd warned her it might. Also inside was the king's shilling he'd given her when he joined up. 'Keep it for good luck,' he had said. But maybe he was the one who needed the luck. She still hadn't heard from him. Hannah looked at Maudie who was lying on her back snoring. She snorted and turned over. Hannah smiled and turned back to the window. Mrs Nosy was running down the street without a coat on, waving something. Hannah moved forward. Mrs Nosy was looking all about her, and appeared very distressed.

Hannah hurried from the bedroom and made her way downstairs. Quickly she pulled on her coat and opened the front door. 'Are you all right?' inquired Hannah.

'No I ain't,' she said aggressively, striding towards Hannah, her face red with anger. 'Look what some cow-son 'as gorn and put under me front door.'

She thrust a feather in Hannah's face. A white feather.

'Who could do a thing like that" asked Hannah in surprise. 'And why?'

'Oh I know why right enough.' She said, straightening her shoulders. 'It's me boy.'

'Your son?'

'Yer, just cos 'e ain't fit ter go in the army, somebody finks 'e's a bloody conshie.'

'What's going on?' asked Mary, coming to the door.

'It's Mrs N . . .' Hannah quickly held her tongue. She still didn't know the woman's name. 'Someone's pushed a white feather under her door, and she thinks it's for her son.'

'I don't fink – I knows!' Her voice rose in anger. 'Always 'ad it in fer me this lot round 'ere 'as!' She was shouting, and one by one the bedroom curtains were being drawn back, faces filling the windows.

Hannah looked at Mary, who just shrugged and walked away.

'Perhaps they did it as a joke,' said Hannah.

'Well, I don't call it a bloody joke.' Fuming, Mrs Nosy walked to the middle of the street, waving the feather about. 'If and when I find out what bleeder done this, I'll murder 'im!' She yelled waving her fist. 'D'yer 'ear? So 'elp me, I'll murder 'im, and willingly swing fer it.'

Maudie appeared at the top of the stairs. 'Wot's all the racket? Wot's going on?'

'I'll tell you later.' said Hannah, closing the front door.

Maudie followed Hannah into the kitchen, where Mary was.

'Well, wot was all that about?' She asked, sitting at the table.

'It seems somebody has put a white feather under Mrs Nosy's front door.'

'Na,' said Maudie. 'Who'd do a fing like that?'

'Don't know,' said Hannah.

'Somebody must feel very strong about her son not being called up,' said Mary. 'Is he exempt?'

'Dunno. 'E was always a weak kinda kid, so I s'pose 'e could be. But then again . . .'

Hannah thought about Jack, Ted, Jeff Owen and all the men at the hospital. They had all answered the call to duty. What would happen if all the men refused to fight?

'Well, if he is fit,' said Mary, 'he should be ashamed of himself.'

''Ere, 'ere,' said Maudie. She gave a little smile. 'Old George Barker and 'is mate always like a joke, especially when they've 'ad a few, and last night was Sat'day.'

Hannah and Mary also smiled, but said nothing.

After the white feather incident, things settled down in Hope Street. Every day Hannah looked for the postman. It had been almost four months since she had last heard from Jack.

'Mary, I'm so worried about him,' she said one evening as they groped their way home through the soaking drizzle.

'If he's driving for the Red Cross, I don't suppose he'll have time to write,' said Mary.

'How would we know if anything had happened to him?'

'The war office would let you know, or at least let Maudie know.'

'Mary? If she heard while we were at work, she would tell me, wouldn't she?'

'Of course she would. Could you imagine Maudie being able to hide her feelings?'

'No,' said Hannah, but that didn't stop her from pondering about it.

Chapter 28

Maudie was busy in the scullery when Hannah walked in.

''Allo, gel, where's Mary?''

'She's been asked to stay on and help the doctor out.'

'Fings bad then?'

'Yes, a bit. Some new patients have arrived, and Doctor James likes to have Mary around when he's working.' Hannah sat at the table.

'Does 'e always work late then?'

'No, but I don't think things are going too well.'

Maudie sat next to her. She nudged Hannah's arm. 'Is 'e nice?'

'Who?'

'The doctor.'

Hannah nodded. 'Yes, I think so. I don't see a lot of him.'

''Ere, yer don't fink . . . 'Er and 'im?' She grinned.

'No, of course not. Besides, he's a lot older than her.'

'Is 'e married?'

'How should I know?' Hannah was getting a little cross with all these questions.

'Still, yer knows what they say: there's no fool like an old fool.'

'Don't talk daft. It's all very professional.'

''Ere, 'ark at you. I bet Mary's good at 'er job.'

'Yes, she is. I wish I could have been a nurse.'

'Still, yer 'appy now, ain't yer?'

Hannah nodded and smiled. 'Yes, I am.'

'By the way, there's a letter up on the mantelshelf fer yer.'

'Oh Maudie, why didn't you tell me before! Is it from Jack?' Hannah jumped up.

'Christ, yer've only just got in. No, it ain't, don't recognize the writing.'

Hannah turned the envelope over. She didn't know the handwriting either. Slowly she opened it. She gasped and, trembling, sat at the table.

'Wot is it, gel? Wot's wrong?'

She looked up. Tears filled her eyes. 'Maudie, it's from a nurse. Jack's in hospital. He's back here, in England.'

Maudie's face turned ashen as she too sank into a chair at the table next to Hannah. 'Wot's wrong wiv 'im?'

Hannah's eyes raced down the page, the paper shaking. Then she read it all over again. 'She said his hands have been injured, but not badly. He can't write at the moment, he sends everybody his love and hopes to see us soon.' Tears ran down her face.

'Does she say where 'e is?'

Hannah nodded. 'He's in Hampshire.'

'Where the bloody 'ell's that?'

'I think it's down south somewhere.'

'Will yer be able ter git ter see 'im?'

'I don't think so. I can't get the time off, not now. I must answer this letter straightaway.'

'I'll git yer tea.'

Tears still in her eyes, Hannah sat and read the short note over and over again. If only there was a clue as to how badly injured he was. Her heart cried out for him. There was so much she wanted to know, and she knew how nurses only told relations half the truth. Hannah pushed her tea to one side as she sat and wrote him a long loving letter. The most important question was, when would he be allowed home?

It was almost ten o'clock when Mary walked in, looking exhausted.

'Take your shoes off, I'll make you a cup of tea,' said Hannah. 'Maudie's gone to bed. Has it been a bad evening?'

Mary nodded and rubbed her feet. 'Doctor James was telling me he's been doing operations all day at St Olaf's; then the poor man has to come over here to do a few more.'

'I didn't think we'd be doing any!' Hannah said in surprise. 'We don't really have the proper equipment, do we?'

'Normally we wouldn't, but these are quite minor compared to what he usually does. It's when things go wrong, that's when he steps in.'

'Here's your tea.'

'Thanks.'

'Mary. Jack's in hospital.'

Mary's head shot up. 'What? How do you know?'

'I had a letter from his nurse.'

'Where is he?'

'In Hampshire.' Hannah took the letter from her pocket.

'Can I?' asked Mary.

Hannah nodded. 'It's quite short.'

Mary read the note and handed it back. 'What are you going to do?'

'I don't know. I've written to him asking lots of questions, so perhaps when I get a reply I'll know more.'

'I'm so very sorry, Hannah,' said Mary.

Hannah smiled weakly. 'Still, at least I know he's safe back here in England.'

Mary gently patted the back of her hand. 'Let's hope he isn't too badly injured.'

Hannah could only nod.

'I'm going on up to bed, what about you?'

'I'll sit here for a while.'

'You'd better not put any more coal on the fire, otherwise you'll have Maudie complaining.'

Hannah looked up at Mary. 'She certainly looks after us. What would we do without her?'

'I don't know. We haven't got time to stand in a queue for hours on end just for a loaf of bread. I did hear the government was thinking of rationing out the food.'

'How would they do that?'

'We'd have coupons or books, something like that. I don't quite know how, but at least it will be fairer that way. Anyway, I'm off. Good-night, Hannah.'

For a long while Hannah sat looking at the glowing embers. She shuddered, the room was getting cold. How badly was Jack injured? She knew when some of the men had lost their hands or arms they would tell her to write as though they had just lost a finger. 'Jack, Jack. I love you so very much, please hurry home,' she said out loud, then put her head in her hands and wept.

Two weeks passed and Hannah still hadn't had a reply to her letter, so when she and Mary walked in from work and found Maudie sitting in the armchair crying, Hannah fell to her knees, desperate with anxiety.

'What is it? Is it Jack?' she cried. 'Have you heard from the war office?'

Maudie shook her head. 'It's poor old Mrs Warren.'

Mary slumped into the chair. 'That poor woman. Is young Ted . . . ?'

'It ain't Ted. It's 'er.'

'Mrs Warren,' croaked Hannah. 'What's happened?'

Maudie blew her nose loudly. 'It's 'er chest. Seems she's bin coughing a lot lately, must be all this damp.' Maudie blew her nose again. 'Well, this morning, she 'ad one of 'er attacks, and it seems 'er poor old 'eart couldn't take the strain.'

'That's awful,' said Hannah softly.

'How's Mr Warren?' inquired Mary.

'Very upset. 'E's bin trying ter git in touch wiv the war office, 'e's bin trying ter see if 'e can git young Ted 'ome.'

'I doubt he'll be able to do that,' said Mary.

'Not if he's fighting,' said Hannah.

'Poor old chap, been going out of 'is mind all day, 'e 'as.'

'She was such a nice woman,' said Hannah.

'Yer,' sniffed Maudie. 'Never fought she'd be the first ter go in this street.'

'Can you find out when the funeral is? Perhaps we could send some flowers,' said Mary.

'Yer, course I will, but I expect they'll 'ave a street collection.'

'I'd still like to send some,' said Mary.

Curtains were left unopened on the day of Mrs Warren's funeral, and Hannah and Mary went to work with heavy hearts. All day, Hannah couldn't get it out of her mind.

Mary was working late again that evening, and Hannah's spirits were lifted when she arrived home to find another letter from Jack's nurse.

As Maudie told her about the flowers, and the carriage that took Mrs Warren to the church, Hannah was only half listening.

'It's a lovely church, ain't never been in there before.'

Hannah quickly looked up from her letter. 'You went to the church?'

'Yer. Fought I'd pay me last respects.'

'What about Brian, did you take him?'

'Yer, 'e was as good as gold. Wasn't many in there though, only a few from the street. Shame, ain't it? Anyway, wot's Jack got ter say this time?'

'Much the same. He does say he's feeling a lot better, but it's very short.'

'Does 'e say when 'e might git 'ome?'

'No.'

'What time will Mary be back?'

'I don't know, it shouldn't be too late.'

Maudie was still up when Mary came home. She looked tired, but Hannah noticed there was something different about her.

Maudie told Mary about the funeral, but she too seemed to have her thoughts on other things.

'I'm glad you're still up, Maudie. There's something I've got to tell you both.'

Maudie plonked herself down in the chair again. 'Wot is it, gel? Wot's wrong?'

Mary laughed. 'There's nothing wrong. It's just that on Sunday I'm going to take Brian out.'

'Is that all? Yer got me all of a flutter then, I fought sumfink was wrong.'

Hannah looked at Mary. 'Where're you going?'

'Don't be nosy,' said Maudie.

'It's all right. You'll know soon enough. I'm going to spend the day with Doctor James. He said he'd like to meet Brian.'

'Doctor James,' gasped Hannah. 'I didn't know . . . I didn't . . .'

'We've been working together for years. I didn't know too much about him till we started working late, and sharing a quiet cup of tea together. He's very nice.'

'Is 'e married?' asked Maudie.

'No, he's a confirmed bachelor.'

'Oh yer, so what does 'e want yer to go out wiv 'im for then?'

Hannah laughed. 'Now who's being nosy?'

Mary's eyes were sparkling. 'You should see the look on your faces. I'm not going out with him, as you put it. Is there a cup of tea, Maudie?'

'Yer, yer, course.' She picked up the kettle and shook it. 'Damn, I gotter fill it up. Don't you dare say nuffink while I'm gorn, I don't want ter miss nuffink.' She left the kitchen in a hurry.

Hannah and Mary laughed. 'What do you want to know?' said Mary loudly, winking at Hannah.

'Anything that's interesting,' said Hannah looking at the door.

Maudie appeared, put the kettle on the fire and sat down. 'Now, come on, tell me all about 'im.'

'Well,' said Mary. 'I've told you he's not married. He lives with an old aunt. It seems they have a nice house over Peckham way, and me and Brian have been invited over to dinner on Sunday.'

'Is that all?' asked Maudie.

'Well, yes. What else did you want me to say?'

'Dunno. I fought yer might 'ave said yer liked 'im.'

'I do like him, he's a very good doctor.'

Maudie stood up and took the teapot from the dresser. 'Go on, yer knows wot I mean.'

'Stop trying to matchmake, Maudie,' said Hannah.

Mary laughed. 'D'you know, I love having you two here. You've changed my life! What would I do without you?' She jumped up and kissed Maudie's cheek.

'Go on wiv yer,' said Maudie, clearly embarrassed. 'By the way, did 'Annah tell yer she got a letter from Jack?'

'No! No, she didn't.'

'Fat chance I've had, you've been blabbering on about Doctor James.'

'Well, how is he? What did he have to say?'

'His nurse wrote it. He said he feels better. Here, read it, it's very short.' She handed Mary the letter.

'It doesn't say much, does it?'

Hannah shook her head. 'It'll be nice when he can come home.' Suddenly Hannah stopped. 'Where will he stay? This isn't his home . . .'

Maudie looked anxious. ''E can't go back ter the wash-'ouse, not now. It's all damp and empty.'

'Perhaps he could stay with Tom,' said Hannah.

'I dunno 'ow much room they've got round there.'

'Look,' said Mary. 'Don't forget we've got the single bed in the front room.'

'But that's for Brian.'

'Yes, I know, but it's a bit cold to put him down there just yet. Besides, I like having him in with me, so Jack could go in there.'

'You mean you don't mind him staying here?'

'Of course not.'

Hannah threw her arms round Mary's neck. 'I can't believe this, all my dreams are coming true. I have a good job, a nice home, and soon I'll have Jack.' She stopped. 'What about when we get married?' For the first time she felt the wedding might actually happen.

'Look,' said Mary again. 'Let's take one step at a time. Let's get him home and see how ill he is, then we can worry about the wedding and where you're going to live, then. He may have to go back into the army if he's not too bad, and then things won't be all that different till after the war.'

'Yes, perhaps you're right.'

'It sounds a good idea ter me,' said Maudie. 'Well, I'm orf ter bed. Night, see yer both in the morning.'

'I'm off as well,' said Mary.

'I'll be up in a while,' said Hannah. She knew sleep wouldn't come easily tonight. She was excited. They had discussed her wedding. She sat in a dream, what would she wear? Clothes hadn't been important since she began wearing a uniform. Mrs Jack Woods. It sounded so wonderful.

Chapter 29

April had been a bright month, and today was a cloudless spring Monday morning with the promise of a fine day ahead. As they walked to work, Mary was telling Hannah about her visit yesterday to Doctor James's house, the third time she'd been.

'Arthur is so kind, and Aunt Helen thinks Brian is wonderful. I'm worried that they'll spoil him.'

'When are you seeing him again – socially, that is?'

'I don't know. I don't want them to get too fond of Brian.'

'What about you? Are you getting fond of them?'

Mary turned her head away from Hannah. 'I'll always be faithful to my Bill.'

Hannah stopped. 'Mary, I know this is none of my business, but if Doctor James . . .'

'Don't talk silly,' interrupted Mary. 'I told you, we're just good friends. Now come on, hurry, or else we'll be late.'

'But Mary,' Hannah persisted, 'you're young and attractive. And what about Brian? Surely he needs a dad.'

'Hannah, if and when I want to get married again, which at the moment is the last thing I'm thinking about, I shall make up my own mind, thank you.'

Mary promptly marched on, and they continued their way in silence.

All day, Hannah thought on what Mary had said. If only her friend could find happiness again . . . She smiled to herself. She was doing it again, trying to run other people's lives.

On Monday, two weeks later, Hannah received another short letter from Jack's nurse. It was almost the same as the others, and she was worried about the lack of information it gave.

'I'll have to try and get down to see him,' she said that evening. 'I must find out how ill he is. Maudie, could you go to the station and find out about the trains? Perhaps I could go next Sunday.'

Yesterday, Mary had been to Doctor James's house again, but Hannah hadn't dared make any comments about it this time. Then, that evening, after they had been sitting quietly discussing Hannah's forthcoming trip, Mary casually announced that Doctor James had asked her to marry him.

'What?' asked Hannah.

'Bit sudden, ain't it?' said Maudie.

'I have known him for a long while.'

'Oh Mary, I'm so pleased for you,' said Hannah. 'When's the great day?'

'I haven't said I would – well, not yet.'

'Wot's gonner 'appen ter Brian?'

'I'll be looking after him. You see, I wouldn't have to work.'

'That would be lovely for you both,' said Hannah.

'Yes, yes it would,' she said wistfully. Mary sat forward. 'But I really don't know. You see, I am very fond of Arthur, but I'm not sure I want to marry him.'

'Why?' asked Maudie.

'I don't know – yes, I do. It's because of Bill.'

'I'm sure he would have liked to see you and Brian settled,' said Hannah.

Mary smiled. 'Yes, I think he would. He was a fine man. Brian looks so much like him.'

'Well, that's up ter you, love,' said Maudie. 'But if 'e's got a nice 'ouse and a few bob, well, it does 'elp.'

Mary laughed. 'Well, at least you don't beat about the bush.'

'Ain't 'ad the time, or the opportunity. Go on, gel, take a chance. If 'e's as nice as yer say, 'e'll make yer 'appy.'

'What will happen to this house?' asked Hannah.

'I think the landlord will let you take over the tenancy,' said Mary.

'But I can't afford the rent,' said Hannah in alarm.

'Yer'll 'ave ter take a lodger in then, won't yer,' said Maudie. 'I ain't going back ter that wash-'ouse, not now, not after living 'ere.'

Hannah tutted. 'Just hark at her. And when I think of the job I had persuading you to move here.'

'Look,' said Mary, 'it'll be a while before, or if, I marry Arthur; and perhaps before then you'll be married and you'll have an army allowance.'

'But what if Jack's too ill to go back?'

'He's always got his driving skills to fall back on.'

'But what if . . . ?'

'Just let's wait and see. I'm sure everything will work out just fine.'

Hannah knew she didn't ever want to leave Hope Street. She would just have to do what Mary suggested: wait and see.

The following evening, Hannah and Mary arrived home from work to find the front door wide open.

Mary was very concerned. 'Maudie should be more careful with Brian running about. He could get out, and with her feet she couldn't run after him,' she said angrily, striding down the passage with Hannah close behind. Mary threw open the kitchen door and stopped so abruptly that Hannah almost fell over her.

Maudie jumped to her feet. ''Annah, 'Annah,' she yelled. 'Look who's 'ere.'

Mary quickly stood to one side. Hannah couldn't speak. All

the things she had planned over the long months to say to him wouldn't come. Jack walked towards her. She felt faint. Tears welled up. He looked wonderful in his uniform, but he was thin and so pale. His right arm was in a sling. She wanted to throw her arms round his neck and kiss him. He was there, it wasn't a dream, he was standing right in front of her. He took hold of her with his left arm and pulled her close. He kissed her mouth. She closed her eyes; she was in heaven and didn't want to wake up. She held on to him and melted with his kisses. In the back of her head she could hear Maudie saying something about a cup of tea. Tea was the last thing she wanted at that moment.

When they finally broke away he led her to a chair.

'All right then, gel?'

This was her Jack. Tears streamed down her face.

''Ere, don't carry on. I must say yer looks a little darling in that there uniform.'

She took hold of his hand. 'How are you, Jack? I've been so worried about you.'

'Not ser bad. Maudie 'ere's been telling me all the news.' He turned to Mary. 'That little un of yours is a proper card. 'Ad me in fits, 'e 'as.'

Hannah was still finding it hard to say the right words. She desperately wanted to be alone with him. 'How's your hand?' she asked.

'Not ser bad, it could 'ave been worse. Lorst the top orf a couple of fingers though.'

'You poor fing. Did it 'urt?' asked Maudie.

'Can't say I recommend it.'

'Will you be invalided out of the army now?' asked Mary.

'Don't rightly know. I'll still be able ter drive, but I can't fire a gun, so I could end up wiv a cushy number over 'ere. Got ter go in front of a board on Friday.'

'How long will you be home?' asked Hannah.

'Till I see the board, then we'll 'ave ter see what the army says.'

'We've only got three days,' said Hannah in panic, 'and I'm at work for all of them! I only get Sunday off.'

'What about Sat'day? I should be around Sat'day, and Sunday.'

'I sometimes finish at four.'

'I'll have a word with Sister to make sure you finish on time,' said Mary.

'Thanks,' said Hannah. 'What about leave, you must be due some leave?'

'I'll be able ter tell yer more after Friday.'

Maudie put the tea on the table.

'Maudie says I can stay 'ere. That's real kind of yer – can I call yer Mary?'

'Of course you can.'

To Hannah the conversations seemed unreal.

'I've put me kitbag in the front room, if that's all right wiv you.'

'Of course. Make yourself at home, Jack. We're all one big happy family here.'

'Ta.'

'Sit yerselves down,' said Maudie.

Tea was a happy, noisy affair, with everyone talking at once, and Brian joining in by shouting and banging on the table.

'It's just like the old days, ain't it?' said Maudie, her face glowing with pride and excitement. She laughed. 'D'yer know, I feel just like a broken pair of curtains.'

'What yer talking about?' asked Jack.

'I can't pull meself tergevver!' Maudie threw her head back and laughed, and everyone joined in.

Hannah felt she was part of a dream. She was aware of

putting food in her mouth, answering questions and chatting, but it all seemed so distant and unreal.

They finished tea, and Mary said she would put Brian to bed. Hannah began to help Maudie clear the table.

'Leave that,' Maudie flapped her hands at Hannah. 'You sit and talk ter Jack.'

'Tell yer what, gel, let's go out fer a spell.'

'I'll get my hat and coat.' Hannah could have kissed him there and then. At last they were going to be alone.

Outside she looked up Hope Street. How she would have loved to walk up and down to show Jack off. She held on to his left arm proudly. 'Shall we go to the park?'

'Why not?'

Although the evening air had a chill, Hannah didn't feel it: she was glowing. She smiled and snuggled against him.

'Maudie was telling me about young Tom. I'm glad 'e didn't 'ave ter go in the army. Always liked Tom, 'e's a good lad.'

Hannah nodded. 'He's happy working and living with Bob.'

'Yer, she said. She was saying Bert ain't been down fer a while. D'yer still write to 'im?'

'I haven't had a letter from him for ages.' She paused and took a deep breath. 'Jack? Why did you two fall out?'

He laughed. 'It all sounds a bit daft really, more so now when yer finks of what's 'appening in the world. Did you know 'e was Maudie's son?'

She nodded.

'I guessed she told yer. We got on all right when 'e first come back, but I fink 'e felt trapped down 'ere, and as we got a bit older I s'pose the truf was, I was a bit jealous Maudie was 'is mum. We 'ad a big row one day when the rozzers came looking for some loot I'd 'alf-inched. I said to Maudie it was 'im what told 'em, but I knew it wasn't, 'e didn't know nuffink about it. I suppose I just wanted to get 'im inter Maudie's bad books.'

'Why did you want to do that?' Hannah asked.

'Well you know what kids are like,' Jack shrugged. 'The old bill didn't find the loot anyway and, ter cut a long story short, 'e upped and went. I never did tell Maudie that I'd lied to 'er, she might 'ave chucked me out. Then it seemed 'e only come back when 'e wanted 'and-out, and I s'pose it just grew from then on.'

'I wish you'd make it up. That would please Maudie as well,' said Hannah as they wandered into the park.

'Yer.' Jack grinned. 'Don't see why not. We could 'ave a go. No point in 'olding grudges now.'

Hannah smiled at him. She was pleased about that. 'Shall we sit down?' They settled on a seat and he put his arm round her shoulders. She felt unbelievably happy.

'Jack, when shall we get married?'

'I'll let yer know after Friday.'

Panic gripped her. Was he going to put her off again? Was everything he had said in his letters untrue?

She turned to face him. 'You do still want to marry me, don't you?'

He pulled her close and his lips were on hers. He kissed her hard and passionately. He had never kissed her like this before, and she was ecstatic, feelings washing over her that she had never felt before. She loved him, and she wanted him to make love to her.

'Jack,' she breathed. 'I love you so much.'

He sat back. 'I tell yer, 'Annah, I didn't know how much I missed yer, not till I was up the Front. When the other blokes was telling me about their missis, and how much they missed 'em, I kept finking about you. 'Annah, I should get some leave, and as soon as I do we can git married.'

Hannah took his head in her hands and kissed his face all over.

He laughed. 'Does that mean yes?'

She laughed, tears running down her face. 'Yes, yes, yes,' she said, sobbing with happiness.

'What yer crying for, yer silly old fing?'

'I love you so very much.'

'And I love you.' He sat back and, with his left hand, fumbled in his left pocket for a cigarette.

Hannah began to help him. 'How are you managing?'

'Not bad, I'll still be able to drive. Fank God. D'yer know, that's the one fing I'm really good at, and I love it, being in charge of a motor.'

'How bad is your hand really?'

'I told you, I only lorst the tops orf two of me fingers. I got a little bit of shrapnel in the top of me leg, too, but the doc over there got it out real quick, and it seems I heal pretty fast.'

'You make it sound so casual, you poor thing.'

'Still, I expect you see a lot worse than that.'

She nodded.

'How's Alice?'

'Still the same. She's very happy living with Betty, and Betty married Rick when he was on leave.'

'Good fer 'im.'

'Alice makes me laugh, when I do get the odd letter. She thinks this war is a big game. Except for the day we had a Zeppelin over. She was scared stiff then, didn't want me to come home.'

'Well, I don't blame 'er.'

'She must have got very brave all of a sudden, because, d'you know, a while back they shot a Zeppelin down at night and she told me she was at a café with Roy and they all rushed outside to see it come down. It was in flames, and she said they all stood there and clapped.'

Jack laughed. 'P'raps it was cos she was wiv 'er boyfriend. I can just see 'er jumping up and down clapping her hands wearing 'er little white gloves.'

'D'you know, her biggest complaint is that the shops are beginning to look shabby. I ask you, men are losing their lives, and all she can worry about is things like that.'

'That sounds like Alice.'

'I suppose it does.'

They laughed together.

'D'yer reckon 'er and this Roy will end up getting 'itched?'

'No. He's just a friend. I think he's a bit . . . funny.'

'From what I've 'eard, and what I saw that time I went and stayed at Rick's mate's place, most of the blokes on the stage are a bit like that. Shall we go over and see 'er on Sunday?'

'That would be lovely.'

'Be then we should know what day we're gonner tie the knot.'

'You mean it, really mean it?'

'Yer, course I do, and I fink it should be as soon as possible.'

'Kate got married by special licence. Could we do that?'

'Don't see why not.'

Hannah snuggled up to him. 'I can't believe this is really happening.'

He kissed her. 'Well, it is, and before long you'll be Mrs Woods.'

'Mrs Woods,' repeated Hannah. 'I hope Alice will come to our wedding.'

'Course she will. She'll be tickled pink.'

'She's never been back to Hope Street, you know.'

'I reckon that's cos she was frightened yer'd make 'er stay.'

'I wouldn't do that, not now. Alice is happy and I don't have to worry about her any more. She's with the kind of people she likes, and living the sort of life she wants too. No, we won't see her back here.'

'Yer, but this'll be different. I know she'll come to our wedding. 'Sides, if I know Alice, she'll wonner show off 'er fine clothes.'

'Yes, I expect she will.' And Hannah knew that this time Alice wouldn't be ashamed of her, for once she was going to outshine her sister. 'I hope you don't have to go away again.'

'Well, we'll 'ave ter wait and see.'

'Was it very bad over there in France?'

Jack drew heavily on his cigarette. 'Seen a lot a rotten sights, but yer 'ave ter try and fergit it. Seen some blokes go clear round the twist, while others don't talk about it.'

Hannah noted a faraway look come into his eyes. Suddenly he looked sad. 'Did you lose any of your mates?' she asked in a quiet voice.

'A few.' He tapped the end of his cigarette nervously. 'I tell yer, 'Annah, war's a bloody 'orrible fing. Makes yer count yer blessings, I can tell yer that.' With the toe of his boot he ground his cigarette butt into the grass. He gave her a squeeze. 'Right, that's enough of that. By the way, I nearly forgot, I met a bloke over there who reckoned he knew you.'

'Knew me, who was that?'

'His name was Alf, said 'e knew you and Alice. Said 'e knew yer when yer lived in Fulham.'

Hannah sat open mouthed. All her fears and past came flooding back. 'Alf,' she whispered.

'Yer knows 'im then?'

She nodded. 'What did he have to say?' Her head was swimming. What had he told Jack? Did he know all about Uncle Harry?

'Not a lot really. I was helping 'em load the ambulance after a really bad day when he recognized me Cockney accent. Asked me where I come from, I told 'im Roverhive, then 'e said 'e comes from Fulham. I told 'im me gelfriend's sister lives in Fulham, 'e asked me 'er name, and I told 'im it was Alice, and 'e said 'e knew an' Alice once, she had a sister, 'Annah. Well, yer could 'ave knocked me down wiv a fevver. I said, me gel's name's 'Annah. By then we'd got to the field 'ospital and I didn't see 'im any more. He was in a bit of a state, poor devil – he didn't even wonner fag.'

'What happened to him?'

'Oh, they said 'e went in the night. Pity, I'd a liked to 'ave found out more about yer wicked past.'

Hannah shuddered.

'Yer gitting cold. Come on, let's git back.' He went to stand up.

'No, wait.' Hannah put her arm out and pulled him back. 'Jack, I must tell you. We mustn't have any secrets from each other, must we?'

He laughed. 'Course not. So, Miss Miller, what deep and dark past 'ave yer got then? Yer making it sound really sinister.'

Hannah sat back and told him everything that had happened. She talked about her father; told him all about Uncle Harry and the way he'd treated her and Alice; and about his wife, Aunt May. She told him how they had run away when they thought she'd killed him, and that was how they'd finished up at Maudie's. She also said how she had met Alf a few years back and found out Uncle Harry was still alive, but out to get them if he could. Jack didn't interrupt. When she'd finished he took hold of her hand, pulled her close and kissed her.

'I fought it must a been somefing like that when yer used ter 'ave all those nightmares. Mind you, I never fought yer'd nearly killed someone. I'll 'ave ter watch me ps and qs; I don't want yer coming at me wiv a 'ammer.' He smiled. 'What about yer poor aunt?'

'I've often thought about her. Alf did say she was all right.

373

I wish I could pluck up courage to go and see her, but I'm terrified of Uncle Harry.'

'I'll tell yer what,' said Jack, patting the back of her hand. 'When we're 'itched, we'll go over and see 'em. Yer old uncle won't be able ter knock yer about then, cos 'e'll 'ave me ter answer to.' He held her close.

'Oh Jack, do you really mean that?'

'Course.'

'My protector.' She nestled in his arms.

Jack threw his head back and laughed. ''Ere, does Maudie know all about this?'

'Yes.'

'She's canny, she never let on then?'

Hannah shook her head.

'Don't look ser serious.'

'You're not annoyed with me?'

'No, why should I be?'

'I thought . . . The way I used to carry on about you stealing, I thought that what I did was worse.'

'Well, yer, I s'pose it is in a way, but fings were pretty bad for you, and yer did 'ave young Alice ter look after.' He sat back. 'Well, at least one fing should please yer.'

'I'm sorry about Alf.'

'I didn't mean 'im. I meant I can't go dipping any more, not wiv this.' He raised his right arm. 'Won't be very good at it now, not wiv these fingers.'

Hannah threw her arms round his neck, and once again her tears fell. 'Jack, Jack, I love you so much!' She was laughing and crying together, wiping her face with the back of her gloved hand. 'After all these years. What will you do?'

'There ain't too many who can drive, so I reckon I'll be able ter git a job anywhere when this lot's over. Now come on, it's getting late, and you've got ter go ter work termorrer.'

They stood up and Jack kissed her again. Hannah was so happy. Although she knew there could be some hard times ahead, with the love she had for Jack and Maudie – her family – together they would get through anything. At last she had everything she had been seeking.

HARRY BOWLING

The new Cockney saga from the bestselling author of GASLIGHT IN PAGE STREET

The Girl from Cotton Lane

Cotton Lane in dockland Bermondsey is one of the many small cobbled streets which serve the wharves. And on the corner is Bradley's Dining Rooms, the favourite eating place of the rivermen, trade union officials and horse and motor drivers. Since her marriage to Fred Bradley, Carrie has been building up the business, and trade has picked up considerably since the end of the Great War. Yet everything is not well between Carrie and Fred. And though they have a little daughter they both adore, neither of them is truly happy.

Carrie's parents, Nellie and William Tanner, live in Bacon Buildings, the tenement they were forced to move into when George Galloway sacked William after thirty-seven years. But their hearts lie in Page Street, their old home, and with their friends there: redoubtable Florrie 'Hairpin' Axford and her gossiping companions; scruffy old Broomhead Smith; the fighting Sullivans, and young Billy, who, unable to box after a wound sustained in the trenches, is determined to set up a gymnasium to help the local youngsters keep off the streets; and new arrivals, Joe Maitland, who's doing well with his warehouse in Dockhead, though his dealings are not always strictly above board, and Red Ellie, the stalwart Communist who brings the street together to fight their slum landlord, George Galloway.

Don't miss Harry Bowling's previous Cockney sagas, GASLIGHT IN PAGE STREET, PARAGON PLACE, IRONMONGER'S DAUGHTER, TUPPENCE TO TOOLEY STREET and CONNER STREET'S WAR, also available from Headline.

FICTION/GENERAL   0 7472 3869 3